IN
BAD
COMPANY

VIVECA STEN

TRANSLATED BY MARLAINE DELARGY

SANDHAMN MURDERS

AMAZON **CROSSING**

IN
BAD
COMPANY

For Tamara,
who survived the Holocaust and
found a new life in Sweden

Horssten

Åbakär
Kersö
Skanskobb
Svängen

Grönskär

Revengegrundet

SANDHAMN

Harö

RUNMARÖ
Pappa's Haven

Svenvik

Stavsnäs
Winter Harbor

Vindö

Värmdö

Ingarö

Nämdö

Stavsnäs
Sandhamn

STOCKHOLM

Almagrundet

0   2,5   5 km

Monday,
March 28, 2016

CHAPTER 1

Mina Kovač scrutinized the draining board. It was spotless, but still she gave it another wipe just to be on the safe side. She'd mopped all the floors and vacuumed the whole house, using the little nozzle to make sure there wasn't a single crumb left in a corner. The bathroom smelled of lemons.

Her precious little boy had slept for an unusually long time, thank goodness, so she'd been able to get the cleaning done in peace. She glanced over at the window. Dino didn't usually bring Andreis home before seven, but she couldn't help checking.

Dinner had to be ready when he opened the door. She'd done most of the preparation: two top-quality steaks with baked potatoes, Béarnaise sauce, and a green salad.

His favorite meal.

Recently Andreis had become more unpredictable than ever. She tried so hard not to irritate him; sometimes she didn't even know why he got mad. She stayed in the background, determined to take up as little space as possible. When Lukas woke, she picked him up immediately so that his crying wouldn't disturb Andreis.

There were many late meetings and phone calls; he would take off with Dino in the middle of the night, giving no explanation.

She didn't dare ask what was going on.

Mina went into the living room and bent over the old crib her father had brought down from the loft and freshened up. Lukas was lying on his back snoring contentedly, just as she must have done back in the day. His incomprehensibly small hands rested on the cover, fingers spread like starfish. His latest cuddly toy, a pale-blue rabbit from Grandma and Grandpa, lay beside him.

She wished she had time to pick him up, press her lips against his downy head, settle down in the armchair and feed him. But it was better to let him sleep, then she could give the guest bathroom another wipe before Andreis arrived home.

A sound from the front door made her jump. Was he back already? It was only six o'clock. She hurried into the hallway and opened the door. She let out a long breath when she saw her father on the porch.

"What are you doing here?"

"I happened to be in the area. Can I come in?"

Mina hesitated.

"Is he home?"

She didn't need to explain, but she found the whole situation embarrassing. "He'll be back in an hour," she said, unable to meet her father's gaze.

"I just wanted to see Lukas; it's been a while. I'll only stay a few minutes; I'll be gone before Andreis gets here."

Mina nodded. "Come in. Lukas is in the living room; he's been asleep for hours, bless him."

Her father slipped past her. She really wanted to make him a cup of coffee, sit down, and chat for a while, but she knew it was a bad idea. There wasn't enough time.

"He's such a sweetheart," her father said when he came back. "He's got your eyes and mouth. Do you think his hair will be as fair as yours?"

Mina managed a faint smile. She also thought Lukas took after her, even though Andreis insisted he looked like his own father.

"We'll see," she said. "Love to Mom."

She hoped it didn't sound as if she were hurrying him along. Her father patted her cheek and opened the front door. Then he stopped. Turned around with a pleading look in his eyes.

"Couldn't you come and stay with us for a few weeks? I'm sure Andreis has a lot to think about right now. Wouldn't it be more peaceful for you and Lukas?"

Mina knew that her parents worried about her. Things had gotten worse; it was impossible to hide the bruises.

"Mom and I . . . we think about you all the time."

They'd tried to get her to move in with them when Andreis was in jail, but she'd known he would have regarded it as a betrayal, and she would have paid the price when he came out. Her father's persistence was making her uncomfortable. She couldn't help looking over his shoulder at the street, but thank God it was still empty.

"We'll talk about it some other time," she said.

"Andreis is no good for you—you know that!" He raised his voice, but Mina didn't have the strength to reassure him. All her energy went into protecting Lukas. And herself.

"Please, Dad. Not now. I've got so much to do."

Her father rubbed his forehead. New lines had appeared on his face over the past few years; she had to remind herself that he was only fifty-five. His graying hair needed cutting.

"Mom isn't well," he said reluctantly.

Mina went cold all over. "What do you mean?"

"There's a problem with her heart."

"No, not Mom!"

The words came out as a reflex. Mom had to be there. Always. Even if it was difficult, sometimes impossible to meet up, Mom was her last refuge. Mom and Dad were there for her, whatever happened.

She could go home.

"You probably haven't noticed, but she gets kind of breathless. It's gotten worse lately. She's been given a priority referral to the Southern District Hospital; she has an appointment next week."

Mina wanted to cry. If only she could grab Lukas and go home to Skuru with her dad. There was nothing she'd rather do. But it was impossible—why didn't he understand?

"I'll call her soon," she promised, digging her nails into the palms of her hands to maintain her self-control.

"Can't you come over and see her? She'd be so pleased if you brought Lukas. How about tomorrow? Or Wednesday?"

The hope in her father's voice was just making things worse. She couldn't let him see how stressed out she was. Lukas would wake up any minute, and before that she had to get the potatoes in the oven and marinate the steaks. She hadn't even set the table yet.

"I'll try," she said, even though she knew it wasn't going to happen. "Bye, Dad. Drive safely. I really must get on now." She kissed his cheek and closed the door.

Lukas was whimpering quietly. Mina grabbed the detergent and a cloth and hurried toward the guest bathroom. With a bit of luck Lukas would go back to sleep for a little while so that she could finish her chores.

CHAPTER 2

Thomas poured meatballs into the frying pan. The "best before" date was the previous day, but he hadn't had time to go shopping.

The pan hissed and spat, and he suppressed a curse as hot oil caught his hand.

He'd had a crap day at work. The reorganization of the police force just wouldn't settle, causing one colleague after another to walk away. This afternoon he'd found out that Kalle Lidwall, one of the people he'd worked with the longest, had decided to leave the force in favor of a security firm. Their civilian assistant, Karin Ek, had also resigned when the investigative department in Nacka had been absorbed into the Serious Crimes Unit in Flemingsberg. She'd said she just couldn't cope with the commute.

Elin was sitting on the sofa watching TV, something with happy children jumping from a sunlit jetty into the water. Thomas tried to ignore the noise; he didn't need reminding that this would be Elin's first summer on the island of Harö without her mother.

He opened the refrigerator and took out a can of low-alcohol beer. He needed to talk to Pernilla about the summer, how they were going to divide up the vacation and who would spend which weeks with Elin. He'd already sent several text messages with various suggestions, but she hadn't come back to him with a concrete answer, just vague indications that she'd think about it.

His cell phone rang; the display showed Pernilla's number.

"Hi, it's me."

She sounded as if she had a cold. He knew her so well, and yet he didn't know her at all. He still didn't understand how they'd ended up in this situation.

"I just wanted to say good-night to Elin," she said. There was a brief pause. It was Pernilla's turn to have Elin tomorrow; they usually swapped over on Mondays, but Thomas and Elin had been away for the Easter weekend. "I have to call your cell since she doesn't have one of her own," she added.

Thomas suppressed a weary sigh. Yet another point on which they couldn't agree. Pernilla wanted to give Elin a phone, but Thomas thought an eight-year-old was way too young. Pernilla argued that it was impractical for her to be unable to contact her daughter directly, but as far as Thomas was concerned that was just an excuse, a strategy to avoid admitting that she was often held up at the office. If Pernilla made an effort to get home on time, then their daughter wouldn't need a phone. Simple.

"What are we doing with Elin over the summer?" he asked, more brusquely than he'd intended.

"What do you mean?"

"I need to schedule my vacation—didn't you get my text messages?"

"Do we have to talk about this now?"

"Human resources has already reminded me more than once. I need to give them an answer."

"Thomas, I don't know what I'm doing yet." She broke off and coughed, then blew her nose. "It's hard to make plans right now—there's a lot going on."

It was like pressing a button. Thomas couldn't stop himself. "It's always hard for you to make plans, Pernilla. But I also have a job that needs forward planning."

"I don't want to argue, but I won't be able to tell you definitely until the middle of May. We have a major product launch in September. I can't make predictions at the moment."

Thomas squeezed the beer can so hard it buckled. Elin looked over at him, and Thomas forced a reassuring smile.

"Can't you show some understanding for once?" Pernilla continued, as if he were the one being unreasonable.

The angry silence grew, until Thomas had had enough. He made a huge effort to keep his tone neutral. "OK, so this is what we're going to do. I'll book my vacation beginning July 1, so that Elin can make the most of the summer here on Harö. At least she'll be able to spend time with her grandparents."

The message was crystal clear: *Even if her mother's not around.*

"You can't do that."

Pernilla sounded upset, but he didn't care. He'd tried to find the best solution, but he couldn't be responsible for her disorganized life. Sometimes you just had to make a decision. "You give me no other option," he said.

"You don't get to dictate what happens!"

"I've been trying to negotiate with you for over a month. What else am I supposed to do?"

"For fuck's sake, Thomas—you're behaving like a child!"

He couldn't talk to her anymore without saying something that he couldn't take back. He went over to the sofa; Elin was laughing at an animated figure doing dumb stuff for the hundredth time.

"I'll pass you over to Elin," he said. "It's Mom, sweetheart—she wants to say good-night."

Elin took the phone, keeping her eyes fixed on the screen as she spoke to her mother. She didn't appear to have noticed the bad atmosphere or the heated discussion between her parents.

At least he hoped she hadn't, even though he still felt guilty. He didn't want Elin to hear them quarreling.

He went back into the kitchen, poured the beer into a glass, and put the buckled can in the recycling bin. He was so tired of the constant sniping. Every conversation ended the same way.

The only form of communication that seemed to work these days was text messaging. They usually managed to agree when they exchanged short sentences, but as soon as they attempted to speak on the phone, it all went wrong.

He'd been too hard on her, he knew that, but did she have to snap right back at him every time? Why did this keep on happening?

He poured the pan of pasta into the colander with such force that boiling water splashed onto his foot.

"Shit!"

This time he couldn't help himself.

CHAPTER 3

Mina allowed herself to relax. The house was immaculate; the food was all prepared. There was nothing that could possibly annoy Andreis when he got home.

She was sitting in the living room with Lukas on her lap, giving him his bottle. He was sucking away with enthusiasm, rosebud lips clamped around the nipple. They would have a nice evening, Mina promised herself. Andreis would be in a good mood when he saw how clean and tidy the house was, and what an excellent dinner she'd cooked. He would look at her with the same adoration as when they first met, when they were so much in love that they could hardly keep their hands off each other. They would sit at the table chatting, just like any normal family. After they'd eaten, Andreis would play with Lukas while she cleared the table and loaded the dishwasher. When Lukas fell asleep, maybe they could settle down with a cup of freshly brewed coffee or a last glass of wine and watch a movie.

She was just about to lift Lukas up to burp him when she heard the front door open. Her stomach automatically contracted, but she pushed aside the bad thoughts and forced herself to take long, slow breaths. There was no reason to fear the worst. Everything was going to be fine. She had to believe that.

Then her blood turned to ice.

The vacuum cleaner was still in the middle of the kitchen floor. Lukas had started crying just as she was about to put it away, and she'd hurried into the living room. How could she have been so stupid?

She listened for footsteps. Could she make it to the kitchen and put it away before Andreis got there?

She didn't dare move. Her head was spinning. Maybe he'd go upstairs first? Sometimes he liked to take a shower as soon as he got home from work. That would give her the chance to correct her mistake before he noticed anything.

Her heart pounded as she waited for the sound of footsteps.

Tuesday

CHAPTER 4

Nora Linde opened the conference room door with her elbow, then put down a pile of documents on the long table. The weekly meeting of the Second Chamber of the Swedish Financial Crimes Authority was due to begin in a few minutes. She really needed to focus, but she had slept badly and was stressed about all the cases she was dealing with at the moment.

Chief Prosecutor Jonathan Sandelin joined her. He must have been in a hurry this morning; he had a bandage on his chin, presumably from a mishap while shaving.

"Morning," he said, pulling out a chair. "Good Easter?"

The question was rhetorical. Nora gave a slight nod as more colleagues arrived. Someone who'd been in bright and early had drawn a flower on the whiteboard and written: *Welcome back!*

Leila Kacim, the detective inspector with whom Nora often worked, came in and sat down on the opposite side of the table.

Jonathan spent a few minutes updating everyone on current issues and relevant points arising from the leadership team meeting before he went through the list of new cases that were allocated to the different chambers within the authority. Over Easter an extreme right-wing member of Parliament had been caught embezzling local party funds, and a construction company had engaged various subcontractors who hadn't paid their taxes.

When he'd finished, he went around the table asking everyone to report briefly on the status of ongoing investigations.

It was Nora's turn.

"How's it going with the tax fraud and the drugs gang?" Jonathan asked. "Are we any closer to bringing charges?"

Nora opened the file in front of her.

The Narcotics Division had been watching Andreis Kovač for a long time. They knew he was heavily involved in dealing, but there hadn't been enough concrete evidence to charge him with drug-related offenses. Then the revenue office had received an anonymous tip-off with supporting material that would enable the Economic Crimes Authority to charge Kovač with serious tax fraud instead. The investigation into his business affairs had taken up the majority of Nora and Leila's time during the spring.

She was close to "doing an Al Capone"—sending a representative of the organized crime fraternity down for financial irregularities, because he couldn't be charged with criminal activity.

"The preliminary investigation into Andreis Kovač is almost done," she began. "I'm going to interview him one last time this week, but I'm confident of a conviction."

The final statement was unnecessary. Everyone in the room knew that a case could only be brought to court if the prosecutor could be sure of a conviction on objective grounds. Anything else would be regarded as professional misconduct.

"Is he still on remand?"

Nora did her best to remain impassive, even though Jonathan's question struck home. She had done her best to convince the court that Kovač should remain in custody until the trial, but the court had refused and chosen to release him.

One point to Kovač and his defense team, unfortunately.

"I'm afraid not. The court released him after a few weeks. No doubt his poor wife would have felt much better if they'd kept him behind bars."

"Has something happened?"

"She was taken into the Southern District Hospital yesterday."

Nora had received the information just before the meeting; it had been a real blow. She took out her tablet and found the message.

"Mina Kovač was admitted last night with two broken ribs, plus a split lip and eyebrow."

"And is it certain that her husband was behind this?"

"More than likely," Nora said. "It's not the first time she's ended up in the hospital." Nora had requested a record of Mina's previous hospital visits; there was a clear pattern.

"Do they have children who are forced to witness the abuse?" Jonathan asked.

"A son. He's only three months old."

"And how old is the wife?"

"Just turned twenty-five. They've been together for four years. Unlike Andreis, whose family fled from the war in Bosnia, Mina comes from an ordinary middle-class Swedish background. She graduated from high school but didn't continue her studies. She hasn't had any kind of paid employment over the past few years. Her parents, Stefan and Katrin Talevski, live in Skuru in the district of Nacka. Her father is an accountant and her mother works in a preschool."

"When are you hoping to go to trial?"

Nora was going for serious tax evasion and accountancy fraud, possibly money laundering. Could she add assault? "I'd like to get a court date before the summer vacation," she replied.

"What sentence are you going for?"

The maximum jail term for tax evasion was six years, but the courts rarely imposed it. It was no secret that sentences for economic crimes were often at the lower end of the range, although the situation was improving.

"Three to four years—maybe a little more, depending on the amount of money involved."

"Is he cooperating?" Jonathan asked.

Nora allowed herself a wry smile. "No chance. Kovač has appointed Ulrika Grönstedt to represent him, and you know what she's like."

Leila caught Nora's eye and gave her an understanding look.

Ulrika Grönstedt had a reputation for being tough. Nora wasn't sure why Ulrika felt the need to fulfill all the clichés about hard-boiled defense attorneys, but she was ice cold and difficult to deal with. She made a point of arguing about everything, including purely procedural issues, as if every detail was a potential battleground.

"Who's leading the domestic abuse investigation?" one of the other prosecutors wondered.

Nora sighed. "I'm not sure if Kovač will be charged. Mina insists that she tripped over the vacuum cleaner, which she'd left in the middle of the kitchen floor. Her husband wasn't even home when it happened. Or so she says."

"No surprise there," Leila said, crumpling a piece of paper into a tight ball and throwing it into the garbage can with impressive accuracy.

"She's never reported him in the past," Nora went on. "The police arrested him last night, but I suspect he'll be out in no time."

Without Mina's cooperation it would be almost impossible to bring charges against her husband, even if she was black and blue. Medical reports meant very little if the victim refused to talk.

"I'm thinking she could be useful to us," Jonathan said. "Have you questioned her?"

"Very briefly. She denied all knowledge of her husband's financial affairs."

Jonathan fingered the bandage on his chin. "She might change her mind if we suggest combining the two cases. Have a chat with her, see how the land lies."

Nora made a note. "I was actually planning to call on her tomorrow," she said.

Bosnia, February 1992

When Andreis walked into the living room, his parents were watching TV, even though it was the middle of the day. His father had a cigarette in his mouth; the column of ash was so long that it was in danger of dropping off at any second. His mother's cup of coffee was untouched.

Andreis tugged at her arm to get her attention. "Can I go and play outside?"

"Not now, sweetheart."

"Please?"

"Later."

His mother shook off his hand without taking her eyes from the television. Andreis had no idea what they were watching. It was just a lot of guys in suits sitting in a great big room with rows and rows of seats. Their expressions were serious, and they were all talking over the top of one another.

An older guy stood up and went over to a lectern. His white hair was still thick, but he had noticeable bags under his eyes.

"We have lived in a multicultural society for many years," he began. "Croats, Serbs, and Bosnians, side by side. We must do all we can to keep the peace in this country so that we can continue to live together in unity and harmony. We do not want war."

He paused, his hands gripping the sides of the lectern.

"The only way to achieve this is through independence." A pleading note crept into his voice. "We have to hold a referendum on the future of Bosnia. We must declare independence and preserve our open society; otherwise we will be torn apart."

He was interrupted by others shouting objections and insults. Andreis had never heard such language. Under normal circumstances his mother would have chased him away, but right now she didn't seem to be aware that he was still there.

"The international community is on our side," the white-haired speaker said in conclusion, although he could barely be heard above the racket.

He went back to his seat, and another man stepped forward. He came from the most vocal group. His face was scarred, his eyes burning with passion beneath bushy brows.

"He's a Serb," Andreis's father explained. "You can see how his party despises the other members of Parliament. The Serbs aren't interested in peace."

His mother stroked her big belly and altered her position on the sofa. Andreis knew there was a baby in there; it was going to come out very soon.

The man on the screen slammed his hand down on the lectern, demanding silence. "There will be war if you hold a referendum," he shouted, raising his clenched fist in a threatening gesture.

Now everyone was yelling.

"Mom, I want to go outside," Andreis whined.

His father shushed him and turned up the volume.

The man with the scarred face raised both fists in the air. "The Bosnians will be trampled to death like a little ant between Serbia and Croatia if you vote for self-government! War will be unavoidable!"

CHAPTER 5

Nora was embarrassed at the state of her desk when she returned to her office. It was covered with piles of paper and folders; it was always the same toward the end of an investigation. She was a tidy person by nature, but right now she would have liked an extra desk for all the paperwork.

She needed to speak to the police about the investigation into the assault on Mina. The easiest thing would be to call Thomas. There were official routes, but this gave her an excuse to find out how things were with him.

He'd had a busy winter, and they hadn't spoken in almost two weeks. He'd spent the Easter weekend in Spain with Elin and his parents. The last time Nora saw him, he'd been really down.

The separation between him and Pernilla was comparatively recent—just a few months. At the moment Thomas was staying in the apartment in the Söder district of the city, while Pernilla had moved out. She traveled so much for work anyway that it seemed like the most sensible option, he'd explained on one of the few occasions when he'd talked to Nora about the situation. Pernilla had found a nearby two-bedroom sublet that she was renting until the summer.

Nora scrolled down to his number.

"Andreasson," replied a familiar voice.

"Is that Detective Inspector Andreasson?" she asked, as if he didn't know who was calling.

They'd been friends for more than half their lives; it was hard to believe they were now middle-aged. She wasn't entirely comfortable with that thought.

"It depends," he said. "Is this personal or work related?"

Nora switched to speakerphone. "You choose."

"OK, work." His tone softened. "Sorry, but I have a meeting in five minutes. How can I help?"

Nora quickly explained.

"Kovač is still in custody," Thomas confirmed after a brief pause. "He's been questioned twice. He denies assaulting his wife, and insists it was an accident. If no other evidence emerges, he'll be released on Thursday at the latest."

"No new witnesses have come forward? Neighbors, for example? Someone must have heard her screaming."

"Not necessarily."

Nora could hear him typing as they spoke.

"They live in an upscale residential area," he went on. "The gardens are pretty big. Only Kovač and Mina were in the house when the ambulance arrived. His wife was taken to the hospital, and a patrol brought him in. Let me see . . . He was arrested at eight thirty last night."

Nora made a note. "Have you heard her version yet?"

"She made a short statement. She refused to cooperate; she claims it wasn't her husband's fault, she just happened to trip over the vacuum cleaner."

None of this came as a surprise.

"What about forensic evidence?" Nora asked. "There must be something to link him to the assault."

"Nothing that can't be explained away by the fact that he was trying to take care of her afterward. He got blood on his clothes when he helped her up." Thomas snorted. "I have no doubt that he beat her up. They were alone in the house, apart from the baby, who was in his crib. With a skilled lawyer Kovač will be able to account for every detail, as long as Mina doesn't say anything."

Thomas hadn't sounded this cynical for many years, but the major reorganization at work had affected both him and his colleagues. He'd been very open about the fact that the constant changes of direction and lack of leadership made the job more difficult than ever. Many experienced officers had left the police force in frustration, and the shortage of skilled forensic technicians didn't make life any easier.

Thomas was now stationed a long way south of Stockholm, in the complex at Flemingsberg, which dealt with crimes throughout Nacka, Värmdö, Södertälje, and the archipelago. Was the job wearing him down, or were the problems in his private life taking their toll?

Someone called out his name.

"Sorry, Nora—I have to go."

"Thanks for your help. By the way, who's been appointed prosecutor?"

"Erik Sandberg."

Nora didn't recognize the name, but there were a lot of prosecutors in Stockholm.

"We'll have to get together soon," she said.

"Absolutely." Thomas sounded stressed, as if his mind were already elsewhere.

Nora thought for a moment. If she could persuade Mina to file a complaint against her husband, that would increase the pressure on Andreis Kovač. He would have two criminal investigations to deal with, and Ulrika Grönstedt would find it more difficult to present her client as an upstanding citizen.

It was worth a shot.

She decided to give Erik Sandberg a call, offer to take over the domestic abuse case, ideally with his blessing and assistance. If she found Mina alternative accommodation, a place where she could feel safe, then maybe she would trust the authorities enough to cooperate.

There was a women's shelter on the island of Runmarö that would be ideal—Freya's Haven. Nora went online to find the contact details for the personal security team so that they could organize a place for Mina and prepare for her arrival.

CHAPTER 6

Anna-Maria Petersén put down the phone and closed her eyes.

There was no end to it.

All these women who were slowly but surely crushed by abuse and hatred and had to hide from violent men. She'd just agreed to take in yet another woman at Freya's Haven; she'd lost count of how many she'd helped.

She gazed out of the window. From her office she could see the lawn and the flower beds, with a shimmer of blue water just visible beyond the sparse pine trees. Freya's Haven was in an idyllic location on the island of Runmarö. It was more like a beautiful summer home than a shelter, and that was exactly the intention. It was meant to blend in with its environment.

Malin, her only child, smiled at Anna-Maria from the photograph on her desk, her eyes sparkling. Anna-Maria reached out and touched the picture to find strength and remember happier times. Her darling girl.

She sat back. She had to keep faith, keep believing that what she was doing made a difference. If she gave up, who would take over? She couldn't let the dark thoughts come creeping in.

Through the closed door she could hear children playing in the common room. This week Freya's Haven had nine women and two children in residence. The sound of the little ones laughing was the best thing in the world; it made her forget her own troubles. They lived in the moment, and just like them she must appreciate the good times, instead of worrying about finances and the needs that always seemed to exceed the available resources, wondering where the women would go when they could no longer stay here.

Why did she always feel so inadequate?

There was a knock on the door, and Beyan Rezazi, one of the permanent staff at the shelter, came in.

"Sorry to disturb you, but the inspector from social services is here."

Anna-Maria sighed and got to her feet. The talk of cuts was becoming increasingly persistent. The local authority had to save money, just like everyone else. She held out her hand to the woman in a navy-blue pantsuit, who introduced herself as Birgitta Svanberg.

"Welcome. Can I get you a coffee?"

"I'm fine, thanks. I'm a little short of time," the inspector replied as she sat down. Anna-Maria didn't recognize her; she must be new. There were frequent changes of staff at the local authority, particularly within social services. The inspectors looked increasingly stressed out.

"Maybe I should start by telling you what we do here," Anna-Maria said, running a hand over her graying ponytail. "Freya's Haven has been here for about ten years. It was founded as a collective based on a nonprofit trust. We offer a shelter for those who need it, and everyone has their own room. The staff are knowledgeable and experienced, providing individually tailored support."

Way too eager. She was spouting clichés, sounding like an advertising brochure, and yet she couldn't slow down.

"The women who are placed here are given a contact who can offer structured counseling sessions with the aim of strengthening their self-esteem and helping them to deal with the trauma they've suffered. This also applies to the children, if they're old enough."

Birgitta Svanberg showed no reaction to this torrent of words, which made Anna-Maria even more nervous.

"We also arrange follow-up meetings with whoever places the women, and with anyone in authority who is important to them," she went on. "We try to offer communal or individual activities, and we run a number of different projects. The aim is for the women who come here to live as normal a life as possible. They all carry out day-to-day chores, and they cook and wash up for themselves."

Still no reaction. What the hell was wrong with the woman? Did she have to sit there like a living statue?

Anna-Maria tried to speak more slowly, with greater weight behind her words. Without the financial support of social services, Freya's Haven wouldn't survive.

"We want the women to be able to return to an independent life, with a job and a place to live," she said. Everything was geared toward building up their self-esteem, making them realize that they had a voice. She could almost weep when she saw how cowed and insecure the new arrivals were; they were so used to a situation where their opinions did not count, where they had no control over their lives. "We achieve excellent results, and we make a real difference to those who come here."

"Do you have data on the percentage who revert to their old ways?" asked Birgitta Svanberg.

She made it sound as if she were talking about prisoners reoffending. Anna-Maria didn't quite know what to say. "Sorry?"

"Women who go back to their husbands in spite of the time they've spent here. What's the situation after twelve months?"

"We don't keep records like that."

"So how do you know you achieve excellent results?"

Anna-Maria's mouth went dry. "We offer follow-up meetings for anyone who wants them." She could hear how lame it sounded.

"I understand," said the woman, who didn't appear to understand anything. She was a bureaucrat, a pen pusher who didn't care about what the women here were going through. As far as she was concerned, they were simply a task to be ticked off. The budget had to balance—nothing else mattered. She wrote something down in her notebook. "As I said on the phone, we're in the process of assessing a range of alternatives within the local authority. It's possible we may need to concentrate our provision to a greater extent than at present."

Anna-Maria knew what that meant. *Concentrate* was code for "cut." The council wanted to get rid of safe, well-run shelters until only a few places remained for the women who were worst affected—the minimum level required by law.

Before long there would be a public bidding process, and whoever offered to take care of broken women for the lowest sum of money would win the contract. It reminded Anna-Maria of the so-called poor auctions in the past, when paupers and orphaned children were handed over to the farmer who demanded the least money to look after them.

"We'll be carrying out an assessment," Birgitta Svanberg continued. "You'll receive a questionnaire by email within the next week or so." She got to her feet. "I'm afraid I have to leave; otherwise I'll miss the ferry back to the mainland."

Her visit had lasted fifteen minutes at the most. Why had she bothered to come, if she wasn't interested in looking around?

Because you insisted on a face-to-face meeting, a little voice whispered. Had Anna-Maria really thought that the mere sight of Freya's Haven would convince this soulless bureaucrat that it should escape any cuts?

"Won't you let me show you around?" she ventured. "The children love being here. Even those who've experienced the most terrible things at home feel better after a few days. There's something about the air and the archipelago that heals damaged souls."

Nothing.

Anna-Maria leaned forward. "I can't overemphasize how important a safe, welcoming environment is for mothers and children who have undergone such trauma. They can stay here as long as they wish, and the children can attend school without worrying about what they'll come home to. Once again—they really do heal with us."

"Unfortunately, I don't have time to look around today. Another time, perhaps."

Anna-Maria nodded, although she wanted to scream at the fucking woman to get out and take her idiotic questions with her. Instead she accompanied her to the main door and said a polite good-bye before returning to her office and flopping down on the chair.

It was bad enough fighting the despair and the feeling that the world was an evil place every time she heard another story about an abusive man. Fighting the politicians and their determination to save money was just too much.

Anna-Maria rubbed her eyes; she was exhausted. Sometimes she wondered if she could get through one more day.

CHAPTER 7

The cell phone on the nightstand beside the hospital bed vibrated. Mina didn't need to check the display to know that it was Andreis. He'd already called three times. She'd put the phone on silent after the first two calls, but she didn't want to switch it off completely because of what her dad had said about her mom's heart.

The call went to voice mail.

Why couldn't Andreis leave her in peace? She didn't want to speak to him. Not yet.

It was too painful, in every way.

If only she could hide under the covers, stay in the hospital, never leave. In here she didn't have to think about the future or make any decisions.

She had no idea how she could go on living with Andreis after what had happened. Or go back to Trastvägen. But she didn't know how she was going to leave him either.

The rain was hammering against the windowpane. A storm had swept in across the city during the afternoon, and the dark-gray heavens had opened. She ought to switch on the bedside lamp, but instead she lay there in the semidarkness.

She didn't even have the strength to press the button.

Her phone beeped; presumably Andreis had left a message. She pictured him sitting there with his phone in his hand in the custody suite. She knew the police had arrested him after she'd been brought to the hospital.

She made a huge effort and picked up the phone. Deep down she didn't want to listen to the message, didn't want to hear what he had to say, but she couldn't help herself.

His recorded voice aroused way too many emotions. She went hot and cold at the same time.

"Forgive me, my darling," he whispered.

He sounded completely different from the previous evening, when his pupils had been no more than tiny pinpricks as she'd cowered beneath his raised fists. This was the real Andreis, the man she'd fallen in love with.

Lukas's daddy.

"I'm so sorry for what I did. You don't know how much I love you. You're my whole life. Please let me talk to you!"

The phone was burning her hand. Tears poured down her cheeks.

"Can't you just answer when I call—"

The message ended abruptly. Mina dropped the phone onto the bed. What should she do? Everything was such a mess, and she was so tired.

The phone rang. Andreis. Again. As if someone else had taken over her body, Mina accepted the call on the fourth ring.

"Darling Mina!" Andreis wept in her ear. "Can you forgive me?" An audible sob. "How are you? How's Lukas? Where are you?"

"We're in the Southern District Hospital."

"I swear I never meant for this to happen. Everything went black, as if I'd turned into someone else. I don't understand it, you have to believe me."

He'd never been like this, so naked and pathetic.

"I can't talk to you," she mumbled.

Lukas had spat out his pacifier and was moving uneasily in the crib beside her bed. Mina reached out and popped it back in his mouth. A stab of pain from her broken ribs made her gasp.

"This can't go on." Every word that passed her swollen lips was agonizing.

"You mustn't leave me. I promise I'll never do it again."

She'd heard that so many times before. His promises. She'd always believed him.

"You need to get help," she said quietly.

"Please, please say you forgive me. I'll do anything if you'll just come home."

"I have to go."

"I can't live without you, you know I can't." He sounded desperate and despairing. "I'm locked up in a cell at Nacka police station. It's unbearable—you know I won't cope."

Andreis panicked in enclosed spaces. Mina closed her eyes.

"You and Lukas are the most important people in my life, Mina. Please forgive me."

The rain was lashing against the windowpane now.

"I forgive you," she whispered.

CHAPTER 8

Nora looked at her watch. It was time to go home if she was going to give the kids dinner at a decent hour. People had started to leave, but she still had so much to go through. She also needed to find a window to meet with Mina Kovač and familiarize herself with the domestic abuse case.

I'll stay for half an hour, no more, she promised herself. Then she would hurry home to Saltsjöbaden.

"Still here?" Leila was standing in the doorway with an overripe banana in one hand. "Did you speak to Stockholm South about Kovač's wife?"

"Yes, we're taking over. It's simpler that way."

Erik Sandberg, the prosecutor, had been happy to accept Nora's suggestion. Everyone had too much to do.

Leila sat down and took a bite of her banana. "Shouldn't you go home?" she said. "I thought Jonas was away all week?"

Nora pointed wordlessly at the files and documents covering the surface of her desk. She had promised Jonathan that the charge against Andreis Kovač would be filed next week. She hoped she would be able to keep that promise, but the case material was extensive and complex—folder after folder containing details of the income streams that had passed through Kovač's multiple bank accounts, making him a wealthy man.

The Narcotics Division had provided enough information to enable them to calculate the turnover from the sale of cocaine, ecstasy, and amphetamines. It was possible to estimate both income and costs, the cash flow necessary to run any business.

Kovač was making millions.

"It's lucky for us that not even criminal networks can deal only in cash these days," Leila said. "Otherwise we'd never have been able to pin him down." She took another bite, then made a face and threw the rest of the banana in Nora's garbage can. "Today's digital society makes things difficult for professional criminals, too."

"Everyone's under scrutiny these days," Nora agreed.

Without the anonymous tip-off they would never have been able to piece the puzzle together. Kovač had a regular income in cash from illegal drug dealing. The amount of profit depended on where you were in the chain, and Kovač was very high up. A kilo of cocaine cost around four hundred thousand kronor, but could be sold on the street for at least twice as much, where a gram was the most common unit. Once the purchase price had been deducted and the minor players further down the chain had been paid, a significant profit remained—in cash.

The problem was feeding this money into the financial system without the banks reacting and reporting a suspected irregularity to the authorities. If large amounts of cash were frequently paid into an account, alarm bells ought to start ringing. Following the financial crisis of 2008, national legislators had introduced a series of control mechanisms. The EU had also increased its regulation through special directives.

"Look what I just got from the IT guys," Nora said. "They've drawn a diagram."

She unfolded a large sheet of paper. Arrows in different colors illustrated all the connections where Kovač was involved in companies or bank accounts in one way or another. The paper covered half the desk, giving a clear overview of the extent of his business interests.

"What do the colors mean?" Leila asked as she studied the diagram.

"Red indicates sole ownership of a company. Blue is part ownership, and yellow shows the income streams."

When Nora and her team had started digging, they had discovered that Kovač owned a group of companies. This enabled him to move money around until it became impossible to trace the profits from his criminal activities.

"This is an empire," Leila said. "He's a smart guy, you have to give him that. He'd have had a glowing career if he'd gone down the academic route instead. Particularly with those looks."

Nora wasn't impressed by Kovač's slick profile, but she had to agree with Leila. He'd built up a wide-ranging and lucrative organization to handle his illegal earnings from the drug trade. He must have had help. A structure of this caliber required expert knowledge of both company law and financial management.

"Do you think Ulrika Grönstedt could be behind it?" Leila added.

Grönstedt was one of Sweden's finest defense attorneys, but this required a different skill set.

"I don't think she could do it," Nora said slowly. "She's good, but this needs both accountants and economists, people who deal with every transaction—companies being bought and sold, corporate decision-making, all the necessary legal documentation." She followed one of the arrows with her finger. "However, I wouldn't be surprised if her practice is involved."

"I'm sure they offer their clients a broad palette of services," Leila said, still studying the diagram.

When the team analyzed all the income streams, a clear picture had crystallized. Kovač chose businesses that handled significant amounts of cash—market stalls, restaurants, cab companies, construction firms. Enough to explain why a considerable volume of liquid assets was generated on a regular basis. The money was paid into small, carefully selected currency exchange offices that specialized in dealing with cash that then moved it on to accounts distributed among a large number of banks. Suddenly the money was in the banking system, and could be sent anywhere with the press of a button.

"What do the broken lines mean?" Leila asked.

"Those are companies he owned for a while, then sold."

By selling these companies, Kovač acquired untouchable profits that could legitimately be transferred to his parent company, which was registered in Bosnia and Herzegovina. However, the country was currently on the European Commission's blacklist of nations deemed to be seriously negligent when it came to combating money laundering. The simple fact that Bosnia and Herzegovina was linked to Kovač's business affairs was enough to arouse suspicion. Other countries on the list included Afghanistan, Iraq, and Syria.

But it wasn't illegal.

"Nicely done." Leila sounded impressed, but Nora wasn't sure if she was referring to the diagram or Kovač's smart moves. "And then he tries to convince us that he bets on the horses," she said with a derisive sniff.

When asked a direct question about how he had built up his lifestyle—the big house, the Rolex watch, and the top-of-the-line cars—Kovač had maintained that he often bet on trotting races and won. His winnings had provided the start-up capital.

Nora could hear Ulrika Grönstedt putting the words into his mouth. "It is what it is," she went on. "The main thing is that the charge holds up when we file."

"So you're going for serious tax evasion?"

"I am."

Nora had no doubt that Kovač was also guilty of money laundering, but after lengthy discussions and due consideration, she'd decided that the chain of evidence just wasn't there.

In other words, she was in the same boat as Narcotics, who didn't have enough evidence to prove that Kovač was behind a major part of the drug traffic in Stockholm's suburbs.

"It's better to focus on a charge where I stand a chance of gaining a conviction rather than taking a risk," she said, massaging her stiff neck. Hopefully it would be enough to put Kovač behind bars for a long time.

Nora's cell phone rang; it was her daughter, Julia.

"Hi, sweetheart."

"When are you coming home?"

The guilt kicked in immediately.

"I'm already on my way," she said, deciding a white lie wouldn't do any harm as she mouthed "Julia" to Leila.

Nora gathered up her papers. It was six thirty; it would take her almost an hour to get home. Far too late to start cooking dinner for Julia, who ought to be in bed by eight.

Leila stood up. "See you tomorrow," she said as she left the room.

CHAPTER 9

There was a gentle tap on the door of Mina's room.

"Come in."

Mina had been dozing, but she propped herself up on her elbows as the door opened. She didn't recognize the elderly woman who came in. It was difficult to make out her features in the semidarkness, but she was wearing a Red Cross badge on her sweater.

"Hi—my name is Irene. I'm a volunteer at the hospital, and I just wanted to check if there's anything I can do for you."

Mina was confused. What did she mean?

"We can have a little chat if you like," Irene continued. "Or I can sit here for a while if you're feeling lonely?"

To her own surprise, Mina nodded, even though the woman was a total stranger.

Irene peeped into Lukas's crib. He was lying on his back, full and contented, completely absorbed by a mobile one of the nurses had hung up for him.

"What a sweetheart! How old is he?"

"Three months."

"He's doing really well."

Mina couldn't hide a proud smile.

"And how are you?" Irene went on. "Are you OK?"

The smile disappeared. "Not exactly," she whispered. She was so embarrassed by her appearance; it was obvious she'd taken a beating.

Irene didn't seem to mind at all. "I'm happy to listen if you want to talk," she said. "I'm in no hurry, and sometimes it's nice not to be left alone with your thoughts."

She pulled up a chair and sat down by the bed. There was something about her that made Mina feel calm. Her white hair was secured by a barrette at the back of her neck; she reminded Mina of one of her elementary school teachers that she'd always liked.

Irene was wearing a gold ring with an ornate floral pattern on the third finger of her left hand. "What a beautiful ring," Mina said.

"Thank you. I never take it off. My husband gave it to me just before he died."

"Oh, I'm so sorry!"

"It's fine. He passed away several years ago." Silence fell, but Irene was still smiling, as if it didn't bother her at all.

"Do you miss him?" Mina asked after a while.

"Every day, but he was very ill at the end, so it was a relief in a way."

Irene's tone made Mina feel she could ask another question. "Did you love each other?"

"Very much. We were married for almost fifty years. We met when we were twenty-one—it was love at first sight."

"I was twenty-one when I got together with Andreis. That was love at first sight, too."

"How did you meet?"

"In a bar in the city. I saw him as soon as I walked in."

Andreis had been leaning on the counter with a beer in his hand when Mina arrived with a girlfriend. His dark eyes and muscular arms had drawn her to him. She hadn't been able to stop wondering what it would feel like to have those arms around her. He was the best-looking guy she'd ever seen.

There was no doubt that he was the center of his circle of friends. When he cracked a joke, everyone laughed. It was as if they were all competing for his attention.

When Mina and Andreis eventually got together, she had loved his self-assurance, his conviction that the world revolved around him.

"How old are you now?" Irene asked.

"Twenty-five."

"You're so young." Irene patted her hand. She didn't know how wrong she was; Mina had never felt older. Where had that girl with the long blond hair gone? The girl who had been so much in love with Andreis that she'd trembled with happiness whenever he touched her.

"Did you and your husband ever quarrel?" she said, unconsciously touching the dressing on her eyebrow.

"You can't always agree in a long marriage, but we were usually on the same page."

"We didn't quarrel either, not at first."

"Would you like to talk about your husband?" Irene said gently, her ring glinting as she clasped her hands.

Mina looked over at the window. The darkness outside was impenetrable; her room was on the top floor. She had stood there, gazing out, earlier in the day, thinking that death would be instantaneous if she leaned too far and fell.

"It was like a fairy tale to begin with," she said without meeting Irene's gaze. "We moved in together after a few weeks, and married within six months."

She had been thrilled when Andreis proposed, floated on fluffy pink clouds on her wedding day. Giving up her old friends and the almost daily contact with her parents had been no sacrifice; it was wonderful that Andreis wanted her all to himself whenever he was free.

They'd done everything together, enclosed in their own bubble.

"We really were happy," Mina whispered. "Andreis spoiled me—he often came home with beautiful presents. It sounds like a cliché, but he gave me everything I wanted."

"That must have been wonderful."

"He was . . . is . . . wonderful."

Nobody could be as attentive as Andreis; nobody could make her feel so loved. His smile was irresistible.

"What happened yesterday wasn't like him at all. He didn't mean to hurt me." Mina ran a hand over her forehead. "He loves me, I know he does."

"And do *you* still love him?" Irene's eyes were full of sympathy; there was no judgment in her words.

Mina hadn't dared to ask herself that question, because she was afraid to hear the answer. She could see her reflection in the window, the swollen cheek, the split lip. As soon as she moved, everything hurt.

Lukas gurgled in his crib.

"I don't know," Mina said quietly.

Bosnia, March 1992

Andreis was woken by someone gently shaking him. When he opened his eyes, Aunt Blanka was perched on the side of his bed. She was his mother's best friend, married to his father's cousin—a big, cheerful woman who lived next door.

"Wake up, Andreis!" she said. "Something fantastic has happened!"

Andreis squeezed his eyes shut. He would rather go back to sleep in his soft, warm bed.

"You have a baby brother," Blanka informed him.

Andreis knew that the baby in his mother's tummy had been ready to come out. A week or so ago a crib had appeared in his room, even though there wasn't really enough space. Now there was just a narrow passageway between the crib and his bed, but his mother had explained that from now on he would be sharing his room with the new baby.

Blanka took his hand. "Come with me."

She led him into the kitchen, where his mother was sitting on a chair with a bundle in her arms. It was whimpering, a bit like a newborn puppy. When he moved closer, he saw a tiny face with red marks on its cheeks and forehead peering out from the blanket.

"Come and say hello to your new brother." His mother seemed tired, but she was smiling at Andreis. She held out the baby so that Andreis could see him better. Andreis didn't really know what to do, but he edged forward.

"It's OK, Andreis. You can touch him if you like."

Andreis reached out and gently stroked the baby's head. He had black tousled hair, just like Dad, but his eyes were closed, so Andreis couldn't see the color.

"You have to take care of him from now on," his mother said. "Big brothers always take care of their little brothers."

"What's his name?"

"Emir."

The front door opened and his father joined them in the kitchen.

"What do you think of your new brother?" he asked with a proud smile. He was holding a half-full bottle in his hand. He went over to the counter and fetched a glass, which he filled to the brim. "Here's to my son!" he exclaimed, knocking back the contents of the glass.

His mother's face stiffened. She looked at Blanka.

"Zlatko, I think Selma needs to get some rest," Blanka said.

Andreis's father didn't seem to hear her. He had already poured himself another drink, and raised his glass to his family.

"Time to celebrate!" he said.

Wednesday

CHAPTER 10

The tiredness crept up on Thomas as soon as he swiped his pass card to enter the police station in Flemingsberg. He plodded up the stairs to the seventh floor and the Serious Crimes Unit.

He would much rather have been on board a boat in the archipelago. He'd worked as a maritime police officer before transferring to Nacka, and in many ways it had been the best time of his career. At sea he had felt confident, and had instinctively found the right solutions. Even when dealing with taxing issues, such as the transportation of a body or a serious collision, he had had no difficulty staying focused.

He had rarely lain awake at night, as he often did now. Somehow any negative thoughts had been blown away as he set his course for home. The archipelago had enabled him to breathe more easily, even when things were at their worst. If it hadn't been for Elin, he would have considered living on Harö all year round.

He ran his hands through his damp hair and opened his office door. Yesterday had been glorious; today it was pouring rain. Typical spring weather in Stockholm.

There was no point in wallowing in old memories.

He hung up his jacket and went in search of coffee; he needed caffeine. In order to be in Flemingsberg before eight, he had to get up by six at the latest. Last night he hadn't gotten to sleep until after two; he'd spent half the night lying there, brooding.

Aram Gorgis, his partner for many years, was already sipping from his first cup of the day as he flicked through the folder containing new cases. He raised a hand in greeting when he saw Thomas. Aram looked fresh and well rested.

Thomas pressed the button for a large cup of coffee. Extra strong, even though he actually preferred tea.

Margit Grankvist appeared, making a beeline for the coffee machine. Another colleague who was finding life difficult.

Margit had been acting head of the department for almost two years, even though she was clearly the best-qualified person for the role of head of the Serious Crimes Unit within the new organization. If she wasn't appointed soon, she was likely to resign out of sheer frustration.

She wouldn't be the first.

"I heard that your friend Nora Linde has taken over a case from Erik Sandberg," she said as she also pressed the button for extrastrong coffee.

There were no secrets around here. Thomas gave her a quick summary of the conversation he'd had with Nora the previous day.

"Don't forget to log anything that might impact the case," she said, taking her cup. Thomas gave her a look; why did she need to say that? Then he realized she was just being kind. The way things were now, everyone was monitored at all times, and the formalities had assumed a disproportionate significance. In an uneasy, stressed environment, the rules were applied with increased rigor, even though this intensified the negative atmosphere. The sense of a lack of faith in leadership was growing with each passing day, while at the same time the media trumpeted the public's diminishing confidence in the police.

"Thanks for the reminder," he said without a hint of sarcasm, and headed back to his office.

He must call Pernilla later, make one last attempt to agree on the arrangement for summer vacation. He'd put it off for too long. The thought didn't improve his mood.

CHAPTER 11

Leila was waiting for Nora by the reception desk at the Southern District Hospital, her long black braid draped over one shoulder, skinny jeans tucked into her leather boots. She waved to Nora.

"It's ward fifty-five." Leila set off toward the elevators, heels tapping on the tiled floor. "You do know she has no intention of cooperating with us," she went on. "She's not going to report him, and she's not going to leave him. This is a waste of time."

Leila rarely expressed herself so forcefully, but Nora decided to let it go.

A stressed nurse pointed them in the right direction. "She has her own room," she said. "Because of the baby."

Leila pushed open the door of a room with white walls and a depressing gray floor. Mina was lying on her back with her eyes closed. Nora inhaled sharply when she saw the young woman's bruised and battered face. A white dressing covered one cheek, and Mina was on a drip.

I could have prevented this, Nora thought.

A man and a woman with gray hair were sitting at the far side of the bed, lines of worry etched into their faces. These must be Mina's parents, Stefan and Katrin. There was no mistaking her resemblance to her mother, in spite of Mina's injuries.

A small crib on wheels stood beside Mina; her baby was sleeping peacefully beneath a pale-lemon blanket.

Nora introduced herself and Leila and explained that they were from the Economic Crimes Authority, but had also taken over the assault case, and therefore needed to ask a few questions.

"How are you doing?" she said to Mina. "Do you feel able to talk to us for a little while?"

No response.

"Who did this to you?" Leila asked.

Mina shook her head.

It seemed incomprehensible that she was still protecting her husband, but Nora knew this wasn't uncommon. She was reacting in exactly the same way as many other women in her situation. Before long she would ask to go home, and on the way she would convince herself that what had happened wasn't too bad. That this was the last time— her husband would never hit her again. From now on, everything was going to be fine.

Stefan laid a hand on his daughter's arm. "You need to talk to the police, darling."

"Please, Mina," her mother said. "You can't stay with Andreis."

"We can help you," Nora assured the young woman. "We can move you into a shelter where he won't be able to find you."

Mina turned her face away. Nora knew it wouldn't be easy to persuade her, but without her cooperation there was no point in asking for Andreis to be arrested, and he could be held for questioning for only three days.

"Andreis will be released on Thursday if you don't change your statement," she went on. "In twenty-four hours he'll be back at home, and it starts all over again."

Had Mina gone paler? It was hard to tell, with all the bruises and the dressings.

"Think about Lukas," Katrin said. "This can't go on."

"I tripped," Mina mumbled. "I'm so clumsy."

Nora tried to hide her frustration; Leila had warned her that this would happen. They had to get Mina to change her mind before Kovač was released. As soon as he was out he would come to see her, beg for forgiveness, and try to put everything right. Had he already called her? Nora had no doubt that Mina would go with him if he promised never to hurt her again. She would talk herself into believing him, and things would be better for a while—until the next time.

There was always a next time.

"I tripped," Mina repeated.

"You do realize he's going to kill you in the end?" Leila said sharply.

Mina's eyes filled with tears, and she clenched her fists on top of the covers. "I can't talk to you. Please go. Leave me alone."

Leila moved closer to the bed. "You have to listen to us—for your own sake. You think he's sorry, don't you? That deep down he loves you. He didn't mean it, not really. You've come up with a whole list of excuses for his behavior. He's stressed about the upcoming trial, he was damaged by the flight from Bosnia when he was a little boy, by all the terrible memories he carries with him."

Mina tried to sit up, but grimaced with pain and fell back against the pillows.

"This is mainly your fault, isn't it?" Leila continued. "If only you made more of an effort, he wouldn't need to get so angry. If only you could stop annoying him, stop making so many mistakes. If only you loved him a little more, everything would be fine. But men who love women don't hit them, Mina. That's not how it works."

Nora didn't know Leila particularly well, even though they had collaborated on a number of cases over the past few years. Leila wasn't particularly forthcoming about her private life, but Nora knew her family had fled to Sweden from Iran toward the end of the 1980s, when Leila was only four. The details were unclear; her parents had divorced a couple of years later. The only personal item on Leila's desk was a photograph of a dog, a Newfoundland by the name of Bamse. He was the apple of Leila's eye, weighing in at 154 pounds.

"Next time he'll kill you," Leila said, softening her tone. "You have to believe me—for your own sake and for your child."

Tears were pouring down Mina's face.

"Listen to her," Stefan said hoarsely. "She's a police officer, she knows what she's talking about." He turned to Leila and Nora. "Can you protect her? He's a terrible person, dangerous and ruthless." Mina tried to protest, but Stefan was having none of it. "You know I'm right! Don't defend him!" He slammed the palm of his hand down on his leg. "For God's sake, Mina, look at the shape you're in! She's right—next time he'll kill you!"

Katrin was beginning to look distressed. "Please, Stefan—I don't want the two of you to argue!"

Nora held up her hand. The situation was getting out of control. If they could get Mina to a place where Kovač couldn't reach her, then maybe she'd feel safer. Safe enough to cooperate. "We can move you and your son to a shelter. No one will know you're there. I've already contacted a place on an island in the archipelago; they can take you tomorrow. It's in a beautiful spot. It's almost like a summer cottage. I'm sure you'd feel at home there."

Leila gently placed a hand on Mina's shoulder. "You don't need to be afraid that your husband will harass you. We'll keep him away, I promise."

"Leila can go with you if you like," Nora offered.

A few seconds passed. Both parents gazed pleadingly at Mina. Katrin let out a sob; her breathing was labored. Maybe it was her mother's reaction that tipped the balance for Mina.

"OK. I'll go."

CHAPTER 12

Nora switched off the bedside lamp and adjusted her pillow. It had gotten way too late by the time she went to bed, in spite of the fact that she'd promised herself an early night. There was always so much to do— piles of washing in the laundry room, and a vegetable compartment in the refrigerator that would be crawling out the door on its own any day now.

Only she and Julia were home. Simon was with his father, Henrik, this week, and Adam was staying over at his girlfriend's. He'd graduated from high school the previous year; Nora couldn't tell him what to do anymore. As long as he did his job as a waiter at a restaurant in the Söder district, she didn't complain.

Jonas was away all week. He was on a long-haul flight to LA, and wouldn't be back until Saturday.

It was eleven o'clock, and she really needed to let go of all the thoughts spinning around in her head: Mina's bruised and battered face, and the nagging feeling that Kovač wasn't going to go down for either tax evasion or assault. It was impossible to relax. She could hear her heart pounding in her ears, even though she was trying to breathe deeply, as her yoga instructor had taught her.

Not that she made it to yoga very often.

If only Kovač had still been in custody, Nora would have felt much better. At least he wouldn't have been able to attack his wife again. But Ulrika Grönstedt had argued persuasively and skillfully, and had gotten him out after only a few weeks, despite Nora's efforts to convince the court that releasing him was a mistake.

The loss still hurt.

Kovač should have remained locked up until the trial, but Nora had never gone head-to-head with a defense attorney of Grönstedt's caliber. She usually dealt with less serious cases, small-time players who were happy with a public defender appointed by the court. Not a purebred professional like Ulrika Grönstedt.

Jonathan hadn't said anything directly, but she knew how he felt about the situation. She should have done better. Instead she had let Grönstedt walk all over her.

Nora stared up at the ceiling. She had been overwhelmed by guilt as soon as she saw Mina lying there in the hospital. If she had died on Monday night, it would have been Nora's fault.

On an intellectual level she knew that wasn't true, but she couldn't help herself.

Henrik had once lost control and struck her during a quarrel down by the jetty on Sandhamn. Nora's lower lip had started to bleed; she'd been so shocked that she was unable to move a muscle. Henrik had been almost as shaken as her. He'd apologized a thousand times, but it had been the death knell for their relationship. There was no saving their marriage after that.

Nora glanced at the clock on the nightstand. She was due to question Kovač tomorrow. The time had been arranged a while ago, but the location had been changed to Flemingsberg, as he was in custody due to the assault. She had to be on top of her game.

But still sleep refused to come.

Thursday

CHAPTER 13

When Nora and Leila entered the interview room, Andreis Kovač was already seated at the table with Ulrika Grönstedt. He was dressed entirely in black, and filled the space with a kind of raw virility. His legs were stretched out in front of him. He was tall and powerfully built. The physical difference alone between him and Mina would be intimidating.

He didn't seem bothered at all by the situation in which he found himself. If he was worried because his wife was in the hospital, it didn't show.

Ulrika Grönstedt was wearing a classic navy-blue suit and pumps, with her Chanel purse looped over the back of the chair.

"Is it really necessary to question my client yet again?" she said before Nora had even sat down. "He's already cooperated fully. How often do we have to plow through all this nonsense before you realize he hasn't committed a crime?"

Nora had no intention of allowing herself to be provoked. She poured herself and Leila a glass of water, taking her time. "We will conduct as many interviews as I deem necessary," she said, keeping her tone neutral. "Is your client worried about something?"

"If he doesn't like being in custody, he has only himself to blame," Leila snapped. "He should have thought of that before he beat up his wife."

Kovač exchanged a glance with Grönstedt.

"As I said before, my client denies all the charges relating to tax evasion. With regard to the alleged assault on Mina Kovač, I don't understand what that has to do with this interview." Grönstedt opened an elegant case and put on a pair of glasses. "Andreis has not withheld any tax payments, nor has his income ever approached the sums you are talking about."

Leila smiled sweetly. "I assume he paid for his fancy house with a win on the lottery, and that his wife just happened to walk into a door the other night?"

"Mina has nothing to do with any of this," Kovač muttered, shifting uncomfortably on his chair.

Nora leaned forward. "I was intending to speak to you about Mina. She's in the hospital, in pretty bad shape. How did that happen?"

Reading a report about what Kovač had done to his wife was one thing; sitting opposite him was quite another. Nora couldn't help glancing at his hands; they must have had Mina's blood on them, but the long fingers bore no trace of the beating he'd inflicted. The nails were beautifully manicured, the knuckles undamaged.

It was only Mina's skin that had broken.

"Mina tripped over a vacuum cleaner," Kovač said. "It had already happened when I arrived home. It's not my fault she's in the hospital, but of course I'm very sorry she hurt herself. I love my wife."

He managed to give the statement a false air of normality, as if he were genuinely concerned about his wife, even though everyone in the room knew the truth.

Leila reacted with a scornful laugh. "Do you actually believe that?"

Her tone was so confrontational that Nora became worried. Leila had to be able to remain objective.

"You beat her up, and now you're scared she's going to testify against you."

"My wife will never testify against me."

"We'll see about that. It can't be good for your son to grow up with a father who beats his wife."

"Don't bring my son into this, or I'll fucking—"

Ulrika Grönstedt interrupted him. "My client didn't mean to get angry." She placed a hand on his arm; her nails were an elegant shade of red, the polish gleaming. "Andreis would never threaten a police officer or a prosecutor. Just so we don't misunderstand one another."

Leila shook her head. "It must be nice to have a female attorney to babysit you," she said. "It's a pity she wasn't there when you attacked Mina. You're clearly incapable of controlling yourself."

Nora cleared her throat. Enough was enough; they had to get on with questioning Kovač. "I'm intending to file charges within a week or so," she informed Grönstedt. "However, I do have some additional queries. The sooner your client responds, the sooner we'll be finished." She selected a document relating to one of the most recently sold companies. "There seems to be an issue with the bookkeeping in—" she began.

Grönstedt stepped in immediately. "It's not my client's fault that all the files were accidentally deleted when they changed to a different IT provider. That's not a crime."

Nora decided to put her foot down. "I suggest you let me finish what I'm saying; otherwise we'll be here all day."

CHAPTER 14

Mina was lying on her back in the bed in her new room, staring up at the white-painted ceiling that was cracked in several places. She'd slept for a few hours; it was almost nine o'clock in the evening.

Andreis would never find her here at Freya's Haven—the policewoman, Leila, had promised her that when she drove Mina and Lukas to Stavsnäs to catch the ferry across to Runmarö. She would be safe on the island. There were no street names or house numbers; it would be impossible for someone who didn't know the place to track her down.

The crossing had taken only five minutes, and they'd been picked up from the jetty.

Freya's Haven was a strange name. Freya was the goddess of love in Norse mythology, according to Anna-Maria, who ran the shelter. Did this mean that the old gods were watching over her? It seemed unlikely. It was a long time since Mina had felt that someone was keeping a protective eye over her.

The split above her eyebrow was aching.

If only she hadn't gone to the club that night. If only she'd stayed home and watched TV. If only she hadn't laughed when Andreis paid her a compliment, if only she hadn't let him buy her a drink.

Those thoughts had come into her mind so many times. What would her life have been like if she'd never met Andreis?

She turned onto her side, even though she felt a stab of pain from her ribs as soon as she moved. Lukas was sleeping in his crib beside her, with his pink cheeks and rosebud mouth.

The answer was simple. She wouldn't have had Lukas.

The room was in darkness. It was decorated in pastel colors, with two armchairs by the window. Two pink pelargoniums stood on the windowsill, and someone had placed an embroidered cloth on the coffee table. There was an old tiled stove in the corner, with a handwritten note stuck to it: *Do not use.*

It was a bit like a nice youth hostel—cozy, but a little shabby here and there.

She moved her head so that she could see the water shimmering over by the shore. When they arrived at lunchtime, she had immediately thought of her maternal grandparents' summer cottage in Roslagen— the wooden house with white eaves and window frames, the lawn surrounded by lilac hedges. She'd been so happy during those long summer days; now she could hardly remember what it felt like not to be afraid all the time.

Her cell phone vibrated. The display came to life, showing Andreis's number.

Hi darling—are you allowed to come home tomorrow?

Mina inhaled sharply. He didn't know she'd already left the hospital. He'd sent her several messages promising that he would change. Everything was going to be all right from now on. The last one had arrived just as she was about to set off for Freya's Haven. She'd almost changed her mind, thought that maybe it would be better to go home. Better for Lukas, so that he would grow up with his mom and dad.

Andreis sounded as if he really meant it; he would never hit her again. Never.

At that moment Leila had knocked on the door. She'd assured Mina that choosing Freya's Haven was the right decision, and had reminded her of how worried her parents had been. Mina hadn't had the strength to argue as Leila gathered up her things and headed for the door. She'd sent a quick reply telling Andreis that she would be in for at least another day, having more tests.

She stared at her phone.

Andreis thought everything was fine between them. He would never imagine that she could say she forgave him, then choose not to come home.

When he found out the truth, he would see it as a betrayal. She was his wife, and family meant everything to him. He often talked about the importance of staying together, whatever happened. He cared deeply for his mother, and called her almost every day. No one was allowed to bad-mouth Selma and Zlatko, not even his younger brother, Emir, who got away with most things.

And now she'd let him down in the worst possible way.

She felt as if her heart was being squeezed in an iron fist. When he realized the truth, he would come after her and Lukas. Somehow he would find out where they'd gone. Andreis always got his own way.

It had sounded so simple when Leila said they were safe here, but she didn't know Andreis. She hadn't seen his face darken when his temper took over and the man Mina loved disappeared, when the veins in his forehead bulged and he grabbed her by the throat, as if he had to obliterate her life in order to save his own.

How could she ever feel safe again?

Lukas let out a little whimper.

Her phone vibrated and the same message appeared again.

Hi darling—are you allowed to come home tomorrow?

Mina replied with trembling fingers.

I hope so.

The answer came immediately.

In that case I'll pick you up after lunch.

Mina hesitated, then she wrote:

Thanks, darling. Good night.

Friday

Chapter 15

Ulrika Grönstedt opened the door of the conference room into which her secretary had just shown Andreis Kovač. He had been released yesterday, just as she'd predicted. She smiled contentedly; she liked being right. And impressing her clients.

She had set aside an hour for the meeting, and hoped that would be enough. She was due in court on another case this afternoon and still had some reading to do. Reporters were likely to be there, which always provided an extra incentive.

"What the fuck did the prosecutor say about charging me with tax evasion?" Kovač said as soon as he saw her. The tray of coffee provided by her secretary was untouched, but he'd helped himself to the dish of sweets. There were a number of crumpled wrappers on the table.

Ulrika had no intention of letting her client see that she was also concerned about Nora's comment. She hadn't been particularly worried when Kovač was first interviewed. His complex company structure ought to be watertight. She herself hadn't been involved, but his advisers were no amateurs. They were experts and well paid for their skills. The prosecutor had nothing, she was sure of it.

Then Kovač had been arrested. That had been a miscalculation. Nora Linde had had him arrested because she claimed there was a risk that he would destroy evidence and impede the investigation. Admittedly the court had ruled that he should be kept in custody for only a few weeks, but that had been bad enough. Kovač had been furious by the time he came out.

Ulrika couldn't understand where Nora had gotten so much information. The questions she had asked yesterday were worrying; they showed that she knew a great deal. She was well aware that the income didn't match the figures in the company books, and she could prove it.

The equation meant that huge sums due in income and sales tax were missing—enough to constitute major tax evasion, and presumably serious money laundering. Which would mean years in jail for Kovač.

"You promised me it would never get to court," he said, drumming his fingers on the oval oak table.

"Someone on your team must have leaked the information to the authorities," Ulrika said, sitting down opposite him. She had no intention of being left holding the bag for this crap; her job was to do her best to get him off once he'd been charged. "There's no chance they could have found all that material without help," she went on. "An insider must have talked to the police."

Kovač frowned. "My guys keep their mouths shut."

"Nora Linde has too many facts," Ulrika insisted. "She has to have a contact who's familiar with your business affairs; otherwise she wouldn't have been able to ask such detailed questions."

She reached for the thermos and poured them both a coffee. The harsh light from the window showed her that it was time for a manicure; her nails were less than perfect. She would ask her secretary to book an appointment for tomorrow.

"I won't have access to everything they have on you until Linde files the charges," she explained. "I don't know which documents she's had access to, but from what I heard during your interviews, and given the way in which the questions were asked, I think she has copies of your accounts."

"That's impossible."

So far, Ulrika had allowed him to keep repeating the same mantra—that the accounts had been deleted by mistake, and everything else that had been brought up by the prosecutor was pure speculation. It was the oldest trick in the book, and it almost made her smile.

But the situation was serious.

If the court bought her explanation, Kovač would walk away, or incur a fine at the worst. There could be no negotiation on the obligation to keep accurate accounts, but failure to do so was a minor offense with little danger of a prison sentence. However, if Linde had gotten hold of the real documentation, Kovač could be looking at a significant jail term.

"You can't think of anyone who's been behaving suspiciously?" she asked. "Someone who's trying to take over your . . . business?"

She hesitated over the last word. She wanted to know as little as possible about what Kovač's "business" involved; her role was to protect his interests in court, nothing else. Everyone had the right to a defense. She had stuck to that principle ever since she started practicing twenty-five years ago. That was what the law prescribed, and she was proud of her role and her reputation as one of the country's most sought-after defense attorneys.

She had nothing to be ashamed of.

Kovač shook his head. "No. I know my guys. Drop it."

Ulrika glanced at her nails again. Why couldn't he be more cooperative? He seemed to have forgotten that she was on his side. Sometimes it was necessary to remind clients of such matters, especially when they were so damaged that they thought everyone was after them.

"You know what I've said all along," she began. "No surprises. You don't need to tell me any more than I ask, but you can't lie to me if you want me to defend you in court."

Kovač took out a cigarette packet that looked like Marlboro, but had the words *Super Drina* on it. Ulrika raised her eyebrows, and he put it back in his pocket.

"Could Mina have anything to do with this?" she asked.

Andreis Kovač burst out laughing. When he smiled, the charm switched on. There was a magnetism about him, which Ulrika assumed he exploited on a regular basis to get what he wanted.

She had no intention of walking into the trap, but she couldn't help responding with a smile. "Mina?" she repeated in a gentler tone.

"Mina has no idea what I do. She's sweet, but she knows nothing about business."

Ulrika decided on a change of tack. "It's unfortunate that you . . ." She searched for the right words. "Had a disagreement with Mina at this juncture."

"That's a private matter."

Did he really not understand, or was he choosing not to understand?

The court was made up of a judge and three to five jurors, who were laymen with no legal training. Photographs of a badly beaten woman wouldn't exactly get jurors on their side. This could seriously damage her credibility when she was arguing that he was innocent.

In this context it was an advantage for once that Ulrika was a woman, even though Kovač probably didn't appreciate it. She was one of the few high-profile female defense attorneys in the country. Men were heavily overrepresented in her profession, particularly those who were known to the wider public. For some reason there were far more women prosecutors and judges, while men were more attracted to criminal law, not least in the cities, where more serious crimes were committed.

"It will be bad news if Mina testifies against you," she said. "It won't look good in court. And there's no doubt that the prosecutor intends to combine both cases."

The charm disappeared as quickly as it had manifested itself. Kovač frowned. "You're not making any sense."

"She's going to file the assault charge and the tax evasion charge at the same time."

"Mina will never testify against me," Kovač said, just as confidently as the day before.

"Are you sure of that?"

"Mina is my wife. She knows how things work within a family."

"Where is she now? Is she still in the hospital?"

"Yes. I'm going to pick her up as soon as we're done here."

"The police will do their best to get her to tell them what really happened."

"I'll take care of Mina."

Ulrika had no doubt that her client was prepared to "take care" of Mina. The problem was that she didn't want to serve up any further opportunities for the prosecutor to file charges. The best thing would be for husband and wife to reconcile, even though the photographs she'd seen made her shudder inside.

They needed to stick together, at least until the trial was over.

"Mina's injuries have been photographed and documented. We're talking about assault, which could result in years behind bars."

Kovač looked at his Swiss diving watch with a wide steel band. Ostentatious, but no doubt the price bracket appealed to him. "Are we nearly done?" he asked impatiently.

"As your lawyer I must advise you to make peace with your wife. Try to get her to come back to you. That would make it much easier to defend you."

"Don't worry. Mina loves me."

Bosnia, April 1992

Selma had laid the table for lunch in the garden; she liked to sit outdoors and look at the flowers. She was very proud of the pink, red, and yellow roses she grew; she put them in vases and gave some away to the neighbors.

The shade of the big walnut tree protected them from the heat of the sun; otherwise it was impossible to be outside in the middle of the day.

Andreis gobbled down his food, eager to run off and play. Her firstborn had as much energy as his stylish father, who unfortunately was as egotistical as he was hot tempered. They hadn't seen each other for many years since they'd gone their separate ways when Andreis was only ten months old.

To her relief, Ivan had never made any claim on the boy.

"Why does Emir have to sleep in my room?" Andreis said. "Why can't he be with you and Dad instead?"

Selma had met Zlatko when Andreis was two years old, and Andreis had always called him Dad.

She patted his cheek. "Why do you ask? Don't you love your little brother?"

The boy looked a little ashamed. "Yes, but he cries all the time."

"That will soon pass." Selma laughed and shook her head. Her long black hair was her pride and joy. Andreis liked to brush it sometimes, using the beautiful hairbrush with mother-of-pearl on the back. It was a present from her mother, who lived far away in Sarajevo, the city Selma had left when she married Zlatko and moved all the way across Bosnia with him.

"Emir will soon be big enough to walk and talk," she assured her son. "Then you'll be able to play and have fun together."

Zlatko emerged from the kitchen doorway. He was limping more than usual; he always did when he was worried. The aftereffects of a motorcycle accident had left him unable to walk long distances.

Why was he home at lunchtime? Selma was immediately anxious; everything was so chaotic right now. "What are you doing here?" she said, getting to her feet with Emir in her arms. "Has something happened at work?"

"They've closed the factory. They sent us all home."

"What do you mean?"

"We're at war."

The words felt like a physical blow. Selma's legs gave way, and she sank back down onto her chair. "What are you saying?" she whispered.

Zlatko sat down and lit a cigarette. "The Serbs have attacked Sarajevo. The city is under siege, the roads are closed."

Mom and Dad. Selma couldn't breathe properly. Had they been imprisoned? Injured? What about Aunt Jasmina and Uncle Adnan, who lived in a small village outside Sarajevo, closer to the Serbian border?

"C-can they do that?" she stammered, pressing her lips to Emir's forehead. She had to keep her children safe. Emir was a baby, Andreis was only five.

"Don't worry, the United Nations won't allow this. They've already recognized us as a sovereign state."

Selma wasn't convinced. "What if the Serbs come here? What will we do then?"

"The international community will intervene."

A couple of walnuts fell to the ground and bounced away across the grass, attracting the attention of one of the chickens.

Zlatko stroked Selma's hair. "Everything will be fine, you'll see. They'll have found a peaceful way to resolve the conflict by the summer. It will all be over in no time."

CHAPTER 16

There was a knock on the door of Mina's room. Anna-Maria, the manager who'd welcomed her the previous day, came in carrying something. Her blue sweater was a little too tight, and there was as much gray as brown in her hair.

"Good morning, Mina," she said warmly. "How are you today? Did you get some sleep?"

"What time is it?"

"Almost nine."

"Oh . . ." Mina pulled herself up into a sitting position. She must have fallen asleep after feeding Lukas at around six o'clock. She was embarrassed by Anna-Maria's searching gaze, and tugged at the T-shirt she'd used as a nightgown. "I didn't sleep very well," she mumbled, without going into detail about the nightmares that had come every time she managed to nod off.

The hands closing around her throat until she couldn't breathe. She'd dreamed that she'd fled from the house to get away from Andreis, running barefoot in the darkness until the soles of her feet were bleeding.

The fear was still there.

"It's difficult for everyone at first," Anna-Maria reassured her. "It takes time to get used to the situation. You'll feel better, I promise." She placed a toiletry bag on the bed, along with a pile of underwear, a pair of jeans, and a sweater. "Just a few things you might need. I hope they're the right size. If not, just let me know—we have a small stock. I don't suppose you brought much from home?"

Mina shook her head. She had nothing. Everything she owned had been left behind at the house in Kolarängen, apart from her purse, which one of the paramedics had remembered to bring.

She pulled the covers up to her neck.

"It's breakfast time," Anna-Maria said. "As a rule everyone is responsible for their own meals, but I've made you a few sandwiches since it's your first day. I thought I'd show you around when you've eaten, go through our routines."

"I'm not really hungry."

"You need something." Anna-Maria smiled at Lukas and straightened the baby blanket Mina had been allowed to bring from the hospital. "You have to be strong enough to look after this little one, if nothing else."

Mina didn't know what to say. She didn't want to leave her room to go to the kitchen and meet the other women. She didn't want to face their curiosity or silent sympathy when they saw the state she was in.

Saw what Andreis had done to her.

She'd worn dark glasses on the way to Runmarö, with a baseball cap pulled down to hide as much of her face as possible. Why couldn't Anna-Maria leave her in peace?

"By the way, a prosecutor has been trying to get a hold of you. She called again a few minutes ago."

Mina didn't understand. "A prosecutor?"

"Nora Linde. Don't you remember—we talked about this when you signed in?"

Mina was trying to keep up, but her brain refused to cooperate. She'd been so tired when they arrived; she didn't remember half of the words that had poured over her. She'd fallen asleep as soon as she'd fed Lukas and changed his diaper.

It was coming back to her now—Leila had mentioned something about the prosecutor.

"She asked if you could call her as soon as you woke up. It's about the investigation into your husband." Anna-Maria waited for a few seconds, then leaned forward with her hand outstretched.

Mina recoiled. Her arms flew up to protect her face.

Anna-Maria immediately stepped back.

"I'm sorry," Mina murmured.

Anna-Maria's cheeks were flushed with embarrassment. "I only wanted to stroke your hair. I should have known better." She turned and left the room.

Chapter 17

Dino Herco looked up when Andreis opened the passenger door.

"Let's get out of here. That fucking lawyer talks too much. She thinks someone working for me has tipped off the authorities about my business affairs."

Dino glanced at his boss. "Like who? Do you suspect anyone?"

"Forget it."

Andreis took out a packet of cigarettes and lit up. He took a few impatient drags before opening the window and blowing out the gray-blue smoke. He preferred a particular brand from the Balkans, which he had imported specially. Dino thought they tasted vile, but apparently Andreis's father had liked them. It didn't take much intelligence to figure out why Andreis insisted on sticking to the tradition.

Flakes of ash landed at the corner of the window.

"Where to?" Dino asked. He put the car in gear and checked the rearview mirror before pulling out of the parking space. No one seemed to be paying any attention to them, but he always made sure he checked their surroundings.

It was the small details that mattered.

"The Southern District Hospital. We're going to pick up Mina and Lukas." Andreis tossed the cigarette stub out of the window. "The last time I texted her she seemed pretty keen to get home."

Dino wondered who he was trying to convince, but he knew better than to say anything.

"My darling Mina. And my beautiful son."

Dino turned off at Skeppsbron, crossing the bridge to the Söder district. There wasn't too much traffic, in spite of the lunchtime rush. They reached the hospital within fifteen minutes. A stream of people hurried toward the main entrance in the glass façade—young and old, wheeled walkers and strollers passed one another beneath the angular letters informing them that this was the Southern District Hospital.

A dark-haired middle-aged woman with a shawl wrapped around her head was crouched down by the door, begging. There was a tin on the ground in front of her, and she was holding out her hand in a pleading gesture. Most people didn't even seem to notice her, but right when Dino drove past, one old lady with a cane stopped dead. She yelled something and shook her fist.

The woman didn't react.

Jesus, imagine sitting there day after day. The Swedes talked about their open, generous society, but they were no better than anyone else. Society was cold and unjust, and it was every man for himself.

Dino concentrated on finding a parking space.

"Wait here," Andreis said as he set off for the entrance. "I'll be back shortly."

There was a police car nearby, but he didn't seem bothered by its presence.

Dino switched off the engine and reached for his newspaper. He could be here for hours—Andreis had no idea how long he was going to be. It made no difference to Dino; he was used to doing whatever Andreis wanted him to do.

With a bit of luck his boss would be in a better mood when he was reunited with his wife and son. Maybe he'd feel like a pizza and a few beers in their favorite bar later?

Dino longed to see the positive side of his childhood friend again. They'd had so many fantastic evenings and nights when the business began to take off, and Andreis wanted to celebrate every success. No one could party like Andreis when he was in the mood, when he thought he owned the whole world.

Stockholm was where it had all started, where they'd made a new life for themselves, far away from the poor areas of Nyköping, where they'd been subjected to a barrage of racist abuse.

Andreis's tall figure appeared in front of the car. He'd only been gone five minutes, and there was no sign of Mina and Lukas.

Dino reached over and opened the passenger door. Andreis got in without a word. He stared at the phone in his hand as if he could force it to come up with a message. Something was wrong, but Dino knew better than to ask questions when Andreis had that look in his eye.

The police car drove off, and a yellow taxi immediately took its place. The woman who was begging got to her feet and shuffled into the hospital. She reappeared a few minutes later, her fingers wrapped around a paper cup containing a hot drink.

Dino waited for instructions. Andreis took out a piece of gum and started chewing frenetically. He still hadn't said a word.

Someone dropped a few coins in the beggar woman's tin. She smiled and nodded gratefully, then lowered her eyes again.

In the end Dino had to ask.

"What happened?"

"Mina isn't there."

"What?"

"Are you deaf? She's not in the hospital. She was discharged yesterday."

"Where's she gone?"

"I don't fucking know! They wouldn't tell me. She's just fucking left and taken Lukas with her." Andreis slammed his hand down on the dashboard. "She can't take my son without asking me for permission!"

CHAPTER 18

Anna-Maria went into her office, but stopped dead by the desk. What had she come in for? She'd been so busy with phone calls and things to do that she just couldn't remember.

She rubbed her nose with her index finger. The shelter was only half full, and yet she felt as if a thousand flies were buzzing around inside her head. She'd found it difficult to concentrate all day, and been short with her colleagues.

The depressing meeting with the inspector from social services was constantly in the back of her mind. Presumably the inspector had only agreed to come over so that no one would be able to criticize her afterward.

The phone rang; Anna-Maria didn't recognize the number.

It was Birgitta Svanberg. Talk of the devil . . .

"I forgot to ask a question the other day," she began, without wasting any time on small talk. "What's the situation re CCTV at Freya's Haven?"

Anna-Maria sank down on her chair. She'd hoped to avoid this discussion. "We have talked about it," she said eventually.

"Talked about it?"

Anna-Maria took a deep breath. Birgitta sounded as if she couldn't believe her ears. What was wrong with her? Didn't she realize that putting up cameras all around the building was tantamount to announcing that it was a shelter? There were no cameras inside, and plenty of shelters had refused to install them for reasons of integrity.

Birgitta made it sound like a dereliction of duty.

"We haven't gone down that route yet," Anna-Maria said, "but we have discussed making a request for tenders to see what it would cost." She tried to sound convincing, even though there was absolutely no money to spare in the budget for that kind of investment. She had no idea where she would find the money if the council came back and insisted on CCTV.

"I thought it was a standard requirement these days," Birgitta said. She ended the call before Anna-Maria could respond.

Anna-Maria remained at her desk, staring at the phone.

The last time Freya's Haven had taken part in negotiations with the council, they had done their best to put in a competitive bid. They couldn't afford to risk losing the funding. They'd cut back wherever they could; it was impossible to save any more money. The women and children must be provided with decent food, and there was nothing to be done about fixed costs.

However, if they weren't successful in the next round of negotiations, the shelter would have to close. They would barely have enough money to wind down in a civilized and organized way. Everything she'd worked for over the past fifteen years would disappear.

That couldn't be allowed to happen.

As always, her gaze sought out the photograph of Malin. Her daughter's smile was usually a source of strength for Anna-Maria, a way to summon up fresh energy in difficult moments.

Now she was overwhelmed by feelings of guilt.

She had failed to protect her own daughter. Was she also going to fail when it came to taking care of the women at Freya's Haven?

CHAPTER 19

Ulrika Grönstedt glanced at her watch. It was almost time to leave the office. She tried to get home reasonably early on Fridays for Fiona's sake, but all too often she didn't succeed. Today she had promised herself that she wasn't going to disappoint her ten-year-old daughter; it had been an intense week with a lot of late nights.

Nico, one of her most ambitious legal associates, stuck his head around the door.

"I was thinking of leaving now, if that's OK?"

He sounded apologetic, as if he were embarrassed for wanting to go home at six o'clock on a Friday. He was young and hungry, with dreams of becoming one of the country's leading defense attorneys.

"It's my mom's birthday," he added.

Nico was often still working when Ulrika left, and God knows she put in the time. "No problem—I'm on my way, too."

Nico lingered in the doorway. *New suit,* Ulrika noticed. It looked like Paul Smith. Nico had been paid a significant bonus for his efforts the previous year; no other associate had billed as many hours as he had.

"How did the meeting with Kovač go?" he asked.

Ulrika grimaced. "I don't think he understands the gravity of the situation with his wife. The timing really is unfortunate."

Needless to say, Nora Linde had been quick to send over the photographs of Mina when she was admitted to the hospital. They were appalling, particularly the images of her bruised and swollen face. Ulrika had had to steel herself in order to keep from looking away or prejudging her client, but she couldn't allow herself to adopt the moral standpoint that the prosecutor was trying to evoke.

Earlier in her career, Ulrika had been eager to work at one of the large practices in the city specializing in business law. Her goal was to make partner with a firm that charged exorbitant fees for company transfers. Then she secured a post as a law clerk in Södertälje, and became fascinated by serious crime, by the feeling of dealing with life and death on a daily basis. The endorphin rush when they triumphed in court, when the press wrote about a case she was involved in.

She had learned long ago to focus on her own client. Mina was not her responsibility.

"I told him to make up with his wife," she went on. "At least for as long as he's accused of tax evasion. Any additional charges won't improve his chances."

"Do you think he'll take your advice?"

Ulrika opened her briefcase and gathered up the documents she needed to go through over the weekend. "I hope so. It's costing him plenty."

CHAPTER 20

Dino Herco looked around before he unlocked the door of the two-room apartment where he'd been living for the last few years; old habits died hard. There was a strong odor of fried food in the stairwell, stale oil and fish. For some reason it reminded him of the refugee center where they'd ended up when they first came to Sweden—the Tre Kronor hotel in Gothenburg.

The apartment was in Farsta Strand. He didn't know any of his neighbors. He just heard them through the walls occasionally when they raised their voices and quarreled. It suited him perfectly; he didn't want close contact with anyone.

The usual advertising leaflets lay inside the door. He stepped over them, went into the kitchen, and got himself a cold beer.

He headed for the living room, with the bottle in his hand, and flopped down on the sofa. He picked up the remote and surfed aimlessly from one channel to another. Nothing but crap as usual. He left Eurosport on—a poor league match from England. Probably a repeat, but who cared?

He took a deep swig of beer and rested his head on the back of the sofa. It had been a long day; it was almost eight o'clock. After leaving the hospital they'd gone to a bar, where Andreis had determinedly knocked back shot after shot of vodka while talking agitatedly on the phone to Emir. Then Dino had driven him to the house on Trastvägen, listening to a stream of curses all the way. The place was in darkness when they arrived; it was immediately obvious that no one was there. More than twenty-four hours had elapsed since Mina was discharged, and she hadn't spoken to Andreis or left a message.

She'd taken off in the past after he'd beaten her, but on those occasions she'd contacted him after a few hours. Andreis always managed to persuade her to give him another chance. No one could resist him when he wanted something. He'd wanted Mina ever since he first saw her. She was the ultimate trophy wife, with her sky-blue eyes and her beautiful blond hair.

But he'd never gone in as hard as he had this time. If the police hadn't intervened and the ambulance hadn't arrived, he would probably have killed her—even though she was the mother of his son.

Dino instinctively knew that Andreis wouldn't have been able to stop himself.

The match was interrupted by a commercial break, and a young girl tried to convince the viewers that the secret to happiness lay in their choice of deodorant.

Dino took another swig of beer.

Andreis had always been temperamental, and over the years Dino had learned how to deal with his violent outbursts. He knew how to handle Andreis, even when most people walked away. Andreis was his boss, but he was also Dino's family.

If he closed his eyes, Dino could still see the green hills around his childhood home, the little village close to Andreis's home in Bosnia. The place where they would both have grown up, if it hadn't been for the war.

Their families had fled at approximately the same time, and they'd ended up in Nyköping, like many of their fellow countrymen. Dino had attended the same Swedish school as Andreis and his kid brother,

Emir. His parents still lived in the town, not far from Andreis's mother, Selma, in the same shabby apartment the city council had allocated them some twenty years ago.

Even back then Andreis had talked about a different life, a life with money, where he'd be treated with respect and not have to kowtow to anyone else. He'd never liked Nyköping; he'd always wanted to get away, and Dino had realized from an early stage that he could accompany Andreis on the journey. He was more than willing to pay the price— unquestioning loyalty to Andreis—for a new life in the capital.

Dino took out his pocket knife and dug out a little dirt from under his thumbnail. The blade glinted in the light; he always carried the knife with him.

Andreis had had a temper even when they were in school, but recently the slightest irritant brought tension. Something had changed when he was released from custody in February. Dino had picked up on Andreis's new frame of mind as soon as he'd gotten in the car. The look in his eyes was different. The stress lay just beneath the surface. In the past Andreis was sometimes unnecessarily suspicious, but now he saw ghosts everywhere. He was convinced that his enemies were out to get him, and he trusted no one.

Except Dino.

Andreis had had problems with the police before, but they'd never had any concrete evidence. They'd never managed to pin him down; he had always flown under the radar. How often had he made fun of the cops, called them idiots because they couldn't find anything?

The new situation made Dino uncomfortable. The other day Andreis had broken the nose of a guy who was late with a delivery. It wasn't good for morale among the boys, and it wasn't good for business. No one was safe when Andreis lost his temper.

If he couldn't take it out on Mina, who would be in the line of fire?

CHAPTER 21

Thomas saw Nora as soon as she walked into the bar on the ground floor of the Sandhamn Hotel. The place was almost full, but he'd managed to grab two seats at a table by the window.

She came over and gave him a hug. "I'm glad you got in touch," she said. "I didn't know you were coming over this weekend."

"You made me feel guilty when you called me the other day," he replied. "You were right—it's been a while since we caught up." Thomas pointed to the beer next to his own. "For you. Lager, of course."

Nora nodded appreciatively and draped her jacket over the back of the chair before sitting down.

"How did the interview with Kovač go?" Thomas asked. Straight to the point as usual.

"No surprises. In other words, it wasn't very productive. His lawyer isn't easy to deal with, and Kovač is even worse." Nora took a sip of her beer. "I'm filing the charge for tax evasion next week anyway. Kovač was released yesterday, just as you expected."

Thomas already knew; he'd checked before leaving work for the weekend. That wasn't all he'd found out, which was why he'd texted Nora to ask if she had time for a beer that evening. "How well do you know Kovač?" he said.

"What do you mean?"

"How much do you actually know about his background?"

"I've been working on this case all spring, so I think I'm pretty clued in. Why?"

Thomas didn't want to offend her, but she had to be told. "I've taken a closer look at him through my own contacts."

They both knew there were other channels than the official ones leading to suspects being remanded in custody, arrested, and charged. The police databases were allowed to store only a certain kind of information, which didn't always tell the whole story.

"He's an unpleasant person," Nora said. She kept her tone light, which worried Thomas; she wasn't taking this seriously.

"I spoke to some guys who work in the area where Kovač operates," he said. "He's regarded as a ruthless individual. The word they used was *brutal*."

"I know that."

Outside the window a ferry slid into the harbor to drop off the last passengers of the day. The sun was going down, and the illuminated lookout at the top of the Sailors Restaurant stood out against the darkening sky.

"I don't think you do," Thomas said. "Andreis Kovač is dangerous. Last year a gang tried to muscle in on his territory. A hand grenade exploded in a café where they often held their meetings."

"A hand grenade?"

"One of the dead was a baby whose mother just happened to be there at the time."

The police hadn't managed to find the perpetrator and had been heavily criticized for the fact that the case remained unsolved.

"According to my sources, everything points to Kovač, but there are no witnesses, no evidence. The usual informants refuse to talk. That says a great deal about his personality."

This information seemed to come as a surprise to Nora. Thomas knew that his colleagues in Narcotics had provided her with background for the tax evasion case, but he suspected that they hadn't gone into this kind of detail.

"Three dead and four injured," he went on. "Just because Kovač wanted to make a point. Now do you understand?" She had to realize that these guys meant business. "I don't think you've come across this kind of criminality before. Your usual white-collar tax dodgers are nothing compared to Kovač."

Nora looked irritated.

"Don't get mad," Thomas said quickly. "I'm only trying to help." He wouldn't have gotten involved in her work if he wasn't worried about her.

"I think I can get a conviction," she said. "Especially if I can get his wife to testify against him on the assault charge. He can't talk his way out of that."

"If you bring in his wife, it becomes personal."

"Sorry?"

"That will only make things worse. He'll see it as a direct insult if you meddle in his family affairs."

"He should have thought about that before he beat the hell out of her."

"It's not about that." Thomas pushed his beer aside and leaned across the table. "Business is one thing, but his wife and child—that's something else. He'll go after anyone who interferes in his private life."

A couple in their thirties pointed to the two chairs at the other end of the table. "Is anyone sitting here?" the woman asked.

"No," Nora replied. Thomas would have preferred not to have anyone else at their table, but the bar was almost full.

The woman took off her dark-gray padded jacket and went to order their drinks.

"You need personal protection until the trial," Thomas said quietly. "Have you discussed it with Jonathan?"

"Are you kidding? Kovač wouldn't be crazy enough to attack a prosecutor!"

"Criminality has changed in Sweden. The climate has become much harsher in recent years. There's no comparison with the way it used to be."

How could he make her understand how serious this was?

The latest official police report on the country's criminality had classed sixty-one districts as vulnerable areas, of which twenty-three were regarded as particularly vulnerable, with high crime rates and social exclusion. The report referred to parallel communities living in close proximity, with blackmail and direct threats as a part of everyday life, to the extent that both the authorities and local industry providers had moved out. Only a few miles from Nora's comfortable workplace on Hantverkargatan, people were living in a completely different world, one where retribution was the norm, human life was a trading commodity, and drug dealing took place openly on the street.

Sweden had changed radically over the past ten years.

Nora turned her beer glass around and around. "I'm not naïve," she assured him. "But I'm not going to start seeing things in broad daylight. If I'm scared, I won't be able to do my job properly, and I can't allow that to happen."

"Kovač is ruthless," Thomas repeated. "Don't be fooled just because he has an expensive attorney and is accused of a white-collar crime."

"I get it, but I have to try and persuade Mina to testify against her husband. Otherwise I wouldn't be doing my job, and as I said, I can't allow that to happen." Before Thomas could say any more, Nora placed her hand on his arm. "I'll be careful. I promise."

Bosnia, June 1992

Emir was lying on a blanket on the living room floor, gurgling happily when Andreis emerged from his bedroom. His mother was sitting, weeping in front of the TV with a cigarette in her mouth. She didn't even notice him.

Andreis edged closer so that he could see the screen. The reporter was talking about a place Andreis had never heard of.

Višegrad.

"Zlatko," his mother sobbed. "You have to come and see this."

The bedroom door opened and his father appeared in his pajamas. His belly protruded through a gap in the jacket, and his hair, as dark as Emir's, was sticking out in all directions. Since the factory had closed, he often slept late in the mornings. He rubbed his eyes and yawned. "What's happened?"

Selma pointed at the TV, where images of the dead and injured were now being shown. "The Serbs attacked Višegrad," she whispered. "Thousands of people in the city and the surrounding villages have been killed. They shot them and threw the bodies in the Drina River."

She could hardly speak.

The camera zoomed in on a bridge made up of stone arches. The name was on a small sign down in one corner: "Mehmed Paša Sokolović Bridge."

"They drove the prisoners up onto the bridge in trucks and executed them, then they dumped the bodies like dead animals."

Andreis saw his father's face harden.

"Serbian pigs," he said. "Karadžić is behind this. He's a devil. A psychopath."

"I'm so frightened." Selma wept.

"The United Nations will intervene. The rest of the world will help us. They're not going to let us go under without doing anything." Zlatko placed a reassuring hand on his wife's shoulder, and she gave it a squeeze. "This is a civilized country, Selma. We're not barbarians."

"Why do the Serbs want to wipe us out?"

Zlatko went over and switched off the television. "Because they're murderers."

CHAPTER 22

The buzzing of his phone woke Dino; he'd fallen asleep on the sofa in front of the TV. He didn't need to check the display to know who was calling. What did he want now? It was almost ten o'clock. He accepted the call.

"I have to get a hold of Mina and Lukas."

Andreis was slurring his words; he'd obviously carried on drinking after they parted company. Dino could hear the television in the background. It was so loud that he could only just make out what Andreis was saying.

"She can't take my son and just disappear. She's my wife."

There was no point in trying to reason with him. Dino sighed. "Where do you want me to start looking?" he said as respectfully as possible. He didn't want to make Andreis even more angry.

"How the fuck should I know? If I knew, I'd do it myself!"

Dino slammed his fist into the arm of the chair—silently, of course. He made his voice even more submissive. "Have you spoken to her parents? Surely they must know where she is."

Andreis's tone changed. "She knows that's the first place I'd go. She's stupid, but not that stupid."

"Exactly—so maybe she's hiding there anyway."

Mina no longer had many girlfriends. They'd fallen away one by one as Andreis's controlling behavior intensified.

"Would you like me to drive over there and take a look?"

"No—I'll do it myself."

"Wait."

Dino didn't trust Andreis not to lose it if he found Mina at her parents' home. More violence or a call to the police by Stefan and Katrin wouldn't help the situation. The cops were already showing too much interest. If Andreis went over there in his current state, all hell could break loose.

"Let me go instead," he said, hoping his boss would listen. "I'll leave right away."

"OK," Andreis muttered after a few seconds. "Call me as soon as you find out what's going on."

CHAPTER 23

How long would she dare to stay at Freya's Haven?

Mina was sitting up in bed, staring at the wall opposite. She'd spent the last few hours trying to rest, but her body was as tense as a coiled spring. The stitches above her eye were pulling, and her broken ribs were agonizingly painful. She'd fed Lukas when he woke up, but stayed in her room more or less all day. When he fell asleep, she'd crept into the kitchen and picked up some fruit. It was hard to get it down, but she'd forced herself. Anna-Maria was right; she had to eat something. She needed to regain her strength.

By this stage Andreis must have realized that she wasn't coming home. If he'd been furious on Monday, that was nothing compared to how he'd be feeling now. He never forgave a betrayal. He demanded total loyalty; he always had.

I will never let you go.

His words haunted her. He'd uttered them so often. She wanted to put her hands over her ears, but they would still echo inside her head.

When they first met, she'd thought it was a loving thing to say. Beautiful, in fact. The promise of a lifelong partnership, just like her parents' marriage—two people who always wanted the best for each other. She'd loved the idea of her and Andreis against the world.

Gradually that sentence acquired a different meaning. It metamorphosed into a terrible reminder that she would never be free again.

If Andreis hadn't been interrupted, he would have killed her on Monday. The realization hurt her more than the physical pain, the conviction that he would have carried on until she stopped breathing.

Who would take care of Lukas if she weren't around?

While she was in the hospital she'd managed to avoid her reflection, but it was impossible here. The battered face in the hall mirror filled her with shame. Her tongue sought out the broken molar. The sharp surface was as damaged as she was, and the gum all around it was swollen and tender.

In spite of the pain she kept on until she cut her tongue, and the taste of blood filled her mouth.

She'd hoped that things would improve when Lukas was born, that Andreis would change. He'd been so happy at the birth. His voice and expression had softened. He had held his son to his chest and whispered in Bosnian in Lukas's little ear.

This is a fresh start, Mina had thought. *Everything's going to be fine.*

How wrong could she be?

Only weeks later Andreis was arrested and held in custody for several weeks. When he came out, he was worse than ever. There were so many accusations; he found fault after fault. He yelled at her, not caring if he woke Lukas. In the end she hardly dared do anything for fear of making yet more mistakes.

It wasn't long before he started hitting her again.

Her room was too hot. She couldn't breathe. With some difficulty she got out of bed and went over to the window. Hiding behind the curtain, she opened it a little way and allowed the cool night air to pour in.

What if he was out there watching her?

She slammed the window shut, and Lukas whimpered. Mina lifted him out of his crib in spite of her broken ribs, and rocked him back to sleep. She lay down on the bed with Lukas beside her. She could feel the warmth of his body, smell his hair, the baby powder after his bath.

For a moment, when madness blazed in Andreis's eyes and her own body was rigid with fear, she had actually wanted to die.

Kill me, she'd thought. *Go on, do it!*

Then at least she would have escaped from everything, the terror and the pain. The shame that never left her. It was Lukas who had made her resist, fight back, fill her lungs with air. She had screamed for Lukas.

It had felt like a miracle when she'd heard the sound of approaching sirens. Someone rang the doorbell, and the police were there. A paramedic touched her gently and whispered reassuring words. Someone comforted Lukas, and Andreis was taken away in handcuffs.

She had been saved, against all odds. But what would happen next time he lost control?

Her phone beeped. She ought to keep it switched off, but she didn't dare. Her parents had to be able to contact her; the results of the tests on her mother's heart were due any day.

The message glowed at her in the darkness. Andreis's number. Two short words.

Come home.

CHAPTER 24

The house in Skuru was at the far end of a narrow cul-de-sac, with nothing but forest and overgrown common land behind it. The sparse streetlamps provided little light.

When Dino arrived, there was a blue Passat parked on the drive. It was almost midnight. A chilly drizzle was falling, and the dampness covered the windshield like a veil of ice.

He pulled up a short distance away and waited in case anyone had heard the engine. Then he got out and checked the neighboring properties in case someone was peeping out to get a look at whoever was visiting at this late hour.

He walked up to the fence and studied the unassuming single-story house. The wood panels were painted gray, and a narrow graveled path led up to the front door, which had a large frosted pane of glass in the top half. The place reminded him of the 1970s homes in Nyköping where the Swedish kids lived; he'd seen them from a distance when he was at school.

The door didn't appear to be particularly robust. It wouldn't take much to break it down.

There was a faint light in the kitchen. Through the window Dino could see clean surfaces and a refrigerator with a white door. The light seemed to be coming from an extractor fan that someone had forgotten to switch off.

Was Mina there?

He looked around again before quietly opening the gate and entering the garden. He headed for the backyard, where a lawn was surrounded by apple trees growing along the fence. Generous picture windows looked out onto a wooden deck; a table and chairs had already been set out, even though it was only April. The main light in the living room was off, but a night-light in one corner made it possible to see the combined dining and living room.

There should be some sign of Mina and Lukas if they were hiding here.

Dino moved closer, stepped up onto the decking, and went up to the window. He scanned the room; he couldn't see any toys or baby equipment or a stroller.

There was a collection of framed photographs on an antique painted cupboard—several pictures of Mina with her parents, and one where she was holding Lukas in her arms, smiling happily into the camera.

But no wedding photo of her and Andreis.

Dino silently stepped off the deck. It was raining harder now. He turned up the collar of his leather jacket, but the cold drops still found their way down the back of his neck.

He continued around the side of the house, sticking to the wet grass so that no one would hear him.

He saw the glow of a bedside lamp behind a closed roller blind, and a shadow moving around. So there was someone home, but he couldn't tell if it was a man or a woman. Was it Mina, or one of her parents?

He stopped. It wasn't a good idea to ring the doorbell at this time of night, for many reasons, but Andreis was expecting answers.

He made his way back to the front door. The external light was off, but he had no difficulty picking the lock and slipping into the hallway. He glanced around in the darkness. Coats and scarves were hung up on hooks, with a shoe rack below. The living room was straight ahead; he'd already checked that. The bedroom where he'd seen the shadow was on the left.

Was Mina hiding in there with her baby?

Dino moved forward without making a sound. The two closest rooms, a study and a bedroom, were empty. He paused by the door of the third room, where the lamp was lit. He could hear the murmur of voices. It seemed as if both parents were still awake.

"What if Andreis finds her?"

That sounded like Katrin, Mina's mother. Dino remembered meeting her briefly in the maternity ward when she came to visit Mina.

"He'll never track her down there," Stefan replied. "It's impossible."

Dino listened hard. Mina and Lukas definitely weren't here, but her parents seemed to know where she was.

"He'll hunt her down and kill her," Katrin said. "He's a monster." She sounded as if she were on the verge of tears. "I wish he'd stayed in Bosnia and never set foot in Sweden. This country should never have taken in his sort."

Dino's jaw tightened.

"Don't say that," Stefan murmured. "I wouldn't be here either if that was the case."

"It's his fault that Mina's had to go into hiding. He should have been deported long ago!"

Dino's fingers closed around the knife in his back pocket; the metal felt cool against his skin. He wanted to fling the door open and put the blade against Katrin's throat, just as his own mother had been threatened before they left Bosnia. He wanted to see the fear in her eyes until she understood that she needed to watch her tongue. What did Mina's mother know about real pain? Torture and rape? Men and women shot dead in front of their children, with the neighbors looking on? Her own husband was an immigrant, and yet she thought she had the right to say whatever she liked.

Dino loathed the supercilious attitude of so many Swedes. The way they boasted about their open borders. The way they took responsibility for the world's war refugees, while other countries turned a deaf ear. They weren't so keen to talk about the fact that they treated immigrants like second-class citizens and refused to let them become a part of society.

"The police assured us that she's in safe hands," Stefan reassured his wife. "They'll take care of her and Lukas."

Dino was breathing heavily.

It would be easy to walk into the bedroom and find out everything he needed to know in order to track down Mina. He was no novice when it came to extracting information. He would have no problem getting the address of Mina's hiding place out of her father—and he could teach her mother a lesson at the same time.

But Andreis had only asked him to find out if Mina was here. Dino had offered to go because he didn't trust Andreis not to lose control.

He let go of the knife. He was not Andreis.

He could always come back.

"We need to get some sleep," Stefan murmured. "Try not to worry so much."

The light went off.

Dino turned and left the house without a sound.

Saturday

CHAPTER 25

Nora ran down to the steamboat jetty on Sandhamn to catch the morning ferry to Stavsnäs. Leila had called her half an hour earlier to tell her that Mina had been in touch, against all odds. She was ready to talk to them about the assault.

Nora didn't want to risk her changing her mind. After a quick check on the timetable, she found a boat that would get her to Runmarö at twelve fifteen.

The deckhand was about to remove the gangway when she arrived.

"Wait!" she shouted, and managed to board just before the captain set off. Slightly out of breath, she made her way to the cafeteria and bought a cup of coffee and a cheese roll. She sat down at a table by the window and took out her laptop in order to refresh her memory before the meeting. It would mean a lot if she could get Mina to testify.

"Next stop Harö" came the announcement over the loudspeaker, and Nora automatically looked up. She saw Thomas's tall figure on the jetty. She waved to him, but wasn't sure he'd seen her. However, a couple of minutes later he came into the cafeteria with a shabby knapsack over his shoulder.

In the daylight the graying hair at his temples was clearly visible. The last few months had taken their toll.

"Morning," he said. "I thought you were spending the weekend on Sandhamn?"

Nora explained the situation before Thomas joined the line to buy something to eat and drink.

"Leila Kacim is in charge of the investigation, isn't she?" he said when he came back with a mug of tea and an egg sandwich. He and Leila had met briefly when Nora introduced them to each other.

"Yes, she's meeting me on Runmarö." She instinctively lowered her voice; not many people knew about the shelter on the island.

"I met someone who worked with her when she was with the city police," Thomas said. "Apparently she's really good."

Nora was a little embarrassed; she hadn't known that Leila had been with the city police before she came to the Economic Crimes Authority. Then again, Leila rarely talked about the past. Nora knew she'd grown up in one of Stockholm's poorer areas, with her mother and younger brother, but that was all. Training to be a police officer couldn't have been an easy choice, and it must have been tough for Leila to establish herself among the veterans in the city when she was newly qualified and came from an immigrant background.

"So why are you going into town?" she asked Thomas. "I thought you were staying on Harö for the whole weekend?"

"Pernilla's sick—she's got a terrible cold." Thomas fished out his tea bag and placed it on the tray. "She texted to see if I could pick up Elin today, even though we usually swap on Mondays. Apparently her temperature is sky-high."

"It's good that you can help each other out when there's a problem."

Thomas shrugged. Nora couldn't decide whether the gesture was positive or negative, or merely resigned.

"So how's it going in general?" she said tentatively. "Has Elin gotten used to spending every other week with you and Pernilla?"

"It works. Of course it would have been better if it could have been avoided. If we hadn't separated."

Nora placed her hand on his. She recognized the bitterness; she'd reproached herself in exactly the same way when she eventually decided to leave Henrik. The anguish at splitting up her family had almost broken her, even though he was the one who'd been unfaithful.

"You can't stay together for the sake of the children," she said. "Believe me. I tried with Henrik, and you know how that went. You can't live with someone when the love has gone, however much you want to."

"I still care about her." Thomas ran a hand through his hair and turned away.

Outside the window the sky was as blue as if it were June. The sunlight sparkled on the waves. Soon the trees would begin to turn pale green, the grass would grow, and the wood anemones would appear. Things always felt better when spring was on the way.

However, Thomas didn't seem to have noticed.

"I really miss her," he admitted, sounding as if he didn't quite know how to explain what he'd just said. "Every night. I hate coming home if there's no one in the apartment. I hate Elin's room being empty when it's Pernilla's week." He stirred his tea with such force that the hot liquid spilled over. "When we're together . . . it's as if we're speaking different languages. We misunderstand each other all the time. We can't reach each other. Or . . . I can't reach her."

Two years earlier Pernilla had taken up a new post as Scandinavian brand ambassador for a telecom company. The role carried a great deal of responsibility, and the salary and benefits were considerably more attractive than Thomas's. In return Pernilla was expected to travel a great deal, and to be constantly available.

Somewhere along the line, things had begun to go wrong.

Nora had noticed the tension between her friends the previous year: the constant sniping about overtime and misplaced priorities. Gibes that were nonexistent during the twenty years they'd been together, jokes with a serious undertone.

On several occasions when they were due to visit, Thomas had showed up alone with Elin, because Pernilla was stuck in some meeting. When Pernilla was there, she always seemed tired but wound up at the same time. She constantly checked her cell phone and disappeared to take calls. Thomas sulked and Pernilla was irritated.

Nora had started to worry. She knew how destructive it could be when one person's career was set against the other's. When partnership tipped over into some kind of competition.

She'd been there herself.

It was hard enough to balance work and leisure, the role of parent and partner in a successful relationship. If the love faded away, then everyday life became impossible.

"The whole thing just feels like a massive failure," Thomas said, pushing away his mug. "First of all losing Emily, then the separation. We could hardly bear to see each other, because we were still alive and Emily was gone. Then we managed to find our way back, and we had Elin. We finally had everything we wanted, life was good—and we had to go and sabotage it."

The rumble of the engine increased as the ferry began to reverse toward the jetty on Idholmen. A woman with a stroller was waiting to board.

"It's so stupid."

Thomas sounded as if he were talking to himself; Nora ached with sympathy for him.

"It makes me so mad," he went on. "It's such a waste. We fucked up, even though we ought to know better."

"Don't be so hard on yourself."

"Well, I can't blame anyone else, can I?"

The harshness of Thomas's tone brought tears to Nora's eyes. She hadn't seen him this low since they lost Emily to Sudden Infant Death Syndrome. He had suffered from depression and been unable to sleep; he'd almost gone under. It had taken him a long time to come back, and a part of him had never really recovered. There was always a streak of melancholy just below the surface.

"Maybe you can find your way back to each other again?" she said gently. "Time apart can give people space to rethink, distance that allows you to see what's good rather than getting stuck in the bad stuff."

Thomas made a sad little noise. "I think we're past fixing. It's gone too far."

"Don't say that."

"You don't understand. The mere sight of her cell phone makes me angry. I'm so sick of her job coming before everything else. We've talked about it over and over again, but nothing changes." He sighed heavily. "She used to say that I was always working, that I couldn't separate my job from my private life, that I put the needs of others above those of my family. Guess who prioritizes their job over everything else now?"

Nora hadn't dared to ask who had initiated the separation, but she suspected she knew now. "It's not easy when you feel you come second," she murmured. "But I can't imagine that Pernilla would choose her job over you and Elin."

"She already has."

CHAPTER 26

Nora was the only passenger to disembark on Runmarö. Leila was already waiting, having taken another ferry direct from Stavsnäs, which was very close.

Leila's black jacket was covered in dog hair.

"New fashion?" Nora joked. "Has Bamse got any fur left, or did you bring it all with you?"

Leila sighed and fished a lint roller out of her purse to get rid of the worst of it. Not that it made much difference. "Don't be like that," she said. "I think we might have an eyewitness to the assault on Mina Kovač."

That would change things significantly. Nora nodded appreciatively. "Tell me more."

They set off up the hill. The road was tarmac, because unlike on Sandhamn, there were about a hundred cars on Runmarö, including taxis to transport children to and from school. However, the island had no public transport. It was roughly a fifteen-minute walk to Freya's Haven.

"The emergency dispatch center finally got back to us," Leila explained. "It was a man who called on Monday night. He refused to give his name or any contact details, but we did get his phone number, which we were able to trace." Leila sounded pleased with herself, not surprisingly. "It's a cell phone belonging to a guy called Dino Herco."

"Does he have a record?"

"No. I've run his ID number through our databases, but there's nothing on him—not even a parking fine. He's registered at an address in Farsta, which means he doesn't live in the same part of town as Kovač."

So Herco wasn't a neighbor who'd happened to be passing and heard Mina screaming.

They'd passed the local store and reached a fork in the road. The medical center and library were in Uppeby to the left; they continued straight toward Freya's Haven, which lay on the south side of the island, not far from the Runmarö Canal.

"The name made me curious," Leila continued. "Turns out it's a Bosnian surname. When I took a closer look, I found out something interesting. Dino Herco came here as a refugee in the mid-1990s, after the Bosnian War. He grew up in Nyköping."

Just like Andreis Kovač.

Nora didn't believe in coincidences.

CHAPTER 27

Freya's Haven blended in perfectly with its idyllic surroundings. It was painted white and looked as if it had been built at the turn of the last century, with leaded windows and ornate carvings above the main entrance. Several small red cabins surrounded the lawn; each had a small patio with a table and chairs. Even though it was only April and nothing was in leaf or bloom yet, it was easy to see how lovely it must be in the late spring and summer.

Nora opened the gate and led the way up the neatly raked gravel path.

Did this peaceful environment make the women feel better, or were those who came here so traumatized that they hardly noticed? Nora had no idea, but before she could ponder the matter any further, the front door was opened by a woman in her fifties with round glasses and graying hair tied back in a ponytail.

She held out her hand and introduced herself as Anna-Maria Petersén, the manager of the shelter. She knew Leila from her visit the previous day, but asked to see Nora's ID before she let them in. She showed them to a pleasant room at the back of the house.

A pretty pink tiled stove stood in one corner, and Mina was sitting in an armchair beside it, with a sleeping baby in her arms. Her blond hair was lank and greasy.

Anna-Maria gently took Lukas without waking him. "I'll look after him so that you can talk in peace," she said, nodding toward a tray with a thermos and a plate of cookies. "Help yourselves to coffee."

Nora sat down on the sofa opposite Mina while Leila set up the tape recorder. She had to find the right words; where should she begin? She needed to persuade Mina to tell her what had happened before the ambulance arrived. Above all, she had to get Mina to trust her and Leila. Mina was terrified of her husband, for obvious reasons, but the only way to protect her was to convict him.

The logic was clear, but fear is not logical.

"Thanks for seeing us," Nora said. "I'm going to do everything I can to make sure your husband goes to jail for a long time, but I need your help."

Mina refused to meet Nora's gaze, even though she was the one who'd called Leila and asked them to come over. Her face was slightly less swollen, but the bruises had darkened.

"If he's locked up, he can't hurt you," Leila said. "It's the only way for you to feel safe again."

Mina started to weep, and Leila passed her a tissue.

"It's OK to cry," she said, gently stroking Mina's arm. "We're in no hurry."

It was a long time before Mina calmed down enough to talk about Monday evening.

"Andreis was already mad when he got home. I was sitting in the living room with Lukas on my lap. As soon as I saw Andreis, I knew he was in a bad mood."

"How did you know?"

"His eyes. They get narrower. Harder." Mina took another tissue out of the packet. "I didn't know what had knocked him off balance this time. He wasn't sober either."

"Is this a regular occurrence?" Nora asked.

"I'm afraid so. Recently he's always been under the influence of either alcohol or something else in the evenings."

"What does he take?"

"I've never asked."

"Were you scared when you saw him on Monday?"

"Yes." The answer was almost inaudible. "I knew he was going to hurt me; he was just looking for a reason to get mad. He needed to take out his anger on someone." Mina grimaced. "On me."

"Do you feel strong enough to tell us what happened next?" Nora prompted her gently.

"I'd forgotten to put away the vacuum cleaner. It was in the middle of the kitchen floor. Andreis is very . . . particular about the house being clean and tidy. He saw it and went crazy. He called me terrible names, 'whore' . . . and worse."

"What did you do?"

Mina's hand crept up to her bruised cheek. "My only thought was to protect Lukas. I just had time to put him down before Andreis . . ."

"Before Andreis did what?" Leila said quietly.

Careful now, Nora thought.

"He grabbed me by the hair, dragged me into the kitchen, and threw me on the floor next to the vacuum cleaner. Then he pulled me up again and started punching me in the face. He wouldn't stop." Mina's voice was no more than a whisper. "I collapsed. I think he kicked me while I was lying there. My chest and side really hurt."

Two broken ribs, one cracked, according to hospital records.

"You had to have stitches in your eyebrow," Leila reminded her.

Tears were pouring down Mina's cheeks. "I tried to crawl away, so he kicked me again, and I banged my face on the sharp corner of a cupboard. I wanted to scream for help, but it was hard to get anything out. I did try though."

"What did he do next?" Nora asked.

"I think he grabbed me by the throat, but I don't really remember, everything was kind of blurred. I couldn't see properly, there was so much blood—it was in my eyes and my mouth."

Lukas had been lying in his crib just yards away, but that hadn't stopped Andreis.

Nora felt a sharp pain in her belly. It was Mina who'd been assaulted, but Nora could hardly bear to listen to her appalling account. She was usually proud of her professional attitude at work, and was embarrassed to discover how thin that veneer was. Thomas had been right in a way; the Economic Crimes Authority was a protected workplace.

Leila was handling the interview much better, asking one relevant question after another. Without coming across as either cold or gratuitously curious, she managed to get Mina to describe the entire course of events. It was important to record every detail if the charge was going to be based on solid ground.

Nora admired her colleague. Why couldn't she be as objective as Leila instead of getting upset? She was furious with Kovač, even though she knew it was unprofessional. She mustn't take this personally; she was there to do her job.

She took a deep breath and forced herself to focus. "We need to talk about Andreis's . . . business affairs," she said, pouring herself another cup of coffee. She immediately regretted her choice of words. *Business affairs* sounded respectable, not like an empire built on getting people addicted to drugs and ruining their lives. However, she didn't want to frighten Mina any more than necessary; she was already fragile enough.

"I don't know anything about his business." The answer came quickly.

"You don't discuss his work?"

Mina shook her head.

"Have you never heard him talking about work on the phone?" Leila ventured.

Mina pulled her cardigan more tightly around her body.

"Maybe you've seen a text message on his cell phone?" Nora suggested.

"I don't remember."

Nora was convinced that Mina knew more than she was prepared to reveal, but she didn't dare push her too hard. It was essential to build up trust so that Mina would feel safe and able to open up to them.

And of course it wasn't just a matter of sitting here, having a private conversation. Mina would have to be willing to testify in court, with her husband in the dock. Ulrika Grönstedt would do her best to tear Mina to pieces if she got the chance.

Leila carried on fishing. "Has Andreis ever left papers lying around? He can't keep everything in his head."

Mina closed her eyes. "I don't remember."

She was clearly exhausted. It was probably best to bring things to a close for the time being.

"We can talk about this another day," Nora said. "Would it be OK if we come back on Monday?"

Mina needed legal representation, an experienced lawyer who could help her deal with the trial and protect her interests. Someone who was purely on Mina's side. Nora would put in an application to the court as soon as she was back at her desk.

"The only way to put a stop to this is for your husband to be charged and convicted," she continued. "With your help I can put him behind bars for many years, which means that you and your son will be safe."

"No," Mina murmured. "Andreis will kill me if I testify against him."

"We can protect you," Leila assured her.

Mina hunched her shoulders but didn't say a word.

"Think about Lukas," Nora said, even though she didn't like using the boy in this way. "Who'll take care of him if your husband kills you the next time he loses his temper?"

Mina's eyes filled with tears once more. "I guess I could try . . ."

Nora leaned forward. "You won't regret this, Mina."

Bosnia, September 1992

Andreis was woken by the morning sun shining in through the window; everyone else was still asleep. Emir was in his crib, his mouth half-open. The house was silent. Andreis pulled on his pants and T-shirt and ran out into the garden.

The little stream was babbling cheerfully in the far corner where the raspberry canes were heavy with red fruit. The grass was damp beneath his bare feet, and the plum tree glowed purple. Andreis reached up to pick some plums and stuffed them in his mouth, the juice running down his chin. Under normal circumstances they would have harvested the plums this weekend, but nothing was normal anymore.

Andreis loved the festivities when the plums were picked to make *šljivovica*, the plum brandy the adults drank. The whole family gathered for the occasion, cousins, aunts, and uncles, everyone working together with great big baskets until the laden trees had been cleared of every last piece of fruit, and the color had changed from purple to green. The plums were poured into old wooden barrels to ferment. In the evening food was served outdoors at long tables, huge plates of grilled meat, corn on the cob, and roasted peppers, plus round loaves of bread that his mother had baked in the oven.

Andreis was allowed to eat as much as he wanted, and to stay up until he fell asleep or his father carried him to bed.

He spat out a couple of plum pits into the clear, sparkling water. It was already warm, even though it was so early. The last white veils of mist over the fields had begun to disperse as the sun climbed higher in the sky.

A dull roar that Andreis hadn't heard before caught his attention. It didn't sound like an ordinary car. Much more exciting.

He placed his foot on the lowest branch of his favorite tree and scrambled up until he could peer over the wall. Something large and a dull-green color was rolling past farther down the street. Andreis had never seen anything like it. It looked like a beetle on a caterpillar band; there was a kind of tower on the top with a pipe sticking out of it.

Andreis watched the vehicle until it turned the corner and vanished from view. He must ask Mom what it was. There didn't seem to be anyone driving it.

A whistling sound sliced through the silence. Andreis looked all around but couldn't figure out where it was coming from.

Suddenly there was an explosion on the other side of the river, creating a wall of flames. Gray-and-white clouds of smoke obscured the view. *So much smoke . . .*

Andreis's ears were hurting, and the blast had almost hurled him to the ground. The door flew open and his mother came rushing out. She crouched as she ran, keeping her head down.

"You stupid boy!" she shouted, wrapping her arms around Andreis. "Quick, we need to hide indoors!"

Until that point Andreis hadn't been worried, just curious about the strange noises. The fear came when he saw his mother's tears.

Chapter 28

Nora and Leila reached the jetty with only five minutes to spare before the ferry to Stavsnäs was due to depart. Nora was planning to wait in the little ice-cream café at the harbor; there wasn't a boat from Stavsnäs to Sandhamn for another hour.

Leila was checking her phone.

"We should have asked Mina if she knew a Dino Herco," Nora said.

"We can do that on Monday. I think she'd had enough," Leila replied. She held up her phone to show Nora an address. "How about going to see him? He lives in Farsta Strand—it won't take more than forty-five minutes to get there if we take Nynäsvägen."

Nora looked at her watch; it was only twelve thirty. The last boat to Sandhamn left at six, and Simon had already promised to watch Julia.

"He must have seen or heard something if he called emergency services," Leila went on. "If we could persuade him to testify against Kovač as well, that would make our case even stronger. And if we can tell Mina we have a witness who backs up her story, that might make her open up more when we see her again."

The ferry was approaching the jetty. Nora adjusted the strap of her purse and nodded. "My car is in Stavsnäs. Let's do it."

Dino Herco lived in Farsta Strand, a scenic area that had been developed in the 1960s. Nora drew up outside the mustard-yellow six-story apartment building. Identical buildings lined the street in a style typical of the era. There were no flower beds to soften the harshness, but a copse of trees was visible a short distance away, next to a square parking lot.

There wasn't a soul in sight when they got out of the car.

Nora found the list of residents in the foyer; Herco lived on the top floor. When they rang the doorbell, a brown-eyed man in his thirties answered. His muscles bulged beneath his spotless white T-shirt; he was clean-shaven, with his hair slicked back.

Leila produced her police ID and asked if they could come in.

"Why would I want to talk to you?" Herco placed his hand on the doorframe, barring the way.

"You don't have to talk to us," Leila said patiently, "but it would be helpful if we could come in, since we're here. It won't take long."

Herco didn't move. "Have you got a warrant?"

"We don't need a warrant to ask a few questions," Nora clarified. "It's only in American cop shows that written documentation is required in order to enter someone's home."

"Of course you can come down to the police station with us if you prefer," Leila said politely.

Herco thought for a moment, then stepped aside and let them into the light and airy two-room apartment. He led the way into a spacious kitchen. The view from the window was like a painting, with the sun sparkling on Lake Magelungen down below. It reminded Nora of the view from the Grönskär Lighthouse just off Sandhamn—sea and sky in harmony.

Leila pulled out a chair, sat down, and explained why they were there. Then she got straight to the point.

"Was it you who called the emergency number on Monday evening when Mina Kovač was being assaulted by her husband?"

"Who?" His Swedish pronunciation was perfect. He was only seven years old when he came to Sweden with his parents and two siblings. Leila had summarized his background on their way over in the car.

"Mina Kovač."

"I don't know her."

"I understand, but was it you who called and reported the incident when her husband almost killed her?"

"No."

Leila opened her notebook and made a careful note of his answer on a clean page. "So you weren't on Trastvägen that evening? You weren't outside the Kovač house at 19:14? That was when the call came through."

"No."

Nora studied Dino Herco while Leila was asking questions. He was good-looking, with deep-set eyes, but his face was marked by a pale scar running from one temple down to his cheekbone. The wound must have been deep and painful. Maybe he'd sustained it as a child in Bosnia, before the family fled?

His black hair was cut short, and he had what used to be called a widow's peak.

"Are you absolutely sure you weren't there?"

"Yes."

"So where were you at 19:14?"

"I don't remember."

"The call came from your number, according to the dispatch center."

"They must be mistaken."

"They seem pretty sure of their facts." Leila took a sheet of paper out of her bulky purse and held it out so that Herco could read it without difficulty. "There's your phone number, right there. No mistake."

Herco's eyes slid to the left. "I remember now. My cell phone was stolen last week."

"Stolen?" Nora repeated. "Why didn't you say so right away?"

"I forgot."

"But now you remember?"

"Yes."

"So the person who stole your phone called the emergency number?"

"How should I know?"

Nora leaned forward. "Tell us what happened when you lost your phone."

Herco got up, opened a cupboard, and took out a glass. He filled it from the faucet, drank the water slowly, then placed the glass in the dishwasher. Nora was still waiting for an answer.

"It was in the back pocket of my jeans on the subway. When we reached the terminal, it was gone. Someone must have taken it on the way there without my noticing."

Herco obviously wasn't the kind of man who would allow his cell phone to be stolen by a simple pickpocket. Therefore, he was the one who'd made the call. Why didn't he want to be involved? Was he scared of Andreis Kovač?

If so, he wasn't the only one.

Nora tried to hide her irritation. There wasn't much that could be done when a witness simply refused to cooperate.

"Do you know Andreis Kovač?" she asked. "Mina's husband?"

"I'm afraid I don't have time for any more questions. I have to go." Herco made a show of looking at his diver's watch. Something about the gesture reminded Nora of Kovač, but Herco seemed like a calmer person, nowhere near as aggressive.

He was already heading for the hallway, and Nora got to her feet. There was no point in sitting at the table, waiting for an answer that wasn't going to come. "Do you know each other?" She tried again anyway.

"We might have met once or twice," he said over his shoulder. "I'm guessing he's from Bosnia, too? Sounds like a Bosnian name."

Leila paused at the front door. "It was lucky someone made that call, even if it wasn't you," she said. "Mina Kovač would probably have been killed otherwise."

Dino Herco opened the door without meeting her gaze.

CHAPTER 29

Nora was on the ferry to Sandhamn. She had found a window seat and was resting her forehead on the cool glass. Fluffy clouds drifted across the blue sky; the weather must have been beautiful out in the archipelago today.

She felt a pang of guilt. She tried to prioritize the kids on the weekends, but she'd been gone for the whole of Saturday. The plan to take Julia to the shore at Trouville to barbecue sausages would have to wait.

A shadow fell over her table.

"Hi there," Thomas said. "We meet again."

Nora looked up. "Are you stalking me?" she said with a smile. "I thought you were going into town to pick up Elin?"

"I decided to bring her over to Harö instead. There was no reason to stay in the city."

Thomas had never been a city person. Elin appeared behind him in a pink coat, clutching a backpack covered in brightly colored Disney characters.

"Hello, sweetheart," Nora said, opening her arms. "Can I have a hug?"

Nora chatted with the little girl while Thomas went to the cafeteria. He came back with a glass of red for Nora, a beer for himself, and a

Fanta for Elin, plus a bag of chips. Elin settled down to watch a film on Thomas's tablet, which he'd handed over with a slight grimace. Nora had overheard a heated discussion between Thomas and Pernilla late one evening when she and Jonas had been over for dinner. Thomas had accused Pernilla of dumping Elin in front of a film whenever she needed to work after they'd eaten.

Today he clearly couldn't cope with sticking to his own principles.

"How did it go?" he asked when he'd taken a swig of his beer.

"Pretty well." Nora raised her glass to him. The ferry wasn't busy; most people had presumably traveled over during the morning in order to take advantage of the good weather. "We met up with Mina, and we're going to talk to her again on Monday. I think she's starting to open up—at least that was the impression I got."

"Have you been there all day?"

"No, we went to see the witness who called emergency services when Mina was assaulted. His name is Dino Herco."

"Dino Herco?"

"Yes—he's from Bosnia, just like Kovač, but he insists that someone else must have made the call on Monday. He claims he was nowhere near Trastvägen."

Thomas stroked his chin. "I recognize that name."

"He doesn't have a record—Leila checked."

"I'm almost sure he was mentioned when I spoke to someone from Narcotics the other day—when I was checking out Kovač for you."

Strictly speaking, he'd done that on his own initiative, but there was no need to correct him. "I actually asked Herco if he knew Kovač, but he made it sound as if they were no more than passing acquaintances. Presumably that was another lie," Nora said.

"Would you like me to see what I can find out?"

"Leila can do that on Monday." No point in creating competition.

"So where did you find Herco?"

"At home. He lives in Farsta Strand."

"You went over there instead of bringing him in?" Thomas's tone left Nora in no doubt about what he thought. "Don't forget what I said about Kovač." He lowered his voice so that Elin wouldn't hear, even though she was completely absorbed in a Disney movie. "You have to be careful with these guys. You have no idea what they're capable of."

CHAPTER 30

There was no one around when Dino reached the shore of Lake Magelungen.

It had been a mistake to let those women in, the cop and the prosecutor. He'd realized it as soon as they started asking questions about Mina. Then it had been an even bigger mistake to pretend he didn't know her. It was an easy enough thing to check, and they'd soon find out that he'd lied.

He couldn't understand why he'd said it, except that they'd taken him by surprise. He'd thought their visit was about something else—Andreis's business affairs, the problems with the tax office. The allegations that filled Andreis's mind at the moment and made him more stressed than ever.

Dino had been so prepared to deny everything that the answers came automatically.

He took out his cell phone and stared at it. The spring sun was reflected in its screen. He looked around, just to make sure no one was nearby, then hurled the phone as far as he could. It landed in the water with a splash and disappeared immediately.

He lit a cigarette, cursing his own stupidity. Why had he used his personal phone to call the emergency number on Monday evening? How could he have been so dumb?

Everything had happened so fast.

He'd remained sitting outside the house for a few minutes after he'd dropped Andreis off, smoking with the window down and trying to think about something other than the way Andreis had ranted at him on the way home. It had been a relief when Andreis got out of the car and went indoors. Dino was enjoying the peace and quiet.

He was just about to leave when he'd heard Mina's screams through the open kitchen window. When he'd looked up, he glimpsed her bloodied face before she was dragged back into the room.

She had no means of escape.

Don't get involved, he'd thought, putting the car into first gear. *It's nothing to do with you, it's between husband and wife.*

Mina let out an even more heartrending scream, and at the same time the baby had started crying in the background.

Dino had acted instinctively. The only way to save them was to call an ambulance. If he went rushing in, Andreis would never forgive him. He couldn't allow Dino to meddle in family matters, but Dino knew he couldn't sit there and do nothing.

He'd grabbed his phone and called emergency services without thinking about the consequences, and now he was in deep shit.

He set off along the narrow path leading back to his apartment. He already had a new burner phone in his pocket. He would never register a phone in his own name again. He'd transferred all the necessary contacts and texted the new number to Andreis before he got rid of the old phone.

He could feel the stress gnawing away at his body.

If that cop kept digging and mentioned her suspicions about Dino's involvement to Andreis . . .

He lit a fresh cigarette from the old one.

If she told Andreis that the call had come from his number, Andreis would realize exactly what had happened. He would regard it as a serious breach of loyalty or, even worse, a direct betrayal.

And Dino would pay the price.

Chapter 31

Mina was sitting in the armchair by the window, with Lukas in her arms. She'd just given him his bottle, and he'd fallen asleep. His little chest was moving up and down, his nostrils fluttering with each breath.

At home she would sit like this for hours, just gazing at her son. Those were the best times in her life—the only good times.

Beautiful little Lukas.

The empty bottle was on the table beside her. She tried to console herself with the thought that there were many children who didn't breastfeed; Lukas wasn't suffering because he wasn't getting breast milk. But she still felt like a bad mother.

She'd had difficulties with breastfeeding right from the start. It just didn't work, however hard she tried. The little milk she'd had dried up as soon as she got home from the hospital—when she quarreled with Andreis because she refused to have sex with him straight after giving birth.

When he started hitting her again.

Mina caressed her son's head and blew gently on his fine, downy hair. He was deeply asleep, his long, dark eyelashes resting on his perfect skin.

He ought to have the chance to grow up in a secure environment. Lukas deserved a peaceful home, not a violent father and a terrified mother.

The prosecutor was right—who would take care of Lukas if Andreis killed her? She had to get away. Nora Linde really seemed to care about Mina; she wasn't just doing her job.

Mina had to make a decision. They were coming back on Monday.

Did she have the courage to tell them about all the money, the bundles of notes she saw on Andreis's desk at regular intervals? The little notebook in which he wrote everything down, the one he always kept with him . . .

She would never be able to talk about the pictures she'd taken. The very idea made her feel sick. Andreis would be furious if he found out what she'd done, but then he was angry anyway.

Mina pressed her lips to the top of Lukas's head, feeling his warmth.

Her cell phone buzzed. Slowly she turned so that she could see the screen. Someone had sent her a photograph. She immediately recognized the gray-painted wooden house. It was Körsbärsvägen 23, her parents' home. The image came from Andreis's phone, so he must have been there.

Mina couldn't breathe.

Then another message came through, exactly the same as earlier:

Come home.

Chapter 32

Nora was almost the last to disembark when the ferry reached Sandhamn. She'd tried to persuade Thomas to come for dinner, but he'd refused, even though Elin would have liked to play with Julia. Nora had even offered them a bed for the night if there was a problem getting back to Harö.

She reached into her back pocket for her ticket and handed it to the deckhand at the top of the gangway.

The air was cooler now—typical April weather. The days were lovely as long as the sun was high in the sky, but the temperature dropped rapidly when dusk began to fall.

It was good to be back on the island.

Nora took several deep breaths and tried to shake off the negativity of the day. Over by the Royal Swedish Yacht Club marina, a few intrepid boat owners had ventured out into the archipelago. Several yachts were moored at the pontoons, although nowhere near as many as in the summer.

She'd texted Simon and suggested eating at the Sailors Restaurant so that she wouldn't have to cook dinner. She was so tired, and Simon loved their steak with Béarnaise sauce and piles of golden fries. Plus he'd watched Julia all day—he deserved a treat.

"Hi, darling."

She looked up at the sound of Jonas's voice. She'd been so caught up in the events of the day that she'd forgotten he was due home. There he was on the jetty, waiting for her. The gesture warmed her heart.

"Hi, yourself."

He'd acquired a slight tan from the California sun. His blue cap was pulled down over his dark hair, but his moss-green jacket was open at the neck. He drew her close and hugged her. He smelled good; she'd always liked his aftershave.

"Back home with my beloved wife at last," he whispered in her ear, then kissed her forehead. "Tough day? Simon said you had to go off to work this morning."

His tone was full of tender concern, with not a hint of reproach because she'd left the kids on a Saturday. They set off toward the Brand villa, past Westerberg's grocery store and the Divers Bar, its outside seating area not yet open for the season.

The bare black branches of the old lime trees along the promenade stood out against the darkening sky.

"I'm cooking your favorite meal," Jonas said. "Seafood pasta—with chocolate mousse and whipped cream to follow."

Nora smiled—he really had made an effort.

"I brought a bottle of bubbly from the US," he added. "A really good Californian label recommended by a colleague."

Nora tucked her arm beneath his and snuggled closer. "Sounds fantastic," she said. "Welcome home!"

CHAPTER 33

Dino's mouth was dry as he parked the silver Mercedes outside Andreis's house. It was almost eight o'clock in the evening, and he hadn't eaten since breakfast. He'd been sitting on the toilet for half the afternoon; his stomach always acted up when he got stressed. The text message from Andreis asking him to come over hadn't made him feel any better.

Another car was already in the drive. Dino recognized the dark-blue Audi belonging to Andreis's half brother, Emir.

That was all he needed.

Andreis was always more intense when Emir was around, as if he had to prove to himself and everyone else that he was the head of the family, the undisputed patriarch taking care of everything.

Emir was an expert when it came to triggering Andreis's inner demons.

Dino got out of his car and locked it. He glanced at the kitchen window but couldn't see anything inside.

Had that cop already spoken to Andreis about the phone call? She and the prosecutor had left his apartment at about four o'clock. He'd watched them drive off toward the city. She would hardly have contacted Andreis after that, not least because all questions were supposed to go through his lawyer.

His stomach contracted anyway.

Instinct told him to get the hell out of there, but he walked up to the front door and rang the bell. When no one answered, he tried the handle. It wasn't locked, surprisingly, so he went in. He could hear voices from the kitchen.

Andreis and Emir were sitting at the table with a half-empty bottle of vodka between them. There were a couple of empty pizza boxes on the counter, and the air was filled with the smell of garlic and melted cheese. Dirty dishes were piled high in the sink.

Emir was just about to refill his glass when Dino appeared. The younger man nodded a greeting, but Andreis barely looked up.

Dino pulled out a chair and sat down. He moved cautiously, trying not to make any irritating noises.

"Have you found her?"

Andreis's voice was quiet and controlled. It was impossible to read his facial expression; did he know about Dino's involvement in the events of Monday evening? Dino did his best to sound relaxed. "As I've already told you, I went to her parents' house last night. She wasn't there, nor was Lukas."

He glanced at Emir, who hadn't yet spoken. The brothers were very much alike, even though they had different fathers. Andreis hadn't offered Dino a drink; he just sat there, idly twirling the glass around in his fingers, the alcohol splashing up the sides.

"So where the fuck is she?" he muttered. "I drove over there this afternoon, but no one was home."

"I've no idea."

Andreis's eyes were unfocused, the stubble on his chin darker than usual. He scratched the back of one hand, where a rash that looked like a distorted flower petal had broken out. "Didn't you speak to her parents?" he said. "They must fucking know where she is."

"They were asleep."

Dino had no intention of telling Andreis about the conversation he'd overheard when he was standing at the bedroom door. If he did, Andreis would go straight over there, egged on by his brother, without a thought for the consequences.

Maybe that would be for the best.

"I went into the house. I searched all the rooms. She and Lukas aren't there."

"So where the fuck is she?" Andreis said again.

"Maybe the police have put her in a safe house. In which case she could be anywhere."

Bad idea.

"Is that all you've got?" Andreis demanded.

"I'm sure she'll be back soon," Dino ventured. "That's what usually happens."

Andreis slammed his hand on the table with such force that the vodka bottle jumped and his glass tipped over. The clear liquid ran across the table and trickled onto the floor, but Andreis ignored it. "Don't fucking come here saying you don't know where she is when I told you to find out!"

"OK, OK. Take it easy—I'll work it out."

Emir watched his brother's outburst with an expectant smile. Dino hated him for that. Emir was five years younger than Andreis; he'd come to Sweden as a baby. He was smart, but lazy. An overindulged little fucker who rode on his older brother's coattails.

No one had picked on Emir in the schoolyard while Andreis was around. Or later on. Emir had never hesitated to use his brother's reputation as a hard man to get what he wanted, and Andreis let him get away with just about anything. Family always came first in his world.

Dino had known Emir almost as long as he'd known Andreis, and he was well aware that Emir couldn't be trusted. Andreis's brother was loyal only to himself.

Dino stood up. There was no place for him here. "I'll go over there again," he said.

"How hard can it be to find the little whore?" Emir sneered. He used his thumbnail to poke at a bit of pizza that had gotten stuck between his teeth.

Andreis also got to his feet. "Forget it. I'll take care of it myself."

CHAPTER 34

Katrin was sitting on the sofa in front of the TV with a blanket over her knees. The nine-o'clock news had just finished, and she was waiting for the late film to start. She had a cup of green tea and a plate of cookies on the coffee table in front of her. Stefan had gone to the bathroom to get ready for bed, but Katrin knew she wouldn't be able to sleep yet. If she went to bed too early, thoughts of Mina and Lukas just went round and round in her head. Last night she'd lain awake worrying for hours.

She didn't even know where they were.

The police had explained that it was better that way. They could keep in touch via their cell phones, but they hadn't been given an address. She had no idea if Mina and Lukas were still in the Stockholm area, or how long they'd have to stay hidden.

Katrin was on the verge of tears. She could never have imagined that a member of her family would be forced to hide from a violent man. Andreis was a monster, and she hoped he would burn in hell for what he'd done to her daughter and grandson. He should have died in the war in Bosnia; she wished with all her heart that he'd never been let into Sweden.

It was terrible to think of another person like that, but she couldn't help it, even though Stefan objected when she expressed her opinion.

His parents had also faced prejudice when they came over from Yugoslavia as guest workers in the 1960s. They still had relatives in Macedonia.

The TV screen was filled with the smiling face of an announcer informing viewers that it was time for the Saturday film, which apparently had been a great success when it was shown in the theaters. It made absolutely no difference; Katrin was prepared to watch anything as long as it took her mind off Mina's situation.

Anxiety was gnawing away at her, causing her physical pain.

The film began and Katrin tried to follow the action, but with little success.

The doorbell rang. Katrin looked at her watch; it was almost ten o'clock. Who on earth could it be at this hour? She folded back the blanket and smoothed down her hair, then got to her feet and went into the hallway. She didn't bother switching the light on. She saw a dark silhouette through the frosted glass, but she couldn't make out who it was. The door handle was pushed down.

Katrin had a bad feeling. She peered through the peephole, one hand on the latch.

Andreis was standing on the porch with a wild look in his eyes. He was holding something.

Katrin snatched her hand away as if she'd burned it.

The doorbell rang again, then he rattled the handle. *Oh God.*

"It's me!" Andreis shouted. "Open the door!"

"What's going on?" Stefan called out from the bedroom.

Katrin was incapable of speaking. She backed away from the door and pressed herself against the wall. Her heart was pounding.

"Can you answer the door, Katrin? I've just gotten undressed," Stefan went on.

Katrin tried to say something, but produced only a hysterical croak that got stuck in her throat. "It's him!" she managed eventually.

"Who?" Stefan appeared in his bathrobe, but stopped dead when he saw her terrified face.

"It's Andreis. He's outside our door. He must have come looking for Mina."

"I know you're in there!" Andreis yelled. "I want to see my wife and son!"

Katrin moved toward the living room as Andreis hammered on the door. "What are we going to do?"

She couldn't hold back the tears. She didn't want to see that terrible man. He had abused their daughter, and now he was after them.

"Let me in!" Andreis roared, in a completely different tone of voice.

He pressed the bell again and kept his finger there. Katrin had never heard such a dreadful noise.

"Open the fucking door!"

Bosnia, December 1992

The loud voices penetrated through the wall of the bedroom where Andreis and Emir slept. Andreis sat up in the darkness, blinking. Mom and Dad were having a heated discussion in the living room.

"It's not safe for the children," Mom yelled. "We can't stay here, we have to leave."

Andreis had never heard her speak to Dad that way. Mom was always calm and gentle. She comforted Andreis when he scraped his knee, and hummed lullabies to Emir when he didn't want to go to sleep.

"We're all going to die if we stay! Why can't you see that?"

"Shut up!" Dad shouted.

"It'll be your fault if we get swept away." It sounded as if Mom was crying. "Why do you have to be so stubborn? Look what happened to the Begović family. They're gone, all of them. They didn't even lock the door behind them. They just disappeared."

Dad slammed his hand down on the table. "And where the hell do you expect us to go?"

"We can go to my sister in Croatia. She keeps calling and asking us to go there before it's too late. Think about Aunt Jasmina and Uncle Adnan. Think about Mom and Dad, trapped in Sarajevo."

"So we leave everything we own to those fucking Serbs? There you go, help yourselves. Take whatever you want—we've gone."

"We can't just sit here waiting for them to shoot us!" Mom's voice was thick with tears. "What use are our possessions if we're all dead?"

"We're staying. This will pass. People are crazy right now, but it will soon be over."

Mom was begging now. "At least think about the boys. We have to save the children. Andreis is only six, and Emir is a baby."

"This is our home."

Andreis didn't want to hear any more. He pulled the covers over his head, muting the sound of their voices. He couldn't make out the words, just the angry tone as the argument raged.

Suddenly the front door slammed so hard that the little house seemed to shake.

"Zlatko!" Mom yelled.

Andreis closed his eyes and pulled the covers even more tightly around him, but he couldn't shut out the sound of his mother sobbing.

Chapter 35

The doorbell was still ringing. Katrin put her hands over her ears, but it was impossible to shut out the terrible noise.

Her body was screaming at her to flee, but where could she go? There was no help to be had. The neighbors probably had no idea what was going on, and no one was safe when that man was around.

It was too late to pretend they weren't home. The lights were on in the living room and the bedroom, and their car was parked in the driveway.

Thank God the door was locked—at least he hadn't been able to walk straight in.

Stefan moved forward, but Katrin held out her hand to stop him. "Mina isn't here," he said. "Go away! We don't want anything to do with you!"

"Open the fucking door!"

Katrin tried to swallow, but her mouth was bone dry. "He's dangerous," she gasped.

"I'm calling the police if you don't leave," Stefan shouted.

Katrin stared at the door as if she were hypnotized. It seemed to be vibrating because of the constant ringing. Stefan took another step forward and put his face close to the glass. "We don't know where she is! Why can't you understand that?"

The ringing stopped.

Please, please go away, Katrin thought. *Go away and leave our family in peace. We haven't done you any harm.*

Was this how Mina had felt, all those times when Andreis had beaten her? Had she experienced the same terror that Katrin was feeling now? Had she also been convinced that Andreis was actually going to kill her?

My little girl.

She almost jumped out of her skin as Andreis started hammering on the door with both fists. *He's going to smash the glass,* she thought. *Or kick the door down.*

"Where are Mina and Lukas? Give me the address!"

Stefan's face was as white as a sheet. "You're the one who's chased her away! We don't know where she's gone. She's in hiding, and it's your fault!"

Tears were pouring down Katrin's cheeks. She had a pain in her left arm, and she felt as if someone were squeezing her chest. She suddenly felt sick, and coughed.

"If you don't open this door, I'll kick the fucker down!"

Katrin looked at Stefan, eyes wide with panic. "What are we going to do?"

"Let me in!"

Andreis's voice was so distorted by rage and hatred that it was almost unrecognizable. He barely sounded human.

Katrin looked over at the floor-to-ceiling glass patio doors, installed a few years ago to let in the light on summer evenings. She'd always liked sitting on the sofa after dinner, gazing out at the garden.

Now those doors posed a serious threat. It would take seconds to smash the glass with a stone. Or a gun.

Would he kill them both if he didn't find out where Mina was? There was nowhere to hide, but they had to try to get away if Andreis got into the house.

She just didn't know how.

Stefan was still staring at the front door, then he glanced toward the cellar steps next to the kitchen. Katrin could almost read his mind. Down there was the gun cupboard containing his hunting rifle and ammunition. A chance to defend themselves against the madman outside.

But everything was meticulously locked away. Stefan wouldn't have time to go down there and fetch the rifle before Andreis broke into the house.

It was hopeless.

The frosted glass in the door shattered into a thousand pieces as a large stone came flying through and landed on the hall floor.

"Listen to me!" Stefan tried again. "We don't know where she is! I'm calling the police."

His voice came from somewhere far, far away. Katrin couldn't breathe. She felt as if an iron fist had seized her chest, crushing her ribs and muscles. Everything hurt. The feeling of nausea was growing.

I can't breathe.

The room began to fade away.

"Blame yourselves if you don't do as I say!" Andreis roared.

Katrin's field of vision was shrinking.

She tried to stay upright, but her legs refused to obey her.

"Stefan . . ." What was wrong with her voice?

Everything disappeared.

Sunday

CHAPTER 36

Mina was woken by the sound of her cell phone. At first she couldn't figure out where she was, then she recognized the wallpaper in her room at Freya's Haven. Reality came rushing back.

Was Lukas all right?

She was overwhelmed by panic before she managed to sit up and check that he was lying in the crib beside her bed. At that moment he opened his eyes and let out a yell. He was hungry, of course. They'd both slept much later than usual; it was almost eight o'clock. She needed to go into the kitchen to heat up a bottle for him.

Her phone rang again, but she ignored it and picked up her son. With one hand she tried to pull on the borrowed bathrobe, but it was impossible while she was holding Lukas. It was slightly too small, and in the end she had to put him down, even though he immediately started crying again.

Her head throbbed as she tugged at the terry cloth. She had virtually nothing of her own here—everything was at home. With Andreis.

Her phone rang yet again. She decided she'd better answer, so she popped a pacifier in Lukas's mouth.

Dad, the display said. Mina quickly took the call.

"Mina?"

He sounded different, weak and unfamiliar. Mina tightened the belt around her waist. "What's happened?"

"It's Mom." His voice broke. "We're at the hospital, sweetheart. Mom's had a major heart attack."

Mina couldn't get those words to make any sense. Her brain was a blank space. "What are you talking about? Is Mom sick?"

"She's pretty bad."

"What do you mean?" Mina knew she sounded hysterical, but she couldn't help herself.

Not Mom. Not now.

"She's in intensive care, under sedation." There was a long pause. "They don't know if she's going to regain consciousness."

Mina dug her nails into the palm of her hand, fighting to remain in control. At least for a few minutes, she couldn't lose it now. "She was supposed to be seeing a cardiologist," she said. "She'd already made the appointment. You told me."

"That man came to our house late last night." Her father didn't need to say the name. *Andreis.* Once upon a time it had meant the promise of love.

"He came to your house?"

"He banged on the door, yelling and swearing and demanding to know where you were."

Mina pressed her hand to her stomach.

"Then he threatened us, he smashed the glass in the door. If a neighbor hadn't come out and shouted that the police were on their way, I'm sure he'd have managed to break in. But your mom . . ."

His voice died away.

"Her heart couldn't cope with the strain."

The guilt Mina felt was unbearable. This was all her fault. She should have warned them after she received the text message with a picture of their house. What had she done?

She undid her belt, started looking for the top she'd worn the previous day, her jeans.

"We'll leave right away," she said. "Which hospital is she in?"

"No!" The word emerged like a scream. "You can't come here."

Lukas spat out his pacifier and started crying again. Mina tried to get dressed, but he bawled even louder. In the end she had to pick him up. She tried to soothe him, but he threw himself back and forth out of hunger, grabbing angrily at her hair with his little hands. "I can't stay here," she said loudly so that her father would be able to hear her over the noise Lukas was making.

"For God's sake!" Stefan was breathing hard. "If you come here, he'll find you. He's counting on it—don't you see?"

"Please, I have to see Mom. What if she . . ." Completing the sentence was too painful.

"Mina, I can't lose you as well."

Lukas's face was bright red now, his mouth sticky with saliva. Mina was crying, too, but silently, so as not to worry her father even more.

"He's dangerous, Mina." She'd never heard him sound so helpless. "He'll kill you if he catches up with you."

"Have you been in touch with the police? You need protection, just like me."

"I haven't told them anything."

"Why not?"

"I can't. That'll just make things worse."

"What do you mean?" Mina dropped to her knees. Lukas was wailing so loudly that she had difficulty hearing her own voice. Someone banged on the wall of the room next door. "Dad?"

"That was the last thing Andreis yelled before he disappeared," her father whispered. "He said he'd kill us if we spoke to the police."

CHAPTER 37

Anna-Maria had only intended to spend a couple of hours at Freya's Haven on Sunday afternoon to clear up some paperwork, but as usual she'd stayed longer. If there was going to be anything left of the evening, it was high time she went home.

She shut down the computer and switched off the desk lamp, ignoring the piles of paper that remained. She never caught up, however hard she tried; she always had a guilty conscience.

She picked up her jacket. Siri, her colleague who worked weekends, came down the corridor just as Anna-Maria was about to close the door. Siri's beautifully styled hair reminded Anna-Maria that it was months since she'd managed to get to the salon.

"How's the new girl getting along?" Siri asked. "Mina—the one who arrived on Thursday with her baby." Siri was carrying a bowl of fruit destined for the coffee table in the TV room.

"I've hardly seen her," she replied. "She seems to keep herself to herself."

Anna-Maria had seen many different kinds of behavior during her years at the shelter: semihysterical women who couldn't stop talking about what had happened and pale, terrified shadows who crept around and didn't say a word. Most apologized for their very existence, as if it were their fault that any vestige of self-esteem had been beaten out of them. Few believed they would one day be able to cope on their own.

Anyone could end up in a destructive relationship—there was no specific personality type—and yet they all took the blame.

Her gaze fell on the photograph of Malin on the desk. She'd always been so like her father, Petter. He had been considerably older than Anna-Maria, and had died of cancer after a long and painful illness. It was as if his death opened the floodgates, and the darkness took over.

Gustav, Malin's partner, had had a certain amount of respect for Petter, and without Petter's calming influence, the situation escalated. Gustav had never been able to handle booze, and he'd started drinking every day.

When he lost his job because of it, things got really bad. Malin became more and more cowed; she lost weight and slept badly. Nervous tics lived a life of their own around her mouth. She knew she was going under, but every time she tried to get out of the relationship, the threats and violence increased. And yet she still couldn't escape.

"He'll kill himself if I leave him," she said.

Anna-Maria was in despair.

Malin defended her abuser, and nothing Anna-Maria said could make her change her view. Anna-Maria begged and prayed, swore and argued. Eventually she came up with a last-ditch plan. She would resign from her job and sell the house. Together they would flee the country. They'd have enough money to hide somewhere overseas, where Gustav would never find them. She had to give Malin the chance to start a new life without fear.

Anything was better than staying with the man who was breaking her down before Anna-Maria's eyes.

"Are you OK?" Siri said, bringing Anna-Maria back to reality.

"Absolutely." She blinked away the tears. "Something in my eye."

She ought to be able to control her feelings after all these years, but sometimes it just wasn't possible. They came over her like a tsunami, obliterating everything else.

She picked up her keys and locked the office door. "Is Mina eating properly?" she asked Siri over her shoulder. Either they didn't eat at all, or they comfort ate the whole time. Moderation was hard when the abnormal had been normalized.

Siri shook her head. "Not really."

"And the baby?"

"She seems to be looking after him well; he's fine."

That was a good sign. Sometimes, when things were really bad, the mothers sank into depression, leaving the child in even more of a mess.

Anna-Maria hesitated, then went along to Mina's room. It had a lovely view over the water. The shelter was built on a raised foundation, so that even the rooms on the ground floor had a pleasant vista.

She knocked on the door, but no one answered. Could she hear sobbing from inside?

"Mina? It's Anna-Maria. Are you awake? Can I come in?"

She waited for a few seconds, then opened the door. Mina was sitting on the bed with Lukas. Her eyes were swollen from weeping.

"Oh, sweetheart—how are you?"

Mina drew her son closer. "Not so good."

Anna-Maria perched on the edge of the bed. "Do you want to talk about it?"

"I can't."

"You can talk about anything here."

Mina shook her head. "Not this."

Anna-Maria gently patted her arm, and this time Mina didn't recoil. There was something about Mina that reminded her of Malin. It wasn't just the long blond hair and blue eyes; it was the trust that they both radiated.

In spite of all the evidence to the contrary, Malin had always believed that she could save Gustav from his inner demons if she just loved him enough. Anna-Maria had fought for her daughter and tried to get her to leave him, but when Malin became pregnant, Anna-Maria knew she'd lost the battle.

Malin had been so happy about the baby, totally convinced that everything would be all right when they finally became a family. Gustav would stop drinking and become a new man.

Anna-Maria clenched her fists and tried to push her grief aside. She had to take care of Mina now. "Sometimes getting things off your chest can make you feel better," she said encouragingly. She took out a packet of tissues and passed two to Mina.

"Thank you," she mumbled, and blew her nose.

Anna-Maria stroked her hair. "What's happened?"

"My mom's in the hospital."

Poor kid. As if everything she was going through because of her husband wasn't enough.

"It's my fault."

Had Anna-Maria heard correctly? "How can it be your fault?"

"Andreis went to my parents' house. He threatened them, and my mom was so scared that she had a heart attack . . ."

The words were almost inaudible. Anna-Maria had encountered many violent men and was well acquainted with their patterns of behavior, but things rarely went this far. "We have to contact the police," she said firmly.

"If we do that, he'll kill them." Mina's voice broke. "Believe me, he'll do as he says. He always has done. It will only make it worse if we go to the police. You can't tell anyone."

CHAPTER 38

Nora switched off the bedside lamp on her side. Jonas was reading a paperback he'd brought back from the US. He was much more of a night owl than she was, and often found it difficult to get to sleep early.

"Good-night, darling," she said with a yawn. "Aren't you tired?"

Jonas patted her shoulder. "Not yet," he said, turning the page.

Nora was just dropping off when Jonas cleared his throat.

"I've been thinking about Thomas," he said.

She'd told him she'd seen Thomas several times over the past few days, and that he'd seemed kind of lost.

"Do you know if he and Pernilla have sought help—counseling, or anything like that?"

"I've no idea."

"Sometimes it can be good to talk to an outsider."

"Mmm."

"It gives you a chance to dissect the relationship. There are lots of options if you need support; even local councils offer marital advice and talk therapy these days."

Nora sighed and tucked one hand under the pillow to find a more comfortable position.

"I mean, if you keep irritating each other, it's not easy to find your way back without help," Jonas went on. He didn't appear to have noticed that Nora was half asleep. "When all the things you loved become a constant source of annoyance, it can really wear you down."

Nora found it difficult to imagine Thomas seeing a therapist; opening up to a complete stranger wasn't exactly his thing. She wasn't sure if it was her thing either, to be honest, but maybe she was just being old-fashioned?

"Good-night," she murmured again.

When she and Henrik went their separate ways, neither of them had even considered therapy. Then again, nothing would have persuaded her to forgive Henrik or take him back. It had been years before she could even have a normal conversation with him without the anger welling up inside her. They'd never reached the stage of irritating each other on a daily basis, because his infidelity had gotten in the way.

Jonas put his book down. "One of my colleagues with the airline knows all about this kind of thing. Or rather his wife does. She specializes in couples counseling, and she has her own practice. We talked about it on the way back from LA yesterday."

"I'm sorry?" Nora propped herself up on one elbow. Jonas had a sheepish look on his face.

"I don't mean I was gossiping about Thomas at work, but the topic came up, and there's a lot of time to talk when you spend ten hours together in a cockpit above the Atlantic."

"I see." She didn't feel sleepy anymore.

"Ingemar said his wife always begins with the same question: What made them fall for their partner in the first place? Why did they fall in love?"

He drew Nora close, and she rested her head on his chest.

"Apparently there are two ways of reacting, which immediately tells the therapist whether there's any hope for the relationship or not. One category immediately remembers the reason why they chose their partner; their faces light up when they talk about happier times, which means the therapist knows there's something to work with."

The warmth of his body passed through Nora's thin nightdress, and the smell of his aftershave enveloped her. "What about the other category?" she asked, even though she could guess at the answer.

"They're so trapped inside their own bitterness that they can't or won't remember. They have no desire to talk about old times. They're seeing a therapist to pick over perceived injustices, not to look for solutions."

"What happens then?"

"Well, there's not much hope, according to Ingemar's wife. It's about finding a way to separate without damaging the relationship even more, which is particularly important if there are children to consider."

Nora adjusted her position so that she could look at her husband, his brown eyes and his light-brown hair, which was often just a little too long at the back of his neck. He hadn't changed much over the ten years they'd been together.

She still knew exactly why she'd fallen in love with him.

They'd met only about six months after she and Henrik had separated. Jonas had rented her old house when she moved into the Brand villa on Sandhamn, and they'd had dinner together a few times at the local restaurant.

She'd been so unhappy back then, struggling because she felt guilty about the split, in spite of the fact that it was Henrik who'd had an affair. Her self-esteem, both as a woman and a mother, was at rock bottom. She couldn't imagine meeting someone new.

Then Jonas turned up, and everything was different.

Through his eyes she changed, became someone she liked much better than the person she'd been during the last few months with Henrik. For the first time in years, she'd felt appreciated. With Henrik she'd gotten stuck in tired, old gender roles, taking care of most of the housework even though they both had demanding careers.

Plus sex with Jonas had been fantastic.

"In that case I guess we belong to the first category," she said, smiling up at him.

He returned her smile. "If Thomas and Pernilla are interested, I've got Ingemar's wife's phone number," he said. "She'll see them at short notice if they mention my name. He could call her tomorrow." He nuzzled Nora's neck.

"Let me think about it," she said. She wasn't sure she'd bring up the idea with Thomas. He might take offense, feel she was meddling. However, the situation between him and Pernilla could hardly be worse.

"It can't do any harm," Jonas murmured as his fingers set off on a journey of discovery over her collarbone and down inside her nightdress.

He seemed to have lost interest in his book, but Nora was definitely wide awake.

CHAPTER 39

A pale half moon was shining into Mina's room. She wished she could sleep, but it was impossible to settle. The other women and children had gone to bed hours ago; it would soon be dawn. Lukas was snoring quietly in his crib, wearing a borrowed pale-blue sleep suit.

Mina longed for home, for her own bed and her own pillow. All the little things she took for granted, but were now out of reach. She wanted to dress Lukas in his own clothes, not the shabby items Anna-Maria had dug out for her. She wanted her own underwear.

Her eyes followed the shadows. The silvery landscape outside was beautiful, the sea was hardly moving, and the treetops looked like ink drawings against the sky.

It was all so peaceful, but she couldn't relax. She pushed back the covers, got out of bed, and went over to the armchair by the window. She tried leaning her upper body against the armrest. It was hard to find a comfortable position; her broken ribs made their presence felt, whatever she did. Her body hurt, but that was nothing compared to the pain in her heart.

Mom.

Her father had called a few hours earlier to let her know that the situation was unchanged. Mom was still unconscious, and the doctors couldn't give a prognosis.

If it weren't for Lukas, Mina would happily have swapped places with her mother. Every night she prayed that she would go to sleep and never wake up again.

There had been a period when she loved the nights, when the darkness hadn't been terrifying. The evenings had been her own special time with Andreis. She couldn't wait to go to bed with him, to feel his strong, muscular body close to hers. He always slept naked, and she would fall asleep with his warm skin touching hers. Even when they were sleeping, they had proved that they belonged together, lying hand in hand.

She had felt so safe.

They would talk for hours. He had wanted to know everything about her, every detail of her life. He asked a thousand questions, almost as if he couldn't quite believe that she'd chosen him. She'd never met anyone like Andreis, never been so deliriously in love, so certain that she'd met The One.

A cloud passed in front of the moon, and Mina shivered in the darkness. She shifted in the chair, but it didn't help.

Gradually Andreis had started to talk about his childhood in Bosnia, before the war broke out and destroyed his life. He told her about the hens, scratching around in the yard. He'd had friends who lived in the same village. They'd climbed trees and swam in a small lake nearby, picked plums that were used to make the plum brandy everyone drank in the local area. She had tasted *šljivovica* on one of the rare occasions when they'd visited his mother in Nyköping.

Life had been simple, without excess, but they'd had everything they needed. Now almost all of it was gone.

Andreis had never said much about what happened when the war broke out, but Mina knew he'd seen things no child should see, terrible atrocities that left deep scars.

Sometimes he was tormented by nightmares. He would talk in his sleep or cry out for help, either in Bosnian or in Swedish. Occasionally he would wake, terrified and drenched in sweat, eyes shining with tears, but those eyes would fill with hatred when he realized it had only been a bad dream, and that he was still alive when so many were dead.

She would know he'd been dreaming of the flight from Bosnia, and she would try to comfort him with her body, caressing him back to sleep and whispering gentle words in his ear to ease his pain.

She had loved him the most when he showed his vulnerability.

He couldn't bring himself to mention the nightmares the following day, but Mina knew that the memories were always there, and would never leave him.

She would have liked to discuss it with her mother-in-law, but they met so rarely, and had never really gotten to know each other. Selma still lived in Nyköping, and it was hard to chat on the phone because her Swedish was very poor. Andreis didn't like going back there, although he did call his mother almost every day. She was often depressed and missed her homeland, in spite of the terrible things she'd experienced there.

Selma had never really recovered from their flight.

If Mina tried to bring it up with Andreis, he told her to mind her own business. His mother had too many harrowing memories from the war; there was no point in digging it all up again. As long as she took her pills, she was fine.

Only Andreis's brother, Emir, was in Stockholm. He was the member of the family Mina had seen most often since she got together with Andreis, and Emir didn't like her. He never had, and he didn't bother hiding his feelings. Mina was wary of criticizing him; Andreis would do anything for his kid brother. He would never take Mina's side against his own flesh and blood.

Her ribs were hurting too much; she couldn't stay in the chair. Laboriously she got to her feet and went in search of a painkiller.

Her phone was vibrating on the nightstand. She'd switched it to silent, but left it on in case her father called.

A message from Andreis. She didn't want to read it, but she couldn't help herself. She immediately recognized the building in the photograph: the Southern District Hospital. Where her mother was. He'd managed to find out where the ambulance had taken her.

It was impossible to escape from him; he would never let her go.

The image grew in front of her eyes until she felt dizzy. The phone vibrated again, the same message as before:

Come home.

Bosnia, January 1993

It was still dark outside when Andreis was woken by the noise, a loud rumbling as if a terrible thunderstorm were passing overhead. The room was illuminated by flashing lights that came and went.

Emir had also woken up and started yelling.

The door flew open and his mother rushed in. She picked up Emir and shouted to Andreis: "Quick, we have to take cover!"

She was still in her nightdress, and Andreis ran after her, barefoot in his pajamas. Dad didn't seem to be home; Andreis couldn't see him.

His mother opened the cellar hatch in the kitchen, where a narrow ladder led to a cramped space that was used to keep food cool in the summer. There were no lights down there. Andreis stared into the pitch-black hole.

"Go on!" His mother was still holding Emir.

"I'm scared!"

"Get down there!"

"Aren't you coming with me?"

"There isn't room for us as well—we'll hide in the pantry. Move!" She sounded beside herself.

Andreis knew he would die if he clambered down that ladder without his mother. "I don't want to, I want to stay with you," he whimpered.

The garden lit up, then there was a bang that made the whole house shake.

His mother slapped him across the face. "Get down there now!"

Andreis stared at her. She'd never hit him before; she'd never even grabbed him tightly by the arm.

Emir was yelling at the top of his voice, mouth wide open.

Light filled the kitchen, followed by an explosion. The roar was deafening, and it was accompanied by a loud whistling noise that hurt Andreis's ears.

"Go!"

Andreis scrambled down the ladder, convinced that he would never see them again.

His mother replaced the hatch, leaving him in complete darkness. He curled up on the cold, damp earth floor. Something scuttled past his foot, and he tried to make himself even smaller.

"Please, Mom," he whispered. "Please let me out."

He couldn't stop the tears from pouring down his cheeks, even though he was a big boy of six. He squeezed his eyes tight shut. There was a horrible musty smell; he tried to breathe through his mouth.

The dampness soon penetrated his thin pajamas, and he began to shiver. He wrapped his arms around his knees and rocked back and forth. He was breathing faster and faster, but somehow he couldn't get enough air.

Panic spread through his body.

If the house were struck by a grenade, no one would find him. Mom and Emir might already be dead. Dad didn't know he was down here.

He was buried alive in the darkness. He would never get out.

The noise above his head went on and on and on.

Andreis opened his mouth and screamed.

Monday

CHAPTER 40

Nora had just flopped down at her desk when Leila stuck her head around the door. They were due to set off for Runmarö shortly, as soon as Nora had had a cup of coffee and checked her emails. She'd rushed around getting Julia ready for school and making sure her daughter had everything she needed in her backpack, only to discover at the last minute that Julia was going on an excursion. Jonas had already left, of course.

"I looked into Dino Herco's story about his missing phone," Leila said, sitting down opposite Nora. "He didn't report it to the police."

As usual Leila had come in much earlier than Nora. She was always there before seven thirty, often after a long walk with Bamse or a visit to the gym. Nora tried not to think about how much exercise Leila did on a daily basis. Or how little she did in comparison.

"He was lying," Nora said. "No surprise there."

She could hear how cynical she sounded, and regretted it. She didn't want to become the kind of prosecutor who'd already seen and heard it all, who was unmoved by any case, however dreadful it might be. It was important to care.

Her phone rang; it was Thomas. She'd considered calling him the previous day, because he'd seemed so down on Saturday, but Sunday had somehow disappeared without her getting around to it. She switched her phone to the speaker function.

"Leila's here and you're on speaker," she warned him.

"I think she'll be interested in what I have to say. I'll keep it brief—I have to leave soon."

She couldn't tell if he was feeling better; she decided to call him when she got home, after Julia had gone to bed. Leila moved her chair a little closer.

"OK, what have you got?" Nora said.

"I made a few calls to check out Dino Herco, the guy you mentioned the other day."

Nora hadn't said anything to Leila, and hoped she wouldn't have a problem with the fact that Nora had discussed the case with Thomas. The domestic abuse fell within Stockholm South's mandate, so it shouldn't be a problem. However, she glanced at her colleague; she didn't want Leila to feel left out. "And you've found something?"

"Dino Herco works closely with Andreis Kovač, just as I suspected."

Herco had made it sound as if they were no more than passing acquaintances. Why was she surprised?

"The guys in Narcotics knew exactly who he was. He's Kovač's driver and his right-hand man. He follows Kovač like a shadow wherever he goes."

"Good to know," Leila said.

Nora felt a stab of irritation. They should already have accessed this information; they must look like amateurs to Thomas.

"They're also childhood friends," Thomas continued. "They went to the same school in Nyköping, and their families know each other."

No such thing as a coincidence.

"Dino is Kovač's creature." He paused. "My colleagues in Narcotics regard both men as extremely dangerous."

Nora knew that was directed at her. "Thanks for your help," she said and ended the call.

"That explains why he didn't want us to know he was involved," Leila said. "He was terrified of Kovač finding out that his own man had gone behind his back."

"How come the link didn't surface during our own preliminary investigation?" Nora couldn't hide her irritation.

Leila shifted on her chair. She clearly wasn't happy either. "We didn't really look at that kind of thing. We didn't put Kovač under surveillance, because we were focusing on tax evasion. If the case had involved drugs or blackmail, for example, I'm sure Herco's name would have come up. Plus we don't have the resources—you know the situation."

She was right, but Nora still wished they'd been better informed when they spoke to Herco. He'd been laughing at them all along.

"He saved Mina's life but didn't have the nerve to admit what he'd done," Leila said slowly. "We should be able to use that somehow."

"Drive a wedge between him and his boss?"

"Why not? Everyone seems to be afraid of Kovač."

"You ought to bring Herco in and lean on him. See how he reacts if we threaten to tell Kovač about the phone call."

Leila was already heading for the door. "I'm on it."

Chapter 41

The sun was shining as Nora and Leila made their way along the neatly raked gravel path to the front door of the shelter. The Swedish flag was flying. It wasn't Anna-Maria who came to let them in this time, but a woman with a plump figure and bleached blond hair. She showed them to the same room as on Saturday. There was a vase of pink tulips on the coffee table, a perfect match with the tiled stove.

Mina was sitting in an armchair opposite a man in a dark-blue suit. He immediately got to his feet when Nora and Leila walked in.

"Herman Wibom—I've been appointed as Mina's counsel," he said, holding out his hand.

He reminded Nora of a genial uncle, in his three-piece suit with a white handkerchief neatly tucked in the breast pocket. He was in his sixties, gray haired, and not particularly tall. A blue bow tie completed his outfit.

Nora had been hoping for an attorney with a stronger personality, someone who could stand up to Ulrika Grönstedt. However, counsel was appointed by the court, and at least Mina had representation. Hopefully Wibom would give her the strength to testify against her husband.

"I've explained to Mina that my role is to support her throughout the legal process until the trial is over," Wibom said. "Both in police interviews and in court. I've also told her that it won't cost her anything, so she doesn't need to worry about the financial side of things."

The state bore the cost of counsel. Deliberations had taken time, but the law was very clear once it had been put in place.

"How are you feeling today?" Leila asked Mina. "Did you manage to get any sleep?"

"Yes."

Leila sat down on the sofa and tried to make small talk, but Mina didn't respond. She was busy studying the buttons on her blue cardigan.

"I didn't mean what I said on Saturday," she said at last.

"Sorry?"

"About Andreis." Mina undid a few buttons, then fastened them again. "When I said he'd hit me. I was wrong."

Nora placed a hand on Leila's arm. "So what actually happened?" she asked gently.

"I tripped over the vacuum cleaner and hurt myself. Andreis had nothing to do with it."

Please don't do this to us, Nora thought. *Don't do this to yourself.*

"Mina, you described everything to us in detail," Leila said. "Are you saying none of that was true?"

Mina began to cry. "I don't know," she said, covering her face with her hands. "I'm so confused, I can't think straight."

Nora exchanged a glance with Leila.

"I want to go home," Mina sobbed.

Nora turned to Herman Wibom. "Maybe we should take a break. Do you have a moment?"

They went out into the corridor, leaving Mina in the room.

"I don't understand," Nora began. "When we were here on Saturday, she seemed prepared to stand up in court and testify against her husband. She described the assault in detail, and there's no doubt that he's guilty."

"I'm afraid Mina's had some bad news," Wibom told them. "Her mother was admitted to the hospital on Saturday night; she's had a major heart attack. Mina doesn't dare go and see her because of her husband, but she's very frightened and upset." Wibom adjusted his bow tie. "It's hardly surprising, under the circumstances."

"Do we know if Kovač had anything to do with it?" Leila asked. "Given the way he's treated Mina, could he have threatened her parents, too?"

"I'm afraid I have no idea, but Mina is extremely concerned about her mother's condition. I think she blames herself for what's happened. I believe her parents have been very worried about their daughter for some time, which of course has taken its toll on her mother's health."

"Protecting her husband won't help," Leila pointed out. "If she doesn't testify, things will only get worse."

Nora took a deep breath. Without Mina's cooperation, there was no assault case. And Mina wasn't going to help with the tax case either.

Back to square one.

"Can't you talk to her?" Leila almost pleaded. "Get her to open up?"

Wibom looked troubled. "My job is to protect my client's interests. I can't try to influence her just because that's what you want."

"The best way to protect your client's interests is to persuade her to testify so that her husband ends up behind bars for many years," Leila snapped. "Otherwise he's going to kill her."

CHAPTER 42

Nora slammed her hands on the steering wheel in frustration. She wished she could pass the slow-moving bus in front of them, but it was impossible on the narrow road from Stavsnäs.

It had been a wasted morning. Mina hadn't given them anything they could use. Quite the reverse—she'd made it clear that she had no intention of cooperating with the ongoing investigation.

Two steps back instead of one step forward, which was what Nora had been expecting. Now her hopes were pinned on Stefan Talevski, Mina's father. After some discussion, she and Leila had decided to go and see him. Maybe he could persuade his daughter to change her mind. Or testify himself, since she was too scared.

Leila had received information about a call to the police late on Saturday night in the area where Mina's parents lived. Apparently one of the neighbors had heard shouting. The window in the front door of Körsbärsvägen 23 had been smashed when a patrol car arrived, but there was no one home.

At almost the same time as that call, Stefan had requested an ambulance for his wife.

Cause and effect.

Leila was nibbling at a thumbnail. She hadn't said much since they picked up the car, but now she broke the silence. "Kovač must have contacted Mina since we saw her on Saturday. That's the only possible explanation. I'm guessing he called and called until she felt she had to answer, and that was that."

Nora had come to the same conclusion. She would have liked to grab Mina's phone and throw it in the sea. Just by leaving it switched on, Mina made herself a target. It was way too easy to get to her. Nora had spoken to Anna-Maria before they left, asked if she knew whether Kovač had been in touch over the weekend, but her response had been evasive. "You need to ask Mina," she'd murmured.

"I don't understand why she continues to protect Kovač," Nora said now, whizzing past the bus that had pulled in at a stop. "She should have left him a long time ago."

She sounded her horn at the car in front, which was traveling almost as slowly as the bus—well below the speed limit. Why had all the useless drivers chosen the same stretch of road as her today?

"I don't understand why she changed her mind. The best way, the only way for Mina to protect herself and her family is to help us put her husband behind bars," she went on.

"Easier said than done."

"Sorry?" Nora hadn't expected that from Leila. When they first spoke to Mina at the hospital, Leila had pushed her almost too hard to testify against her husband. "Are you defending her decision?"

"No woman wants to accept that she's with a man who hits her," Leila said. "So she convinces herself that he'll change, and that's why she stays."

"Surely she must realize that's not going to happen in this case." Mina's medical records told their own story.

"Of course she does, deep down." Leila stroked her long braid. "The men know they're doing wrong, too. A man shouldn't hit a woman—most guys learn that when they're children."

"And yet they still do it. I don't know how they can look at themselves in the mirror."

"They make excuses." Leila paused. "They develop a range of strategies to justify the violence, because they know the world is judging them. They're probably judging themselves, too, on some level. Almost all men believe it's wrong to use violence in a relationship, if you ask them straight out."

"So why don't they stop?" Nora slowed down as she approached the bridge. A de-rigged sailboat was moored by the gas station, looking depressingly mutilated.

"The problem is that these men just can't do it. It takes great courage to confront your own behavior, and violent men are usually afraid." Leila sounded as if she were quoting from a textbook.

"How do you know all this?" Nora asked.

"I took a couple of subsidiary courses in psychology at college before I applied to the police academy."

"Did you consider a degree in psychology?"

"No, I . . ."

Nora glanced at Leila. There was more to this than just curiosity.

After a while Leila continued. "My father used to hit my mother when I was little," she said quietly. "It was horrible. I could hear Mom crying in the kitchen after I'd gone to bed. The more she cried, the angrier he got, as if her distress somehow provoked him, even though he'd caused it." She tucked her hands under her thighs. "Mom was so lonely; she had no one to turn to. They'd come here from Iran, and she could barely speak Swedish. She had no friends or family around."

Nora wanted to place a hand on Leila's arm, but instead she asked: "What happened?"

"They separated when I was five years old. Mom got some help from a women's organization; she learned Swedish and found a job." Pride shone through when Leila talked about her mother. Her features softened, and the relief in her voice was unmistakable. "She works as

179

an interpreter today. She's always been interested in languages, and now she's fluent in five: Farsi, Swedish, English, French, and Arabic."

"How did things go for your father?"

"Not too well. He's never really adapted to life in Sweden. He's not happy here, but he can't move back. He doesn't belong anywhere."

It had begun to rain.

"He wasn't like that before we left Iran," Leila said. "Something changed when we got here. I think he was knocked off balance when he lost his status, if that makes sense. He had a good career in Iran; he was a teacher with a college education, but that counted for nothing in Sweden, and we were always short of money. It was impossible to find a job that matched his qualifications. He's a cab driver these days."

"Are you still in touch?"

"Yes, but not much—it's too hard. I couldn't accept the way he treated Mom . . ."

The children always suffered, and yet many women stayed because they thought it was best for the kids.

"Did you ever find out why he became violent?" Nora asked after a while, as they passed Fågelbro. The road was deserted now.

"We've never talked about it." Leila's expression was distant, as if she were half in her childhood, half in the present. "I think he was scared that my mom would leave him. He didn't feel good enough for her in their new situation, in this new country where everything was so different from home. That was why he used the wrong method to achieve control, even though he was obviously driving her away." Leila rubbed her index finger under her nose. "He became so desperate that he kind of got stuck, if you know what I mean. It's indefensible, but it makes it easier to understand. He was so frustrated, and the only person he could take it out on was Mom."

Nora wanted to say something empathetic, but all the phrases in her head seemed banal and meaningless. Leila must have had a tough time. How could Nora, who had grown up in the most secure environment imaginable, possibly put herself in Leila's shoes? "Do you think that's why Andreis Kovač behaves that way toward Mina?" she asked instead.

"I'm sure there are lots of explanations. Who knows what he went through in Bosnia before the family came here, what terrible memories he carries with him? Trauma at an early age can scar a person for life."

"That's no excuse."

The same could be said of Leila's father. Nora realized how clumsy she'd been as soon as the words left her lips.

"Or it could be a part of his personality," Leila mused. "It's impossible to reach a diagnosis without investigation. I learned that much from my courses. Not everything can be explained by looking at the past. There are countless other factors that come into play, from genetic predisposition to chance events. Human beings are complicated."

Nora slowed as she approached the roundabout just past Värmdö Golf Club. Mina's parents lived in Skuru; it shouldn't take more than fifteen minutes to get there. She sincerely hoped it would be possible to make Stefan Talevski see sense. She couldn't think of any other way to get Mina to change her mind.

CHAPTER 43

Ulrika Grönstedt was on her way to the Svea Court of Appeal, high heels tip-tapping across Birger Jarls Square, when her cell phone rang. She was moving as fast as her black pencil skirt allowed. She was already late, after driving Fiona to the clinic for an injection during her lunch break. The trial was due to begin in fifteen minutes, and she needed a word with her client beforehand.

She dug her phone out of her purse.

"Hello?" she said breathlessly, still heading toward the impressive Wrangel Palace, where the court was housed.

"Have you heard from Mina?"

Andreis Kovač. He hadn't bothered to introduce himself, even though his number was withheld; he assumed she would recognize his voice. "Who is this?" she said, mainly to make her point.

Without success.

"Do you know where she is?"

"She hasn't come back yet?"

"If she had, I wouldn't be ringing you, for fuck's sake."

During the weekend Ulrika had pushed aside all thoughts of her hot-tempered client, hoping that his problems with his wife would solve themselves.

Clearly that hadn't happened. She tightened her grip on her heavy briefcase crammed with documents and her laptop.

"Have you checked with her girlfriends?"

"No one seems to know anything. Including her parents."

The way he said the last three words gave Ulrika a bad feeling. "When did you speak to her parents?"

"Doesn't matter."

"Has something happened?"

"They don't know where she is."

Ulrika had reached the stone steps. Sometimes it was better not to insist on an answer. "Have you tried to speak to her yourself? Isn't she answering her phone?"

"Not for the past few days."

"How about texting her?" Ulrika glanced at her watch, less than ten minutes to go. She needed to end this call and go inside.

"You're my lawyer," Kovač said. "It's your job to fix this. She can't just take Lukas and disappear—he's my son, too."

Ulrika paused on the top step. "I've got an idea—I just need to check on a couple of things. Come by my office at four thirty this afternoon."

Chapter 44

Nora was immediately struck by the idyllic charm of Körsbärsvägen. Every house seemed to have a perfectly manicured lawn and apple trees. In a month or so the gardens would begin to bloom.

"Look at that," Leila said, pointing to the front door of number twenty-three. The frosted glass was broken, and someone had stuck a piece of cardboard on the inside. There were shards of glass on the ground. "I wonder what happened here?" She moved closer. "That's a thick pane of glass—it took some breaking."

Nora pushed the shards aside with her foot.

"How about this for a theory?" Leila went on. "Andreis Kovač turned up and threatened Mina's parents. Her mother had a heart attack, and when Mina found out, she changed her mind about talking to us."

"That would certainly explain a great deal."

"Let's hope her father is more talkative than Mina," Leila said as she rang the doorbell. They heard the sound echoing through the house, but no one came.

Leila had contacted the hospital on the way over, and had been told that Stefan had gone home to rest for a few hours. He ought to be here. She rang the bell again, and eventually Stefan appeared.

He looked haggard. His hair was all over the place, his chin covered in gray-white stubble. The last time they saw him he'd been a different man.

"What are you doing here?"

"We wondered if you could spare us a few minutes? It's about your son-in-law."

The flash of fear in Stefan's eyes confirmed their suspicions. Kovač had definitely been to the house and threatened them. "It's not very convenient," he mumbled.

"It won't take long," Nora countered.

"No one needs to know about this," Leila added. "But it would be best if you let us in." She made a sweeping gesture with her hand. "In case anyone wonders why we're standing on your doorstep."

Stefan rubbed his forehead, then stepped aside. There was glass on the floor of the hallway, too. A white dustpan and brush stood in one corner.

"Coffee?" Stefan offered, leading the way into the neat and tidy kitchen. The house was beautifully kept, with typical Swedish furniture in pale wood. Nora recognized the beige corner sofa from the IKEA catalog; it was one of their most popular models.

A safe, secure, middle-class home.

Stefan switched on the coffee machine and placed two blue mugs on the table. He was clearly taking his time in order to avoid answering their questions.

"So how are you?" Nora asked.

Stefan continued to busy himself over by the counter. His shoulders were hunched, his movements jerky, as if he couldn't quite remember which parts of his body served which purpose. "Do you have children?" he said over his shoulder.

"Two sons and a daughter. The boys are twenty and sixteen, and Julia's almost seven."

Viveca Sten

Stefan turned around. "Mina's our only child. You think you're going to be able to protect them from all the bad stuff, make sure no one ever hurts them . . ." His voice died away. "We were wrong."

The last of the coffee dripped down into the pot.

"What happened to the front door?" Nora asked.

"It was an accident."

"What kind of an accident?"

Stefan searched for the right words. "Some kids throwing stones. I need to call a glazier, but I haven't had time." He poured their coffee.

"How's your wife? We heard she was in the hospital."

His pale face lost even more color. "How do you know that?"

"We saw Mina this morning."

"Mina?" He sank down onto a chair. "Did she tell you? She wasn't supposed to—" He broke off.

"What were you going to say?" Leila encouraged him gently.

He hid his face in his hands.

"We'd really like to hear it from you, too, in your own words—if you feel up to it," Leila added.

"If Katrin dies, it's his fault," Stefan mumbled between his fingers. "He's a monster."

"Start at the beginning," Nora said.

Stefan lowered his hands and gazed in the direction of the front door. He clenched his fists, the thin blue veins standing out. "I think I ought to speak to Mina first," he said, getting to his feet as if he'd already said too much. "I really need to get back to the hospital. Maybe we could discuss this some other time?"

He almost threw them out; they hadn't even touched their coffee. Back on the pavement, Leila sighed. "Someone else who's terrified of Andreis Kovač."

Nora clutched her car key. "We're not scared," she said. "We're going to make sure we put him away."

186

Bosnia, February 1993

Selma was sitting on the sofa in the living room with an old magazine. She hadn't turned the page for a long time; she was simply staring at the pictures and listening to the erratic rhythm of her heartbeat.

Fear had become such a normal state of mind that she no longer remembered how she had felt before all this. The helplessness was the worst, knowing that she couldn't do anything, that her fate was determined by factors beyond her control.

The phone rang.

Selma knew it was her sister. She called at this time most days to try to persuade them to leave, to come to her in Croatia until everything calmed down. Their parents were still trapped in Sarajevo. It was months since they'd heard anything.

Maybe they were already dead.

She couldn't cope with watching the news reports anymore, the starvation and desperation in the city. The population of Sarajevo had been under siege and bombardment for almost ten months. Her father was almost seventy, her mother sixty and diabetic. Selma knew in her heart that their chance of survival was very small, but she tried to push the thought away.

The village where Aunt Jasmina and Uncle Adnan lived had also been attacked, just as she'd feared. It was impossible to contact them; she'd tried to call many times, but she couldn't get through. The small amount of information that had trickled out was so horrific that she couldn't bring herself to believe the whispers.

Selma shivered and rubbed her hands together, but it didn't help much. Andreis was sitting by the window, staring out at the snow-covered garden.

The only good thing about the snow was that it made the days lighter. The electricity came and went. Sometimes rockets illuminated the sky, but then she hid in the pantry with the children and hoped the attack would soon be over.

Last night Andreis had crawled into bed beside her once again. Emir was already there; it was too cold to leave him in the crib. The three of them had lain there, close together. Her beautiful little boy was scared of the dark now. He was too frightened to be alone at night, and refused to hide in the cramped cellar beneath the kitchen, even though it was the safest place in the house. He suffered from nightmares and had sudden, inexplicable outbursts of rage.

Zlatko was often missing at night, but Selma didn't dare ask where he went. He was rarely sober when he got home, and he was always in a bad mood.

They'd stopped talking to each other.

The more he sensed her silent reproach, the more aggressive he became. Sometimes she wished he didn't have a bad leg so that he would have been called up, like most other men. It would have been easier if he'd been at the front. Then she could have worried about his safety instead of dreading him coming home drunk and spoiling for a fight.

She saw Andreis blow on his fingertips. She knew he was cold in spite of the two sweaters he was wearing, plus long johns under his jeans. She hoped he wasn't hungry, too; the little food they had was earmarked for dinner.

There was a knock on the door.

Blanka brought the cold into the house. She was wearing a coat that was far too big. Her cheeks were red, eyes wide.

"Have you heard what's happened in Gornji Vakuf?" she said before she'd even taken off her scarf.

Selma put down the magazine. "I don't want to hear any more bad news. Please tell me something that will cheer me up instead!" She could see from Blanka's face that wasn't going to happen. Her friend was on the verge of tears.

"Croatia has attacked the Bosnian army!" she sobbed. "Now we're at war with them, too!"

"That's impossible." Selma felt sick. Was that why her sister had tried to call not long ago? To pass on the unthinkable? "They're our allies," she whispered. "We're fighting the Serbs together."

Blanka sank down on the sofa and pressed her hand to her mouth, struggling to stay in control. "Everyone's fighting everyone now," she said quietly.

Selma's cheeks were already wet. Blanka reached out and placed a hand on hers.

"There's no hope for our country now. We're all going to die before this war is over."

CHAPTER 45

Nora yawned; it was definitely time to go home. She gathered up the documents she'd been studying for the past hour and put them in the filing cabinet behind the desk.

It was a relatively simple case, but she'd found it difficult to concentrate on the details. Mina kept coming into her mind, which was frustrating; she'd already spent far too many hours on Andreis Kovač over the past few days. Jonathan wouldn't be impressed if she neglected the rest of her commitments. Each individual prosecutor's statistics were meticulously analyzed, especially after the latest media outcry over the length of time it took the Economic Crimes Authority to deal with its cases. The Authority had been heavily criticized for the fact that preliminary investigations seemed to take forever before charges were even filed.

Her office phone rang; she didn't recognize the number.

"This is Herman Wibom," a polite voice informed her. "Am I disturbing you?"

"Absolutely not." Nora leaned back on her chair. They were both on the same side, after all, and she needed Wibom to help her persuade Mina to testify against her husband.

"I've just spoken to Ulrika Grönstedt—she's Andreis Kovač's attorney."

"Yes, I've met her."

"She's been informed that I'm representing Mina."

"Oh yes?" Nora was doing her best not to hurry him along. She wanted to say *get to the point*, but that probably wouldn't help. He was like some long-winded old relic from the eighteenth century.

"I'm afraid she's delivered an ultimatum."

Nora sat up straight. "Sorry?"

"She claims that Mina has removed her client's child without permission, and has therefore committed a criminal act." He sighed. "If Mina doesn't return the boy to her client, Ulrika Grönstedt is going to file a complaint with the police."

It couldn't be true. "Seriously? Her client has beaten his wife black and blue! Are you telling me he wants her reported to the police because she's too scared to stay at home?"

Wibom sounded deeply unhappy as he went on: "She is unilaterally preventing the other parent from having contact with his child."

"You've got to be joking!"

So Grönstedt was intending to use the Penal Code in order to force Mina to return to that appalling man. Nora grabbed the blue book and quickly turned to chapter 7, which dealt with family law. There was no ambiguity in section 4:

> *A person who without authorization separates a child under fifteen years of age from the person who has the custody of the child, shall, unless the crime is one against personal liberty, be sentenced for arbitrary conduct concerning a child to a fine or imprisonment for at most one year. The same applies if a person having joint custody with another of a child under fifteen years of age without good reason arbitrarily carries off the child or if*

> *the person who is to have the custody of the child without authorization takes possession of the child and thereby takes the law into his or her own hands.*

She quickly skimmed through the rest. Her attention was caught by the final sentence:

> *If the crime against the provisions of the first or second paragraph is gross, the accused shall be sentenced to imprisonment for at least six months and at most four years.*

"Grönstedt repeated several times that the mother had taken Lukas without his father's agreement," Wibom said. "He's determined to fight for his rights."

"She can't be serious! Mina certainly has *good reason* in the eyes of the law to take the child—surely there can't be any doubt about that?"

"The parents have joint custody, as I understand it. Andreis Kovač is adamant that Mina had no right to remove the boy from his home. Grönstedt stressed that he's begged her to come back many times, but Mina has refused to accede to his demands." He still sounded like a legal textbook. "As far as I'm aware, there is currently no proof that Mina's husband assaulted her, and Mina denies that any such assault was perpetrated. Therefore, the court cannot take such an allegation into account."

Theoretically, Wibom was right. Mina had never formally altered her original statement, in which she'd said that she'd tripped and fallen. As long as she refused to testify, she couldn't cite Andreis's violence as a reason for leaving him and taking Lukas with her.

The idea that this could be exploited in order to force her to give up her son was totally unacceptable. If Mina had been terrified of standing up in court before, that was nothing compared to the situation in which she found herself now.

Admittedly Ulrika Grönstedt's job was to represent her client, but this was one of the worst things Nora had ever experienced. Did the woman have no integrity? Was she really prepared to go to any lengths to help Kovač force his wife and son to come home?

She must know her client; she must realize what a total shit he was.

"That's absolutely ridiculous," Nora said, slamming the Penal Code shut.

What precedents were there in this kind of case? Nora had no idea; she'd never dealt with family law or custody issues. Before moving to the Economic Crimes Authority, she'd been employed as a legal adviser with a bank for fifteen years.

A couple of colleagues passed her door, and the sound of their lively conversation penetrated into Nora's office.

Herman Wibom sounded very unhappy. "Ulrika Grönstedt stressed that there's going to be a custody battle over the boy, and that things don't look good for the mother. Even if her actions aren't deemed punishable by law, she could lose custody on a temporary basis if social services carry out their own assessment." He cleared his throat. "I thought you ought to be made aware of the situation, given what you said to me this morning about persuading Mina to testify."

Nora thought it was unlikely that Grönstedt's new tactic would make Mina more inclined to stand up in court. "Have you spoken to Mina about this?"

"I think it's better if I do it face to face. It's too late today; I'll go over there tomorrow."

Nora pushed the Penal Code away. She wanted to hit someone or something but didn't quite know who or what. "Did Grönstedt have anything else to say?"

"She's demanding that Mina hand Lukas back to his father within three days—so on Thursday at the latest."

"And if Mina refuses?"

"Then she'll go ahead and report Mina to the police, and at the same time she'll contact social services and request that the father is granted sole custody."

"Sole custody."

"'Because the mother is unstable, and isn't prepared to cooperate with the child's father.' I'm sorry, but that's exactly what she said."

Chapter 46

Leila opened the door of the interview room at the Economic Crimes Authority. Dino Herco was already there. She'd deliberately made him wait for a few minutes; there was no harm in marking her territory.

Interestingly, he'd arrived without a lawyer. Presumably he wanted as few people as possible to know he'd been asked to come in, or he was hoping that this was the end of it, and that they'd get tired of him if he repeated his lies often enough.

Whichever it might be, Leila had every intention of exploiting the situation.

She shook hands and sat down at the table; someone had scratched the surface with a sharp object.

She read out the obligatory details for the tape, then opened her file as she considered the best way to begin. She should have brought a colleague along, but no one was available. It would be fine; she didn't want to postpone the interview until tomorrow.

Dino Herco couldn't sit still; he kept changing position. His nails were bitten to the quick, and there were little sores around his cuticles. Leila hadn't noticed this when she was in his apartment; she was sure she would have if his fingertips had been in such a state.

This was a good sign—she was determined to do her best to increase the pressure on him.

"We've checked out the information you gave us the last time we saw you. There's no doubt that the call to emergency services came from your cell phone."

"I told you—it was stolen."

"There's no record of the offense."

"I didn't get around to reporting it."

"And there's no insurance claim."

"I didn't get around to that either."

Leila decided to take a risk. "Where were you last Saturday night?"

"Sorry?"

"Someone went to the home of Mina Kovač's parents and threatened them at about ten o'clock in the evening. The window in the front door was smashed; there was glass everywhere. The police were called."

Herco tried to maintain a neutral expression but didn't entirely succeed. He blinked, and Leila had a strong feeling that this information hadn't come as a surprise.

You knew that Andreis Kovač had been over there, she thought. *Does that mean you were there, too?* "Was it you who threatened them?"

"No." He shifted position yet again.

"Mina's mother was so terrified that she had a heart attack." Leila allowed her words to sink in. "She's still in the ICU. Do you know what the sentence for unlawful aggressive and threatening behavior is?"

No response.

"Up to four years. If she survives. Otherwise we're talking about causing the death of another person."

Herco leaned back, eyes half closed.

"So where were you?"

"I was with my boss, Andreis Kovač. His brother, Emir, was there, too."

Leila looked up; Herco had made a mistake. "You said you didn't know each other. Now you're referring to him as your boss. Interesting."

"You must have misheard." His jaws were working.

"I don't think so."

Herco wasn't good at playing it cool. He was trying to adopt a poker face, but it didn't come naturally. Leila let him sweat.

"Can *your boss* confirm your whereabouts?" she said after a while.

"Yes."

"Maybe we should take the opportunity to ask him if he's aware that it was you who called emergency services a week ago, when he almost killed his wife." Leila tapped her pen on the table, emphasizing her words.

Herco's eyes darted from side to side. "I didn't make the call. I've already told you that. How many times do I have to repeat myself?"

"In that case you won't mind if we mention it to your boss, just to be on the safe side," Leila said innocently.

Herco went pale. He looked up at the ceiling as if he were hoping an alternative explanation might appear out of thin air. "Don't do that," he said eventually.

Leila sat back and waited. She had him now. He'd reacted exactly as she'd hoped. "What's the problem?" she almost purred. "Talk to me, if you don't want me to speak to Kovač."

There was still a possibility that Herco might simply walk out, demand to have his lawyer present before he said another word. Or tell her to go to hell.

Instead he rested his forehead on one hand, the corners of his mouth drooping.

"That will just cause a whole lot of trouble," he muttered. He was clearly losing heart, much to Leila's satisfaction.

"What kind of trouble?"

"You don't know Andreis. He'll . . . misinterpret the situation."

"In what way?"

"I can't explain."

"I'm guessing he'll see it as a betrayal, a lack of loyalty," Leila said, putting words into his mouth.

Silence.

"So what do I get from you if I don't mention it to Kovač?"

"What do you mean?"

"Well, you made the call, so you must have seen what happened when Kovač assaulted his wife."

"Sorry?"

"I want you to agree to testify, so that we can charge him with serious assault."

Herco's expression changed with lightning speed. "Are you fucking crazy?" he spat.

Leila tried to hide her surprise. "Surely it's reasonable to expect you to do something for me, if I'm doing something for you?"

"You think I'd testify against my own brother?"

"He's not your brother. You're not related."

Herco stared at her as if seeing her for the first time. His eyes traveled slowly down her body, returned to her face, and focused on the thick, dark braid, such a contrast to the blond hair of her fellow students at the police academy. "You're not Swedish either. You know exactly what I mean."

"Enough."

Herco's eyes were full of contempt. "Working for them doesn't make you any more of a Swede," he said. "Are you so stupid that you think it'll change anything? They'll never accept you—you're just a dirty foreigner like the rest of us."

Leila thought he was about to spit on the floor, but he changed his mind at the last minute. She'd been so sure that he was going to go along with her suggestion, but now something had shifted in the room. She had to take back control.

"You think you're something special just because you're wearing a police badge." Herco snorted. "Who are you trying to fool?"

"You leave me no choice but to speak to Andreis Kovač," Leila said. "Your decision."

Before she had time to react, Herco lunged across the table and switched off the tape recorder. "Do that and I'll kill you," he said hoarsely.

CHAPTER 47

Ulrika Grönstedt felt more than happy once she'd summarized everything for Andreis Kovač. They were in the small conference room, the one with four upholstered chairs around a beautifully polished mahogany table. The view over Strandvägen reminded clients of the firm's status.

Herman Wibom had been an irritation. She hadn't met him before, but knew his type. He probably ran a private practice, possibly with one associate, and made a living from the cases allocated to him by the court.

Ulrika wasn't interested in that kind of client. She'd always known that she was aiming higher, from the day she got her first post with a well-known criminal law firm after passing the bar. She'd been their first female associate, and the skeptical joint owners had called her *sweetheart* and placed bets among themselves on how soon she would give up.

None of them had won their bet.

"I threatened to file a police report and to apply for sole custody via social services," she summarized. "That should show your wife that we mean business. I was very clear when I spoke to her counsel."

Andreis Kovač seemed less than convinced about this new strategy. At close quarters Ulrika could see how bloodshot his eyes were—he'd been crying or partying all weekend.

She suspected the latter.

"She's going to have to hand Lukas over to you," she added, smoothing out a crease in her black woolen skirt. It was cut just above the knee, which was the most flattering length for her legs.

"I want Mina back, too." His expression was unreadable. "I can't take care of Lukas on my own."

Maybe you should have thought of that before you beat the crap out of your wife. "Don't worry. From what I've heard, Mina wouldn't dream of giving up Lukas—she'll be home. This is a neat and tidy solution to the whole situation. We avoid any further dispute, and we eliminate the risk of unpleasant testimony in court."

Kovač still looked doubtful, but Ulrika gave him an encouraging smile. She couldn't help feeling pleased that she'd found such a constructive way forward, removing a major problem.

"Your wife will be back soon," she continued. "Herman Wibom will explain the situation very clearly to her. Trust me, he'll do a good job."

"Who?"

"Herman Wibom—he's been appointed as Mina's counsel by the court. I found out today."

Kovač's full lips narrowed until his mouth was no more than a thin line. And yet he was still just as attractive; it wasn't fair. "Does he know where she's hiding?"

"I'm sure he does, but that's irrelevant right now. You need to focus on the upcoming trial."

"Why?"

"Have you given any more thought to what we discussed last time we met? Whether anyone you know could have leaked information to the tax office?"

Kovač shook his head. "The guys are like my family, my brothers. None of them would betray me."

"That information has come from somewhere," Ulrika said. "Nora Linde couldn't possibly have found out all that without help." A nearby clock in a church tower struck five. "Let's go over it one more time. Who has access to those details?"

Kovač folded his arms. "My cousins, and my younger brother, of course. Emir knows more or less everything."

"Anyone else?"

Kovač fiddled with his coffee cup as he thought. "Dino, my driver. He's always with me, but we grew up together. He's my right-hand man."

"That's it? You haven't forgotten anyone?"

"No."

"Are you absolutely sure that none of them has talked?"

"They're my own flesh and blood. They would never betray me."

"Are you related to Dino?" Kovač's face darkened, but Ulrika didn't care. He was paying her very well to protect his interests. It was better for her to ask the tricky questions now than to have them come up in court.

"We've known each other since we were kids. Dino would take a bullet for me."

"OK, if you say so. In which case that just leaves Mina."

"I've already told you—Mina has no idea about what I do."

Kovač got to his feet and went over to the window. His broad shoulders certainly filled his expensive leather jacket.

"She wouldn't dare," he said over his shoulder. "She knows what would happen if she betrayed me."

Ulrika was in no doubt about that. "All I can say is that someone talked. Someone who is very familiar with your business affairs. If you want to walk away without a conviction, then you need to find out who that person is."

CHAPTER 48

Elin settled herself on Thomas's lap with her favorite cuddly toy, a rabbit she'd had since she was a baby. A long, floppy ear tickled Thomas's chin. The rabbit had been white to begin with. Its soft fur was much grayer these days, but it was essential if Elin was to get to sleep at night. It shuttled between Thomas and Pernilla on a weekly basis, just as Elin did.

"Don't you think it's bedtime?" Thomas murmured in her ear. The seven-thirty news had just begun.

She shook her head firmly. "I'm not tired."

"Just a little while longer then. Promise me you'll go to bed when the news is over."

Elin made herself comfortable. Thomas felt his shoulders drop and his tense muscles relax as the warmth of his daughter's body reached his. This might just be the best time of the day.

Sometimes he wished that Elin would never grow up, just like Pippi Longstocking, so that he would always have an eight-year-old who loved to sit on Daddy's knee. He couldn't get his head around the fact that she would be a difficult teenager in only five years.

A reporter was talking about the upcoming presidential election in the US. Thomas yawned. He'd had endless meetings and routine tasks to deal with all day, and yet he felt as if he'd achieved nothing.

He had no energy these days. The winter darkness had been more difficult than ever to deal with; the short hours of daylight had vanished as quickly as they'd come, and had never been enough.

"Why are you mad at Mommy?" Elin asked.

Thomas gave a start. The familiar feelings of guilt came flooding back. "That's a funny question, sweetheart," he said with a poor attempt at a laugh.

"You and Mommy are always arguing."

"No, we're not. I'm not mad at Mommy."

"You sound mad when you talk to her."

Thomas had wanted to keep Elin out of his disagreements with Pernilla. It was bad enough that their relationship had broken down; he didn't want it to affect his daughter, too. But sometimes his jaws ached in the evenings with the sheer effort of pretending that everything was OK. "It's just because I'm tired when I talk to her. Mommies and daddies get tired when they've been at work all day, and that means they can sound a bit mad even when they're not."

"Are you tired all the time?"

A child's logic in one sentence. Thomas had to smile, although he wanted to cry at the same time. He gave Elin a hug. Her hair was freshly washed and still damp at the ends. "No, sweetheart."

Elin turned her head away. He gently cupped her chin, brought her face around so that he could look into her eyes. They were as blue as Pernilla's.

"Is that how it seems to you?"

"Mmm."

He kissed her forehead. "Mommy and I love you very much, even if we don't always agree about everything."

Elin's lips trembled. A tear rolled down her cheek, followed by another. Thomas gently wiped them away with his index finger.

"Don't get upset, honey."

"Is it my fault?" Elin mumbled.

Thomas could see the news anchor's mouth moving, but he had no idea what she was talking about. Elin's words echoed inside his head as she buried her face in her rabbit. "Whatever gave you that idea? Of course it's not your fault."

"You always fight when you talk about me."

Thomas stroked her hair. "You must never, ever think that. None of this has anything to do with you. Mommy and Daddy love you. You're the best thing we have."

A sob shook Elin's body. "I want Mommy to come back home! I want her to be here all the time!"

The news was over; the logo filled the screen, then the next program began.

That's what I want, too.

He held his daughter close. She curled into his chest but didn't stop crying. She was so precious to him, and it was his fault that she was sad. She was only eight years old, and he could no longer protect her.

"Time for bed," he said firmly, turning to routine in the absence of a solution. "How about coming in with Daddy tonight? Would that make you feel better?"

Elin nodded, and he carried her into the bedroom. He settled both her and the rabbit on Pernilla's side—or rather what used to be Pernilla's side—and sat with her until she fell asleep and her breathing slowed. One last sob passed through her body, and she clutched the rabbit a little tighter.

Thomas stood up and crept out of the room, weighed down with guilt.

What should he say to Pernilla? He knew exactly how she'd react if he told her what Elin had said. She would accuse him of upsetting

Elin, insist he was to blame for the fact that the child felt this way. If he hadn't been so unreasonable, the three of them would still be together. He could already hear her hissing: *What did I tell you?*

He rarely drank alcohol during the week, but he went into the kitchen and took out a beer. He opened the bottle and took several swigs before putting it down on the counter and returning to the living room.

The television was still on—yet another idiotic reality show about people looking for love with complete strangers. How the hell could anyone bring themselves to do that kind of thing?

Pernilla thought it was his fault they'd separated. That he was the one who'd left her. But she'd let him down—he didn't understand why she couldn't see that.

CHAPTER 49

Dino parked in front of Andreis's house and got out of the car. He opened the back door and took out the pizzas Andreis had ordered. Three boxes, which meant that Emir was there, too. That didn't make him feel any better.

He'd hardly slept over the past forty-eight hours. The thought of Andreis finding out what he'd done had kept him awake until the small hours, and today's interview had made things so much worse.

He knew that threatening a police officer was crazy, but that girl had left him no choice. If she contacted Andreis about the phone call, he was a dead man. And testifying against Andreis would be like signing his own death warrant. Whatever he did, he was in deep shit, and it was his own fault for meddling in something that had nothing to do with him. If only he'd driven away a few seconds earlier, before he saw Mina's bloodied face at the window. Then this situation would never have arisen.

Someone waved to him from inside the house; was it Emir or Andreis, smiling broadly? For a second it was like being back in Nyköping, when he'd ring the Kovačs' bell to collect his friend on the way into town to check out the girls on a Friday night.

Life had been simple then, even if it was always Andreis who picked up the prettiest girl.

Dino tried the front door, but it was locked. He rang the bell and Emir appeared.

"Pizza delivery!" he shouted with a grin, then headed for the kitchen without bothering to say hi. Dino would have liked to punch him hard, but instead he followed him.

The kitchen looked worse than on Saturday. Crumbs on the floor crunched beneath his feet, and yet more dirty dishes were piled up by the sink. There was a terrible stench coming from one corner, as if no one had taken out the trash for quite some time.

Andreis was sitting at the table. His face was in shadow, his expression unreadable. He was holding a black pistol, slowly rotating it between his fingers.

Dino almost shit his pants.

He knows. The police have been in touch.

His brain worked feverishly. Should he try to explain himself before it was too late? Admit everything, then throw himself on the floor and beg for mercy? Would Andreis forgive him if Dino reminded him of what they'd been through together?

His hands were so sweaty that the boxes almost slipped from his grasp, but he couldn't say a word. He felt as if something were stuck in his throat, and he tried to cough.

Andreis put down the pistol, but continued to stroke the black barrel with his fingertips. The light glinted ominously off the metal. Dino recognized the model—it was a Glock. He had learned how to handle guns a long time ago, and knew his stuff.

This was it. The pizzas had just been a ruse to get him here. He'd walked into the trap like a sacrificial lamb to the slaughter.

Andreis caressed the Glock; any second now he would pick it up and point it at Dino.

Dino was screaming inside, but kept his face expressionless. There had to be a way out of here . . . He glanced around the room. Emir was standing between him and the door. Would he be able to force his way past? No chance, Andreis would take him down before he got anywhere near.

Plus it was two against one.

His knife was in his back pocket as usual, but by the time he got it out to defend himself, it would be too late. Emir would regard it as a bonus if he got the chance to smash him over the head with something. Dino got ready to react.

Emir gave a wolfish smile and moved closer to the table. Dino was about to throw up when Andreis pushed the gun aside. He sniffed the air and pointed to Dino. "I'm fucking starving—what are you waiting for? Pizza!"

Dino slowly put the boxes down on the table without taking his eyes off the Glock. He was sweating like a pig, and prayed no one would notice. Fear has its own smell. Dino knew that, and so did Andreis.

"Another five minutes and he'd have taken a bite out of that thing," Emir said, pointing to the gun.

Dino obediently forced his lips into a smile. Emir grabbed a slice of marinara. The mussels on top of the cheese began to move in front of Dino's eyes; he felt sick.

"Andreis scared the shit out of Mina's parents the other night," Emir went on before taking a big bite of pizza. The tomato sauce turned the corners of his mouth red.

Andreis nodded with satisfaction. "They thought it was their last moment on this earth."

Dino cleared his throat, hoping his voice would hold up. "Did you go over there on Saturday?"

Andreis nodded again. "Useless fuckers," he mumbled through a mouthful of food. "Scared of their own shadows."

Dino had to ask the question. "Did you find out where Mina is?" Andreis shook his head but didn't seem particularly bothered. Did he have a new plan?

"My lawyer's working on it," he said.

"Mina's mother had a heart attack," Emir confided, taking a swig from a can of beer. "She was so frightened she nearly pissed herself."

Something about Andreis's posture made Dino feel he could breathe again. He opened his own pizza box in spite of his churning stomach.

Andreis's thoughts seemed to be elsewhere. His movements weren't as tense as the other night, and the look in his eyes was less suspicious.

Dino took a bite of pizza and chewed. It tasted of ashes. He didn't dare reach for a beer; he didn't want them to see that his hands were shaking. His armpits were wet with sweat, and he could feel it running down his back. He pressed his spine against the chair and hoped they wouldn't notice.

The situation was under control. Andreis hadn't found out what he'd done, and everything was just the same as usual. He was safe. For now.

Bosnia, March 1993

Mom was busy peeling potatoes for dinner. Andreis was hungry; it was a long time since lunch, which had consisted of soup with no meat. They hardly ever ate meat these days.

However, at least the air was warmer. He wasn't constantly shivering as he'd been all winter.

He was sitting at the kitchen table, drawing with his colored pens. He wanted to do a really nice picture for Mom to cheer her up. She always looked so sad, and she never laughed.

"This is for you."

He held out the picture for her to admire. He'd tried to draw their garden, the berry bushes, the fruit trees, and the pretty flowers. Mom used to like puttering around out there, although she didn't really bother anymore.

"Thank you," she said, putting it aside without looking at it.

Andreis swallowed his disappointment. "Will you play with me?"

"I don't have time right now."

She said that whenever he asked. She was always too busy for him. Andreis was bored; almost all his friends had left the little village. There was one thing he wanted to ask his mother, but he wasn't quite sure how to do it. "Why is Dad always mad at you?" he said eventually.

Mom put aside the potato peeler. She reached for a cigarette and lit it. "What do you mean?"

"You keep yelling at each other."

Andreis didn't know how to continue. His eyes were inexorably drawn to the bruises on his mom's forearm. Last night he'd been woken yet again by another terrifying argument.

"You never kiss and cuddle anymore," he said, lowering his head.

Mom put down the cigarette and dropped to her knees in front of him. "Sweetheart, sometimes moms and dads disagree—that's just the way life is. It's nothing for you to worry about." She kissed each of his eyelids; that was their special thing. "Your dad and I have a different opinion about certain matters. It's not unusual." Her eyes shone with unshed tears. "Our country is at war, Andreis. It's not easy for anyone right now. Dad's having a hard time, just like everyone else."

"Is that your fault?"

Mom sighed. "What makes you say that?"

"Dad's so angry."

Mom pushed back her hair and picked up the cigarette again. She took a deep drag, turned her head, and blew the smoke away from Andreis's face. "Dad's frustrated," she said, stroking her son's hair. "He wants to go and fight, but his bad leg means he can't do that. He's worried and scared, just like me."

Andreis had another question that kept him awake at night. He gathered up his courage. "Are we going to leave Dad?"

Mom pulled him close and gave him a big hug. "Of course not, you silly boy. We're a family. Families stick together, whatever happens."

CHAPTER 50

Thomas cautiously turned down the covers so that he could slide into bed without waking Elin. She was fast asleep on Pernilla's side, still clutching her rabbit. He switched off the lamp, knowing he wouldn't be able to concentrate on a book. Elin's words had had a profound effect on him.

When Emily died he'd been devastated, but the despair he felt now was almost as excoriating, though in a different way. When Elin was born, he'd vowed to do everything in his power to protect her—and look where they were now. Elin's life had been torn apart, and she wondered if it was her fault.

He propped himself up on one elbow and gently stroked her soft cheek with his index finger. Nothing was more important than Elin; why couldn't Pernilla see that?

They'd had a huge fight back in June. He thought Pernilla was away too much, and when she finally came home, she was stressed and irritable. He couldn't bear to see the sadness in his daughter's eyes when Pernilla disappeared for weeks at a time. He had found it increasingly difficult to cope with his own job, even though his mother willingly helped out. He had obligations, too, something his partner didn't seem to understand.

He'd tried to explain that he felt more and more like a single dad, so maybe it was time to accept the situation: they'd reached the end of the road.

Eventually they'd decided to try again. They loved each other, and they'd already been through so much together. They couldn't simply give up again; they had to think of Elin.

Thomas had really believed Pernilla's assurances that this would be a fresh start. He'd been optimistic all summer, and enjoyed the weeks they'd spent on Harö. The usual bickering had disappeared. Pernilla had made a real effort and had barely looked at her laptop or cell phone during the vacation.

It had almost been like before, when they nurtured their love.

Thomas lay down on his back. That was the last time they'd been happy.

Once the fall came, Pernilla started traveling again, and her days at the office grew longer. Elin cried for her mother in the evenings, and Thomas seethed with anger when he saw how disappointed she was.

Things came to a head late one night early in October, when Pernilla admitted that she'd accepted a more demanding role in the company without even discussing it with him. Thomas had lost his temper.

"You lied to me!" he'd shouted in the bedroom, ignoring the fact that Elin was sleeping next door. "Everything you said back in the summer about putting the family first—did you mean any of it?"

He'd been holding a book, and without realizing what he was doing, he'd hurled it onto the floor with a crash that reverberated through the whole apartment.

Pernilla had been white-faced as he continued: "You don't give a shit about me or Elin. Nothing's more important than your career."

They'd yelled at each other like never before, said things that could never be taken back.

He didn't know who she was anymore, and he couldn't forgive her. What made it worse was the fact that he'd actually believed her when she promised to change and put the family first. It had meant so much more than he'd realized at the time.

Darkness descended on their relationship. He'd slept on the sofa in the living room, and the following day Pernilla had gone off on a long-planned business trip to the US. When she returned to Sweden, she'd found alternative accommodation.

"You're impossible to live with," she'd explained on the phone.

He felt exactly the same about her.

He turned onto his side. He had to find a way to get along with Pernilla. They couldn't let their daughter suffer like this.

The problem was that he had no idea how to fix the situation.

CHAPTER 51

Mina lay curled up on her side, wishing she were dead. It was all her fault—Mom was in the hospital, and Dad was in a terrible state.

Why hadn't she left Andreis the first time he hit her?

She still didn't understand why she hadn't done it. How many times had she read in her magazines about women who'd been abused? She'd always wondered why they didn't simply walk away. Every article advised readers to leave at the very first sign of violence, and Mina had nodded to herself. It was obvious—what woman would stay with a man who beat her?

Then she ended up in the same situation, and forgave and stayed and forgave again.

Andreis had been so upset the first time it happened. He'd bathed her wounds and kissed her bruises one after another. He'd sworn by all he held sacred that he'd never do it again. They had wept together, and he had clutched her hands, apologizing over and over.

She loved him so much; how could she ignore his distress and leave him?

Then it happened again and again and again.

Gradually she began to recognize the warning signs. She learned to be afraid when the bathroom door slammed in a particular way, or when he came into the kitchen with an ice-cold look in his eyes. She knew what to expect when he called her from the car using a certain tone of voice, or when he sat down at the dining table without even bothering to say hello. The way he put down his glass. Her body reacted instantly. Her heart began to race, and she broke out into a cold sweat before she even realized what was going on.

The waiting was almost the worst part, the knowledge that he would soon unleash his anger and violence, and that there was nothing she could do to prevent it. She had no control whatsoever.

Sometimes she just lay there wishing it would come quickly so that at least it would be over—this time. Afterward things calmed down for a while. Every blow, every bruise earned her a kind of respite. When he grabbed her by the hair and pulled so hard that she almost blacked out, she consoled herself with the thought that he'd be nice to her for a week or so.

She looked over at the crib. Lukas was the only thing that made her life worth living, and he needed her.

She couldn't allow herself the luxury of death.

CHAPTER 52

Nora was brushing her teeth when Jonas came into the bathroom.

"I've put Julia's gym clothes in her backpack," he said, reaching for his own toothbrush. "I can drop her off tomorrow if you want to leave early for work."

"Thanks," Nora mumbled through a mouthful of toothpaste.

Jonas turned the cold water on at the faucet. "By the way, did you manage to speak to Thomas about therapy?"

Nora felt a pang of guilt. She'd had so much on her mind that she'd completely forgotten to call him. She spat into the sink. "No, I haven't gotten around to it yet."

"We should have him over to dinner one evening."

Jonas's thoughtfulness made her so happy. It was good that he cared about her best friend. He'd quickly become friends with Thomas and Pernilla, and liked them both very much. There had never been any tension between Jonas and Thomas, as there had been with Henrik. The two of them had never really gotten along, and that had become even clearer when Nora finally decided to leave Henrik. Thomas had encouraged her every step of the way.

"Maybe next weekend, when Simon's back with us?" Jonas went on.

Thomas was Simon's very committed godfather. Nora had always suspected that he'd have liked more children.

"I really hope he and Pernilla can sort things out," Jonas said. "It's not easy being single with a young child."

He knew what he was talking about. When they first met, his daughter, Wilma, had been only thirteen years old, and Jonas had spent a long time as a single dad. He and his partner Margot were only twenty when she got pregnant, and their relationship had been short lived. Over the years the two of them had built up a strong friendship as they coparented Wilma.

"I hope so, too," Nora said. "They've split up before and managed to start afresh. Plus they have Elin to consider; it's not just about what they want." She picked up the jar of night cream that presumably promised far more than it could deliver, dipped her finger in, and began to work the cream into her face. "It seems as if Thomas is the one who's taken it hardest—or maybe that's my impression because I've talked to him more than Pernilla. She travels so much it's hard to get a hold of her."

Nora felt a little guilty that she hadn't spoken to Pernilla over the past few months, but then Thomas was her oldest and closest friend. It wasn't a competition; Nora was doing the best she could—and to be fair, Pernilla hadn't contacted her either.

"I thought he was the one who decided they should separate," Jonas said.

"Did he tell you that?" Nora realized she sounded offended, but Thomas hadn't confided in her.

"Not exactly, it was just something he said back in the summer. You remember that weekend when Pernilla rushed off from our crayfish party? After you'd gone to bed, Thomas and I had a beer down by the jetty."

Nora nodded. They'd held the annual crayfish celebration on Sandhamn, together with friends and neighbors. Pernilla had taken a phone call and announced that she had to leave for London immediately.

"He was furious. It was obvious that things weren't right between them, and that he really didn't want her to go, but she went anyway."

Pernilla hadn't been happy either. She'd clearly felt guilty, and had left after profuse apologies.

"It's not easy to balance a job like that with a partner and a child," Nora said. "There are bound to be conflicts along the way."

"That's not what it's about."

"So what is it about?" she asked, putting down the jar of cream with a little too much force. "The fact that Thomas can't cope with his wife being a highflier and earning more than he does?" Jonas's analysis of Thomas and Pernilla's relationship irritated her. Thomas was *her* best friend, not his.

"Are you mad at me?"

Nora shook her head and tried to smooth things over. "What were you going to say?"

Jonas scratched the back of his neck. "I think Thomas would be able to cope with Pernilla's job if she just made him feel that he came first in her life."

He drew Nora close.

"It's not about the hours she works or how much she earns," he murmured in her ear. "Thomas isn't that kind of guy—we both know that."

"As I said—so what is it about?"

"She makes him feel irrelevant, and he can't handle that. He'd rather be alone."

Tuesday

Chapter 53

She didn't even have her own hairbrush. Mina gazed at her reflection in the bathroom mirror. She'd just washed her hair with the cheap shampoo she'd been given. It was a million miles from her usual brand, which smelled divine and was specially made for long blond hair. The strands felt dry and brittle, even though they were still damp.

Everything except her purse was still back home in Kolarängen. Every stitch she and Lukas were wearing was borrowed. Nor did she have any money. The little she had squirreled away was hidden in the house, where Andreis wouldn't find it.

She sank down on the toilet seat. She didn't want to stay here among all the other abused women who also wept at night. She wanted to sit in her own kitchen with a cup of coffee as the morning sun streamed in through the window.

She wanted to go home.

She stared at the shampoo bottle next to the sink, then swept it onto the floor. It bounced on the cheap vinyl and rolled into a corner.

If only things could go back to the way they used to be . . .

Mina got to her feet and contemplated her reflection again. The bruises had begun to fade, and the stitches were healing. She still looked battered, but not quite as bad as before. She would soon be able to show herself in public without attracting the wrong kind of attention.

She bent down and picked up the shampoo. She longed for her own home in a way she'd never thought it was possible to long for material possessions. The simplest details, like opening a drawer and seeing lingerie she'd bought herself. Being able to dress Lukas in something cute and new instead of the faded clothes another baby had already worn.

She'd never realized how much it all meant. Maybe that was how Andreis's mother had felt when she'd been forced to leave her old life behind—a yearning for the everyday, for some kind of normality, even though the world was on fire and the life she knew had been smashed to pieces.

Mina closed the bathroom door and went to make herself some breakfast. Lukas had already eaten, and was sleeping peacefully in the crib by her bed. She'd hoped to find the kitchen empty, but Anna-Maria was standing by the coffee machine.

There were crumbs all over the wooden table. Someone else had eaten without clearing up. Mina always wiped the table when she'd finished; Andreis had made her very meticulous about such matters.

Anna-Maria gave her a warm smile. "Good morning, Mina—how are you today? Would you like a cup of coffee?"

"Please." Mina opened the refrigerator and took out cheese and butter. She wasn't hungry at all, but knew she ought to try and get something down. She'd already lost weight.

"Don't you think it's time you took a walk to explore the area?" Anna-Maria said. "You could take Lukas and check out the grocery store. The idea is that everyone shops for their own food here."

Mina hadn't left the shelter since she arrived. She'd taken Lukas out into the garden for some fresh air occasionally, but that was all. The first few days had passed in a kind of fog. If the staff hadn't reminded her to eat, it would never have occurred to her.

"There's a stroller by the front door—you're welcome to borrow it if you like," Anna-Maria continued. "I put it there a little while ago. It's a beautiful day, and it would do you good to get out for a while."

Mina mumbled noises of agreement without turning around.

"It's not far, it's a lovely walk. You just go to the gate and turn left. You could try Uppeby, too—that's where the local community center is. It's open for a few hours each day."

Anna-Maria disappeared into her office with her coffee. The silence when she'd gone was such a relief. Mina quickly made a sandwich and forced it down in tiny bites. She carefully wiped every surface, then swept the floor with a broom she found in one of the cupboards.

The stroller.

She opened the front door. The sun was shining, though it was still hidden behind veils of mist. There was definitely a hint of spring in the air; on another day she might have appreciated it.

There was a blue stroller at the bottom of the steps. The fabric was stained and worn, and the wheels were dirty.

Mina reached out and touched the handle. Lukas's own stroller was much nicer. It was back home in Kolarängen, of course.

She went back inside and closed the door. There was a timetable for the Vaxholm ferries in the hallway. Boats plied the route between Runmarö and Stavsnäs on an almost hourly basis, with bus connections into the city. The trip to Stavsnäs took only five minutes, while the bus journey was just over an hour.

The idea suddenly came to her. If she changed at Nacka Forum, she could go home, get some money, and pick up her own things.

She looked around; there was no one in sight. The shelter was only half full at the moment. Several women had left, and there had been no new arrivals. She took out her phone and quickly photographed the timetable. There was a departure at nine forty-five. She could be in Kolarängen by eleven fifteen, and back at the shelter in the early afternoon.

Anna-Maria would never know.

Everything would seem so much better if she had her own clothes. She felt lost, like a homeless person, like one of those unhappy women in the city, carrying their possessions around in plastic bags. She hated asking to borrow yet another essential item.

She wasn't like that; she had a home and a family. She wasn't like the other women in the shelter either.

Mina checked the timetable once again, tried to make up her mind. Did she have the courage to risk it, to go home?

Andreis was rarely there during the day; he was always busy. She could sneak in and out, and he'd never even realize she'd been there. Her keys and bus pass were in her purse. She would be so careful.

She thought about Lukas. He'd already been exposed to so much in his short life. If he couldn't lie in his own bed, at least he ought to be nicely dressed and have his own cuddly toys. She hated the horrible washed-out sleeper he was wearing now.

Mina straightened her shoulders. She would do it for Lukas.

Andreis need never know.

Chapter 54

Andreis had asked Dino to pick him up at ten thirty. The day usually began much earlier; Andreis didn't need a great deal of sleep. Even when he was up late at night, he woke early. There was no end to his restless energy.

But nothing had been the same as usual recently.

When Dino left the freeway and headed for Kolarängen, he was seized by a strong impulse to turn the car around and drive straight out of Stockholm, just keep going until he reached a new town where nobody knew who he was.

Make a fresh start.

He continued toward Kolarängen. His life was here in the capital; he couldn't simply take off. There had to be another way to solve his problem, but right now he couldn't work it out. He was driving himself crazy thinking about it.

His guts were still like jelly, and he was running to the bathroom all the time.

Nothing had been said the previous evening. Dino's heart rate had eventually slowed down. Andreis and Emir had behaved normally, talking and joking, drinking one beer after another before moving on to vodka shots. It was only when Dino had to go to the bathroom that

Emir had let out a whistle and pointed to his back. "Did you take a shower with your clothes on?"

Dino's shirt was drenched in sweat. He'd muttered something and hurried out of the room.

He turned onto Trastvägen and parked in the usual place outside the terra-cotta-colored house. This was a very "Swedish" neighborhood, not unlike the street in Skuru where Mina's parents lived. It was Mina who'd wanted a nice house not too far from her mom and dad. Dino knew that Andreis had enjoyed showing off to his in-laws how easy it was for him to come up with the purchase price.

Presumably he also relished the fact that no one could really see in, except through the kitchen window. The previous owner had planted a dense evergreen cypress hedge around the perimeter of the garden, protecting the house from nosy neighbors.

Andreis might like it here, but it wasn't for Dino. He could never feel at home in a place like this.

It took a long time for Andreis to answer the door. He was wearing only his underpants, his eyes were bloodshot, and his breath stank.

"Late night?"

Emir had stayed when Dino left. They must have carried on drinking, judging by Andreis's appearance. The house still reeked of stale cigarette smoke.

At least Emir wasn't here now; his car was gone.

"I won't be long," Andreis muttered as he disappeared into the shower.

Dino went into the kitchen and sat down to wait. It really was disgusting. Andreis clearly hadn't lifted a finger since Mina left. He'd always insisted that everything should be spotlessly clean and tidy; more than once Dino had heard him yelling at Mina because something didn't meet his exacting standards. Now he'd let the place go to hell, as if he were punishing her.

The pizza boxes on the counter smelled unpleasantly of yesterday's cheese and tomatoes. Dino went into the living room. Lukas's stroller was still in the corner, with a cuddly toy poking out. He picked up the toy and gazed at it, then put it back.

For the first time he wondered if Mina wasn't coming home. Had she actually left Andreis?

She ought to know him well enough to realize that he would never allow such a thing. Lukas belonged to him; he would never let her leave with his child. Even if he ended up in jail, he would find a way to hold on to her.

An unwelcome thought came into Dino's mind. If Andreis were charged with assault and Mina testified against him in order to help the prosecutor secure a conviction, would Emir take his place?

Dino sincerely hoped not.

He glanced at his watch. Almost eleven o'clock, he'd been waiting for twenty minutes. Andreis was taking his time. They were due to meet some guys in Södertälje at midday, and Andreis didn't like to be late.

Dino went back into the kitchen and sat down at the table. He knew better than to hassle his boss.

CHAPTER 55

The bus to Kolarängen was virtually empty. There were just a couple of retirees and Mina, who'd positioned the stroller by the back doors. Her hair was tucked beneath a baseball cap, and she kept her head down. To be on the safe side, she was also wearing sunglasses. No one must recognize her.

Not that they would, given the condition of her clothes.

She almost gave a wry smile at the thought, but found herself suppressing a sob instead.

Boarding the ferry had been straightforward, and the bus had already been waiting when they arrived in Stavsnäs. Changing at Nacka Forum had also been problem free.

They were approaching Kolarängen; the soulless cityscape had given way to more verdant areas. It was an attractive location near Lake Älta, not far from Skarpnäck. Mina often used to go for long walks with Lukas in his stroller in the mornings. There were plenty of places to swim nearby. It was perfect for families with young children. That was why she'd wanted to live here; she'd thought they'd be so happy in an area like this.

She'd thought everything would be wonderful.

Mina stared out of the window. She could still change her mind, stay on the bus until it reached the terminal, then go back to the shelter. Everyone would assume she'd been out for some fresh air, as Anna-Maria had suggested.

A little voice pointed out that that would be the most sensible thing to do.

Lukas woke up and started whining. Mina dangled a plastic toy in front of him, and he soon calmed down.

Her cell phone rang. She didn't recognize the number, so she rejected the call. Then she put it on silent; she couldn't cope with talking to anyone right now.

"Sävsångarvägen," the driver announced over the loudspeaker. He slowed down and stopped with a jolt. An elderly lady with a cane got off, pulling a small shopping cart. The doors closed with a hiss, and the bus began to move.

The next stop would be Mina's. She rested her forehead against the cool glass. She had to make up her mind. What should she do? She had only minutes to decide. The bus was traveling fast. There wasn't much traffic at this time of day.

The stained fabric on Lukas's stroller caught her eye; the borrowed sweater felt scratchy at the back of her neck.

Not long now.

She promised herself she'd be careful.

She reached out and pressed the "Stop" button. It immediately glowed red. She adjusted Lukas's blanket and got to her feet.

CHAPTER 56

Anna-Maria was busy filling in the online questionnaire from the council when she was interrupted by her office phone.

"Hello?"

"Good morning, this is Herman Wibom. Am I disturbing you?"

Mina's counsel. They'd met briefly when he visited the previous day.

"Not at all—how can I help?"

To be honest, she was glad to take a short break. Whoever had put together the form seemed to have no idea how a shelter was set up. The questions were idiotic. She was getting increasingly irritated about all the cost specifications required, while the qualitative aspects were clearly not a priority. She wouldn't be surprised if Birgitta Svanberg was behind the whole thing.

Bitch.

"I've been trying to reach Mina on her cell phone, but unfortunately she's not answering."

"If you hold on, I'll see if I can find her," Anna-Maria offered.

"That's very kind of you."

She put down the receiver and walked over to Mina's room. She tapped on the door, waited a few seconds, then tried again. No response.

She pushed down the handle and peeped in. There was no one there. Presumably Mina had gone for a walk, as Anna-Maria had suggested at breakfast time. That was good; the girl needed to get out and about instead of sitting indoors, brooding. Fresh air did everyone good; it helped to dispel the demons.

Anna-Maria returned to her office. She glanced through the window and saw that the blue stroller was gone.

"She seems to be out," she said. "Her jacket isn't on the hook, and our stroller isn't here either."

"Have you any idea where she might be?"

"I expect she's gone for a walk. We discussed it earlier."

"I've tried to contact her several times."

"Maybe she's put her phone on silent by mistake?"

"The thing is, I have bad news. I'd actually prefer to come over and tell her face to face."

"I'm sure she'll be back soon. When were you thinking of?"

"There's a boat at one o'clock—would that be OK?"

"I'm sure she'll be back by then—I'll let her know you're coming." Anna-Maria hesitated. "Can I ask what you mean by bad news? Is it to do with her mother?"

"No, no, not at all."

The answer came quickly; Wibom sounded troubled and concerned. Anna-Maria didn't like this at all; Mina had enough problems. "So it's something else?"

"I think it's best if we wait until I see Mina. Client confidentiality . . ."

"Of course. I'll see you this afternoon."

Anna-Maria ended the call. After a few seconds she picked up the phone again and dialed Mina's number. No answer. She tried again—straight to voice mail. Slightly worrying.

She left her office and went in search of one of her colleagues. Siri had just finished a therapy session and was writing up her notes.

"Have you seen Mina?" Anna-Maria asked. "I can't find her."

Siri closed her file. "I think she took the stroller and went for a walk. I saw her heading toward the road a while ago."

"What time, roughly?"

"Shortly before ten, I think."

Anna-Maria thanked her for her help and returned to her office. She tried Mina's number again. Still no answer.

She glanced at the clock on the wall; it was just after eleven. Mina had been gone for a little over an hour. She had probably decided to go for a long walk and was enjoying the fine weather.

There was nothing to worry about.

Bosnia, March 1993

There was a knock on the front door. Selma put Emir down on a blanket on the floor and went to see who it was. Zlatko had just taken Andreis to the grocery store, because someone had said there was meat for sale.

She couldn't help exclaiming when she saw who her visitor was.

"Aunt Jasmina! You're alive!"

After all the terrible news, she hadn't dared to believe that her aunt had survived. Her aunt's little village had been attacked; the story had been on the news. Selma hadn't managed to get through on the phone, and had feared the worst as time went by and she heard nothing from her aunt and cousins.

"Can I come in?" Jasmina said in a hoarse voice.

"Of course—I'm sorry. I thought you were . . . I heard about . . ." Selma gave her aunt a hug. "You took me by surprise."

"Well, I'm here now."

Selma took a step back and tried not to stare.

Jasmina was only fifteen years older than her, and had always been regarded as a beauty, with her dark eyes and her long, thick hair. Now she looked like an old woman. Her gaunt, lined face was almost unrecognizable, and her short gray hair was lank and greasy. She moved laboriously, as if everything hurt. Slowly she took off her shabby jacket and sat down at the kitchen table. Selma set out bread and jelly and put the water on to make tea. She forced herself to hide her shock, in spite of the alarming change in Jasmina.

"Have you heard anything about Mom and Dad?" she asked, against her better judgment.

"There's no point in asking. All hope for Sarajevo is gone."

Jasmina almost sounded as if she didn't care about Selma's parents and their fate; that frightened Selma even more. Emir had fallen asleep on his blanket. Jasmina hadn't touched him or acknowledged his presence in any way, in spite of the fact that they hadn't seen each other since he was born. Under normal circumstances she would have picked him up and sung his praises.

What had happened to her?

Selma placed two cups of tea on the table. Jasmina lit a cigarette and stared blankly at the blue smoke. Her hands were dirty, her nails broken.

"Aunt Jasmina?" Selma ventured after a while, when the silence became unbearable.

Jasmina gave a start; she must have been far, far away. She took a deep drag, then stubbed out the cigarette. "I just came to say good-bye. You're my last living relative."

Selma gripped her cup tightly. "Don't say that."

"They're all dead. There's nothing left to live for. I'm a widow, your cousins are gone."

Alija and Mehmed—they were only twelve and fourteen. Gone? Alija, who had a slight squint, and Mehmed, who loved playing football and fishing in the stream near their house.

Jasmina's eyes were bottomless pits. "I want you to know what happened to me and my family. Someone has to know. If I don't survive, then someone has to tell the world what they did to us."

Selma wished she could avoid hearing whatever it might be. "Wouldn't you like to have a rest?" she suggested. "We can talk some other time. Don't you want to get cleaned up first?"

"I can't stay long. I'm going to try to get to Bihać, it's supposed to be a safe zone. I'm being picked up shortly."

"You're leaving so soon?"

"Listen to me. It wasn't easy to get here, even for a short visit."

Jasmina's eyes held Selma's, her gaze simultaneously present yet distant.

"It began at dawn. First they fired shells, I woke up and pulled on some clothes. When I stepped outside, there were explosions everywhere. I could smell blood and gunpowder, rockets lit up the sky. I saw little Aiša, my neighbor's granddaughter, she was only six years old. She was standing in the road, staring at something white on the ground. It took a little while before I realized what it was. She'd lost her arm."

Selma couldn't speak.

"It was lying there, bleeding in the dirt, even though it was no longer attached to her body. She didn't make a sound." Jasmina clasped her hands. "Her face . . . I carry it with me."

Selma glanced at Emir. So far he was unhurt; how long would he remain safe? How could she protect her sons?

"The noise of the shells was relentless. We ran down into the cellar and hid. I was shaking so much with the horror of it all that my muscles ached for hours afterward." Jasmina sat up a little straighter. "Then the soldiers came. They went from house to house forcing everyone out onto the street. Some people were in their nightclothes, some were barefoot. The soldiers separated out all the men, including young boys of no more than ten or twelve, and old men who couldn't walk without a stick. They made them get up onto flatbed trucks, packed tightly together like a wall of human flesh."

For the first time Jasmina's voice almost broke.

"They took your uncle," she said, wrapping her arms around her body.

"What happened to him?" Selma whispered.

"The trucks drove toward the forest. We heard the sound of many shots, then silence. None of them came back. Not one."

Uncle Adnan. Selma couldn't hold back the tears. Uncle Adnan, who always had candy in his pockets when she was a little girl. He used to carry her on his shoulders.

"They took Alija and Mehmed, too." For the first time Jasmina let out a sob. "My fine boys. I never saw them again." Her face was contorted with pain. "One young man tried to run away, but they caught him within minutes. They dragged him back and lifted him onto the roof of the truck. Then they threw him to the ground—headfirst."

Jasmina rubbed her eyes.

"I'll never forget the sound when his skull hit the concrete. It sounded like an egg breaking. They kicked and beat him until he stopped moving. His legs twitched a few times, but that soon stopped. The ground where he lay was sodden with blood. His face was no more than a bloody pulp."

Selma had no words. Thank goodness Andreis wasn't home to hear this.

Jasmina groaned. "They raped us all. Little girls, old women, new mothers clutching their babies to the breast. Over and over again, there was no end to it. They slit the throat of anyone who wept or protested. No one escaped."

"Wasn't there anyone who could save you? Weren't there any UN forces nearby?"

The pain in Jasmina's eyes was replaced by something resembling hatred. "The UN forces were on the other side of the hill, but they did nothing. They must have heard our screams, our desperate cries for help, but no one came. They ignored our suffering when they could have saved us."

"Couldn't anyone else do anything? Neighbors with a different background?"

Jasmina looked as if she would have liked to spit on the floor. "They stood behind the soldiers, egging them on. They told them which of us were Muslims and where we lived. Our families have been neighbors for generations, but they pointed out our houses."

Selma glanced at the silent radio on the shelf. "I heard about the attack on the news, but I didn't want to believe it. I thought it couldn't possibly be true—that people could do such things to one another in our country."

"No one came to help us."

They heard the sound of a car engine outside the door, and Jasmina got to her feet.

"I have to go."

Selma inhaled sharply. The time had passed so quickly. Jasmina was her last link to her own family, to her parents.

To life as it was before the war broke out.

"Can't you stay a little longer? Please?"

"No. I'm sorry." Jasmina pulled on her grubby jacket, weary but determined.

The car sounded its horn, but she paused, stroked Selma's hair, managed an exhausted smile. For a moment Selma caught a glimpse of the aunt she remembered.

"Take your children and get away from here," Jasmina said, fighting to keep control of her emotions. "There is nothing left for us in this country."

She headed for the door, then turned back.

"Never forget what they did to us. Tell the rest of the world."

CHAPTER 57

Andreis emerged from the bathroom with a gray towel wound around his hips and disappeared into the bedroom.

"I'm going to get dressed," he grunted over his shoulder.

Ten minutes later he looked considerably better than when he'd opened the door. He was freshly shaved and had put on a clean white T-shirt under his leather jacket. His hair, still damp from the shower, was swept back.

In fact, he almost looked like his old self.

Dino relaxed; for a few seconds life was back to normal. When Andreis was in a good mood, there was no one better to be with. That was how it had always been, from their days at school together in Nyköping. Andreis energized any gathering; when he wanted to party, no one was bored.

He went into the kitchen and switched on the Nespresso machine, choosing the strongest pod—metallic blue. "Want one?"

Dino nodded.

"What a fucking mess," Andreis continued, nodding in the direction of the sink and counter. "Looks like a fucking crack den. I'll have to ask my mom to come over and clean up before long. It'll give her something else to think about, apart from all the pills she takes."

He grinned at his own joke and sat down at the table with his coffee. Dino made himself a cup and sat down opposite his boss. The aroma filled the kitchen, going some way toward disguising the smell of dirty dishes, stale pizza, and the overflowing trash can.

Andreis's cell phone rang. "It's Mom." Selma said something, and he answered in Bosnian. "I'm fine, Mom. Don't worry about me."

He had joked about her pills, but his voice changed when he spoke to her. It became softer, more tender. He'd always taken care of his mother. He'd bought her a little dog, a black poodle, when he and Emir moved to Stockholm.

"Lukas is doing great," he went on, as if everything were OK. "You'll have to come over and see him soon. He can't wait to see his grandma. You'll have to teach him Bosnian so he can talk to you." He glanced at his watch. "I have to go. Speak to you later."

He put down his phone and lit a cigarette. Dino tried to read him, to work out if there were any suspicions bubbling away beneath the surface. Andreis could usually tell if someone was scared of him; it was one of his greatest talents. Along with his brutality. That was why he was the boss, unlike Dino.

At least Emir wasn't there. Always a plus.

Dino pointed to his own watch. "Shall we get going?"

Andreis shrugged. "No rush." He gave an enormous yawn.

"It can take a while to get to Södertälje," Dino pointed out.

"I need another coffee." Andreis got up and inserted another pod in the machine. Dino put his cup in the only available space on the counter. He could see dust motes dancing in the sunlight coming through the window. He turned and found himself eyeball to eyeball with Andreis.

"You look like shit," Andreis said, draping an arm around Dino's shoulders. "What's going on? You haven't been yourself over the past few days."

241

"What are you talking about?" Dino kept his voice casual, even though his guts were churning.

"I know you, my friend. Something isn't right." Andreis's face came even closer. "Don't give me any fucking bullshit." The arm tightened its grip on Dino's shoulders.

"It's a girl who won't leave me alone, if you must know."

Andreis grinned. "You've got trouble with a lady! I could tell you had something on your mind!"

Dino tried to look embarrassed. "I met her in a bar last week, and now she keeps calling me, wanting to get together again. She's driving me fucking crazy!"

Andreis removed his arm and thumped Dino on the back. "Girls, eh?"

He finished his coffee and left the cup on the table next to his cigarette packet.

"OK, let's go. We have business to attend to. Mustn't keep our associates waiting."

Dino swallowed hard, then picked up his keys and went to unlock the car.

Chapter 58

Mina got off the bus, pushing the stroller in front of her. The stop was on a street that lay at right angles to Trastvägen, only a five-minute walk away. She stuck close to the trees as she turned into her own road.

They lived at number thirty. She passed number fifteen. She would be able to see her house at any second. She'd loved it from the moment she found it online; she could hardly believe she'd reached the point where she was afraid to go and open the door.

She pulled her baseball cap even farther down and clung on to the handle of the stroller. Lukas had fallen asleep, thank goodness.

Her heart was pounding.

She glanced at her watch—a Rolex, a twenty-fifth birthday present from Andreis. Far too big and ostentatious for her taste, but she'd thanked him profusely as he expected when she opened the elegantly wrapped gift.

Eleven fifteen.

She would just dash in and collect her things. She'd worked it all out on the bus, exactly what she was going to do when she got there. The blue sports bag in the bedroom closet would hold everything she needed, plus it would fit under the seat of the stroller. She would take only the most essential items—her underwear, a few tops, a couple of pairs of jeans, little things she couldn't bear to be without. Some nice clothes for Lukas, and the yellow sleeper with teddies on it that Grandma had given him.

What about the stroller? She really wanted to take Lukas's own, but then she'd have to leave behind the one she'd borrowed from the shelter—there was no way she could manage two. Andreis would notice the difference and realize she'd been there. Although of course she'd be gone by then.

It didn't matter.

There. Her house was only a hundred yards away.

Mina slowed down, squinting against the sunlight to see more clearly. There was no car outside; the street was deserted.

Lukas was sleeping like an angel.

Mina paused for a few seconds to make sure there was no one in the yard. She felt as if a thousand ants were crawling across her skin; the fear was palpable.

She could still turn around and go back the way she'd come.

The house was calling to her.

She was suddenly filled with a deep sense of injustice. Why shouldn't she go and pick up her things? It was her house just as much as his. Why should Andreis be allowed to drive her away from her home?

Mina set off again at a brisk pace.

CHAPTER 59

Leila appeared in the doorway of Nora's office, her black hair gathered up in a loose bun instead of a stiff braid for once.

"Can you spare a few minutes?" she said.

Nora beckoned her in. She'd been planning to spend the morning reading up on a new case, but she couldn't get Herman Wibom's conversation with Ulrika Grönstedt out of her mind. If there was any way of reporting that woman to the Bar Association, she would do it.

Leila sat down in the visitor's chair and crossed her legs. A little mud dropped to the floor from the sole of her boot.

"Did you get a hold of Dino Herco?" Nora asked, closing the file in front of her.

"I spoke to him late yesterday afternoon. I asked him to come in, but unfortunately there was no one available to sit in with me, so I interviewed him alone."

"How did it go?"

Leila looked uncomfortable. "He threatened to kill me."

"What?" Leila's cheeks flushed red. Nora had never seen her lose her composure. What the hell had happened in that room?

"Herco made it very clear that he will kill me if I tell Kovač that he called emergency services."

Threats of violence were commonplace for most police officers, but not usually during the course of a formal interview.

"We'll have him arrested immediately," Nora said, turning to her computer.

"There's no proof."

"I'm sorry?"

"As I said, I was alone with him." Leila scratched the back of her hand.

"Surely there should have been two of you?"

Leila's flush deepened. "Like I told you, I couldn't find anyone else. I had to go ahead or send him home. I made a judgment call."

"Tell me exactly what happened."

"He switched off the tape recorder and immediately made the threat. It all happened very fast. I was so taken aback that I didn't have time to react. Then he switched it on again, but refused to say another word."

"And what did you do?"

"Nothing. I just sat there like an idiot. I don't know what was the matter with me." Leila slammed her hand down on the arm of the chair. "I thought I'd got him. The interview had gone really well. I was sure he was going to agree to testify against Kovač. He must have seen the assault on Mina, because he made the call. Instead the whole thing turned into a fucking mess."

Leila didn't usually swear.

"So what do we do now?" Nora said. "Mina's too scared to stand up in court, and her father seems to feel the same."

"I have absolutely no idea," Leila replied. "I think I'll just go and shoot myself, if you'll excuse me."

Chapter 60

A little bird had landed on the drive and was pecking at the asphalt in search of something to eat. There was no one around.

Mina practically ran to the front door. She rummaged in her purse for the key, and eventually found it in the jumble. Her fingers were slippery with sweat, but she managed to insert the key in the lock and turn it.

At last.

The seven-lever dead bolt had been on, which made her feel safer. When someone was home, they usually used only the bottom lock.

She turned and scanned the neighborhood one more time, then she swiftly pushed the stroller into the spacious hallway so that it couldn't be seen from the street by anyone passing by.

Or by Andreis, if he came home.

She gasped when she saw the state of the kitchen. And the smell . . . her beautiful kitchen, which she always kept spotless. Pizza boxes and leftover food on the counters, crumbs and dirty dishes everywhere. What a mess! How could he have let it get like this, when he demanded perfection from her?

She didn't have time to think about that. She'd allowed herself half an hour, not a minute longer.

She could see Lukas's own stroller in the living room, but she didn't dare transfer him in case he woke up and started yelling. It would be much easier if he stayed asleep while she gathered everything together.

She hurried into the bedroom. The bed was unmade, the sheets in a tangle, dirty underpants on the floor. Fortunately the blue bag was in the closet, just as she'd hoped.

First she had to retrieve the money, the secret fund she'd gradually built up. She didn't have a bank account of her own—Andreis controlled all their finances—but occasionally she'd managed to squirrel away a little of her housekeeping allowance. Over time she'd saved ten thousand kronor, hidden in a stocking inside a pair of boots in one of the closets.

She opened the door and moved a stack of shoeboxes until she found the black leather boots she'd chosen. She stuck her hand into the left one, praying that the money would be where she'd left it.

Someone up there was looking after her. The bundle of notes was pushed into the toe. She felt a wave of relief, followed by a surge of fresh courage. At least she had her own resources now.

Freedom.

She replaced the shoeboxes and closed the door, then went over to the chest of drawers. There was so much she wanted to take, but she knew it was impossible. She had to choose carefully, ignore the fact that she'd have to leave most of her possessions behind.

She opened the top drawer and gazed at her underwear, neatly folded and arranged according to color. Her fingers shook as she picked up a black lace bra. The material was soft and silky smooth against her skin. It reminded her of the way Andreis used to bring her such beautiful presents. She closed her eyes, remembering happier times.

The sound of a car engine brought her back to reality.

Please, please, don't let it be Andreis.

He mustn't find her here. Mina crept over to the window and peered around the curtain. There was no sign of a silver-gray car on the drive, nor Andreis's black BMW. Had Dino dropped him off and left? If so, she would hear the key in the door at any second.

Panic flooded her body.

She hadn't thought of that—Dino almost always picked Andreis up and brought him home in the Mercedes. The BMW stayed in the garage, virtually unused. She'd been so busy thinking about what she'd come here for that she hadn't given Dino a thought, even though he'd been a part of their lives ever since she first met Andreis.

She was stupid, just as Andreis so often yelled at her when he was mad.

Mina held her breath, waiting for the sound of the key. She should never have come here. How could she have been so foolish? She reached for her cell phone to call for help, but the back pocket of her jeans was empty. She almost fainted when she realized that the phone was in her purse. Hanging on the handle of the stroller. In the middle of the hallway. Andreis would see it as soon as he opened the door. She might as well have put up a big sign outside, saying she was home.

She couldn't move. She was paralyzed by the same fear she'd felt just before the ambulance arrived.

He's going to kill me.

She heard a scraping noise, growing fainter. After a moment her brain figured out what it was.

One of the city road sweepers had just driven past the house. At this time of year they swept the whole area, clearing away the sand and grit from the winter.

She didn't need to be afraid.

She sank down and wrapped her arms around her knees. It was OK.

She wasn't going to die today.

Mina didn't know how long she'd been sitting on the floor when she eventually found the strength to move. She grabbed hold of the windowsill and pulled herself up. Cold sweat trickled down the back of her neck.

She couldn't give up now. She had to do this, in spite of the fact that her legs felt like jelly and all she wanted to do was to curl up in a dark corner.

She would cry later, when she was back at the shelter and both she and Lukas were safe.

The blue bag was waiting on the bed. She unzipped it, her movements jerky. She had to hurry now, gather up what she needed. Far too much time had passed since she got here.

Andreis could be back at any minute.

CHAPTER 61

Dino increased his speed and moved into the outside lane to overtake a blue Toyota with a smashed rear light. He would need to fill up with gas when they arrived. The gauge was getting close to the red zone, and he didn't want to run out on the way back.

He also needed the toilet, but clenched his buttocks in an effort to keep control.

In the passenger seat, Andreis was staring at his cell phone; he was scrolling up and down, but Dino couldn't see exactly what he was looking at. Instead he concentrated on driving, and hoped there wouldn't be any more questions he'd need to answer with more lies.

Andreis hadn't commented on his "confession" since they left the house.

Yesterday Dino had really believed it was all over as far as he was concerned. He was getting in deeper and deeper—somehow he had to find a way out of this situation.

"Shit," Andreis said suddenly, dropping his phone on his lap. "I left my cigarettes in the kitchen." He refused to smoke anything but his own specially imported brand.

"Do you want me to turn around?"

They were twenty-five miles from Södertälje; there was no chance of covering the distance by twelve, but sometimes Andreis liked to keep people waiting—especially if he thought they needed to know exactly who was in charge.

To make sure they behaved themselves.

"Do we have time?"

"That's up to you." Dino deliberately kept his tone neutral. Out of the corner of his eye, he saw Andreis grin. He was the buyer; he didn't need to kowtow to the guys they were meeting.

"You're absolutely right."

Today was purely an initial sounding out of possible suppliers recommended and screened by another contact. Andreis had become more cautious since he was released from custody—he didn't embark on any new deals without extensive background checks.

Of course, nothing that was said at the meeting would touch on the real business or be expressed in a way that could link Andreis to the final deal. Others would take over at that stage, those who physically handled the goods once terms had been agreed on. The organization consisted of many layers, with different people fulfilling different roles.

In a corporate context, Andreis would be described as adept at exploiting the particular skill set of each member of his team.

"I can turn off up ahead," Dino said, pointing to the exit ramp for Nacka a few hundred yards away. "It won't take more than twenty minutes to drive back to the house."

Andreis stuck his hand in his pocket where the cigarettes should have been. "OK," he said. "But step on it."

Chapter 62

Nora found it even more difficult to concentrate on the new case when Leila left. She was well aware that time was running out. She'd already postponed filing charges against Kovač so that she could include the assault on Mina, but there was a limit to how long she could wait. The prospect of Mina changing her mind was fading.

Maybe it would be wiser to focus on the financial crimes? That was her area of expertise, after all. She had solid evidence against Kovač; perhaps she ought to take a step back and let the police worry about Mina. File the charges as she'd originally intended and leave the rest.

She closed the folder. She was getting nowhere fast. She stood up, grabbed her purse and jacket, and left the office. She needed fresh air and the chance to clear her head. When she stepped out onto Hantverkargatan, the lunchtime rush had already begun in the nearby cafés and restaurants. She wasn't hungry anyway and set off toward Kungsholm Square.

Without really knowing how it had happened, she found herself sitting on the bus to the Southern District Hospital. She was going to take one last shot at persuading Stefan to testify against his son-in-law.

Andreis Kovač was much too dangerous to be allowed to walk free. Thomas had said that Andreis would take it personally if Nora insisted on dragging Mina into the court proceedings, but Nora had taken his assault on his wife personally, too.

It took less than twenty-five minutes to reach the hospital. She showed her ID at reception and learned that Katrin Talevski was still in intensive care on the fourth floor. She was in critical condition.

Nora spotted Stefan as soon as she entered the unit. He had just emerged from a room opposite the door. Beyond him, Nora could see Katrin lying in bed. Various tubes were attached to her body, with a battery of machines bleeping and humming away.

Stefan stopped dead when he recognized Nora. His face was gray and haggard. He didn't look as if he'd had much sleep since they met at the house on Körsbärsvägen.

Poor guy. First the worry about his daughter and grandson, and now his wife.

"What are you doing here?" he exclaimed.

"Can you spare a few minutes, Stefan?" Nora felt extremely uncomfortable. She shouldn't have come here. She hadn't spoken to Leila; she'd just taken off like some kind of private eye.

Stefan glanced over his shoulder at Katrin. "What's it about?"

"I have a few questions about your son-in-law's actions when he came to your house and threatened you and your wife."

"I have nothing to say. I made that clear yesterday."

"I promise it won't take long."

How could he be so blind, with Katrin lying unconscious just yards away because of what Kovač had done?

"Don't you realize that things will only get worse if both you and Mina choose to keep quiet about what happened? If you choose to protect Andreis Kovač?" Before Stefan could interrupt, she went on: "A week ago, you tried to persuade Mina to testify against her husband, but she couldn't find the courage. Now he's attacked both you and your wife, and you're doing exactly the same thing. How long are you going to allow him to terrorize your family?"

Stefan blinked several times.

"Help me to put him away. Burying your head in the sand isn't going to improve the situation." Nora took a step closer. "You'll never be free of Kovač if you don't help us now. We need both your and Mina's cooperation to send him to jail for a long time."

"I need to talk to Mina first."

"You haven't spoken to her?"

Stefan shook his head and moved to the side. When he opened his mouth again, his gaze was so unfocused that Nora wondered if he even remembered why she was there. "I've been sitting here the whole time," he said. "Katrin's condition deteriorated during the night. I haven't had the chance to call—"

A loud beeping noise came from Katrin's room. A nurse immediately appeared and hurried past them. The light above the door was flashing frenetically.

"You need to leave," Stefan said, following the nurse.

CHAPTER 63

Lukas's room was decorated in soft shades of blue. Mina had put up the wallpaper herself; it was adorned with cute little ducks. His crib was against one wall, with the nursing chair beside it. A pure white fleece was draped over the back of the chair.

Mina glanced around quickly. She'd spent far too long in the bedroom. Where had the time gone? She had to decide what to take with her, but her heart was racing, and she couldn't think clearly. She'd developed a kind of tunnel vision; she could only look at one thing at a time, with no comprehension of how it connected with anything else. Time after time she picked up an item of clothing, then put it down again. She couldn't decide what was most important. She felt as if every single object were essential.

Her mind was a syrupy mess.

She opened the top drawer in Lukas's chest and rummaged through his clothes. She chose two snowsuits, a few warm tops, and two pairs of pants. She added Lukas's favorite teddy bear and a couple of pacifiers. At the last minute she remembered to close the drawer—she didn't want to leave any obvious traces of her presence.

She ran into the bathroom but avoided looking in the mirror. She'd stood in this spot too often, covering up her bruises and flushing a split lip with water. She didn't need a reminder; that was provided by the painful stitches in her eyebrow. She filled her toiletry bag with makeup. She would have liked to take her electric toothbrush but didn't dare. Its absence would be too obvious.

She hurried into the hallway and grabbed her favorite jacket.

Lukas was still fast asleep. Mina hesitated. Should she take his lovely new stroller, or leave it behind? The borrowed one was smaller and lower; it would be difficult to fit the blue bag underneath. But it was already twenty to twelve. She had to get out of here.

Make up your mind.

The other stroller was in the living room, exactly where it had been when Andreis got home that Monday. Her last evening in this house.

Mina released the brake and pushed the stroller into the hallway. Gently she transferred Lukas and tucked him in. He whimpered and his eyelids flickered, but he didn't wake up. She managed to stuff the blue bag underneath and placed her purse in the carrier.

She hesitated again. Should she try to take both strollers or leave the borrowed one behind? She didn't know which would attract the least attention, but in the end she put the stroller from the shelter in the spot where Lukas's had stood. Hopefully Andreis wouldn't notice the difference. If there was a problem as far as the shelter was concerned, she would pay for a new stroller. At least she had her own money now.

She took out her keys, glanced around to make sure she hadn't forgotten anything, and headed for the door.

Chapter 64

Ulrika Grönstedt leaned back in her office chair and contemplated her neat and tidy desk, where the photograph of Fiona took pride of place. The mahogany shone. She'd bought it at Svenskt Tenn, and it conveyed precisely the discreet elegance she wanted.

Their clients might engage in shady activities, but the law practice was totally respectable.

Kovač's thick file was in front of her, with Nico's memo on custody disputes and removing a child without permission right at the top. He was the associate who had looked into her idea of bringing Mina back by threatening to bring in social services.

Ulrika had weighed the ethics of using a child to force an abused woman to return home, but had decided once more that Mina's well-being wasn't her problem. Herman Wibom could worry about his client.

Nico hadn't seemed particularly concerned about the moral issue. He was sharp—there was no doubt about that—and so far he'd gotten most things right. His latest suggestion was that the practice should set up an Instagram account. He had argued with great enthusiasm that they should be building up their image on social media.

Nico was going to do well.

Her cell phone rang. She considered not answering; she didn't have time for a long conversation. She was due at Riche for a lunch meeting in ten minutes. Then her professional persona took over, and she accepted the call. If worst came to worst, she could continue talking as she walked to the restaurant.

"Ulrika Grönstedt."

"Have you spoken to her?" As usual, Andreis Kovač didn't bother introducing himself.

"Are you talking about your wife?"

"Is she coming home?"

Ulrika put on her coat. "I haven't spoken to her myself, but as I've already told you, I have spoken to Herman Wibom, her counsel. He was going to pass on our demands, exactly as we agreed."

"Will she obey?" There was no emotion in Kovač's voice; he could just as easily have been talking about a dog.

"I underlined the seriousness of removing a child against the will of the other parent," she said, using the severe tone she normally saved for the courtroom.

"She needs to come home right now."

"We gave them three days. I can't change that after the fact."

"I want her back here by tomorrow," Kovač snapped. "I've had enough of this crap."

Ulrika took a deep breath. "They haven't responded yet," she said, heading for the elevators. "We'll have to wait until her legal counsel contacts me."

"Do your job and make sure she comes home." He lowered his voice, but there was no mistaking the menace. "I won't tell you again."

Bosnia, April 1993

The aroma of freshly brewed coffee filled the kitchen. Blanka had gotten hold of some eggs and had baked a sponge cake. Both Selma and Andreis had had a big slice. It tasted divine.

They didn't have sweet treats in the house these days—or even bread. Selma used to make big round loaves, but recently the little flour she could get had been enough for no more than a small slice with each meal. She often let the children have her share. The shelves in the grocery store were virtually empty, and anything that was available to buy cost a fortune.

"Go and play, sweetheart," she said to Andreis when he'd finished his cake.

He went over to the corner and lined up his toy cars. He had three—one red, one blue, and a black-and-white police car.

Selma worried about him every single day.

She tried to protect him as best she could, but what was growing up under these conditions doing to his young soul? He heard the quarrels between her and Zlatko, saw the bruises she did her best to hide. There was no avoiding the terrible news pumped out by the TV and radio day after day.

Would he be marked forever by the terrible things that were going on all around them?

The other day he'd gone crazy and hurled the police car to the floor, even though it was one of his most prized possessions. A wheel came off and was beyond repair. He was inconsolable but couldn't explain what had made him do it.

Blanka lit a cigarette. "How long are you intending to stay?"

Selma wished she wouldn't ask. She didn't want to talk about it; the question was already going around in her head all the time.

"We're looking into every possible way to get out," Blanka went on. "The Serbs have almost cleared eastern Bosnia now."

Selma ran her fingertips over the surface of the table. "There's no talking to Zlatko—he won't leave. He refuses to abandon our home and possessions."

"He's always been stubborn."

"He keeps saying it will pass, the war will be over soon. We just have to be patient."

Blanka tapped the ash into her saucer. "What if he's wrong, Selma?"

Even Jasmina's story hadn't changed Zlatko's mind. He didn't want to listen.

Tears scalded Selma's eyes, but she tried not to cry when Andreis was around. He was already so nervous. Over the past few weeks he'd become increasingly restless; her sunny little boy had disappeared. He'd always had a lot of energy, but now there was nowhere for it to go. He should have been in school, but it was closed until further notice. No one knew when it would open again.

She didn't dare let him play outside—she panicked as soon as he was out of her sight. The bombings had stopped temporarily, but she was still anxious.

"Don't say that!" she snapped. "It will all sort itself out somehow. It has to."

Blanka was clearly taken aback by the sharpness of her tone, and Selma immediately regretted it. Blanka was her best friend; she meant well.

"I'm sorry," Selma said quickly. "I don't know what to do. Zlatko's determined to stay and defend what we have."

"You need to talk to him again."

"He just gets mad if I try to bring it up."

Blanka leaned forward and pushed up Selma's sleeve, exposing an ugly bruise. Selma's cheeks flushed deep red, and she pulled the fabric down again.

"He's not the same man I married," she whispered.

"War changes people. It brings out the worst in them."

Selma buried her face in her hands. "Zlatko can't admit that he's wrong," she mumbled. "That we should have fled to Croatia as soon as the war broke out. Now it's too late. We argue about it all the time." She looked up and rubbed her forehead. "He's hardly ever home. He spends his time drinking with the other men, the few who are left. I don't know what to do. I don't know anything anymore."

Blanka finished her coffee. "He's going to condemn his family to death if he doesn't change his mind. Would you like me to ask Dario to talk to him?"

Selma shook her head. Admittedly Blanka's husband was Zlatko's cousin, but he was considerably older and already retired. If Zlatko found out that she'd been moaning and dragged the family into their private affairs, it would only make things worse.

Her stomach contracted at the thought of bringing up the subject of leaving with Zlatko yet again, but Blanka was right.

"I'll try and talk to him," she said.

CHAPTER 65

The street was still deserted when Mina cautiously opened the front door and looked around. She slipped out quickly and carefully locked up behind her. Everything must be exactly the same as when she'd arrived. She didn't want Andreis to suspect anything.

She decided not to think about switching the strollers.

With her heart in her mouth, she hurried down the drive and made for the bus stop, sweating as she pushed the heavy stroller in front of her. The exertion was hurting her ribs, but she felt stronger than she had for a long time. She'd done it! She'd found the courage to go home, in spite of her fear of Andreis. For once she'd stood up for herself.

Mina laughed nervously at her own boldness.

Lukas whimpered, but she couldn't stop and pick him up yet. She would comfort him as soon as she was safely on the bus. It was due in ten minutes; her timing was perfect. Soon she would be back at the shelter with her own things.

Please don't wake up, she silently begged her son, increasing her speed as she rounded the corner. She could see the bus stop now.

The last patches of snow were melting in the spring sunshine, and even though the old snow was ugly and brown around the edges, it gave her hope. The leaves on the trees would start to appear in a couple of weeks, and the first snowdrops were already out.

Something clean and beautiful was about to replace everything that was dirty.

She had to step off the sidewalk in order to skirt a pile of gravel. *Not far now.* She could hear her labored breathing.

She became aware of the sound of an approaching car, much too loud on the quiet street. The speed limit in this residential area was twenty miles per hour, but this driver didn't seem to care. The roar of the engine grew louder behind her. Mina couldn't help turning her head.

She knew immediately where the car was going.

It was a silver-gray Mercedes.

It was no more than a hundred yards away when she began to run for her life.

CHAPTER 66

Dino turned onto Trastvägen. He was driving fast; they'd been held up at several red lights, and the journey back had taken too long. There were no other cars around, and he didn't care about the speed limit.

Andreis had called his lawyer from the car, and was in a foul mood. He'd cursed Ulrika Grönstedt, but she'd come with the highest recommendations from others who'd engaged her services. She was "good," according to the word on the street.

There was a woman pushing a stroller up ahead. Was she running?

"Look!" Andreis yelled, just as Dino realized who she was. Her hair was tucked inside a baseball cap, and he could only see the back of her, but there was something familiar about her posture, the odd strands of blond hair that had escaped and were blowing in the wind.

It was Mina!

She was pushing Lukas's stroller; Dino had often seen it in the corner of the living room over the past few months.

What the hell was she doing here? Surely she would have the sense to stay away after everything that had happened.

"Put your foot down—follow her!" Andreis was pointing and waving his arms.

The woman turned and looked back, and in spite of the distance, Dino could see the panic in her eyes. It was definitely her.

"She's heading for the bus stop—get after her!" Andreis shouted.

CHAPTER 67

Anna-Maria took a walk around the shelter to see if Mina had returned. Her room was still empty, and the stroller was gone. She'd been out for almost two hours; she ought to be back by now.

Anna-Maria stuck her head around the kitchen door and said hi to Sanna and Lori, who were sitting at the table. Lori was thirteen, and Sanna's only child. Her long, shiny red hair was tied up in a ponytail. Her features were well defined, but her cheeks were pale, her eyes sunken. Her nails were so badly bitten that they were barely visible.

Sanna reached across and patted her daughter's arm. It sounded as if she was trying to persuade the girl to eat something; Lori was as skinny as a rake, bordering on anorexic.

Anna-Maria left them in peace.

Sanna had left her husband after years of physical and mental abuse. When he attacked her in front of their daughter for the first time, something snapped inside Sanna, and she took Lori and fled. They'd been at the shelter for a few weeks, deeply upset about everything they'd had to leave behind. Sanna was depressed, while Lori missed her friends and wept over the boyfriend she wasn't allowed to see.

The violence of men against women.

Anna-Maria sighed and went back to her office. She tried Mina's cell phone again, but just as before it went straight to voice mail.

Something was wrong, she could feel it.

Should she call Leila Kacim? The police officer had left her card, told Anna-Maria to get in touch at any time. Maybe she should contact Herman Wibom as well?

Then again, what would she say? That Mina had gone for a walk, and hadn't returned after two hours? They'd think she was overreacting. Mina would be back soon. There was no point in worrying about nothing.

CHAPTER 68

Dino put his foot down and shot past the terra-cotta-colored house. He approached the junction, ignoring the stop sign, and was about to turn left when a red Golf appeared, coming from that direction.

It was also driving too fast.

The two vehicles were so close that he could see the other driver's wide-open eyes and mouth. He slammed his foot on the brake; the seat belt cut into him, and he was flung forward as the car came to a halt.

"What the fuck are you doing?" Andreis yelled.

Dino was waiting for the sound of screeching metal, but the Golf whizzed past with only inches to spare. The woman at the wheel sounded her horn angrily, and Dino gave her the finger.

"There she is—move!"

Mina had almost reached the bus stop, and the bus was pulling in. The doors opened, and Mina almost threw herself on board with the stroller.

Andreis had opened the window and was leaning out. "Stop! Mina, wait! I need to talk to you!"

Dino drew up behind the bus. Andreis opened the door and leaped out while the car was still moving. Mina was shouting hysterically at the bus driver.

"Mina, wait!" Andreis roared again. "Get off!"

The doors were closing as he grabbed hold of the black rubber edging and tried to force them open. He did his best for one endless second, but had to let go. The doors slid shut right in front of him. He started hammering on them with his fists.

"Let me in or I'll fucking kill you!"

Mina looked absolutely terrified.

Dino got there just as Andreis produced the heavy Glock from his inside pocket and pointed it at Mina.

The bus began to move.

Dino could see from Andreis's eyes that he'd lost control. He had to do something, and fast.

"Calm down, for fuck's sake!" he shouted. "You can't force her off the bus with a gun in your hand."

"I can't let her get away again!"

"You'll be put away for life if you shoot her in front of a bus full of passengers."

Andreis's face was bright red; a vein bulged at his temple. Dino had never seen him so angry. He took hold of Andreis's shoulders.

"There are witnesses on board—they've already seen too much. The driver will have called the police. We have to get out of here—right now."

Andreis was still breathing fast, with his mouth open.

"Come on." Dino half pushed, half dragged Andreis toward the Mercedes, listening for the sound of sirens. He opened the passenger door and managed to push Andreis into the seat, then he ran around to the other side, jumped in, and started the car.

The tires screeched as he drove away.

Andreis seemed to be in shock. He couldn't believe that Mina had actually defied him. That she'd dared to go home, against all odds.

"I'm going to kill her for this," he said quietly. "As soon as I find her, I'm going to kill her."

CHAPTER 69

Nora heard Leila's rapid footsteps approaching along the corridor.

"Has something happened?" she asked when her colleague appeared.

"It's Mina."

Nora's stomach flipped. Had her mother died? Or had Kovač managed to track Mina down? She had no illusions about what he was capable of. "Go on."

"She left Freya's Haven this morning and went back to her house, but her husband saw her."

"Is she still alive?" Nora exclaimed.

Leila raised her hand. "She's fine. She managed to get away at the last minute, and she isn't hurt. Not physically, anyway."

"Where is she?"

"On a bus, hysterical and terrified. Kovač came after her, but she just made it on board and the bus driver took off. She called me two minutes ago, crying so hard that I could barely make out what she was saying."

"She's still on the bus? What if he comes after her in his car?"

"I don't think he'll dare—too many witnesses. I've sent a patrol car to pick her up, then I'll go back to Freya's Haven with her, make sure she stays there."

Nora tried to digest the information. "Where's Lukas?" she said. "Tell me he's at the shelter, safe and sound."

"He's with her." Leila's face hardened. "I don't know what she was thinking. How could she take such a risk?" She checked her watch. "I have to go."

Nora got to her feet. She couldn't sit at her desk reading legal cases about tax fraud. "I'll come with you," she said, pulling on her coat.

CHAPTER 70

Leila was driving an unmarked police car, a Volvo V70 she often used when she didn't want to attract attention.

Mina and Lukas had been taken off the bus by the officers in the patrol car without further incident. They were safe, although Mina was very upset, according to the report.

Nora was able to breathe a little more easily.

"Where are we meeting them?" she asked when they reached the freeway heading toward Gustavsberg. "In Stavsnäs?"

Leila shook her head. "That would be too obvious. They're taking her to Mölnvik. I told them to wait behind the helicopter hangar; it's quiet there."

Nora ran a hand over her hair. It felt oddly stiff. She hadn't had time to wash it this morning, but had used a new dry shampoo that made it resemble old hay. At least it didn't look greasy. "Have you spoken to anyone at the shelter? Do they know what's happened to Mina?"

Leila slowed down as two lanes merged into one. "I haven't got around to it, I'm afraid."

"I'll do it."

Anna-Maria answered right away, and Nora explained the situation.

"I knew it! I had a feeling something was wrong when she didn't come back," Anna-Maria exclaimed.

Nora switched to speakerphone so that Leila could hear. "We should be with you in about forty-five minutes. Could someone pick us up from the jetty? I'm not sure if Mina will be in any shape to walk, even though it's not far."

"No problem."

Leila reached the roundabout, skirted a McDonald's, and continued toward the helicopter base. The façade, with its huge panes of glass, looked dirty and gloomy in the sunshine.

There was a police car by the wall, with a uniformed officer waiting by the driver's door. Leila parked beside him, got out, and showed her ID. Mina was sitting in the back with her son in her arms.

Leila opened the door and Lukas's screams filled the air. Nora could have wept, too, when she saw Mina's shocked face. Instead she went over and collected Mina's things from the other officer. Leila helped Mina out of the car.

"How are you doing?" she asked.

"He tried to shoot me," Mina whispered. "He had a gun." She staggered, and Leila put her arm around her, providing much-needed support.

"OK, let's get you back to Freya's Haven," she said.

Chapter 71

Ulrika was at her desk when the door to her office flew open. Andreis Kovač was standing there, shoulders hunched, his normally slicked back hair standing on end. He was clutching his cell phone.

Behind him Ulrika could just see the receptionist, looking distressed. "I asked him to wait while I called you, but he wouldn't listen," she said.

Ulrika got to her feet and smiled. "It's fine." She pointed to the visitor's chair and turned to Kovač. "Please take a seat."

For a moment she thought he was going to kick the armchair, but then he sat down. Ulrika returned to her place behind the desk and consulted her schedule. "Did we have a meeting today?"

Kovač was breathing hard.

"Have I missed something?" Ulrika continued. Why was he so worked up? He looked as if he were about to kill someone.

"I want to get a hold of my wife!"

Ulrika tried to gather her thoughts. She'd already explained the situation to him, several times. She'd given Wibom until tomorrow to respond, and there wasn't much they could do before then. "I'm afraid that will be rather difficult to organize at the moment, but as I said this morning, I expect both Mina and Lukas to be home soon."

"I need to see Mina. Make it happen—you're my fucking lawyer!"

Ulrika clicked her pen, fighting to remain calm. "That's not possible."

"She was at the house today, but she took off. Fucking whore! She had Lukas with her!"

This was followed by such a tirade of swearing that Ulrika seriously considered asking him to leave.

"She came to the house behind my back! She was in *my* house with *my* son! Do you understand?"

He was almost spitting. The conversation was spiraling out of control. Ulrika took a deep breath. "To be honest, there are other things you need to focus on right now," she said. "We've decided on a strategy. Have patience."

Kovač leaned across the desk and grabbed Ulrika's left arm, his fingers digging into her flesh. "I have a right to speak to my own wife, for fuck's sake! Don't tell me to be patient, or I'll—"

"Let go of me!"

He immediately released his grip. Ulrika glared at him as she rubbed her wrist. Red marks were clearly visible on her skin.

"If you do that again, you can find yourself another lawyer. Is that clear?"

At least Kovač had the sense to look ashamed of himself. Ulrika poured herself a glass of water and took a few sips, keeping her hand steady to show that she was unmoved by what had just happened, in spite of the fact that her heart was racing.

She had to keep her composure.

"OK, let's move on," she said, reaching into the drawer for his file. "There are other things we can discuss today. The leak within your organization, for example."

Kovač was already on his feet. "I'll take care of it." He walked out before she could say another word. Ulrika sat there with the file in her hand. She'd had many ruthless clients charged with serious crimes over the years, but Andreis Kovač made her feel more than uncomfortable.

Her arm was still painful.

She was starting to wonder whether she ought to withdraw from the case. The Swedish Bar Association wouldn't like it, but . . .

A court order would be required for her to be relieved, because she was Kovač's designated public defender. Better to grit her teeth and go through with the trial. It would be easier to step away before the case went to appeal.

She put down the file and rubbed her arm again. She really needed to give this some thought.

CHAPTER 72

Nora could see Anna-Maria through the window as the ferry slowed down. The crossing took only five minutes, but they'd chosen to sit on a sofa in a quiet corner. Leila had managed to get Mina to take a few sips from a can of Coke, but the girl was still dangerously pale, except for the half-healed sore above her left eyebrow glowing an angry red.

"Have a little more," Leila cajoled her.

Mina drank a mouthful.

"Next stop Styrsvik," the captain's voice boomed from the loudspeaker.

"This is us," Nora said, gently touching Mina's arm. Mina stood up and held on to the handle of the stroller. Lukas had fallen asleep from sheer exhaustion.

Mina hadn't said much during the drive to Stavsnäs. She should really have gone to the hospital to be checked over, but after a brief conversation with Anna-Maria, Leila had decided it would be better for mother and son to return to the safety of the shelter. They had trained staff who could take care of her. She was badly shaken; it didn't take medical expertise to realize that she was at the breaking point.

Anna-Maria had ordered a taxi. Ten minutes later they pulled up in front of the old wooden building, where Siri was waiting anxiously in the doorway.

The idyllic setting should have been reassuring, but for Nora the contrast was too stark, given what Mina had been through. The beauty of the archipelago merely served to highlight the ugly reality.

"Mina has a visitor," Anna-Maria said when they got out of the car. "Herman Wibom is here. He arrived about an hour ago."

She placed a gentle hand on Mina's shoulder.

"Do you feel up to talking to him? I know it's been a difficult day, but it sounded important—otherwise he wouldn't have come all the way out here. He said it wouldn't take long."

Mina's eyes widened. "What's wrong? Is it Mom? Has she gotten worse?"

Anna-Maria bent down and picked up a cigarette butt. She carefully wrapped it in a tissue and put it in her pocket. "I think it's best if you talk to him. He didn't tell me what it was about."

Mina turned to Leila and Nora. "Will you come with me?"

"Of course." Nora suspected she knew why Wibom was here. Ulrika Grönstedt's threat of a custody battle was bad news for Mina. There was a risk that she might break down completely when she heard what Grönstedt had cooked up. If she did, it would give Grönstedt even more ammunition, and Nora knew she wouldn't hesitate to use it.

Mina had to stay calm and show that she was more than capable of looking after her child; otherwise social services would step in with a temporary care order.

Or give him to his father.

As long as Kovač hadn't been convicted of anything, he was still eligible to be granted custody of Lukas. The rule stating that a child had the right to both parents was open to absurd interpretations in the Swedish courts. Even fathers who were palpably unsuitable, including some who were actually in jail, had been given custody when the mothers were out of the picture.

Anna-Maria picked up Lukas and adjusted his pale-blue hat. He blinked in the sunlight, only half awake. He opened and closed his mouth like a little fish; he was obviously hungry. He'd start screaming again at any minute.

"I'll go and find this little man something to eat," Anna-Maria said. "Don't you worry about him."

CHAPTER 73

Herman Wibom was already waiting in the common room. As soon as they'd all sat down, he leaned toward Mina. "Your husband, or rather his lawyer, Ulrika Grönstedt, has been in touch with regard to Lukas." He paused, as if he wasn't quite sure how to continue. "He claims you've taken his son without his permission."

Mina stared at him. "What?"

"I spoke to his lawyer yesterday, and she's demanding that you return Lukas within three days, or they'll file a police report."

"Return Lukas to Andreis?" Mina groped for the arm of the chair. "He's not having my son," she whispered.

Nora couldn't keep quiet. "I've already spoken to Herman about this. It's just a clumsy trick on the part of your husband. He wants to scare you into keeping quiet, and he's trying to force you to go back home. This is about preventing you from testifying against him, nothing else."

"I can't go home. He'll kill me. I realized that today."

Her voice was dull, almost as if she were commenting on the weather forecast. And yet this was the father of her son, a man she must once have loved deeply.

Maybe she still loved him.

"If your husband and his lawyer go ahead and file a report to the police, I'll fight it every step of the way," Wibom assured her. "There's something called 'mitigating circumstances,' a kind of excuse for the alleged crime. That will be my argument in your case."

Mina blinked.

"The way things stand, I can't imagine the police stepping in to forcibly remove Lukas from you and return him to your husband," Wibom added.

"Forcibly remove . . . ?" Any remaining scrap of color had drained from Mina's face. Leila squeezed her hand, but Mina didn't react.

"If the court should decide, against all odds, that the father has grounds for his allegation, then social services would be brought in."

Nora wanted to tell Wibom to build up his client's self-confidence instead of frightening her to death. She desperately needed support and encouragement. It was his job to help her stand up to Kovač. He ought to be making it clear that he was on her side, that he would guide her all the way through the legal proceedings, be a fixed point in the chaos. Instead he was doing exactly the opposite. His timing to deliver Grönstedt's ultimatum could not be worse.

Nora had to intervene. "That's all hypothetical—pure scare tactics on their part. You have nothing to worry about."

"Defense lawyers come up with all kinds of crap," Leila said, ignoring the fact that Wibom was also a lawyer. "Believe me, I've heard it all."

It didn't help; Mina shrank before their eyes.

"I would strongly recommend that you don't give in to this kind of pressure," Nora said firmly. "I'll fight for you every step of the way."

"As long as you stay at Freya's Haven, he can't get to you," Leila assured Mina. "You or Lukas. You're safe here—you can rely on us."

"Herman will help you, too," Nora added, as Wibom still hadn't responded.

Mina wrapped her arms around her body. "I thought the worst that could happen was Andreis finding our hiding place." She began to rock back and forth on the sofa.

Enough, Nora thought.

"I think we should call it a day," she said to Wibom, even though he was Mina's counsel. "Mina needs to rest; she's been through a great deal."

She got to her feet, and Mina did the same.

"I'll call you tomorrow when you've had the chance to sleep on it," Wibom said. "We don't need to give them an answer just yet."

Nora could have wrung his neck.

Bosnia, April 1993

Andreis was in the bathroom brushing his teeth when his father came home. He'd been out since breakfast time, and they'd had dinner without him, as they often did nowadays.

Andreis ran out to say good-night.

His father was trying to hang his jacket on a hook, but he missed and it fell on the floor. His eyes were bloodshot, and he wobbled on his bad leg. He lurched at Andreis and hugged him much too tightly. His breath smelled of booze; Andreis didn't like it.

His mother emerged from the kitchen. She stopped dead in the doorway and folded her arms. Her lips narrowed to a thin line. Andreis knew she was furious.

"We've got hardly any money—how can you spend it on drink?"

Dad waved a dismissive hand. "Not now."

"I'm doing everything I can to make sure your children have some food in their bellies, and you do nothing to help!"

"Shut up, woman!"

"This has to stop—I can't do this anymore!"

"Shut your mouth!" Dad staggered into the living room and sank down on the sofa in front of the TV, but Mom followed him.

"Please, Zlatko." She didn't sound angry now, just desperate. "We're all going to die if we stay here. Blanka was here today. Things are getting worse and worse, the shells rain down almost every night now. The Serbs are advancing—the Croats, too."

Dad switched on the television and turned the volume up so high that the sound filled the room. Mom went and stood in front of the screen so that he couldn't see.

"This can't go on," she sobbed.

"Move."

"We have to leave!"

"I'm warning you."

"We're going to die if we don't leave!"

Dad got up from the sofa, his face dark with anger. Andreis curled up in a corner and closed his eyes so that he wouldn't have to see. When he opened them again, Dad was leaning over Mom, who was lying on the floor, staring up at him with something close to hatred. One cheek was dark red, the mark of Dad's palm standing out against her pale skin.

"Not another word!" Dad yelled. "I'm doing the best I can!" He grabbed his jacket and stormed out, slamming the door behind him.

Mom started sobbing. Andreis ran over and tried to comfort her as best he could.

"Don't cry," he whispered. "He's drunk, he didn't mean it."

"We're all going to die because of your father."

CHAPTER 74

When Nora got home, dinner was almost ready. Jonas had cooked Julia's favorite—spaghetti Bolognese.

Nora took off her coat and shoes and went into the kitchen. The previous year they'd knocked down the living room wall, creating an open-plan apartment. She loved the feeling of space, but could do without the smell of food spreading everywhere.

Jonas was standing at the island. "Hi, sweetheart—how was your day?"

Nora perched on a high stool opposite him. "Do we have any red wine?"

Jonas reached for a bottle of Californian Pinot Noir they both enjoyed. "You look like you need this."

Nora rested her chin on both hands. "To be honest, I've had a horrible day."

Jonas poured her a drink while she told him about Mina and the unplanned trip to Runmarö. He handed her the glass and was rewarded with a kiss on the cheek. She really wanted to feel his arms around her.

"What the hell is wrong with Andreis Kovač?" she said, taking a deep swig of her wine. It tasted soft and fruity, and her tense muscles began to relax as the alcohol spread through her body.

Julia came running in and gave her mother a quick hug before settling down in front of the TV. There were only the three of them for dinner; Simon was with Henrik this week, and, as usual, it wasn't entirely clear where Adam was. Presumably with his girlfriend, Freya. They'd been together for two years, with a short break in the middle, and they'd both graduated from high school. Freya's parents lived in a house with a separate apartment on the ground floor, where the teenagers spent most of their time.

Her little boy had grown up.

"I wish I'd never taken this case," Nora said, sipping her drink. "I can't maintain a professional distance as I should."

"I'm sure you're doing wonderfully."

Jonas couldn't possibly know, but it was nice to hear him say it anyway. "Over twelve thousand women are abused by their husbands or partners every year," Nora said. "Seriously enough to have to go to the hospital."

The figure was shocking, and in all probability, the real tally was much higher. There were far too many who had "just" been given a slap or two and didn't report it.

Jonas tasted the sauce with a wooden spoon, then put the messy spoon down on the counter. Nora decided not to say anything, even though she knew who'd be cleaning up after dinner.

"Between thirty and forty women a year are killed by their husbands or partners," she went on. "That's a third of all murders committed in Sweden."

"In that case I'm grateful that you're brave enough to come home," Jonas said. He was trying to be funny, but Nora found it difficult to respond. If he'd seen Mina's face, he would never have expressed himself so clumsily. She didn't have the energy to embark on that particular discussion. Instead she took another sip of wine and wondered how Thomas was. He'd seemed so down the last time she saw him. Exactly the way she was feeling right now, in fact.

When did life get so depressing?

Chapter 75

There was a sound from the door. Mina raised herself up on one elbow and turned her head. The handle was slowly being pushed down. The room was in darkness, apart from the glow of a night-light. It was almost midnight, and the house was silent. Everyone had gone to bed long ago.

Someone was trying to get into her room.

Before she had time to react, the door opened to reveal Andreis standing there. He was wearing his black leather jacket and holding a gun in his hand.

He'd found her.

It was impossible. The police had promised she'd be safe at the shelter, and yet here he was.

They'd lied to her.

Andreis took a step forward and closed the door behind him. Mina couldn't move, couldn't even shout for help, even though she knew why he'd come looking for her.

He was going to kill her.

She managed to shuffle backward on the bed and pressed her spine to the wall, but the distance between them increased by only a few inches. There was nothing she could do to get away from him.

She stared at the barrel of the gun pointing straight at her face, saw the finger squeezing the trigger.

"You knew I'd track you down before long." Andreis parted his lips, exposing his teeth in a smile that reminded Mina of a predator.

The walls of the room bellied out.

"Did you really think you could escape?" he whispered. "You ought to know me better than that." The childhood scar beneath his lip glowed white in the darkness.

Lukas woke up, but Mina didn't dare glance in his direction. He started to whimper, but there was no way she could pick him up. If Lukas was in her arms when Andreis fired, the bullet might hit him, too.

Her son must live, even if she died.

"Please, Andreis. Think of Lukas . . ."

Andreis didn't react in any way.

"Think of your son . . . ," she pleaded.

Lukas began to cry, and Mina held up both hands, palms outward, in a silent prayer.

"You knew this would happen," Andreis said.

He was enjoying her terror, her suffering. She had loved him once, but now it was impossible to understand how.

"You have only yourself to blame."

Those were the last words she registered. Mina closed her eyes and heard herself screaming until she woke up.

CHAPTER 76

Dino was sitting at the table in his apartment with a half-full glass of vodka in front of him. He'd opened a bottle of Smirnoff as soon as he arrived home, and had slowly and methodically begun to drink himself into a stupor.

The level in the bottle had fallen as his intoxication increased, but he didn't feel any better. His nerves were in shreds.

By this time the sun had long ago disappeared over the waters of Lake Magelungen. The last rays had colored the sky pink. The apartment was in darkness; he hadn't even bothered to switch on a light.

The only source of illumination was the red glow of his cigarette. The ashtray, which was actually an old saucer, was piled high with stubs. The air was thick with smoke, and his throat hurt. Tomorrow he'd feel like crap, but that didn't matter.

For the first time he seriously wondered whether Andreis was losing control. Whether he'd actually crossed a line.

If that was the case, what would happen?

Dino had been deeply shocked when Andreis pulled a gun in front of a bus full of passengers. Andreis had always been hot tempered, but the rage he'd displayed today had been verging on suicidal. If he'd gotten hold of Mina and shot her, with all those witnesses looking on, he'd have been jailed for life. Not even his fancy lawyer would have been able to keep him out of Kumla.

Dino had never imagined that Andreis would be prepared to take such a risk just to punish his woman. He couldn't grasp the fact that Andreis hated her so much. She was the mother of his child; they'd built a life together. He remembered how happy and proud Andreis had been when Lukas was born.

It didn't make sense.

However hard Dino searched for an explanation, there were no mitigating circumstances. Andreis hadn't been under the influence of either booze or drugs; he'd known exactly what he was doing.

They'd grown up together, but Dino felt as if he no longer knew his childhood friend.

As the bus drove off, Andreis had looked at Dino with hatred in his eyes, as if Dino were to blame for the fact that Mina had managed to get away yet again. He'd decided to forget the meeting in Södertälje, and had told Dino to drive him straight to Ulrika Grönstedt's office in the city center instead.

After he'd seen her, he was even more furious.

He'd ordered Dino to take him home. On the way he'd called Emir and told him to come over with something to drink. He hadn't asked Dino to stay, thank God. Dino just wanted to get out of there before Andreis decided to take his anger out on him.

He emptied his glass and refilled it. The condensation on the chilled bottle had long since disappeared, and the vodka had almost reached room temperature, but he couldn't be bothered to go and fetch ice.

The doorbell rang.

Dino looked up. It was late; he wasn't expecting anyone.

The bell rang again, more insistently now.

He pushed the glass away and slowly got to his feet. He was more drunk than he'd realized, and had to lean on the kitchen counter for support. His feet dragged as he headed for the door.

The bell rang again, and this time the visitor kept his finger on the button.

"I'm coming!"

If it was one of those kids from the other apartments, he would soon find out what Dino thought of little fuckers who disturbed their neighbors in the evenings.

He breathed through his nose and tried to peer through the peephole, but it was hard to focus. The walls were moving; everything was kind of blurred. He blinked over and over again, but it didn't help.

"Open up!" someone shouted.

The familiar voice penetrated the boozy fog. What the hell was he doing here?

Dino fumbled with the security chain, but his fingers felt fat and clumsy and refused to obey. Eventually he managed to unhook the catch. The door opened, revealing what Dino had been unable to see through the peephole.

Three against one.

"You're coming with us," Emir informed him.

CHAPTER 77

Anna-Maria came into the room.

Mina blinked, utterly confused. Her cheeks were wet with tears. She'd been so sure that Andreis had shot her.

Anna-Maria came and sat on the bed. She stroked Mina's damp hair, which was plastered to her scalp with sweat. "You had a bad dream. I heard you screaming."

"It was Andreis . . . he found me . . . he . . ."

Mina looked around. She was lying on top of the covers, and she was fully dressed.

Lukas wasn't crying.

Anna-Maria shook her head. "This hasn't been an easy day for you. It's hardly surprising that you've had a nightmare." She drew Mina close and stroked her back with long, soothing movements. "How are you feeling now?"

Mina began to cry. "I don't know what to do."

"It's OK, honey, you're exhausted. I'm going to give you a sleeping tablet. I'll stay overnight and watch Lukas. I've missed the last boat anyway."

"I'm too scared to go home, and I'm too scared to stay," Mina whispered. "I'm too scared to sleep."

"You'll never get away if you go back to him now," Anna-Maria said firmly. "I've seen so many women in your situation. These men never change, because they don't know how. Eventually they go too far. Almost always."

Mina couldn't stop crying. Anna-Maria carried on stroking her back as if she were comforting a small child. "Why does he treat me this way?" Mina sobbed.

Anna-Maria sighed. "There are no excuses. Presumably he has so many demons eating him up from the inside that he couldn't even explain it himself."

"I'd never do that to someone I loved."

"It's not about you—it never is. It's hard to accept, but it's important to understand that."

Anna-Maria got up and fetched some wet wipes from Lukas's changing table. Mina wiped her face; it was nice to feel the coolness against her skin. Her eyes were swollen from weeping. Anna-Maria lingered by the crib and adjusted the baby's blanket before sitting down again.

"These men kill the very people from whom they should be accepting help and support," she said. "The only way they can handle their emotions and their frustration is to take it out on those closest to them."

"I should be able to help him."

"No!" The sharp reply was instant. "You can't help him. He needs years of therapy, plus he has to want to change. He has to be receptive to the professional support that's offered, otherwise it's pointless."

"What am I going to do?"

Anna-Maria's tone softened. "Don't give him the opportunity to kill you. That's all you can do in this situation." She looked away. "My daughter was with a man like yours. She was pregnant with their first child . . ." Her voice died away. She gathered up the used wet wipes and threw them in the trash can.

"He's trying to take Lukas away from me."

"It's not that easy." Anna-Maria gave her a comforting pat on the cheek. "The prosecutor and Herman Wibom have every intention of fighting for you—put your trust in them. Back in my day, legal counsel wasn't automatically appointed, but you have someone who's totally on your side."

Mina nodded shakily. She tried to remember the feeling of strength she'd had when she left the house on Trastvägen, just before Andreis spotted her. "Do you really think I can do it? Testify against Andreis?"

Anna-Maria took Mina's face between her two hands. "You *have* to testify against him. It's your only chance. If you can help put him in jail, then you have to do it. There's no other way of escaping from that bastard."

CHAPTER 78

Dino was sitting in the back seat of the silver-gray Mercedes he usually drove. The streets were dark and empty as the car pulled into the deserted parking lot. He did his best to focus, even though he was drunk.

"Where are we going?" he asked.

The gorillas on either side of him didn't react. He'd met Jovan and Nermin many times in Andreis's company when things were a little tense and Andreis needed extra protection. Nermin was also related to Andreis.

Right now they were acting as if they'd never seen Dino before.

He really needed to pee.

Emir was driving. He stopped the car and switched off the engine. "OK."

Dino tried to orient himself. They'd traveled for no more than twenty-five minutes. They must be outside Stockholm, but he couldn't figure out where. They were surrounded by trees; no sign of any houses. They'd left the freeway and taken minor roads for the last few miles.

"Are we meeting Andreis?" he asked Emir, making an effort to sound as if everything were perfectly normal.

"Shut the fuck up."

Jovan pushed Dino out of the car and gripped his arm firmly. They set off toward a dilapidated building. Dino recognized it now; it was the disused factory in Lännersta. Andreis had used it in the past when dealing with people who were causing him problems.

He forced down a sudden surge of bile. Gravel and garbage crunched beneath his feet with every step. He attempted to turn his head to see where the others had gone, but Jovan dragged him over to a metal door, then pushed down the handle and nudged it open with his elbow. He shoved Dino so hard that he stumbled and fell to his knees on the concrete floor.

Dino looked around, but the room was pitch black. He registered the sound of dripping water just before the ceiling light came on, blinding him. He blinked several times, then saw Andreis leaning against the wall with his arms folded.

Andreis studied Dino without saying a word.

All trace of intoxication disappeared. Dino got to his feet, every nerve on full alert. His mouth was so dry that his tongue was sticking to his palate. "Andreis! How's it going?" His voice shot up into a falsetto in spite of his efforts to sound normal. "Why did you want to meet here?"

"Sit down."

Andreis pointed to a wooden chair in the middle of the floor. Dino knew exactly what was going to happen; he'd been in similar situations with others who feared for their lives.

His heartbeat was pounding in his ears, and he felt dizzy.

Andreis knew everything. He'd found out the truth, and now he was going to punish him.

"What's this about, Andreis? I don't know what you think I've done, but whatever it is, you're mistaken."

"Sit down."

Andreis's tone was ice cold. Dino knew better than to argue. He moved toward the chair, although every instinct was telling him not to. He had no choice; he was caught like a rat in a trap. Jovan was between him and the door, and Nermin was on guard outside. Emir couldn't be far away.

Dino perched on the very edge of the chair.

"Look at me," Andreis said.

Dino obeyed, suddenly aware of footsteps approaching from behind. Someone grabbed his hands and secured them with cable ties. Dino let it happen; he knew how this worked. The more you struggled, the more the ties cut into the flesh.

He'd used them himself on other people.

Andreis's face was expressionless.

Another sound behind his back made Dino break out in a sweat, but he had no way of defending himself. Something cold was slipped over his head and pushed down until it reached his neck. A wire garrote, pulled just tight enough to press on his Adam's apple.

The gag reflex kicked in immediately.

"For fuck's sake, Andreis!"

He could hardly get the words out. They came one by one, hoarse and desperate.

"I haven't done anything," he rasped. "I'd never betray you, you know that. You know me."

Andreis came closer until his face was only inches away from Dino's. His eyes were bloodshot, the pupils enormous. Dino could see the same madness staring at him as earlier in the day when he'd tried to stop Andreis from shooting through the doors of the bus—but now Andreis was also drunk and high. "Are you the one who talked, you little shit?"

Dino searched for an answer that would appease his boss. "What's this about?" he managed to say, even though every syllable was agony. "I've always been loyal to you."

The man holding the garrote hadn't said a word, but the aftershave was all too familiar. Emir.

Andreis wasn't in the mood for a discussion. The garrote was tightened until it became hard to breathe. Dino felt an intense urge to swallow, but resisted for fear that the pressure would increase still more. His field of vision was filled with little black dots; there was a rushing noise in his ears, and his temples were throbbing.

Andreis brought his face closer. "You talked to the cops—admit it."

The pressure eased a fraction; it was possible to breathe. Dino filled his lungs with air. "It's all a misunderstanding," he gasped. "I swear on my mother's grave, I've always got your back." His head exploded with pain as Andreis struck him hard with the gun. Warm, sticky blood trickled down from his eyebrow. Through a dark-red curtain he whispered: "Please."

"Admit it was you."

He hadn't called for Mina's sake; he'd done it to save Andreis from himself, but Dino knew he would never be able to make Andreis understand. "I swear. For fuck's sake, Andreis. We grew up together. You're my brother."

If he could just make eye contact with Andreis, make him see that the whole thing was a terrible misunderstanding. They'd been friends for over twenty years—it couldn't end like this.

I don't want to die.

"How could you betray me?" Andreis was almost in tears. "We were brothers, you and I, yet you sold me down the river." He kicked out at a broken pipe on the floor; it crashed into the wall. "You let me down! You let me down, you bastard, just like everyone else! I can't trust anyone!"

Dino pressed his back against the chair in a futile attempt to get farther away from the man who seemed to have decided that Dino had to die.

Andreis raised his hand again and smashed the gun into Dino's jaw. The blow was so powerful that Dino felt as if his head might actually come off. He bit his tongue, and his mouth filled with blood and fragments of tooth. He spat and swallowed at the same time, convinced that he was about to choke on his own blood. He could taste nothing but iron.

"Why are you making me do this?" Andreis yelled. "I trusted you!"

"I did it for your sake," Dino managed to snivel, blood pouring from his eyebrow and chin.

"What did you say?"

"If you'd killed her . . . ," Dino sobbed.

The words were hard to make out; they were more of a pathetic grunt emerging through a sodden mess of blood and mucus.

"That's it, he's confessed!" Emir rejoiced. "I knew he was the leak, I told you from the start."

The pressure from the garrote disappeared, and instead Dino felt the barrel of the gun against his temple.

A warm stream of urine soaked his pants and ran onto the floor.

"Look at that!" Emir yelled, somewhere above his head. "He's fucking pissed himself!"

Andreis's contorted face came even closer.

Then everything went black.

Wednesday

Chapter 79

When Mina woke up, her body felt heavy. For the first time in weeks, she'd slept deeply, without nightmares. The sheets weren't crumpled and sweaty as they usually were, but she still felt exhausted and disorientated, as if she were surrounded by a thick fog.

She glanced over at the crib. It was empty.

Lukas!

Her heart missed a beat, then she remembered Anna-Maria's promise to watch him during the night. She'd taken him away so that he wouldn't wake Mina. He was absolutely fine. She didn't need to worry about him. She was still safe at Freya's Haven, and Andreis was far away. He didn't know where she was, and he would never find out.

Anna-Maria's words came back to her. She wanted Mina to fight; otherwise Andreis would kill her. Mina had to stand up for herself.

She rolled onto her side and closed her eyes. How was she going to find the courage to do that? Maybe she could talk to Herman Wibom, tell him about the secret email account? The pictures she'd hidden away online?

The very thought gave her palpitations.

Andreis would be furious if he found out. He'd never stop trying to hunt her down. She wouldn't be able to hide from him, because he wouldn't give up. She knew him well enough to realize that.

But she had to break free. Anna-Maria was right.

Mina reached for her phone and logged in to the email account she'd registered eighteen months ago. She'd used it to send pictures to herself—she didn't dare save them on her cell in case Andreis found them. She entered her password with trembling fingers. It was all there.

Images of the cuts and bruises Andreis had inflicted on her, photos of her medical notes when she'd been forced to seek treatment for her injuries . . . the doctors and nurses had logged everything.

She might have lied about what had happened in order to protect Andreis from the police, but the official record was there. She'd documented as much as she dared on her phone on a regular basis, and it was all accessible online.

She closed down her account. If Anna-Maria was right, there was only one way to escape from Andreis. She got up and pulled on her robe—time to fetch Lukas. She hesitated for a moment.

If she didn't cooperate with the police, there was a strong probability that Andreis would walk free, as Leila had said. Then she would never know peace.

But she was so frightened of him.

There was no one to ask for advice; her mother was in a coma, and she didn't want to bother her father. She sank down on the bed again. What should she do with the pictures? Could she show them to someone?

Was she brave enough to do that?

CHAPTER 80

Aram stuck his head around the door of Thomas's office.

"Margit wants to talk to us."

Thomas looked up. "Now?"

"Now."

Thomas followed Aram to Margit's office at the end of the corridor. She was on the phone, but beckoned them in and pointed to the visitor's chairs.

The only photograph on her desk showed her grown-up daughters smiling at the camera with blond hair, tanned and relaxed—the polar opposite of Margit's troubled expression. Bertil, her quiet husband of thirty years, wasn't in the picture.

"I'll send a team over right away," Margit said, ending the call. She put down the phone and leaned back, clasping her hands behind her neck. Thomas realized this was something serious. When Margit frowned like that, it was never good news. "A jogger has found a dead body in the Nacka Nature Reserve," she said. "Buried."

"What happened?" Aram asked.

"The jogger had his dog with him. It started scratching at the ground and barking, so he went to see what was wrong."

"Do we know anything about the cause of death?" Thomas said.

"Shot at close range. The victim's face looks like ground beef."

"Any sign of a murder weapon?" Aram wanted to know.

Margit smiled wearily. "Is it ever that easy? The body and the murder weapon served up together?"

Aram shrugged and touched the small gold cross he always wore on a chain around his neck. "Sometimes God is good."

"Not this time."

Thomas got to his feet. "Is Staffan on his way?"

Staffan Nilsson, the most experienced forensic technician on the team, had been persuaded to stay on for a while longer, even though he should have retired several years earlier. If Margit wasn't formally appointed as head of department soon, Thomas knew that Staffan would quit.

"The CSIs are on the way, but I don't know who's on duty," Margit said, picking up her phone. "There are so many of them these days—it's hard to keep track."

CHAPTER 81

Nora was on her way up from the subway by the courthouse when her phone rang. She stopped and rooted around in her purse. Why was it always at the bottom? Was it dictated by some law of nature?

It was Anna-Maria from the shelter. "Good morning. I'm sorry to call you so early, but I have something important to tell you."

"No problem—I'm just on my way to work." Nora popped in her white earbuds as she waited her turn to pass through the gate. There was the usual crush, with everyone in a hurry.

"Mina's going to testify against her husband," Anna-Maria said.

"Sorry?" Nora stopped dead, and a woman in a bright-red duffel coat pushed past her, giving Nora a hard shove in the ribs as she did so. Nora gave her an angry scowl, which she ignored.

"She's changed her mind," Anna-Maria went on. "She's decided to do it."

At last.

When Nora left Runmarö the previous day, she hadn't had much hope that Mina would stand up in court. She clearly couldn't cope anymore. Nora had told Jonathan she would file the charges today; there was no point in waiting any longer.

"Are you absolutely certain?" she asked Anna-Maria.

"We had a long talk yesterday, then she had a good sleep while I watched Lukas. We talked again at breakfast. I think she's reached a point where she's realized it's the only way to free herself from her husband." Anna-Maria sounded relieved. "Between you and me, it's the best that could happen. Nothing else will stop that man."

Nora had to agree.

"Of course she'll need protection, or she won't do it," Anna-Maria added. "She has to be able to rely on you."

"Don't worry, we'll look after her." Nora hoped she wasn't promising too much. She would have to speak to Leila; the lack of resources was a constant concern.

She'd reached Hantverkargatan, and turned left toward the Economic Crimes Authority's offices. A red bus pulled up at the stop outside.

"Mina's ready to speak to you today, if that's convenient," Anna-Maria told her. "It might be a good idea to strike while the iron's hot."

Nora tried to remember what her schedule looked like. She had no meetings this morning, as far as she could recall. It felt as if they were shuttling back and forth to Runmarö all the time, but it was worth it if Mina really had changed her mind.

"We'll be there as soon as we can," she said. "Tell Mina she's definitely made the right decision."

CHAPTER 82

When Thomas and Aram reached the clearing in the forest, the area had already been cordoned off with blue-and-white police tape. There was no sign of Staffan Nilsson, but another technician whom Thomas vaguely recognized was on his knees by the body, a look of intense concentration on his face.

A short distance away, a man in his forties was sitting on a tree stump, with a black Labrador at his feet. As soon as the dog saw Thomas and Aram, it got to its feet and started wagging its tail.

Thomas showed his ID and introduced himself to the jogger, who was clearly still in shock.

"We have one or two initial questions," he explained. "If you feel up to answering them now, that would be very helpful. We can take a full statement at the station later."

The man, whose name was Linus Roslund, had no objections. His blue tracksuit pants were damp, with noticeable grass stains. He must have dropped to his knees by the grave when he realized what the dog had found.

Thomas took out his notebook. "Can you remember what time it was when you found the body?"

"Around seven thirty. I usually leave home shortly after seven, and do a circuit of just over three miles."

"Do you often run out here?" Aram asked.

Roslund nodded. "Every other morning—sometimes several days in a row. I live nearby, so this is my home area."

Exactly the answer Thomas had been hoping for. "Did you come here yesterday? Do you always follow the same route?"

Roslund didn't seem to understand the point of the questions. "Yes."

"And do you always bring your dog?"

"Yes. He enjoys a good run."

"But he didn't react yesterday—no scratching or barking?"

"No."

"Are you sure?"

"Absolutely. You should have seen him when . . ."

Roslund broke off, the color draining from his face beneath the stubble. He scratched his cheek, his fingertips and nails still grubby with earth. He must have started digging with his hands before he realized he ought to call the police.

"Labbe went crazy," he said. "I've never seen him behave like that."

He reached out and stroked the dog, who wound himself around his master's legs, overcome with joy.

"I came back to see what he was doing. He usually sticks pretty close to me." Roslund blinked at the significance of what he'd just said. "If the body had been there yesterday, Labbe would have reacted."

Thomas nodded. They might not have a murder weapon, but they did have a time frame.

At least it was a start.

Bosnia, May 1993

It was late afternoon when Blanka turned up on the doorstep. Selma was sitting at the kitchen table, feeding Emir, while Andreis was playing in the garden.

Blanka's voice was far from steady. She came over to Selma and hugged her for a long time. "We're leaving now."

Selma had feared those words. "Please, no!"

She could hear her own despair bouncing off the walls. Blanka was the one who'd kept her going as the world collapsed around them; now she was going to disappear, too. Would they ever see each other again?

Blanka sat down. "There's no future here, Selma, even though we're Catholics. The Serbs are burning and destroying everything. They'll kill us all if they break through the line of defense and come here." She took a packet of cigarettes out of her pocket. "There's no alternative. We're running out of time."

"It will pass."

Blanka shook her head. "You heard about what happened in Ahmići," she said quietly. "They say the Bosnians and Croats burned down the entire village—everyone died. The young men were gathered together and tortured before they were killed. Even the babies were shot."

"Zlatko is a Croat. They won't touch us."

"But you're a Muslim." Blanka's tone was sharp.

"We're not religious," Selma protested. "I don't even know how to pray in Arabic. Think of all the times we've celebrated Catholic festivals with our friends outside the village."

"Things were different then. Under Tito, no one cared about religion or talked about ethnic origins. You know that as well as I do, but now the whole country is on the verge of collapse."

"Andreis's father is a Serb," Selma said quietly. "He has a European name, and he was baptized in a church."

Blanka lit a cigarette and took a deep drag. "That doesn't matter. In the eyes of the world, you and your children are Bosnian Muslims. They won't spare you, even if you show them Andreis's birth certificate."

Selma began to cry, which in turn upset Emir. She stood up and walked around the kitchen, jiggling him up and down in her arms. "We've nowhere to go," she said. "We can't go to Croatia—they've turned against Bosnia and declared war on us." Her voice broke. "We should have left when my sister did her best to persuade us."

Blanka's cigarette smoke rose to the ceiling. "I've heard about a country in northern Europe that's accepting refugees from Bosnia—Sweden."

"Sweden?" Selma wasn't sure where Sweden was. All that came into her mind was snow and darkness and blond hair.

"We're going to try and get there via Hungary," Blanka explained. "They say the route through Croatia is open at the moment. You ought to come with us." She stubbed out her cigarette. "We're leaving tomorrow morning—at first light."

Chapter 83

Staffan Nilsson called out to Thomas just as he and Aram finished questioning Linus Roslund.

Thomas turned to see Nilsson standing by the grave with the other technician, Hasse something or other. Thomas was relieved that Nilsson had been brought in; he trusted his colleague's judgment completely.

Aram followed him over to the shallow grave. Whoever had buried the body didn't seem to have cared whether it was found or not—or maybe they'd been in a hurry.

Officers were searching the forest for tire tracks or anything else that might indicate how the perpetrator or perpetrators had gotten to and from the location. A dog handler was also on the way.

Nilsson slipped something into an evidence bag, sealed it, and placed it in a large leather case on the ground. "So," he said. "Here we are again."

Every homicide had its own story. An investigation must never become pure routine, but this situation was a familiar part of their profession. Thomas could feel the surge of adrenaline that always came hand in hand with the weariness at yet another wasted human life. At the thought that a bullet could pass so easily through a head and extinguish that life.

Nilsson pointed to the corpse, laid out on its back with the legs slightly parted, arms by its sides. The clothes were damp and filthy, strewn with pine needles and withered leaves.

Thomas scrutinized it. A man, probably in his thirties, slightly above average height, broad, muscular shoulders. Dark hair, shiny with some kind of gel. Expensive watch.

"He hasn't been there very long," Nilsson said. "Rigor mortis has only just set in."

"Any ID?" Aram asked.

"Nothing—no wallet, no phone. I'd check the missing-persons database."

"How are we supposed to recognize him?" Aram pointed to the mutilated face covered in congealed blood. It had darkened to the same color as the earth that had settled on the shredded skin. From this angle, there didn't seem to be many of the man's original features left. Thomas moved closer.

The right side of the face was gone; the shot must have been fired at very close range, possibly straight into the eye. The bullet had exited through the back of the head, which mainly consisted of a large wound. It was a horrible sight, even for a hardened cop—no wonder Linus Roslund had looked kind of green.

Death must have been instantaneous.

The chin was also damaged, the skin discolored, as if someone had delivered a powerful blow with an object. A clenched fist wouldn't have caused that level of injury.

The right eye, the right side of the chin. That could mean that the perpetrator was left-handed, if the same person had beaten and then shot the victim. Or he was right-handed and he'd been standing on the other side . . .

There was something familiar about the face, the little that remained, but Thomas couldn't quite put his finger on it.

"He was killed elsewhere," Nilsson said, interrupting his train of thought. "There's very little blood. If he'd been shot here, there would be a lot more, given the severity of his injuries."

So the body had been moved. With a bit of luck, there would be a car with bloodstains in the trunk. It wasn't easy to transport a heavy dead body without leaving any traces—DNA could be identified from the smallest fragments.

A short distance away several torn black plastic garbage bags were being examined by another technician; had they been used to wrap the body? Thomas estimated the victim's weight at around 190 pounds, so at least two people must have been involved.

"He's wearing a leather jacket," Nilsson said. "Either he was grabbed while he was outdoors, or he went willingly with the perp."

In which case he hadn't been abducted by someone he didn't know. Not that it had made much difference to him.

"Do you think he was tortured before he was killed?" Aram asked, pointing to the discolored wrists. "The broken skin suggests the use of cable ties."

Thomas agreed; the damage to the chin supported this view. It must have been agonizingly painful. The victim had certainly suffered during the final hours of his life.

A tooth was missing from the lower jaw.

"I wonder if they were trying to get some kind of information out of him? And if so, what was it?" Thomas asked.

"Could be a dispute between rival gangs," Aram suggested.

"It's not a very sophisticated approach," Nilsson said. "Pure violence, nothing else. By the way, he pissed himself—but that could have happened at the moment of death."

"How do you know?"

"Just use your sense of smell." Nilsson grinned in spite of the tragic circumstances, pointing to a large, dark stain around the victim's crotch.

"Maybe he knew he was going to be killed," Aram said.

"Poor bastard," Thomas murmured. Tortured and murdered with the full knowledge of how things were going to end.

"If he was a gang member, it goes with the territory," Aram said dryly.

Thomas shivered. There was a chill in the air, even though the sun was shining through the mist. Patches of grubby snow still lay here and there beneath the trees, and the ground was sodden. He walked around the body to take a closer look at the undamaged side of the face, crouching down on the damp moss. From this angle the features were better preserved. He could see a hint of dark stubble against the ashen skin. The smell of urine was unmistakable.

One dark eye stared straight ahead.

Thomas realized that he knew exactly who the victim was.

CHAPTER 84

Herman Wibom had just sat down with a cup of coffee at his desk, which was cluttered with papers as usual. The dark wood was barely visible. Gunilla, his secretary, often took him to task over his untidiness. His defense was that he had his own system; so far he'd never lost an important document.

"It's only a matter of time," she would say with a snort. They'd worked together for many years.

He pushed aside one of the piles and put down his coffee just as the phone rang. It was Mina Kovač's number. To tell the truth he hadn't expected to hear from her so soon. He'd thought he'd have to chase her to find out how she was going to react to her husband's demands.

"Good morning," Mina said. "Am I disturbing you?"

"Not at all. How are you today? Are you feeling better?"

The state she'd been in the previous day had worried Herman, in spite of the professional distance he always tried to maintain when it came to his clients. He'd hoped that his role as Mina's counsel wouldn't be too arduous. After a long career he was nearing retirement, and definitely ready to step aside. The firm had shrunk more and more, and he no longer employed a legal associate, only the ever-loyal Gunilla, and she was happy to cut back. There were too many newfangled ideas that he couldn't cope with, such as the demand for an increased online presence and electronic accessibility. He'd reluctantly agreed to post a recent photograph of himself on the company's home page.

"I've made up my mind," Mina said. Her voice was a little unsteady, but there was a note of determination there. Herman could hear the baby whimpering in the background; maybe she was holding him in her arms to give her strength? The power of a mother protecting her offspring was unique. It wasn't the first time he'd noticed this, in spite of the fact that he had never been in a long-term relationship and had no children of his own. Herman was definitely a confirmed bachelor. Being part of a couple wasn't for everyone.

"Oh yes?" he said, trying to sound encouraging. "I'm pleased to hear it."

"I will never give up Lukas." Mina paused. "And I have no intention of going back home."

"I see." Herman rested his chin on his hand and thought for a moment. Deep down he'd expected Mina to give in to her husband's demands.

He'd obviously underestimated her.

"You can tell Andreis and his lawyer that I will *never* let him have Lukas. I'd rather die!"

Herman wasn't particularly fond of dramatic outbursts. To be honest, there was a great deal he didn't like about this case. Too much violence, too many threats, and children always exacerbated the situation. He was too old for this kind of thing.

He opened the drawer and took out his favorite black-and-gold Montblanc pen. The familiar weight in his fingers made him feel better. A sense of normality returned.

"I also intend to file for divorce," Mina continued. "I won't be going back to him."

Herman made a careful note.

"You can inform Andreis that I'll be testifying against him. I'll tell the court about all the times he's abused me. I have photographs of the injuries he's inflicted on me." Her voice gave way. "And I'll be helping the prosecutor as much as I can." Mina began to cry, but Herman could hear the resolve beneath the surface. She mumbled an apology and blew her nose. "There's no point in him threatening me—I'm not going to change my mind."

Herman had no illusions about the consequences of Mina's decision, but this wasn't the time to go into all that. Mina was his client, and she'd made up her mind.

"Understood," he said. "I'll do whatever I can to support you. You can rely on me."

He ended the call, but kept his hand on the receiver. He would have to contact Ulrika Grönstedt.

She would be disappointed, to say the least.

Maybe he could email her instead? Her tone had been sharp and unpleasant the last time they'd spoken. She was the kind of lawyer who enjoyed attacking others—the kind Herman preferred to avoid.

However, the thought of upsetting her was surprisingly appealing. It was a long time since he'd had a case that filled him with enthusiasm. This was almost like the old days.

He drew the Penal Code toward him and looked up the section on no-contact orders. Best to summon up the whole artillery now that Mina had made her position clear.

Chapter 85

Ulrika Grönstedt ended the call with Herman Wibom and put her cell phone down on the table, although she would have preferred to hurl it at the wall with all her strength.

The guy was a has-been, but he'd conveyed his message with admirable clarity. He had more backbone than she'd thought. He'd even informed her that he would be filing for a no-contact order as soon as possible. This new threat on Mina's behalf infuriated Ulrika.

She'd expressly asked Kovač if his wife had anything on him, sensitive information that might harm his defense. He'd dismissed her concerns and said it was out of the question. Mina was too dumb for that.

Now what?

She called her client. There was no point in putting off the conversation, even if it was likely to be unpleasant.

"Hello?" He answered almost right away, but sounded as if he'd just woken up. It was ten fifteen, and Ulrika had been up for four hours. If he slept all morning, he had only himself to blame if she disturbed him.

"Were you asleep?" she asked, almost hoping he'd say yes.

"What do you want?"

When he didn't bother to turn on the charm, he really was an asshole.

"I've just spoken to Herman Wibom," she said, walking over to the window, which was ajar. A white Vaxholm ferry was just moving away from the quayside in front of the entrance to the Diplomat Hotel. In a month the summer timetable would begin, with direct boats traveling to the outer archipelago.

Ulrika longed for a vacation.

"He had new information," she said, not bothering to hide her irritation.

"Who are you talking about?"

"Herman Wibom, the lawyer who's been appointed as your wife's counsel." She must have mentioned his name to Kovač at least five times by this stage.

"When is she coming home?"

There was no point in sugarcoating it. "She's not."

"What do you mean?"

"Mina's decided she's not coming back to you."

"What the fuck?!"

"She's filing for divorce."

"She can't do that! I won't allow it!"

Kovač started yelling and swearing, but Ulrika had no intention of letting him get away with that. "Listen to me!" she snapped.

He stopped immediately.

"If we contact social services, then Mina and her lawyer will produce documents that could harm you." She'd caught his attention; he didn't say a word. "Wibom was very clear. According to him, Mina has collected evidence that can be used against you, and will give her sole custody of your son."

"What the fuck are you talking about?"

"Apparently Mina has documented the injuries, which, according to her, you have inflicted on her over the years. She has photographs of everything, including her medical notes."

"I didn't know there were photographs," Kovač muttered. There was no trace of regret in his voice.

"That's not the worst of it," Ulrika continued. "Your wife has decided to cooperate fully with the prosecutor. If she knows anything about your financial affairs, that information could come out, too."

For once Kovač seemed to be lost for words. Ulrika hoped the seriousness of his situation had sunk in. Maybe he'd be prepared to listen to her advice.

"Are you still there?" she said after a few seconds.

"Yes."

"Do you remember my asking you if Mina was involved in your business affairs? If there was any risk that she could reveal your secrets?" A fire truck raced by, the sound of its sirens filling the room. "You assured me that she had no idea about anything. That there was nothing to worry about."

"She hasn't a clue. I've found the leak and dealt with it."

Ulrika didn't want to know what that meant. "What if you're wrong?"

"Mina doesn't know what she's fucking talking about."

Kovač sounded slightly less sure of himself now. "If what Wibom says is true, then there could be serious consequences," Ulrika informed him.

"That won't happen. I'll talk to her."

Ulrika was losing patience fast. "She's in a shelter. All contact has to go through me or her counsel."

"Find out where she is."

"I can't. That would contravene the Bar Association's rules." Ulrika paused. "Maybe you could speak to her parents, see if you can reach her that way?"

"You do it. I want to know where Mina is!"

Chapter 86

Nora was in her office waiting for Leila to finish conducting an interview on another case, so that they could go to Runmarö together. There was a boat from Stavsnäs at eleven. If they left within fifteen minutes, they should be able to catch it.

Her phone rang.

"You have a visitor," the receptionist informed her. "There's a detective here; he wants to see you as soon as possible."

"Just a second." Nora checked her schedule to be on the safe side. "What's his name?"

"Thomas Andreasson."

"I'll come down."

Thomas's tall figure was indeed waiting for her when the elevator doors opened. In spite of the fact that they knew each other so well, she was struck by his air of calm authority. Something serious must have happened for him to show up unexpectedly.

"Thomas—what are you doing here?" She almost gave him a hug, but stopped herself just in time. He'd obviously come to see her in a professional capacity.

"We need to talk about your current case," he said. "Could we go somewhere more private?"

Nora checked the schedule and found an empty interview room. At that moment Leila appeared with a thick file under one arm. Nora beckoned her to join them, then swiped her pass card and led Thomas through the security barrier.

"Coffee?" she said as they passed the small staff kitchen.

"I'd prefer tea at this time of day. As you know," he said with a wink. It almost felt like normal as they stood in the kitchen, chatting about nothing in particular. Then reality took over. Thomas wasn't here for midmorning refreshments.

They went into one of the smaller conference rooms equipped with green upholstered chairs and a whiteboard with old notes still faintly visible. Nora sat down opposite Thomas.

It felt weird, being here like this. They had been friends for many years, but had never worked together, although she had acted as an informal sounding board in several investigations. Their paths had never crossed professionally while she was working as a legal associate at the bank, and this was the first time it had happened since she'd been appointed as a prosecutor with the Economic Crimes Authority.

Thomas took out his notebook. "Sorry to turn up out of the blue like this, but something's happened in the Nacka Nature Reserve, and we think there's a connection to Andreis Kovač."

Nora had had a feeling that might be the case, but she still felt a tremor of anxiety in her stomach.

"A body was found in the forest this morning. We have reason to believe that the victim is a man by the name of Dino Herco, who worked closely with Kovač."

Leila inhaled sharply. "What? Herco's dead?"

Thomas nodded.

"How did he die?" Nora asked.

"He was shot at close range, probably during the past twenty-four hours. A bullet through the brain—a straight execution."

"Shit," Leila muttered, tugging at her long black braid.

"His injuries suggest that he was tortured, or at least badly beaten before he died."

Only a few days ago they'd been sitting in Herco's kitchen, questioning him about the call to the emergency dispatch. Now he was dead.

Nora felt as if she'd entered some kind of parallel universe. "How did you find him?"

"He was buried in a shallow grave in the nature reserve. A jogger and his dog practically tripped over him. Almost as if he was meant to be discovered."

"It wouldn't surprise me if Kovač wanted to make an example of him," Leila said. "A kind of warning: *Don't interfere in my affairs if you want to live.* He seems the type."

"Do you think Kovač is behind the murder?" Nora asked. "Is there anything to connect him to the crime?"

Thomas shook his head. "It's way too early to say. I've come straight from Nacka; we haven't located the murder scene yet."

Leila tugged at her braid again and moved it to the other shoulder. "What forensic evidence do you have?"

"None at all. No bullet, because it passed right through the head, no fingerprints on the body. A team of CSIs is heading over to his apartment now."

"We only spoke to him a few days ago," Nora said.

Leila quickly filled Thomas in on their conversation with Herco and his involvement in the assault on Mina. She also told him about her interview with Herco two days ago.

"He was terrified that Kovač would find out what he'd done," she said, turning to Nora for confirmation. "So terrified that he actually threatened me while he was here."

Nora nodded.

"This was exactly what he was afraid of," Leila continued. "He became incredibly uncomfortable when we pushed him. He lied about basic facts, details that we could easily check."

"Which we did, of course," Nora added.

"If Kovač knew that Dino Herco called emergency services, there's your motive," Leila said.

"We're keeping an open mind," Thomas replied. "We can't rule out other motives or even different perpetrators. However, this does seem to have been a planned execution; there's nothing spontaneous about the modus operandi."

"What's your next move?" Nora asked.

"We want Kovač's phone tapped immediately. It's going to take time for all the tests and analyses—strands of hair, blood, DNA. We'll be waiting at the end of a long line."

"What else will you be focusing on, apart from forensics?" Leila said.

"We're putting Kovač under surveillance."

"He must have realized that the murder of Dino Herco would lead straight back to him," Leila mused out loud. "Given how closely they worked together. That suggests narcissistic arrogance and a predilection for risk."

Or sheer ruthlessness, Nora thought.

"Not necessarily," Thomas said. "I recognized the victim by pure chance—thanks to you, Nora."

"Me?"

"We were talking about him on the boat the other day. Otherwise I would never have seen a photograph of him, so I wouldn't have had a clue who the dead man was."

"You'd have found out eventually." Nora was unwilling to accept an undeserved accolade.

"Yes, but it would have taken a lot longer. He had no ID on him, and no phone. He lives alone, so there were no family members to report him missing."

That was true. And all the indications were that Dino Herco had been single.

"Kovač can't possibly have expected you to be on his trail so fast," Leila said. "That has to be a big advantage for you."

Thomas nodded. "I hope so."

"What are the odds that someone else would kidnap and murder Kovač's right-hand man just two days after Herco admitted he was terrified of his boss?" Leila folded her arms, as if she were challenging Thomas to contradict her. "Come on—you know I'm right. You ought to bring him in immediately."

Chapter 87

Ulrika Grönstedt shifted position on her chair behind her desk. She just couldn't get comfortable.

Her carefully planned strategy hadn't worked, and the conversation with Andreis Kovač had made her uneasy. She doodled one meaningless shape after another on her pad and tried to think.

Eventually she got up and closed the door. Then she took out the packet of cigarettes she kept in the bottom drawer for emergencies. She lit up, inhaled deeply, and gazed at the glowing tip of the cigarette.

Her brain was still empty.

She hated the feeling of having played all her cards, yet, at the same time, something wasn't right. Mina wasn't behaving the way Ulrika had expected. She'd been certain that Mina would give in as soon as the issue of a custody battle was raised.

Ulrika stubbed out her cigarette in the screw-top tin she kept in the same drawer, well out of sight of her colleagues. She never smoked at home, for Fiona's sake.

There was only one reasonable explanation for Mina's change of attitude, and it didn't make the situation any better. Something must have happened yesterday, when Mina returned to the house on

Trastvägen. Presumably Kovač had scared her so much that she didn't dare go back to him.

He'd been given a chance to fix everything, to show her how much he loved her. Instead he'd fucked it up. The guy was his own worst enemy.

"Damage control," she murmured to herself, without any idea of how to achieve that. There had to be a solution, a way of reconciling the couple. It was their only chance of stopping Mina from testifying against her husband.

She needed a new plan.

Ulrika leafed through the file. Kovač had suggested using Mina's parents as a way of reaching out to her. The last she'd heard was that the mother was in the hospital for some reason. Maybe she could talk to the father? Plead for compassion under these difficult circumstances? She could hint that the mother would feel better if she didn't have to worry about her daughter's conflict with her husband.

It was worth a shot.

Ulrika looked longingly at the half-full cigarette packet, but resolutely closed the drawer. She went over to the window and flung it wide open to get rid of the smell of smoke.

Contacting Mina's father was risky; the Bar Association would hit the roof if they found out, but the lack of alternatives left her no choice. She'd worry about the ethics some other time.

She googled the name, found the cell phone number, and dialed before she could change her mind.

Stefan Talevski answered just when Ulrika thought the call was going to voice mail. She introduced herself politely, and explained that she was representing his son-in-law, Andreis Kovač.

"Why the hell are you calling me?" he spat.

She hadn't expected a warm response, but this open hostility took her by surprise. "My client is eager to see his wife and son," she said, her tone as warm as she could possibly manage.

"He should have thought of that before he beat her half to death."

Ulrika tried again. "He's very sorry. He doesn't know what came over him. He's prepared to do whatever it takes to win her forgiveness. What he did was reprehensible, but it will never happen again."

She laid it on as thickly as possible, without saying anything that could be used as evidence against her client. If Stefan ever brought up this conversation, she would insist that she had been referring to a nasty quarrel between Andreis and Mina, nothing else. She had never in any way admitted that Andreis had used violence against his wife.

"He's desperate to see his son. Lukas is his only child. If your daughter goes back to him, he's promised to seek help with his anger issues."

She would deal with Kovač's response to that particular suggestion later. If the cost of getting Mina back was signing up for a counseling program, then he would just have to do it. There must be a way of getting him to agree if she managed to deliver Mina and Lukas back into his arms.

"He really does want to change," she added for good measure.

"Are you out of your mind?"

"I'm sorry?"

"Do you seriously think I'd advise my daughter to go back to that lunatic after what he did to us on Saturday?"

"I don't understand."

"My wife still hasn't regained consciousness; she's in a coma because of your so-called client."

The conversation was spiraling out of control.

"I have no idea what you're talking about," she said. The background noises suddenly made sense. Mina's father was in the ICU, and the beeping and humming came from various machines.

A carpet of sound in death's waiting room.

What the hell had Kovač done?

Mina's father let out a guttural groan, somewhere between a laugh and a sob. "Are you trying to tell me that you don't know he came to our house on Saturday? That he threatened us, hoping to frighten us into telling him where Mina's hiding?"

Contacting Stefan Talevski had been a mistake. Ulrika needed to end this call as soon as possible. "Unfortunately I have to—"

"He smashed the glass in our front door. I thought he was going to kill us. My wife was so terrified that she suffered a major heart attack. Her condition has deteriorated since she was brought in. The doctors don't know if she's going to make it. My daughter is never going back to that man!" Stefan yelled.

"I didn't know any of this."

"Do you have children?"

Instinctively Ulrika glanced at the photograph of Fiona beaming into the camera. She would be eleven in June.

"How can you defend such a piece of shit? How can you live with yourself?"

CHAPTER 88

They'd been in the conference room for almost an hour. Thomas and
Leila had gotten caught up in a technical discussion about some of the
details from the scene of the crime.

Nora opened her notepad and drew a diagram of the situation.

If Kovač became the subject of a homicide investigation, then
things became a lot more complicated from her point of view. That
would give her three parallel investigations to take into consideration,
with another prosecutor brought in—presumably someone who was a
lot more suited to handling a murder charge than she was.

She'd held off filing the tax evasion charge because of the assault on
Mina, but in the end she'd decided she had to file today. Now she had
to think about the implications of this new information.

A homicide investigation could take months. It might be better to
postpone the tax evasion case until a later date; it wouldn't be the first
time something similar had happened.

Before making a decision, she needed to hear what Mina had
to say.

Leila and Thomas were now talking about Kovač's mental state.

"I wonder if he's starting to lose control," Leila said. "The violence and aggression he's displayed are worrying."

She got up and went over to the whiteboard, picked up a black marker, and drew a timeline, with a cross for each incident in which Kovač had been involved. It began with the assault on Mina just over a week ago, and ended with today's date and the murder of Dino Herco. Kovač's visit to Mina's parents was there, with a symbol to indicate that Mina's mother was in intensive care.

Nora shuddered.

"It feels as if he's under increasing pressure," Leila said, tapping the board with her pen. "One incident after another within the space of ten days. It's escalating."

People under pressure did desperate things.

Nora thought back to her interview with Kovač, the impression that she was sitting opposite a predator. What would happen if the pressure increased even more?

Leila stared at the board. "The question is how far he's prepared to go." She put down the pen and sat down.

"What about the visit to his in-laws?" Thomas said. "Can't we charge him with threatening behavior?"

"Mina's mother is still unconscious," Nora told him. She'd checked with the hospital, and Katrin's condition was unchanged.

"Her father refuses to go into detail," Leila said, "even though we're pretty sure about the course of events. He's too scared to talk, which is understandable, given what happened yesterday."

Thomas looked up. "Yesterday?"

"Kovač was about to shoot Mina in broad daylight," Leila explained. "She managed to get on a bus with the baby in his stroller at the last minute, and the driver took off." She filled Thomas in on the rest of the day's developments, and Mina's return to the shelter with a police escort.

"So why hasn't he been arrested?" Thomas asked.

Leila grimaced.

"The bus driver had his eyes on the road. He says that because of the angle of his seat, he didn't see anything. The patrol that picked up Mina from the bus didn't take the names of the passengers. We've issued an appeal, but nothing so far. We have no witnesses apart from Mina, who is still refusing to testify against her husband."

Nora realized she hadn't told Leila about the call from Anna-Maria. The news about Herco's death had taken all her attention. How could she have forgotten? It almost constituted malpractice. There was too much going on in her head right now.

"Mina seems to have changed her mind," she said. "We need to go back to Runmarö as soon as we're done here."

Leila raised her eyebrows.

"Anna-Maria called me earlier. Mina wants to see us again, and it sounds as if she's actually ready to tell the truth about her husband. I've double-checked with Herman Wibom, and he says the same thing."

Leila's face broke into a smile. "At last—some good news!"

Nora glanced at her watch. She didn't want to hurry Thomas, but they ought to get away before Mina regretted her decision. She didn't really trust Wibom's assurances that Mina was determined to leave her husband and testify against him.

"We really should make a move," she said apologetically.

Thomas closed his notebook.

"I'll send you everything we have on Dino Herco," Leila said. "Then you can form your own opinion."

"Much appreciated. One more thing, do me a favor and ask Mina if her husband is left-handed. The injuries to Herco's face suggest a left-handed perpetrator," Thomas said.

Nora stood up. "By the way, Kovač has a very sharp defense attorney—Ulrika Grönstedt."

"So much the better—she'll know what's what. We won't have to provide him with representation."

"Kovač will deny everything if you bring him in," Nora said.

Leila nodded. "Plus you can assume he'll have a perfect alibi—but you were probably expecting that."

"Bring it on." Thomas didn't seem particularly concerned. "I'm looking forward to having a conversation with him."

Bosnia, May 1993

Andreis spotted Aunt Blanka through the window, and ran to open the door. Selma had just settled down on the sofa with Emir on her lap. She inhaled audibly when she saw Blanka.

"Have you changed your mind?" she exclaimed. She'd wept when she said good-bye to Blanka earlier in the day, convinced that was the last time they'd see each other.

Blanka went over to Selma without taking off her coat. "Is Zlatko home?" she asked quietly. Selma shook her head, and Blanka sat down beside her. "You and the children have to come with us tomorrow. There's room in the car. I've spoken to Dario, and we're both in agreement."

"It's impossible." Selma was holding Emir much too tightly. He started twisting his body around and whimpering until she loosened her grip and put him down on the floor. He immediately crawled across the room to Andreis, who was playing in the corner.

Blanka unbuttoned her coat. "You need to think about the children."

"I can't talk to Zlatko. I've already tried. You know what he's like."

Bright red patches had appeared on Blanka's cheeks. "You can't stay here! Please come!"

"I know we ought to . . ." Selma's voice gave way; she couldn't go on.

Blanka rested her forehead against Selma's, blinking back her own tears. "I'm not trying to scare you, Selma. I'm just so worried about what will happen to you and the boys after we've gone." She wiped her eyes with her sleeve, then got out her cigarettes. It took her three attempts to light one; the hand holding the match was shaking too much. She couldn't suppress a sob. "Please come," she said again. "Don't say anything to Zlatko."

Selma glanced at Andreis; he seemed to be fully absorbed in his cars. Emir was staring in fascination at the toys as Andreis moved them back and forth.

"Otherwise you're all going to die," Blanka continued. "It's only a matter of time until the Serbs get here."

CHAPTER 89

The winding road that began at the jetty in Styrsvik was a familiar sight by now. Nora's feet found their own way to Freya's Haven. How many times had she followed this route over the past week? Considerably more than she could have imagined when she came back to work after the Easter break.

Anna-Maria opened the door when Nora and Leila rang the bell, but her usual energy was missing.

"How are you?" Nora asked as they took off their coats. The manager had dark circles under her eyes, and a few strands of hair had escaped from her ponytail.

"I'm just a little tired." Anna-Maria rubbed her forehead with her right hand. "I had Lukas last night so that Mina could get some sleep. She was completely exhausted, poor soul."

Nora took a closer look at her. The lines between her nose and mouth had deepened, even though it was only twenty-four hours since Nora had seen her. She seemed to be carrying bigger problems than a baby who needed a bottle in the middle of the night.

Leila's phone rang. She excused herself and moved away.

"Is that all?" Nora said. "You look pretty worried, if you don't mind my saying so."

"We've got problems with the local authority," Anna-Maria admitted, adjusting the cloth on the little table in front of the mirror; it had been perfectly straight to begin with. "They need to save money, they're on us all the time. Someone called just now with bad news."

All the local authorities were trying to economize. Where did the money go?

Swedish taxes were high, and yet whenever you opened a newspaper, it seemed as if most public services were on their knees. There was a shortage of resources in health care, education, and, not least, the police, as Thomas often pointed out. Everything was operating on a deficit.

Anna-Maria was clearly so upset that Nora didn't feel she could let it go. Leila was still on the phone, so Nora pointed to the sofa in the empty living room. "Let's sit down for a moment."

Anna-Maria reluctantly complied, perching on the very edge of the seat.

"Tell me about the phone call."

Anna-Maria flushed. "I shouldn't have said anything. You don't have time for this kind of thing; that's not why you're here."

"Don't you worry about that." Nora was happy to help if she could. "Tell me. I'm an attorney, after all—maybe there's something I can do?"

"Do you know anything about public-sector tenders?" Anna-Maria uttered the words as if they were in a foreign language.

"Not much," Nora admitted.

"The local authority is putting women's shelters out to tender." Anna-Maria sighed. "I'm sure the intention is good, but the way they've chosen to do it will mean the end for us. We're a charitable foundation, but we're totally dependent on the authority's contribution to make ends meet."

"And why would the tender process have such serious consequences for you?" Nora asked.

"It seems as if the criteria are going to be so narrowly defined that we won't be able to fulfill them. Which means we won't be given an allocation, and that in turn means no financial support." Anna-Maria rubbed her hand up and down her thigh. "We've run this place for twenty years with excellent results, but that appears to be irrelevant. It's all about what it's going to cost in the future—nothing else matters." She was speaking more and more quickly, and Nora was finding it difficult to process the information.

"Take a deep breath and explain it to me slowly," she said. "What exactly has the local authority said?"

A skinny, fair-haired teenage girl stuck her head around the living room door. When she saw Anna-Maria and Nora, she quickly withdrew. Anna-Maria didn't even notice her.

"They're going to weight the tender so that previous experience dealing with traumatized women and children doesn't count," Anna-Maria said.

"What do you mean by 'weight the tender'?"

"In the public sector–tendering process, there's a points system to clarify the extent to which a provider fulfills the various criteria. Whoever has the most points wins the contract."

"Go on."

"If you give high points for 'competitive prices' and low points for 'expertise and experience,' then what do you think is going to happen?"

The penny dropped. Nora silently forgave herself; this was an area of the law she'd never worked in. "It's all about offering the lowest price," she said.

"Exactly. We don't stand a chance. We can't compete with the other bidders. They're huge care providers who see this as purely a business opportunity. They can even put in a tender that will run at a loss, just to get the contract. As far as we're concerned, the writing's on the wall." Anna-Maria had tears in her eyes. "Now do you understand? Our knowledge is regarded as unimportant, despite the fact that it's vital. This is a complex operation. The women who come here are frightened and broken. They need help from qualified therapists and proven support mechanisms."

Anna-Maria's shoulders slumped. "I sat up late last night going over the figures. It's impossible to put in a competitive bid while maintaining the quality of what we do here. It simply can't be done. We're going to have to close."

"Surely it can't be that bad?"

"I'm afraid it is. There's no money for anything, even though these women are so vulnerable. I just don't know what we're going to do."

Leila ended her call and came over to join them, slipping her phone into her pocket. "Sorry—I had to take that."

Anna-Maria quickly got to her feet. "Listen to me, babbling on!"

"It's fine." Nora gently placed a hand on her arm. "I wish I could do something to help."

Anna-Maria managed a wan smile. "It was good of you to listen, but you're not here to solve my problems. I'll take you to Mina's room. She's probably feeding Lukas."

CHAPTER 90

The day had started badly, and it was getting worse.

Ulrika Grönstedt had already smoked two more cigarettes this afternoon, even though she'd promised herself she'd stop. Or at least stick to one a day.

It couldn't be helped. To be honest, she hadn't expected things to move so fast when Herman Wibom informed her that Mina was intending to testify against her husband, and that as her representative he would be applying for a no-contact order. She hadn't thought the old fool would be prepared to go so far.

Clearly she'd been wrong. Nothing was going according to plan. One of her contacts had informed her that the police were out looking for Kovač in connection with a new investigation. She had to get a hold of her client.

This time he answered right away.

"Yes?"

That told her everything she needed to know about his mood. "Apparently the police are looking for you."

"So?"

He was in his car. She could hear the hum of the engine in the background, and the automated voice of the GPS telling him to take the next right. Presumably he was on the way to conduct yet more illegal business. Ulrika was under no illusions. "Why are they looking for you?"

"How the fuck should I know?"

"It must be because of the assault on your wife," Ulrika speculated. "Now she's decided to testify against you."

"For fuck's sake . . ."

He had only himself to blame. "Tell me what happened yesterday, when she went to your house," Ulrika said.

"Later."

"When?"

"Later, I said!"

"I can't prepare your defense if I don't have access to all the facts. Things seem to have taken a fresh turn over the past twenty-four hours."

The automated voice instructed Kovač to take the next left, then turn left again.

"Maybe it's about your visit to Mina's parents," Ulrika went on. "We need to talk about that, too."

"No, we don't."

"I spoke to your father-in-law a little while ago. He gave me a detailed account of what happened on Saturday night. His wife is in a coma at the Southern District Hospital, and he holds you responsible for her condition."

The memory of her conversation with Stefan Talevski was painful. There were limits to how far she was prepared to go for her client.

"You can't do that kind of thing if you want me to defend you. This is getting worse and worse. I have to be able to do my job as your lawyer if we're to have any chance of getting you acquitted."

"Fuck that."

Ulrika almost ended the call there and then. "Anyway, the police are looking for you," she said with a sharp edge to her voice.

"I don't have time for this. Am I wanted as a suspect?"

Ulrika was suddenly unsure, and Kovač picked up on that immediately. "Am I a suspect or not?"

"I don't think so."

"There you go then."

Ulrika wasn't used to being spoken to like this.

"Have you found out where Mina is yet?" Kovač snapped.

"No—I've already told you, that's not how it works."

"I need to speak to her."

Did she have to tell him yet again that Mina was in a shelter? The most sensible thing he could do would be to stay away from his wife. Every time they were in contact, he made his own situation worse.

Ulrika stood up. "You can't," she said with more patience than he deserved. "It's out of the question. Any communication has to go via me and her counsel."

"We'll see about that."

"Those are the rules." Ulrika's jaws ached with the effort of holding back. "Her legal representative is in the process of requesting a no-contact order against you. That means that all contact between you and your wife is banned. It wouldn't surprise me if the order comes into effect tomorrow. Just so you know." She had no idea if that was true, she didn't care anymore. If she'd been representing Mina, she'd have had a no-contact order in place long ago.

"What did you say his name was?"

"Mina's counsel? Herman Wibom."

"In that case I'll speak to him directly, if you can't manage it."

"Andreis, please don't do anything stupid."

Silence. Her client had already gone.

CHAPTER 91

When Nora and Leila knocked on the door, Mina was standing in the middle of the room, rocking Lukas in his stroller. It looked brand new, and was, without doubt, the most expensive stroller Nora had ever seen.

She hadn't really noticed it yesterday, in the midst of all the chaos. Was that why Mina had gone home and risked her life? For the sake of a stroller?

It seemed incomprehensible, but maybe something else was going on here. Maybe this was about Mina's right to visit her own home, to collect items that meant a great deal to her. An attempt to preserve an ounce of normality.

"Hi, Mina," she said, holding out her hand. "How are you feeling today?"

"A little better, thank you." Mina pushed the stroller into the corner by the tiled stove. Lukas was fast asleep, with a cuddly toy beside him. "I slept right through the night, thanks to Anna-Maria."

"We really appreciate the fact that you have changed your mind and are ready to talk to us," Leila said. "We realize it's not easy."

"Anna-Maria helped. She made me think." Mina was pale, but radiated an inner strength compared with yesterday. Her hair was clean and brushed, tucked neatly behind her ears. "I want to show you something," she said, sitting down on the sofa. She took out her phone and entered her password. "Here," she said with no hesitation, turning the screen toward Nora and Leila.

Nora inhaled sharply.

She was looking at a close-up of a faceless woman in her bra and pants. From the navel upward the skin was badly discolored, covered in large purple contusions. There was an ugly red mark around the neck.

"Is this you?" Nora had to ask.

"Yes. That was just over a year ago."

"What's this?" Nora said, pointing to the mark on the neck. "Did he try to strangle you?"

"Not on that occasion. It must have been a kick, but I don't really remember what happened toward the end. I was completely out of it."

Mina swiped left; the next picture showed her face. Her lower lip was swollen and split, and her right eye was closed. There were scratches all over one cheek, and her chin and throat were streaked with blood.

Nora wanted to look away. She could still see the traces of Kovač's latest attack on his wife, even though the bruises were fading and her lip had almost healed. She couldn't understand how a couple could make up after such violence. How could they even speak to each other again?

"You must tell us if this gets too difficult," Leila said gently. "We'll understand."

"There's more," Mina said. She must have been living in a minefield, where one false step could trigger an explosion. What kind of marriage was that? It was almost impossible to imagine existing in constant fear of your own partner. Was it possible to heal from something like that?

Nora blinked back the tears.

Mina moved on to a third picture, where a lump the size of a one-krona piece had appeared above her eye in shades of blue and purple.

Nora thought about figures in Greek mythology with grotesque horns on their foreheads. Once again, Mina's face was badly scratched.

"He usually struck me on the body where it didn't show so much," Mina said. "But sometimes he'd lose control and go for my face. This happened just before I became pregnant with Lukas." She pointed to the lump. "He hit me so hard that I fell against the edge of the kitchen counter. I passed out on the floor."

"Why didn't you leave him?"

Nora regretted the words as soon as she'd spoken. She ought to know better than to ask a question like that. There were many reasons why abused women stayed with violent men, when the violence gradually broke their spirit and destroyed their self-esteem. The sick behavior became normalized over time until even the abused partner accepted the perpetrator's view of reality.

Comments that could make the victim feel guilty were no help at all.

"Sorry," Nora said immediately. "That was a really stupid question."

"I don't know why I didn't leave him," Mina said, bringing up another picture of bruised flesh. "I never thought this could happen to me." She looked over at Lukas, then up at the ceiling. "When it did, I was so ashamed."

"None of it was your fault," Leila said quickly.

"I know that now. I wish I could explain why I stayed with Andreis, at least before Lukas was born. After he came along it was impossible to leave."

Nora hardly dared ask the next question. "Were you able to talk to your parents about what was going on?"

"No. Absolutely not."

Mina put the phone down on the coffee table. She pushed her hair back from her forehead; the sun shining in through the window by the stove left half her face in shadow.

"Mom and Dad never liked him. They were worried because he was five years older than me, and they had concerns about his background.

I think they suspected pretty early on that he didn't have a proper job, that he did . . . other things . . ."

"So they knew nothing about the abuse?"

"At first I didn't want to admit to them that they'd been right, that he wasn't good for me. I couldn't do it—it was too hard. When things got really bad, I didn't dare. My dad would have confronted Andreis, and I was terrified about how Andreis would react."

Lukas whimpered. Mina went over to give him his pacifier.

"I really thought everything would be all right when I got pregnant," she continued. "Things did improve for a while; Andreis was almost like the man I fell in love with. He was wonderful when we first got together. I guess it's hard for you to believe it, but he really was. I'd never been so much in love with anyone else. The first few years were so good—until he became stressed by his business affairs and started drinking too much and taking too many drugs." Mina's voice was thick with unshed tears.

"Thank you for showing us the pictures," Leila said gently. "You're very brave."

"Those pictures will be used as evidence," Nora explained. "It's important that you understand. Other people will need to see them."

"I do understand." Mina sat down again.

"I hope you realize how important it is that you saved those images," Nora added. "We'll use them against your husband. You won't need to worry about him for many years."

Mina turned her head toward Lukas. "I'm doing it for his sake," she said.

Chapter 92

The air-conditioning was humming quietly in Thomas's office, a monotonous sound in the background that he never usually noticed. For some reason it was disturbing him today. He was finding it very difficult to concentrate, and he really needed to gather his thoughts before the briefing Margit had called in half an hour.

He stared at his notes without enthusiasm. He ought to call Staffan Nilsson, find out if forensics had come up with anything new. He also had to contact Pernilla, which he wasn't looking forward to at all. He'd already spoken to his mother and asked her to pick up Elin.

When his phone rang, he felt as if he'd been let off the hook.

"This is Ulrika Grönstedt."

Thomas had encountered Grönstedt's type before, lawyers who regarded the legal process as a competition, and took every case personally. Their tone was always supercilious and critical; it was all about winning. She would do her best to complicate matters by querying every detail in the police investigation.

"I hear you're looking for my client," she went on.

How did she know that?

"Unfortunately he's sick. He's in bed with the flu."

"We have sickbeds in the custody suite," Thomas informed her.

"He's very ill. He has a high temperature."

Thomas was under no illusions about Kovač's health. Presumably Grönstedt had told him to make himself inaccessible for as long as possible so that she could formulate a suitable strategy before he was questioned by the police. He hadn't been home when officers went to the house, but someone must have seen the patrol car.

"I can provide a doctor's note if you wish." Grönstedt's attitude was matter-of-fact. She was good at her job and 100 percent on the side of her client, whatever he'd done. She cleared her throat. "The question is why you want to speak to my client. It would be simpler if you could tell me why he's under suspicion."

So that was why she'd called. She didn't know about the homicide investigation, but sensed that there was a problem. Of course it would be simpler for Grönstedt if she found out that Kovač was the main suspect in another inquiry; how else would she be able to fabricate a suitable story for her client to reel off like a parrot when he was interviewed?

She wasn't the only one who could make life difficult.

"You'll find out when we bring him in," Thomas said and put down the phone.

CHAPTER 93

The clock on the wall at Freya's Haven struck the hour. It was time to round off the conversation with Mina and head back to the mainland, but Nora had one more key issue to raise.

The murder of Dino Herco.

"There's something else we need to talk about," she said. "It's about a man called Dino Herco, who works with your husband."

Mina leaned forward. "Dino? Why?"

"I'm afraid he's dead."

Mina's hand flew to her mouth. "Oh no!"

If Herco had been close to Andreis, she must have met him on a regular basis. That didn't necessarily mean they were friends, but judging by her reaction, she'd liked him.

"His body was discovered this morning, deep in the forest at the Nacka Nature Reserve," Leila said. "I'm very sorry."

"Was it an accident?"

Leila shook her head. "He'd been shot in the head; death would have been instantaneous. We're pretty sure he was murdered."

Mina took several deep breaths. How much bad news could one person deal with?

Leila was about to ask another question, when Nora stopped her with a discreet gesture. Mina needed a few seconds.

"Dino was kind to me," she murmured.

Nora patted Mina's arm in an attempt to express her sympathy and support.

"Unfortunately we believe he was killed by your husband," Leila continued.

"Andreis?"

Leila nodded. "We know that it was Dino who intervened when you were assaulted last week. He called the emergency number, which is why the ambulance and the police arrived."

"It was Dino who saved me?" Mina bit her lip. "I don't understand . . ."

Nora poured her a glass of water from the carafe on the tray. Mina took a few sips.

"We spoke to him a few days ago," Leila explained. "He wasn't prepared to admit that he'd made the call, but it came from his cell phone, and his voice was recorded."

"He was terrified that your husband would find out," Nora said.

"Andreis would never have forgiven him . . ."

"We think he did find out, and . . ." Leila broke off and gave a little shrug, which said it all. "As I'm sure you understand, this means there's now another ongoing police investigation in which your husband features."

"I had no idea it was Dino," Mina whispered. "I thought it was one of the neighbors."

"Did you know each other well?" Nora asked.

"He was always with Andreis. I've seen him almost every day since I first met Andreis."

"We're looking into every possibility, even though most of the evidence points to your husband," Leila said. "Do you think he's capable of doing that to an old friend?"

"I don't know . . ."

"I just want your spontaneous reaction. What's your gut feeling when I ask that question?"

Mina couldn't speak.

"OK," Leila said after a moment. "That's fine—let's move on. Do you know if Dino had any enemies? Someone who didn't like him, maybe wanted him out of the way?"

Mina tightened her grip on the glass. "Have you spoken to Andreis's younger brother, Emir?"

Nora glanced at Leila. Emir's name hadn't really come up so far. On the other hand, they hadn't known about Herco either; the focus had been on Kovač and his financial transactions.

"Emir spent a lot of time at our house," Mina went on, "just like Dino did. But he's different."

"In what way?"

"They're half brothers, as I assume you know. Same mother, different fathers. Emir's not as hot-tempered as Andreis; he plays the long game." Mina drank more water. "Andreis can be cruel because his anger gets the better of him, but he's not nasty, if you know what I mean." She noticed Nora's reaction to her choice of words. "OK, it sounds weird. But Emir—"

She broke off.

"Deep down I'm sure that Andreis never planned to beat me. It just kind of happened when he lost control. He always apologized afterward—well, in the beginning anyway. He was ashamed of himself, he regretted what he'd done."

Nora knew that Mina was being honest, that she believed what she was saying, even though everything her husband had done to her proved the opposite. She wasn't sure whether to despair at such loyalty, or be moved by it.

"But Emir . . . he's not like that. He does things on purpose."

"You mean he deliberately hurts people?" Leila asked.

"Not only that—he enjoys it."

CHAPTER 94

A fine drizzle was falling by the time Herman Wibom locked his office for the day and headed home.

The apartment on Roslagsgatan wasn't far from the practice, and he enjoyed the daily walks to and from work. Stockholm was a beautiful city, and he'd lived in Vasastan, with Vanadislunden Park just around the corner, all his life. He put up his black umbrella and set off along Döbelnsgatan in the direction of Sveaplan.

He'd spent all afternoon on the application for a no-contact order against Andreis Kovač. He'd called Mina to explain why he couldn't come over to Runmarö for the meeting with the prosecutor and the police, and she'd assured him that was fine.

Now everything was ready to file. He hadn't stayed at work so late for years; it was after eight o'clock, but he felt unusually satisfied with the day's efforts.

He hadn't just applied for the standard order, where the husband (in this case) was not allowed to visit, contact, or follow his wife. Instead he had argued at length for an extended ban, which would place even greater restrictions on Andreis Kovač. Not only would all communication between him and Mina be forbidden, the order would also prevent him from going near her place of work or other locations where she normally spent time.

Mina would be fully protected.

Herman had considered including the house on Trastvägen, but suspected that Mina wouldn't feel safe there, at least for the foreseeable future. They could always discuss the possibility further down the line, if she wanted to move back home. With the documentation she had, it shouldn't be difficult to achieve.

Herman was particularly pleased with his assessment of how dangerous the husband was. Kovač had played straight into his hands by producing a gun and threatening Mina and Lukas in broad daylight. There was no better argument from a legal point of view; that alone should be enough to warrant granting the order, even if Mina's photographs didn't live up to expectations.

The young police officer Leila Kacim had informed him that they were looking for anyone who'd witnessed the incident. She was hopeful that someone would come forward very soon.

Herman stopped at the crossing on Odengatan and waited for the light to change to green.

Gunilla had made an appointment for him to see Nora Linde at the Economic Crimes Authority tomorrow at one o'clock so that a decision could be made on the no-contact order as quickly as possible. He doubted whether Ulrika Grönstedt would raise any objections or appeal once the order had been granted. She'd sounded much less feisty than usual the last time they'd spoken.

Herman smiled at the thought.

He'd made an important decision during the course of the day. He would fight for Mina, do his very best. When the case was over, he would leave the legal profession and close down the practice. It was time to step back, but if he could make a real difference for Mina and her son, he would be leaving with his head held high.

The rain was heavier now, but his big English umbrella was a godsend. In a few weeks it would be May, and spring would finally arrive. He'd always found March and April to be quite miserable months, just waiting for that real feeling of spring.

As he turned the corner onto Roslagsgatan, a large black BMW sped past him, splashing water all over Herman's pants.

"Have some consideration!" Herman muttered, but the driver didn't slow down. People were so thoughtless these days. Herman glared after the car, then continued toward his apartment building. He was looking forward to a peaceful evening with a small brandy. He'd earned it after all his hard work today.

CHAPTER 95

The dinner Ulrika Grönstedt had agreed to attend was taking place at Sällskapet, the long-established gentlemen's club by Kungsträdgården. The club described itself as a meeting place for networking and socializing. In reality it was yet another illustration of the fact that company directors like to hang out with other company directors, preferably without women around. Only men were allowed to be members, according to the club's old-fashioned rules.

Ulrika felt irritated every time she walked through the door. It was incomprehensible that associations where women weren't welcome still existed in Sweden, but Sällskapet endured. Women were admitted only as invited guests at specific times.

Like tonight.

She loathed the patronizing attitude embedded in the richly decorated walls, but she also knew that networking could be very useful. This evening's charity dinner aimed to raise money for some kind of research, although she couldn't remember what it was—presumably cancer or diabetes. As far as she was concerned, the guest list was a lot more important than the goal. She had already exchanged a few words with several colleagues and key decision makers who regularly appeared on Industry Today, the country's leading business website, and in various financial journals.

The guest speaker, a professor from the Karolinska Institute, stepped up to the podium, which was surrounded by impressive flower arrangements. The main course had just been served; the food would grow cold. No doubt the speech would be long and tedious, as was so often the case when academic gentlemen of a certain age were given the opportunity to hold forth.

Ulrika had no appetite anyway. She cut a small piece of the tender fillet of lamb, but found it difficult to force the meat down. She couldn't shake off the events of the afternoon. It wasn't like her to allow a client to get under her skin; she prided herself on her ability to be professional at all times.

She put down her knife and fork and discreetly took out her cell phone to see if Kovač had been in touch. She'd tried to call him before she left the office, just to make sure that everything was OK—she was seriously worried. Surely he wouldn't be dumb enough to go and see Herman Wibom to ask for Mina's address?

The screen was blank; he hadn't returned her call.

Ulrika had resolutely trained herself to leave her work at the office. Her clients had full access to her intellect and expertise during the day, but she didn't take their troubles home with her. And yet . . . she couldn't forget Kovač's final words.

What was he capable of?

Anxiety had settled in her stomach like a hard lump, and she couldn't shift it. She was under no illusions about Kovač. He was no stranger to violence, but surely even he must realize the folly of seeking out a lawyer and trying to force him to reveal the location of the shelter where his wife was staying.

She tore off a small corner of her napkin, spat out the piece of meat, and hid it under a lettuce leaf on her plate. Then she checked her phone again.

Everyone's attention was focused on the speaker, who was droning on about his distinguished research and his constant need for funds. A major breakthrough was just around the corner.

Blah blah blah.

She should have sent her apologies, but now she was here, and she couldn't simply stand up and walk out in the middle of the speech. Her dinner companion, Per-Johan Aller, was a lawyer with one of Stockholm's major business-law practices. He was listening with interest. If he knew what was on her mind, he would be horrified.

She glanced at him in his perfectly tailored suit. He'd never sat across the table from criminals with a record as long as his arm, never pleaded for a lenient sentence following a conviction for a brutally violent crime. Presumably he'd never felt the same surge of adrenaline as she had when the jury delivered a not-guilty verdict against all odds, because she'd managed to convince them that there was reasonable doubt.

In his world robberies were carried out through elegantly worded business contracts, where companies were bought and sold regardless of the consequences for employees and suppliers. Per-Johan had never consorted with clients from the underworld; he soiled his hands in different ways.

The professor was still talking. Would he never stop so that she could get out of here?

She couldn't eat another thing. She placed her knife and fork neatly side by side, then took a large gulp of red wine, quickly followed by another. There was nothing she could do, she told herself for the hundredth time. She'd already tried to contact Kovač on the phone, but he wasn't answering. She couldn't text him—what would she say? That he mustn't go anywhere near Herman Wibom?

If anything happened, her message could be used in evidence, and she wasn't prepared to take that risk. Calling Wibom herself was also out of the question. She would have to admit that she was afraid her client might be on the way to see him, that there was a risk he would use violence to get the information he wanted.

She would be thrown out of the Bar Association if it emerged that she'd portrayed her own client as a violent man—Herman Wibom would make sure of it. After her threat of a custody battle, he wasn't exactly kindly disposed toward her; he'd made that clear during their last conversation.

And yet she couldn't clear her head. She'd repeatedly told herself to forget about Kovač, but one disastrous scenario after another played out in her mind.

She couldn't be held responsible for the actions of her client, but . . .

She emptied her wineglass. *There is nothing I can do.* She took out her phone one last time, just in case Kovač had been in touch. Nothing. She felt as if the casing were burning her fingers.

Should she call Wibom and warn him?

Bosnia, May 1993

Selma was lying in bed wide awake, waiting for Zlatko to fall asleep beside her. For once he'd come home sober, which made things more difficult. She'd hoped he would be so drunk that he'd pass out immediately.

As usual.

Blanka and her family were leaving at first light, at about five o'clock. They wanted to get away as early as possible to avoid attracting attention.

Selma had made the most difficult decision of her life.

She was going to take the children and go with them. Deep down she knew that Blanka was right. Their homeland was lost. They would all go under if they stayed in Bosnia. She couldn't let Zlatko's stubbornness condemn them all to death. By the time he woke up, they would be far away.

She had packed a small case with things for the boys, plus just one change of clothes for herself, her jewelry, and a handful of photographs. As much as she could carry with Emir in her arms.

An entire life reduced to a few bits and pieces.

At long last she heard Zlatko's slow, even breathing.

She slid out of bed as quietly as possible. She reached into the pocket of his pants, which were draped over a chair, searching for his wallet. She had almost no money of her own, and had to take whatever was in the house.

Zlatko grunted and turned over. Selma froze; he mustn't wake up.

The seconds passed, stretched into minutes. She couldn't see his face in the darkness, but he sounded as if he was fast asleep. Selma hesitated, then took out the wallet, opened it, and removed the notes it contained.

Her forehead was damp with perspiration. She was about to replace the wallet, when she felt dizzy and had to lean on the chest of drawers for support. Her hand caught the lamp on the end, and it fell to the floor with a crash.

"What the . . . ?" Zlatko reached out and switched on the bedside light. He stared at Selma; she was still holding the wallet.

He sat up, his voice sharp.

"What are you doing?"

CHAPTER 96

Herman was sitting in the library, reading, with a glass of good Cognac beside him. The solitude was restful after a busy day with many phone calls. The first thing he'd done when he got home was switch off his cell and put on some Bach, his favorite composer.

The library was the finest room in his spacious apartment, with walnut shelves from floor to ceiling and a crystal chandelier that spread a warm, pleasant light. Two English leather armchairs by the fireplace created the perfect spot for reading, where Herman could leave the troubles of the day behind and be drawn into another world.

He'd picked out a book in the Stockholm Series by Per-Anders Fogelström. He often returned to Fogelström's work; there was always something new to discover in his account of the city that developed when Stockholm became industrialized at the end of the nineteenth century. The author wrote about the workers who paid the price for the transformation to a modern capital. He described the dirt, the misery, and the unacceptable working conditions. Progress took its toll in the form of human suffering.

The question was whether the city had changed for the better.

Herman put down the book and reached for his glass. He didn't really feel at home in Stockholm these days; it was so different from the place where he had lived ever since he was a child and used to take the tram out to Djurgården to go for a walk with his parents on Sundays.

These days there was construction going on everywhere, with cranes and road closures. Buildings were either being pulled down, or "renovated" beyond recognition. It was ridiculously expensive to buy, and the waiting list for a rental apartment in the inner city was an incomprehensible twenty-seven years.

What did that mean for young people who came to the capital with dreams of a great future but couldn't find anywhere to live?

Herman warmed the crystal balloon in his hands to release the aromas. He prided himself on being something of a connoisseur, well versed in the noble drink and in the various French wine producers. It was an interest he had shared with his late father, who had left behind an impressive cellar.

A flowery bouquet of cinnamon and vanilla with a distinctive oakiness filled his nose as he sipped the XO.

The doorbell rang.

Herman looked at the clock: almost nine thirty. It must be a neighbor.

With a sigh he put down the glass and pushed his feet into his slippers, then stood up and went to the door.

CHAPTER 97

Nora had cuddled up with Julia on the bed and read her a story, then they'd both fallen asleep; it was nine thirty when Nora opened her eyes.

Julia was lying on her back beside her, with her teddy bear tucked under her arm, her breathing slow and even. Her round cheeks were slightly pink, her blond hair spread across the pillow. Nora gently stroked her forehead and adjusted the covers.

Darling Julia.

She had started school back in the fall, and she loved it. The years had sped by since she was born, despite the fact that Nora had done her best to enjoy those childhood years this time around.

It had been different with the boys; she'd always felt exhausted, juggling home and work, with everyone vying for her attention all the time. Then one day they were suddenly grown up, and she wondered where those years had gone.

Adam would be twenty-one in August, and Simon was in high school. Two tall young men at the point of flying the coop. She longed to hug them, tell them they weren't allowed to grow up, but she didn't want to make herself any more embarrassing than she no doubt already was in their eyes.

When they were little, so many people had told her to make the most of their childhood, but back then she hadn't understood how that could possibly work. How could she stop and enjoy it, when she was always so tired? If she had any spare time, she just wanted to sleep. Then came the divorce and so much pain; it was a struggle to get out of bed each day.

Then everything sped up.

Sometimes she wished someone had warned her that the years between the ages of ten and twenty went even faster than the years when they were little, but that this was worse, because it would soon be over for real.

She would look at her boys, almost unable to believe that she'd carried these young men in her belly, that she'd fed and changed them when they were helpless babies.

Julia had given her a second chance. The shock at an unplanned pregnancy had quickly turned to joy. She was determined to savor every moment. She still worked long hours, but was more present in the moment.

She was grateful for her daughter every single day.

The night-light gave a soft pink glow; Julia didn't like the room to be dark.

Nora quietly got to her feet. She needed to spend a few hours on the documents she'd brought home, plus she ought to call Thomas. Jonas was away and wouldn't be back until Friday.

She went into the kitchen. Yesterday's bottle of wine was on the counter, and contained just enough for a well-filled glass, which she took into the living room, along with her laptop.

Chapter 98

Someone started banging on the door before Herman Wibom had even reached the hallway. It wasn't like his neighbors to be so rude. After all these years he knew most of them; there wasn't a high turnover of occupants in the apartment block.

"I'm coming," he muttered. "What's the problem? Where's the fire?"

His foot slid out of one slipper on the parquet flooring, and he had to stop to put it back in.

Someone rattled the handle, and the bell rang again.

A new neighbor had moved into the two-room apartment next to his a few months ago; it must be him. Herman couldn't imagine anyone else behaving like this.

"I'm coming!" he called out. He turned the key and opened the door without bothering to check the peephole.

There was something familiar about the man in front of him, but Herman couldn't quite place him. The ceiling lamp in the stairwell was too weak, and the dark-green marble walls consumed most of the light.

Herman looked inquiringly at his visitor. The man's eyes were shadowed, and it took a few seconds for Herman to see what was lurking within them.

Madness.

"Yes?" he said uncertainly.

The man took a step forward and shoved him backward, then slammed the door behind him. His black hair was wet from the rain, and there were drops of water on the shoulders of his leather jacket.

"What are you doing?" Herman exclaimed.

"Where is she?"

"What?"

"Mina."

Herman reached out to the wall for support when he realized whom he was talking to.

Mina Kovač's husband, Andreis.

He was here, in Herman's home.

His hand instinctively flew to his throat. "You're not supposed to be here," he whispered. "It's inappropriate." He tried to swallow but couldn't. At close quarters, Andreis Kovač was terrifying.

He was tall and well-built, and there was no mistaking the cruel line of his mouth. That was what frightened Herman the most—the brutality streaming toward him.

"Tell me where she is!" Kovač said in a voice that came from far, far away, even though he was so close. Too close.

Herman didn't know where he got the strength to answer as he did. There was a terrible pressure in his chest. "I can't do that."

"Tell me where she is!"

"I can't."

CHAPTER 99

It had gotten late by the time Thomas left work. They'd had a brief final meeting to allocate tasks and plan for the next couple of days. He'd been on the go for twelve hours, sustained by nothing more than a hot dog after his visit to the Economic Crimes Authority.

Elin had fallen asleep long ago by the time he wearily inserted his key in the lock. His mother, Lotta, was already waiting in the hallway; she must have heard the elevator.

"Thanks for helping out," he said. "I'm sorry I'm so late—we've got a lot going on at the moment."

"You look tired."

"I'm fine." The answer came automatically, just like the false smile underlining the message: *Don't worry about me.*

He'd said those same words even when he was at rock bottom. It was just possible to hold it together if he could pretend to himself and those around him that everything was perfectly OK.

As long as no one tried to scratch beneath the surface.

"I think you're doing too much," his mother said. "You're working way too hard. Don't forget you're not so young anymore."

She was seventy-six, his father seventy-seven. Thomas couldn't help smiling—a genuine smile this time.

"There's a plate of beef stroganoff in the microwave for you, if you want it," Lotta added.

"Thank you, that's great." Thomas gave her a grateful kiss on the cheek.

"By the way, Pernilla rang," she said.

"What did she want?" The suspicion was there immediately. He couldn't do anything about the sharpness of his tone as soon as he heard her name.

"Just to say good-night to Elin, I think." The concern was clear in his mother's face. "There's no need to get mad."

"Sorry."

Lotta reached for her coat and scarf, then picked up her purse from the hall table. "You always sound so angry when you talk about Pernilla these days. Can't the two of you try to be friends, for Elin's sake, if nothing else?"

Thomas wasn't in the mood for that particular conversation. "Not now, Mom. It's been a long day."

"Forgive me—I didn't mean to interfere, but it makes me so sad that the two of you don't seem able to talk anymore."

"We do talk." He knew he sounded like a truculent child.

His mother sighed. "Your dad and I have always been very fond of Pernilla."

Thomas wanted to yell: *Me too!* Instead he took off his jacket and placed it carefully on a hanger; he usually threw it over the chair in the hallway. Then he removed his shoes and put them away.

"I'd better get going." Lotta sounded hurt.

Thomas was saved by the phone; the display showed Nora's number. She couldn't have called at a better moment.

"I have to take this," he said apologetically. "Maybe we can discuss my relationship with Pernilla some other time?" They both knew that Thomas would do his utmost to avoid any such discussion. "Love to Dad," he said.

His mother nodded and waved good-bye. He heard the old metal elevator doors screech as she closed them.

"Hi, Nora."

"Sorry to disturb you so late." Nora also sounded tired, but cheerful—as if she'd had a good day at work.

"No problem, I just got home. How was your visit to Runmarö?"

Thomas was hoping to make it over to Harö for the weekend, if the new investigation didn't get in the way.

Or Pernilla.

As Thomas headed for the kitchen with the phone to his ear, Nora told him about what Mina had said. There was indeed a plate of food ready to be reheated in the microwave, and the table had been laid. He shouldn't have snapped at his mother like that; without her help his life would collapse.

He went to check on Elin. She was fast asleep, surrounded by a sea of cuddly toys. He kissed her gently on the cheek.

He sank down on the sofa in the living room, still listening to Nora's account. He moved a small collection of Elin's dolls onto the coffee table—half the apartment looked like a toy store.

"Mina mentioned Andreis's brother, Emir," Nora said. "Apparently he was a thorn in Dino's side—did you know about him?"

Only fourteen hours had passed since Herco's body was found. They'd brought in extra staff, who'd worked intensively all day, but there was still so much to do. It was like doing a jigsaw puzzle the size of the Atlantic; they'd made a start on one corner, nothing more. And most of the pieces were missing.

Thomas got up and fetched a pen. He grabbed the morning paper, which, as usual, he hadn't had time to read, and made a note in the margin: *Check out brother, Emir Kovač, thorn in side.*

It was something at least.

"According to Mina, Emir's worse than his brother—deliberately cruel. She liked Dino, but loathes her brother-in-law," Nora went on.

"Charming family."

"Did you manage to pick up Andreis Kovač?"

"I'm afraid not. A patrol car went to his house, but he didn't seem to be home. His lawyer claims he's sick."

Nora snorted. "I told you she was tricky. Ulrika Grönstedt regards manipulating the legal process as a sport."

"Maybe we ought to speak to Mina instead," Thomas said slowly. "We are going to need to question her."

"OK, but just take it easy. She's very fragile at the moment."

Thomas could hear the sound of Nora's fingertips flying across a keyboard. He pictured her in the apartment in Saltsjöbaden; it was on the top floor of a three-story building, with a fantastic view of the sea. It almost felt like being in the archipelago, yet it was only a twenty-minute drive into town. The Baltic Sea right in front of your eyes, and acres of forest just around the corner. What more could anyone want?

Thomas was suddenly overwhelmed with a longing for Harö.

"Did Mina say anything else of interest?"

"She's given me plenty," Nora said. "I'm going to go through everything with a fine-tooth comb tomorrow, but it should be enough to have Kovač arrested, even if your investigation hasn't quite reached that stage."

"I don't need a particular reason to bring him in."

Nora laughed. "Well, there's nothing wrong with your self-confidence. By the way, you asked me if Kovač is left-handed. The answer is yes."

Chapter 100

Herman backed away. Kovač followed, making sure the distance between them stayed the same.

Herman had never been a brave person. He knew he was no match for a man like Andreis Kovač, but he couldn't tell him where Mina was. If he did so, he would be condemning her to death—he knew that with absolute certainty.

Kovač had crossed a line. His eyes were wild, and he had only one goal: to force Herman to reveal Mina's address so that he could track her down.

Herman's brain had never worked so fast. His mind raced as he tried to weigh his options. His cell phone was in his briefcase. Kovač would be on him before he got anywhere near it. He'd gotten rid of the landline last year, because only the odd cold caller used it.

He could hear his heart pounding in his ears.

He was alone in the apartment with a hardened criminal, a man who had almost beaten his own wife to death. A man who seemed prepared to go to any lengths to punish her for leaving him.

Herman was finding it hard to breathe.

The dim light reinforced the sense of unreality. A large dust bunny lay in one corner; he hadn't noticed it before. The cleaner must have missed it.

The shadows were closing in.

"Tell me where she is!" Kovač yelled yet again. He hadn't shaved and the dark stubble made him look even more menacing.

This isn't happening.

Herman looked for a weapon, anything at all that he could use to defend himself. There were knives in the kitchen; could he get that far?

Kovač seemed to realize what he was thinking. He raised a warning hand. "Otherwise I'm going to have to hurt you," he said.

Herman backed into the library, where he'd been sitting only minutes ago, enjoying his book and his Cognac in peace and quiet.

Everything looked the same. Bach's Fugue in D Minor was playing in the background.

Kovač didn't take his eyes off Herman as he walked over to the CD player and turned the volume up high. The room was filled with loud, dramatic organ music, increasing in intensity as it reached a crescendo. The sound bounced off the walls; Herman could feel the vibrations right through his shaking body. Sweat was dripping from his upper lip, but he didn't dare wipe it away.

He didn't dare do anything at all.

His eyes darted between the three windows and out toward the street. The apartment opposite was in darkness; there was no one home to see that he was in danger. Shouting for help would be pointless— none of the neighbors would hear him above the deafening music.

Kovač was waiting for an answer. He filled the doorway of the library, the light from the hallway forming a blurred halo around his head.

He took a step forward.

Herman stared at him, transfixed. He'd already backed so far into the room that he was right in front of the open fire. His shirt was drenched in sweat, the fabric so wet that it was sticking to the gray mantelpiece.

His glass was on the table where he'd put it down when the doorbell rang.

The room closed in, then receded.

Kovač came closer. "Tell me where she is!"

As if in a dream, Herman reached out, picked up the glass, and, after a second's hesitation, threw it at Kovač with all his strength.

Kovač turned his head, and the glass went sailing past, some distance from its target, and shattered on the floor.

Herman stared at his failed attempt to fight back.

Kovač was smiling in a most peculiar way. He bent down and picked up the stem, which was still intact. It was crowned with sharp edges, the light sparkling on the broken crystal, and it was pointing straight at Herman.

"Please," Herman whispered.

Bach's rich melodies filled his head as Kovač moved toward him.

Thursday

Chapter 101

When Mina woke up at about five o'clock needing to go to the bathroom, she felt as if something was missing. It took her a few seconds to realize what it was. The weight in her chest, the sense of approaching disaster, was gone.

She'd done it. She'd told someone about what Andreis had done to her, shown her photographs to an outsider. She had taken a stand against her husband.

Her heart skipped a beat at the thought. Had she really been so brave, finally dared to stand up for herself and Lukas?

The pictures of her battered body had been her deepest secret. She was so ashamed; it had been impossible to share them with anyone. No one must know what was going on. Now she'd taken irrevocable action.

She slipped into the bathroom, then returned to her bedroom. It was beginning to grow light outside; she caught a glimpse of the gray dawn through the gap at the side of the roller blind. The sun was rising.

She got back into bed and closed her eyes. Anna-Maria had assured her that she'd done the right thing. She would never have to be afraid of Andreis again.

Still the tears came.

It was hard to believe that it was really true, that she was safe, but she felt safer than she'd been for years. She trusted Nora and Leila when they assured her that Andreis couldn't get to her.

Leila wasn't like the other police officers she'd met—tall, well-built men who'd tried to persuade her to testify against Andreis. They'd made no attempt to hide their frustration when she refused to cooperate; sometimes they would roll their eyes and sigh at her explanations for her injuries. One of them had gone so far as to say that she had only herself to blame if she came out with excuses so transparent that anyone could see they were made up.

Leila was different. She was tough, but she was on Mina's side. Anna-Maria had been a huge support, too. Mina would never have imagined that there were so many people who wanted to help her.

She got out of bed and took her blanket over to the armchair by the window. She'd often sat there over the past few days. There was something peaceful about the view of the water; from time to time a boat would pass through the sound, even though it was early in the season. It was easy to picture how beautiful it would be in a month or so, when everything was in bloom. The birch trees were already showing the first tiny leaves, like a mouse's ears, suggesting that spring would be early this year. A few weeks of warmth and the hawthorn would be out. Nothing smelled as sweet as white hawthorn blossom.

Mina curled up and wrapped herself in the blanket. The dawn chorus of birdsong was beginning; it would soon be May, the best month of the year. The light evenings grew longer, and the promise of summer was in the air.

Everything was going to be fine. She would make a fresh start with Lukas.

She wouldn't be afraid anymore.

Chapter 102

The conference room was already pretty full when Thomas walked in, his eyes gritty. Yet another night when he hadn't managed to fall asleep until the early hours. His body felt slow and heavy, and Elin had been especially difficult on the way to school.

It had been a crap morning. He still hadn't spoken to Pernilla, and he knew he ought to call his mother, smooth over yesterday's disagreement.

Aram was sitting beside Staffan Nilsson, and raised a hand in greeting. Most of the extra officers were gathered at the far end of the table. Thomas hardly recognized any of them; since the move to Flemingsberg, everything had grown bigger and more anonymous.

Nothing had improved.

"Late night?" Aram asked as Thomas sat down opposite him.

Was it that obvious? He was about to mumble some excuse when Margit arrived and saved him. She closed the door behind her, balancing a pile of papers and a coffee cup in one hand.

She nodded to Nilsson. "Staffan, can you tell us where we are?"

Nilsson pointed to the photographs of Dino Herco and the location of the shallow grave displayed on the whiteboard. The enlarged shots clearly showed the injuries to his face and wrists. Other pictures had been taken elsewhere in the forest, where a dog team had found signs of a parked car. There were no distinguishing features on the tire tracks, unfortunately. There were thousands of cars with that type of tire.

It was like looking for a needle in a haystack.

"If we start with the victim, he's now with pathology in Solna for the autopsy. They're pretty busy at the moment, so it's likely to be a week or so before we have the results," Nilsson began.

Margit sighed.

"However, I'm pretty sure they'll confirm our own conclusions," Nilsson added.

"Which means?" Margit said.

"That the gunshot was fatal, and that it was delivered by someone beside him or diagonally behind."

There was nothing new about this information. Was it Nilsson's way of dealing with his own frustration over the constant delays at the medical examiner's office and the National Forensics Center? The lack of resources irritated everyone.

"Can you tell us something we don't know?" Margit snapped.

"It's only been twenty-four hours," Nilsson countered. "We have no crime scene, no murder weapon, no bullet." He leaned back and folded his arms. "What do you expect?"

Less than ten minutes, and the atmosphere in the room was already tetchy.

Thomas tried to get his weary brain cells to focus. Maybe they were wrong to suspect Kovač? Herco's death could be an act of revenge from some rival narcotics gang who wanted to take over the territory, making their point to Kovač by taking out his right-hand man.

Then again, Leila had sounded very sure of herself when she said they ought to concentrate on Kovač. As far as she was concerned, there wasn't a shadow of doubt that he was guilty of murdering Herco.

Nilsson was still talking about his conclusions, but Thomas wasn't really listening. Until Margit's voice brought him back to reality.

"Over to you, Thomas."

"Sorry?"

Suddenly everyone was staring at him. Margit frowned and repeated her question. "You were going to liaise with the Economic Crimes Authority. Did you find out anything useful?"

"Absolutely. I spoke to the prosecutor in charge of the case yesterday evening," he said without mentioning Nora's name. Margit already knew she was involved. "The ECA is convinced that Andreis Kovač is behind the murder, given his history and previous relationship with the victim. They describe him as dangerous and ruthless. I've also spoken to Narcotics, who've been keeping an eye on Kovač for a long time, and they share that opinion."

His mind went blank; he couldn't recall anything else that Nora had said on the phone last night, or anything else from Narcotics. Somehow he had to get a full night's sleep, or he wouldn't be able to do his job.

Aram shot him a worried look, and his brain started working again.

"The prosecutor also confirmed that Kovač is left-handed, which fits with the injuries to the victim's face."

Nilsson appeared to be slightly mollified; this backed up his own hypothesis.

Margit made a note. "In that case I think you'd better bring him in for questioning as soon as possible."

"We'll do our best," Aram said quickly, as if he didn't trust Thomas to respond.

Bosnia, May 1993

Zlatko's gaze bored into Selma. She was still standing there, clutching his wallet.

In seconds he was out of bed and by her side. She instinctively cowered, although he hadn't yet raised his fist.

"What are you doing?" he said, his eyes filled with suspicion.

"It . . . it fell out of your pocket," she stammered, trying to come up with a reasonable explanation. "I was just picking it up off the floor." She placed it on the chest of drawers, hiding the notes in her left hand.

"Have you stolen money from me?"

For the first time during their marriage, Selma wished her husband had drunk himself into a stupor. Then she could simply have walked out on him, consoled herself with the knowledge that they had loved each other once, before the war broke out.

Before everything was reduced to ashes.

The tension was unbearable.

"We're leaving first thing in the morning," she sobbed. "We can't stay here any longer. We'll die if we do."

He still didn't understand what she was talking about.

"I'm so sorry," she said, her voice thick with tears. She could hear the desperation in her voice. "I still love you," she whispered, knowing it was true. "But I have to save the children."

Any second now, he would lose control, but she couldn't let him stop her from getting the boys to safety. Even if he beat her half to death, she was determined to make sure that Andreis and Emir grew up in a country free from war and bloody massacres.

The love for her husband remained, in spite of everything that had happened between them over the past year, but nothing was stronger than her love for her children.

"We're going with Blanka and Dario. She says it's possible to drive to Hungary via Croatia. We're aiming for Sweden; they'll accept us."

Zlatko's expression changed. The anger and bitterness that had tainted their relationship for so long disappeared. He pulled her close and held her.

Selma didn't know what to think. Could she allow herself to relax in his arms?

"In that case I'll come with you," he murmured, stroking her hair. It had begun to turn silver at the temples in recent months. "You were right all along. I was just too stubborn to see it."

Selma couldn't quite believe what she was hearing, but at last she was weeping tears of joy, not sorrow.

"I'm not losing my family," Zlatko went on, hugging her tightly. "We'll all go, at first light. Families stick together."

CHAPTER 103

Ulrika had found it impossible to concentrate all morning, even though she had a great deal of preparation to do for the afternoon's trial. Her client was accused of stealing goods in transit, and had already been remanded in custody for quite some time. He was also teetering on the brink of depression.

In a couple of hours she would have to get in the car and drive to the courthouse. Before then she needed to polish her opening address, and check a few legal details. Nico was going with her.

There was a knock on the door.

"Yes?"

Nico came in clutching a pile of documents—presumably the cases she'd asked him to dig out at short notice.

"I just wondered—what time are we leaving?" he said.

"Twelve fifteen." Ulrika gave him a look. "Don't you have a calendar where you can keep track of your appointments?"

"Yes, sorry." He placed the papers on her desk, then turned away.

"Close the door behind you," she called after him. She knew she sounded disproportionately annoyed, but her nerves were as taut as violin strings. Kovač still hadn't been in touch, although she'd left even more voice mail messages.

She'd also tried Herman Wibom, but he wasn't answering his cell phone. She was reluctant to contact his secretary; she didn't want to arouse suspicions unnecessarily.

When her office phone rang, she grabbed the receiver with such force that the whole thing nearly fell on the floor.

It was her dishwasher repairman. He couldn't make it today— would next week be OK?

Ulrika put down the receiver, then took a swipe at the documents Nico had brought, scattering them in all directions like oversized snowflakes.

Shit!

One last sheet of paper drifted down onto the carpet.

Where the hell was Kovač?

She picked up her cell phone and called his number one last time.

"Hello?" a voice mumbled. Ulrika couldn't determine whether she'd woken him, or he was drunk.

"Didn't you get my messages?"

"I'm sleeping. I can't talk to you right now."

The call ended, leaving Ulrika staring in disbelief at her phone. Who the fuck did he think he was? She sent a message:

Call me!!!

Three exclamation marks to underline the urgency of the situation. He would no doubt ignore that as well, just as he ignored anything he didn't regard as important.

She couldn't settle; the restlessness was eating her up.

She called Herman Wibom yet again, listened to the signals ringing out until voice mail took over. She didn't leave a message. She took several deep breaths, then looked up the number of his practice.

His secretary answered. Ulrika recognized her voice; she had a good memory when it came to people.

She didn't bother introducing herself. "I need to speak to Herman Wibom."

"Who's calling?"

Ulrika hesitated. No one could dispute the fact that she had a legitimate reason for contacting Wibom. She was representing Andreis Kovač; she could always claim that he wanted to know how his son was.

"Ulrika Grönstedt. I'm an attorney," she said reluctantly.

There was a brief pause. Ulrika held her breath. She was still hoping to be put through to Wibom, in which case her fears would prove to be unfounded.

"I'm afraid he's not here," the secretary said.

"When will he be in?"

"I don't actually know. I haven't heard from him this morning."

Chapter 104

The sky was overcast, but the day was pleasantly warm. Mina decided to take Lukas out for some fresh air.

She settled him in his stroller and set out along the road. Anna-Maria had mentioned Solberga farm, a family-run business in the south of the island. They grew crops and farmed sheep, and apparently there was a really nice store. Maybe she could find a soft sheepskin blanket for Lukas's stroller.

He fell asleep after only ten minutes.

She still had that secure feeling from earlier this morning, a kind of warmth in her heart. It was a long time since she'd felt that way.

She was almost happy.

It was good to get out. Her ribs didn't hurt so much anymore, and with a little makeup, she looked perfectly normal. She missed the opportunity to exercise; maybe she could ask someone at the shelter to watch Lukas tomorrow morning so that she could go for a run?

She passed the bridge leading to Storö and continued beside the narrow channel between the islands. There wasn't a soul in sight, but she didn't mind. In fact she appreciated the peace and quiet. Several new women had arrived at the shelter over the past couple of days, and there were people everywhere.

Her phone rang just as the road curved away from the water. Mina accepted the call without checking who it was. Her heart began to pound. How could she be so stupid? She stared in horror at the display, then realized there was no need to be afraid.

It wasn't Andreis calling to hassle her; it was her father.

"Hi, Dad," she said cheerfully. "How's Mom?"

"Darling Mina." His voice broke, and she could hear what sounded like sobs.

"Dad?"

His distress turned her blood to ice.

"What's happened, Dad?"

"It's Mom."

"What do you mean 'It's Mom'?"

"She . . . she's not with us anymore."

"I don't understand."

"Mom passed away an hour ago."

Mina swayed. It couldn't be true. She was having a nightmare, just like the other day. She was asleep in her bed; she would wake up in a minute, and everything would be back to normal.

Like this morning, when she'd almost felt happy.

"Sweetheart, I'm so sorry."

Her father's voice penetrated Mina's consciousness. She let go of the stroller and doubled over. The phone slipped from her grasp and fell to the ground.

No, no, no.

She was violently sick, right in the middle of the road. From a great distance she heard her father calling out her name.

"Mina? Mina! Hello? Are you still there?"

She vomited until there was nothing left in her stomach. In the end she was bringing up clear phlegm that hurt her throat.

"Mina? Mina?"

Slowly she began to breathe. She picked up the phone, leaned on the handle of the stroller for support, and managed to straighten up.

How could anything hurt so much?

"Sorry," she whispered eventually. "I dropped my phone." Her hands were shaking so much that she could hardly hold the phone to her ear. She forced her voice to obey. "What happened?"

"Her condition deteriorated during the night. I thought they were going to be able to save her. She got worse the other day, too, but they stabilized her. She . . . she just stopped breathing."

Mina couldn't speak.

"There was nothing they could do. They tried, but it was too late. She'd had a cardiac arrest, and her heart was too weak."

He let out a sob.

"She passed away at twenty to nine this morning. I've been sitting with her ever since. I couldn't just get up and walk away, so I sat beside her and held her hand until they came for her."

Mina stared at the remains of her breakfast in the dusty gravel. It stank, and something pink and half digested, with little lumps in it, had splashed onto one of her boots.

Bright green blades of grass were sticking up in the middle of the disgusting slop.

Tears poured down her cheeks.

"She looked so peaceful lying there," her father went on. "I think she murmured your name before she . . . fell asleep. She was thinking of you right to the end. Always remember that."

Mina couldn't take it in. Her mother would never give her another hug or a reassuring pat on the cheek, never hold Lukas in her arms.

She was sweating and shivering at the same time.

"She loved you so much, Mina." Dad's breathing was uneven. "She wasn't in pain. The staff assured me of that; she didn't suffer."

Guilt sucked all the air out of her lungs.

This was all her fault.

If she hadn't gotten together with Andreis, none of this would have happened. He wouldn't have gone to her parents' house and threatened them. If she hadn't married Andreis, her mother would still be alive.

Mina turned the stroller around and set off back the way she'd come, when everything was fine.

Nothing would ever be fine again.

"I'm coming to the hospital," she said. "I have to see her one last time."

"You can't do that."

Her father had told her not to come before, and she'd listened to him. Now Mom was dead, and she hadn't said good-bye. She couldn't stay here on the island; he had to understand that. "I need to see her."

"Please, Mina—do this one thing for me." He was crying now. "I can't lose you as well. Promise me you'll stay where you are. I'll come to you instead, when everything's taken care of here. I'll come as soon as I can—tomorrow at the latest."

Mina gave in. "OK," she whispered.

"I'll see you very soon, darling girl. Where are you?"

"I'm at a shelter called Freya's Haven on Runmarö—directly opposite Stavsnäs."

CHAPTER 105

Nora's shoulders were stiff after several hours at her computer. However, it had been well worth it; she'd gone through picture after picture from Mina's secret email account, analyzing the information and its legal significance.

This evidence had changed the situation instantly. It was more than she'd dared hope for. Kovač had long since crossed the line when it came to assault, but now he could be charged with gross violation of a woman's integrity.

The maximum sentence was six years.

She could have him arrested and remanded in custody on the basis of this material. She also intended to share it with Thomas to bolster his investigation into Kovač.

It was time for her meeting with Herman Wibom. He'd asked to see her at one o'clock; it was now ten past, and there had been no call from reception to say he'd arrived. Surely he would have gotten in touch if he'd been delayed? He'd already told her he was filing for a no-contact order against Mina's husband, and Nora was more than happy to cooperate.

Where was he? She couldn't sit around waiting for him all day. She had another meeting with auditors working on a different case at two o'clock.

She called his cell phone, but there was no answer. She hesitated, then googled the number of his law firm.

A woman answered almost right away, and Nora introduced herself as a prosecutor with the Economic Crimes Authority. "Do you happen to know if Herman's on his way here? We were supposed to have a meeting fifteen minutes ago."

"To be honest, I don't know where he is," replied Wibom's secretary, Gunilla something or other.

"You don't?"

"It's very unlike him not to get in touch."

Something in her voice made Nora react. "What do you mean?"

"He hasn't come in at all today, even though we have a great deal to do. He actually worked late last night, which doesn't happen very often these days." She gave a nervous laugh.

"So you haven't spoken to him today?"

"No."

"Have you called his cell phone?"

"Yes, but there's no answer."

Nora stood up and stretched in order to get her circulation going. "I've also tried his cell, but without success," she said, rotating her neck to extend the muscles. When she touched her shoulders, it felt as if there were hard knots beneath the skin. She would have to start exercising more; otherwise she was going to have problems.

"Do you think something might have happened?" Gunilla said. She sounded as if she had been thinking along those lines, but hadn't dared admit it to herself until Nora called. "What if Herman's fallen, or been taken ill? He lives alone, as you perhaps know."

Nora had had no idea about Herman Wibom's marital status, but wasn't particularly surprised. He had all the signs of being a confirmed bachelor. "Is there anyone who could go and see if he's OK?" she said. "Just to be on the safe side?"

"I don't know who else has a key to his apartment."

"Maybe a neighbor?"

Gunilla suddenly sounded resolute. "I'll go over there when I've finished for the day. He lives in Vasastan—it's not far from the office."

"Good idea. I'd appreciate it if you'd give me a call when you've spoken to him."

CHAPTER 106

Freya's Haven was very quiet when Mina arrived back. At first she wondered where everyone was, then she remembered that Anna-Maria had mentioned a day trip to Sandhamn earlier in the week. Mina had said no, but it seemed as if all the others had gone.

She parked the stroller and picked up Lukas. When she heard his contented gurgles, the emotion hit her again. Mom would never hear his first words, never watch him take his first steps. Mina would never see her again.

The door of Anna-Maria's office was ajar. When Mina walked past and saw her sitting at the desk, she couldn't hold back the tears. Her face crumpled.

Anna-Maria stood up and hurried over to her. Gently she took Lukas and led Mina to the sofa in the living room. "Sweetheart, what's wrong?"

"Mom," Mina whispered.

Anna-Maria started to take off Lukas's dark-blue zip-suit. His face was already bright red, and he was waving his little hands around. He soon settled when the outer garment was removed. "Tell me what's happened."

"Dad called . . . ," Mina began. She couldn't finish the sentence.

Anna-Maria put Lukas down in the corner of the sofa so that he could lie there safely without falling off.

"Mom died," Mina managed eventually. She was sobbing so hard that her whole body was shaking. "She died this morning, in the hospital. Dad was with her, but I wasn't there."

"I'm so very sorry, Mina."

"I wasn't there," Mina said again. "She died without my being there. I didn't get to say good-bye."

Anna-Maria put an arm around her shoulders and hugged her gently. She, too, had tears in her eyes. "You couldn't help that."

"You don't understand. It's my fault that she's dead." Andreis had done this to her parents. To her. She hated him. "I can't do this anymore. I'm done."

She rested her head on her knees and closed her eyes. Not even childbirth had been this painful.

Anna-Maria held her and let her cry. Mina's face was wet with tears and snot when she finally straightened up.

"You'll feel better in a while," Anna-Maria reassured her quietly. "I know that's hard to believe right now, when it's all so fresh, but I promise you won't always feel this bad." She held out a wad of the tissues she always seemed to carry around with her, and Mina wiped her face. "Why don't you go and lie down?"

"I have to go to Dad. He needs me."

"Would he really want you to do that?"

Mina looked down at the floor.

"It's way too dangerous for you to leave Runmarö at the moment," Anna-Maria went on. "And I'm sure he realizes that."

"He told me to stay here," Mina admitted. A sudden exhaustion came over her; she could hardly hold up her head. Her neck felt weak and thin, her eyelids as heavy as lead. She was so cold that her teeth were chattering.

"You're in shock," Anna-Maria said in a tone that brooked no disagreement. "You need to rest for a while."

"I have to take care of Lukas."

Anna-Maria got to her feet and picked up Lukas, then held out her hand to Mina. "Let's get you to bed. Lukas can stay with me in the office; he'll be fine."

Mina stood up and followed her like a robot. She climbed into bed, and Anna-Maria tucked her in with an extra blanket. "Try to get some sleep."

"Thank you," Mina murmured, her eyes already closed.

"None of this is your fault," Anna-Maria said quietly before she left the room. "You mustn't blame yourself for your mom's death."

Mina knew she was wrong.

CHAPTER 107

It was three thirty by the time Nora got back to her office. The meeting with the auditors had dragged on, then she'd spent some time with Leila, going through the new criteria for Kovač's arrest. If they could be sure that Mina wasn't about to change her mind again, she was prepared to have him picked up this evening.

She decided to speak to Thomas, assess the situation. "How's it going?"

"Not great—we can't find Kovač. We'll have to put out a call for him soon."

"We need to liaise on that—I'm thinking of issuing a warrant for his arrest." Nora filled Thomas in on the latest developments.

"He's a popular guy."

Thomas's ironic comment fell flat. He sounded so tired; Nora wished there was an easy way to make him feel better—a pill, a button to press, a witch's brew to put everything right. He'd been with Pernilla for so many years. Why was it always the people you loved best who hurt you the most?

"I really need to talk to Mina," Thomas went on. "The information Leila sent over is very useful, but I have a few questions I'd like to ask Mina myself, face to face."

Nora kicked off her shoes under the desk. She would also like to see Mina one more time before making her final decision on Kovač. Depriving someone of their freedom was no small matter, and she still didn't entirely trust Mina to keep her promise and testify against her husband.

"Why don't we go over there together?" she suggested. "How urgent is it?"

"I'd like to see her today."

Nora glanced at her watch; she had no more meetings. "We can go right away if you like. I'll be ready to leave in fifteen minutes. Actually, how about this: we'll go over to Runmarö together and talk to Mina, then we can have dinner and catch up."

The therapist Jonas had mentioned was in the back of her mind. If she brought the subject up on the phone, she knew exactly how Thomas would react. He would dismiss the idea immediately, without giving her a chance to put across her point of view. Over dinner she might be able to persuade him to give it a try.

Before it was too late.

"We could even go over to Sandhamn and eat at the inn," she added. "An evening in the archipelago would do you good. You're welcome to stay with us."

He might lower his guard in the archipelago; Thomas always felt better when he was by the sea.

"That's kind of you, but I don't have time."

"Steak with Béarnaise sauce and fries," she cajoled. "You'll be twice as efficient tomorrow. We'll catch the first boat back. I need to be in the office bright and early."

"I don't know . . ."

"Is Elin still with you?"

"No. Pernilla's picking her up today, because she came to me early last weekend."

"There you go then. There's something else I want to talk to you about, but not on the phone."

Thomas capitulated. "My boat is in Stavsnäs. I'll meet you there at five thirty, then we'll go over to Runmarö, see Mina, then on to Sandhamn."

Nora nodded with satisfaction. "Good decision. See you in Stavsnäs."

CHAPTER 108

Mina woke to find Anna-Maria by her bed with Lukas in her arms.

"What time is it?"

"Five o'clock. How are you feeling?"

Mina was so groggy that she didn't know what to say. Then the realization hit her with full force.

Mom was dead.

Why did Anna-Maria have to wake her? Why couldn't she just go on sleeping?

"I need to pick up a few things from the store," Anna-Maria said. "Could you take care of Lukas for a while? He's had something to eat; he'll probably fall asleep soon."

Mina nodded weakly.

"I've spoken to your father," Anna-Maria continued with a sad smile. "He called a little while ago, and I promised him you wouldn't leave Runmarö. You're much safer here than anywhere else."

Another nod.

"He's going to try and come over tomorrow. The others should be back from Sandhamn at around seven, but I'll be here long before then."

She carried Lukas over to his crib and gently laid him down. His contented babbling reminded Mina why she had to make the effort and sit up.

Chapter 109

Nora was on the subway. She had to change at Slussen, then continue to Stavsnäs. She was so pleased she'd managed to persuade Thomas to have dinner on Sandhamn, even if she was meddling with his relationship more than she should. She couldn't just stand there and say nothing when he was clearly unhappy.

The way he spoke about Pernilla showed that his feelings hadn't changed; there was just too much crap in the way.

Nora had been devastated after her divorce. If there was any way of saving Thomas's marriage, it was worth a shot. Adam and his girlfriend had agreed to watch Julia overnight in return for a pizza of their choice.

Her phone rang; it was Herman Wibom's secretary.

"How did it go?" Nora asked. "Did you get a hold of Herman?"

"No. I went to his apartment and rang the bell, but there was no answer." Gunilla sounded out of breath. "I looked through the letter box, but I couldn't see anything. I called out his name, but he didn't come."

"Does he have any relatives you could contact?"

"He has a sister in Karlskoga. I've already called her, and she hasn't heard from him."

It would soon be twenty-four hours since anyone had spoken to Herman Wibom.

"I don't like this," Gunilla went on. "By the way, you're not the only one who's wondering where he is."

"Oh?"

"Ulrika Grönstedt has called several times."

Nora had a bad feeling. Of course Grönstedt could have a perfectly legitimate reason for wanting to contact Wibom, but too many factors just didn't fit.

Herman Wibom never missed a meeting, nor did he fail to answer his phone.

"Where are you now?" she asked.

"At the office."

"Do you think you could go back to Herman's apartment if I send a police officer over there? Her name is Leila Kacim."

"Absolutely."

"I'll ask her to go right away."

CHAPTER 110

The turn-of-the-century apartment building on Roslagsgatan was nowhere near as opulent as the elegant architecture in Östermalm dating from the same period, but the high ceiling in the foyer was equally impressive when Leila walked in.

She ran up the stairs to the third floor. A woman in her early sixties was waiting by one of the doors; this must be Gunilla, Wibom's secretary. She was wearing a pale camel-hair coat.

"Leila?" she said immediately, her voice shrill with nervous tension. Leila held out her hand and smiled reassuringly. "I keep ringing the bell, but there's no answer," Gunilla said, pointing to the door behind her. A small brass plaque above the letter box bore the name "H. Wibom."

"Have you checked with the neighbors to see if anyone has a key to the apartment?"

Gunilla tightened her grip on her purse. "No, sorry, I didn't think of that."

There were three apartments on each floor; Wibom's was closest to the elevator. Leila rang the bell of his next-door neighbor, but it soon became clear that no one was home. She moved on, and after a moment a sleepy voice called out: "I'm coming."

The door opened to reveal a young man in jeans and a T-shirt. His light-brown hair was tousled; he must have been having an afternoon nap. Leila showed her ID, explained why she was there, and asked if he had a spare key to Wibom's apartment.

"I'm afraid not," said the young man, who'd introduced himself as Dagge. "I haven't lived here very long—only since the start of the autumn semester. It's a sublet."

"Do you happen to remember when you last saw your neighbor?"

Dagge shrugged. "I'm not sure. We keep different hours. I'm studying biology at the university, so I often work late, and if I don't have lectures in the mornings, I sleep in." He yawned and scratched the back of his neck. "Sorry, I was up late last night."

Leila considered her next question. If the guy was sometimes home during the day, he might have noticed if anything unusual had gone on in Wibom's apartment. "Is there anything that's struck you lately? Anything out of the ordinary?"

Dagge shook his head as if he didn't really understand the question.

"Strangers on the stairs? Weird noises from your neighbor's apartment?"

"No . . . actually, yes."

Leila waited for him to go on, her nerves on edge.

"Last night . . . he was playing his music really loud."

"And that's unusual?"

"He's so considerate. I've never heard a sound before, to be honest, but this was deafening."

"What kind of music was it?"

"I've no idea." Dagge spread his hands apologetically. "It was kind of old fashioned, like church music."

Gunilla inhaled sharply. "Could it have been an organ? Herman likes to listen to Bach's fugues." Suddenly she was overcome with embarrassment at having interrupted. "Sorry, I just meant . . . he must have been at home then."

"What time did you hear the music?" Leila asked.

"Around ten o'clock, maybe. I'm not sure." He leaned against the doorframe, and Leila was able to see into his apartment. It didn't look as if cleaning was high on his list of priorities. Dirty clothes were strewn across the floor, and there was a faint smell of stale cigarette smoke. The bedroom wall adjoined Wibom's place.

"What did you do when the loud music started?"

Once again, Dagge didn't seem to understand the question. "Nothing, really. I was studying, so I put my earbuds in and turned up my own music. It wasn't that bad."

"Do you know when the music stopped?"

"Sorry, no. I've got an exam soon; I was concentrating on my work."

"When did you go to bed?"

"After one, maybe?"

"Was the music still playing then?"

"I don't think so—I guess he'd turned it off."

"And you didn't hear anything else?"

"No."

"All night?"

"No."

Only now did he begin to realize that there was a problem.

"Has something happened to Herman? I hope he's OK," he said.

"We can't get a hold of him," Gunilla replied, pushing her hands deep in her coat pockets. "He's not answering his phone, and he didn't come into work today. That's not like him at all."

Leila took a closer look at the door to Wibom's apartment. There was no sign of forced entry. Everything appeared to be normal.

Except that Herman Wibom had gone up in smoke.

The logical approach would be to wait for twenty-four hours, which was the accepted time frame before a person was officially regarded as missing. If Wibom had been playing Bach last night, then only nineteen hours had passed since there had been any sign of life from him. Maybe he was on his way home from a wild party, with a killer hangover and a cell phone that needed charging.

Which didn't fit with his personality at all.

A small mark on the marble floor outside Wibom's door caught Leila's attention. She bent down and peered at it.

Dark brown—the color of dried blood.

Something wasn't right.

She took out her phone and called the locksmith they used in an emergency.

Bosnia, May 1993

Selma couldn't sleep. She lay there wide awake with her mind racing, fear and anxiety building a nest in her breast. The darkness was too compact; in the end she switched on the night-light to keep the demons away.

Shortly after four, she gave up and got dressed.

The first light of dawn crept into the house as she walked around saying good-bye to her beloved home. She ran her fingertips over the back of the sofa, the piece of furniture she had coveted and saved for. She touched the mats her mother had crocheted, the little porcelain figurine she'd inherited from her grandmother. She'd taken such good care of it, made sure the children didn't break it.

Finally she went into the kitchen and looked through the window. The garden was a riot of color. Was there any other country where the plants were so lush, where the roses were so beautiful, so perfect?

Selma blinked away the tears.

Maybe another family would move in and tend her lovely flowers. She would like to think so, but she knew there was a good chance that the place would be shelled and destroyed in a firestorm.

She fetched her keys and put them on the table. There was no point in taking them with her, or locking the door behind her.

She would never see her home again.

With a heart so full of despair she thought it might burst, she opened one cupboard after another, trying to imprint every single thing on her memory.

She must remember what it looked like; there was nothing else she could take with her.

Then she went and woke Andreis. He whined and refused to get up. She had to dress him while he was half asleep, and as soon as she'd finished, he rolled over and closed his eyes. She made a few sandwiches with what she had, then changed Emir's diaper for the last time before leaving.

The only positive thing was that Zlatko was going with them.

All the bitterness, all the anger that had built up over the past year had dispersed like veils of mist over the meadow early on a summer's morning.

Zlatko came into the kitchen and stroked her cheek. Selma looked out and saw Blanka's car approaching.

Was it possible to die of sorrow?

Zlatko picked up Andreis and their bag and walked out of the door. Selma followed with Emir in her arms.

CHAPTER 111

It usually took about fifteen minutes to walk to the store. Anna-Maria was reluctant to leave Mina right now, but Lukas's formula was running out and wouldn't last the night. It was better for Anna-Maria to deal with it than for Mina to realize later in the evening.

She felt so sorry for the girl. This morning there had been color in her cheeks and a spring in her step for the first time, and now she was in an even worse state than she'd been when she arrived, floored by grief.

Anna-Maria had long ago stopped believing in a benevolent higher power, but surely there ought to be some form of justice. Mina had already gone through so much; when would it end?

Why couldn't God strike down Mina's husband instead, before he caused even more trouble? Why was he allowed to live and do whatever he pleased, while Mina had to hide away, and her mother was dead?

There was no one around. Anna-Maria pushed her hands into her pockets and realized she'd left her phone charging in the office. It didn't matter; she wouldn't be gone for long.

The gravel on the narrow lane crunched beneath her feet. It was nice to get some fresh air, escape from the misery within the walls of the shelter. Mina's troubles had brought back her own terrible memories.

A little hare bounded in front of her and disappeared toward the field, where the sheep had been let out to graze.

Anna-Maria angrily dashed away the tears. The pain of losing Malin never eased, no matter how many years passed. The day she took the call from the emergency department was forever etched on her mind, like a fresh tattoo on sensitive skin that refused to heal. The invisible burden of agony.

She had hurried to the hospital and raced through the corridors, searching for her daughter, calling out her name and flinging open doors, finding only other sick and injured patients.

Eventually someone had shown her where to go.

She had hardly recognized her daughter's bruised and battered face. This time Gustav had gone too far—he'd used a hammer. The injuries to Malin's body bore witness to such rage that Anna-Maria couldn't take it in. It was an evil too great to comprehend.

How could one human being do this to another?

She was worried about the baby, concerned that the unborn child might have been harmed by the attack on Malin. She could never have imagined that things would get worse—that it would prove impossible to save the baby or Malin.

That they would both die that night.

Afterward she had sat alone with her despair. The nurses had lit a candle and folded Malin's shattered hands over her breast. The hands with which she had tried to protect her belly.

In the semidarkness Anna-Maria could almost convince herself that her daughter was sleeping. For the first time in many years, Malin's face had been peaceful. The fear had finally gone.

In death there was no need to be afraid.

The solitary flame had flickered through the night. The hours had passed; the candle had burned out. Eventually a nurse had whispered that Anna-Maria had to leave, Malin was to be taken to the mortuary.

It was time to say good-bye.

Anna-Maria increased her speed, marching along, the dust whirling up around her feet. The sun had disappeared behind lead-gray clouds; it was going to rain.

Mina would not suffer the same fate as Malin. Anna-Maria had no intention of allowing that to happen. Maybe there was a higher purpose behind Mina's arrival at Freya's Haven rather than another shelter? Maybe Anna-Maria had been given the chance to save another young woman, as she'd been unable to protect her own daughter?

The future of Freya's Haven might be uncertain, but she was determined to make sure that Mina had a new life.

As the lane curved, she saw a broad-shouldered man approaching from the opposite direction. He was wearing a black leather jacket, and his dark hair was slicked back.

Anna-Maria didn't recognize him, but he didn't belong on Runmarö; his clothing was all wrong. Almost three hundred people lived on the island, and she usually met familiar faces on her way to the store, which was only a few hundred yards away now.

She sensed danger instinctively, even though it was broad daylight and she knew there were people not far away. He was striding along purposefully.

The hairs on Anna-Maria's arms stood on end as he came straight toward her.

CHAPTER 112

"There you go."

The locksmith stepped aside. Leila pushed down the handle, and the door of Herman Wibom's apartment swung open. The hallway was in darkness, and she couldn't hear a sound apart from Gunilla breathing heavily behind her.

Leila glanced around.

She could see a corridor with dark wallpaper leading to the dining room and presumably the living room. There was a closed door—a bedroom? The farthest room was the one that adjoined the neighboring apartment; that was where the music had come from.

"Hello? Anyone home?"

A worn leather briefcase was propped up against the wall. If Wibom had left for the office, it shouldn't be here. Another sign that he was in the apartment. She waited a few seconds.

"Hello?"

A Persian runner in shades of blue lay on the floor of the corridor. Leila recognized the design from her childhood home. It was an elegant Nain rug patterned with ornate flowers, their stems intertwined. Her father had been very fond of that particular style.

Several irregular reddish-brown stains marred its beauty. The distance between them suggested that someone had walked to the door with something unpleasant on the soles of their shoes.

Someone who'd been in a hurry.

The locksmith was leaving; the sound of his footsteps echoed in the stairwell, then the outside door slammed shut.

Silence.

Leila knew she ought to call for backup, but instead she drew her gun. "Stay here," she said to Gunilla.

The adrenaline was pumping as she edged forward, holding the gun in front of her.

She checked the kitchen. Wibom wasn't there. She stopped outside the bedroom, took a deep breath. Then she flung the door open in a single movement with her left hand, not knowing what she might find.

A neatly made up bed stared back at her. Herman Wibom hadn't slept there last night.

Which left only one more room.

Chapter 113

The man was only fifty yards away when Anna-Maria recognized him. Andreis Kovač.

The deep-set brown eyes, the broad mouth with well-formed lips—it couldn't be anyone else. He'd found out where Mina was hiding.

How the hell had that happened?

She reached into her pocket for the phone that should have been there, remembering too late that it was out of reach in her office. She had no way of calling for help or warning Mina.

What was she going to do? She stopped dead. He was only a couple of yards away now. She stared at him, and fear took over.

"Oh my God!" she gasped. As soon as the words left her lips, she saw her mistake. He would realize that she knew who he was. And where Mina was hiding.

What had she done?

Kovač strode right up to her and grabbed her by the wrist, twisting the skin so that she cried out in pain. "I want to see Mina," he said. "Take me to her."

A flash of insight. He had no idea where Freya's Haven was. There were no street names on Runmarö, just one red-painted wooden building after another. They all looked the same to anyone who was visiting the island for the first time.

This could be Mina's salvation.

As long as Anna-Maria could hold out.

She looked around; there still wasn't a soul in sight. On one side of the lane a flock of sheep were grazing contentedly, on the other lay the forest, dense and inhospitable.

No one would hear her scream.

Kovač twisted her wrist a little more; Anna-Maria thought she was going to faint.

"Where is she?"

The underlying aggression frightened her more than anything. Suddenly she understood why Mina was so afraid. Her own daughter must have felt the same. The thought gave her strength. She couldn't allow him to get to Mina.

"I'll call the police if you don't let me go," she managed to say. She had to keep quiet for Mina's sake. For Malin's sake.

Kovač smiled, exposing even white teeth, as if she'd said something amusing. Then his eyes narrowed. His wedding ring glinted. "Tell me where she is."

"No—let me go!"

"I don't care what I have to do to find out where Mina is—don't you understand that?" He sounded terrifyingly normal. He altered his grip on her hand and bent her little finger back at a dangerous angle. "Where is she?"

The pain was unbelievable. Anna-Maria dropped to her knees as tears sprang to her eyes. "Please, no," she gasped. She heard herself scream as the finger snapped like a chicken bone.

"Where is she?"

Anna-Maria shook her head.

Kovač produced a knife and brought it close to her face. She felt the touch of cold metal; he slowly stroked the blade over her skin from temple to chin. "Tell me where she is or I'll cut you."

"No," Anna-Maria sobbed. "I can't."

Chapter 114

Leila hesitated outside the last closed door in Herman Wibom's apartment. Her mouth went dry when she saw another dark-red stain. Slowly she pushed the door open.

The sun wouldn't set for a few hours, but the room was gloomy. It faced northeast, and the building opposite took most of the light. The dark furniture and crowded bookshelves reinforced the impression of a cave.

There were two wing-backed leather armchairs by the fireplace.

Leila took a step forward, her feet crunching on broken glass on the floor. It took her a second or two to register the leg sticking out from behind one of the armchairs. She moved closer.

Herman Wibom was lying on his back with his eyes closed, his face battered. Blood had run down onto the parquet flooring, discoloring the herringbone pattern. Both palms were badly cut, as if he'd tried to defend himself against his attacker with his bare hands.

Was he still alive?

Leila slipped her gun back in its holster and knelt down beside Wibom's unconscious body. His face was deathly white; she couldn't tell if he was breathing. She placed two fingers on the side of his neck, checking for a pulse.

"Oh God!" she heard from the doorway. Gunilla was standing there, eyes wide with horror. "Is he dead?"

At that moment Leila felt the faintest beat beneath her fingertips. "Call an ambulance!" she shouted. "He's still alive!"

Suddenly Wibom opened his eyes. The whites were bloodshot. He tried desperately to say something; his lips moved, but nothing came out. He groaned.

"What are you trying to say?" Leila leaned closer and put her ear to his mouth.

"He was here," Wibom mumbled eventually.

"Who was here?"

"Mina's husband . . . knows where she is."

He tried to raise his hand, but his eyes rolled back in his head and he lost consciousness.

CHAPTER 115

Thomas left his car in the parking lot at Stavsnäs and headed for the small marina where he usually moored his boat when he went into town. He looked around for Nora. He was a few minutes early, so maybe she hadn't arrived yet. The Vaxholm ferry was still at the main quay, waiting for the bus from Slussen.

He continued toward the Buster. The sky was overcast; he hoped it wouldn't start raining before they reached Runmarö.

At that moment the bus pulled in. Thomas saw Nora as soon as the double doors opened. Most of the passengers made their way toward the ferry, weighed down with shopping bags. It must be the last trip of the day.

Nora waved to him, but stopped when her cell phone rang. She fished it out of her purse and answered it. Her face changed immediately; shock and horror were written all over it. She broke into a run. "Kovač has found out where Mina is!" she shouted. "We have to go!"

Thomas moored the Buster in Styrsvik as quickly as he could. Every second counted, bearing in mind what Kovač had done to Herman

Wibom. Nora had tried to contact Anna-Maria during the short crossing, but there was no answer.

Mina's phone was switched off.

Even if they used a helicopter, backup wouldn't get there in time.

Nora's face was white as she slipped her phone into her purse and jumped ashore before Thomas had tied the last knot.

Dusk was falling, rain hung in the air, and the water was the color of lead.

Nora had a head start, but Thomas soon caught up with her. They ran past the store and around a corner. A small group of people had gathered in the middle of the lane.

A car with the driver's door open and the engine running was parked behind the group.

Someone was lying on the ground.

Thomas felt a surge of adrenaline. He increased his speed, even though he knew Nora wouldn't be able to keep up.

"I'm a police officer," he shouted when he was about fifteen yards away. "What's happened?"

A young man in blue dungarees turned toward him, looking horrified. "She was just lying there," he stammered. "I think I might have hit her, but it was an accident. I couldn't avoid her." He broke off and swayed where he stood. "She's covered in blood, and there's something wrong with her hand . . ."

No one else spoke, but people stepped aside to let Thomas through.

An unconscious woman was lying on her back. She had a slash wound to one cheek, and the blood had run down her chin. Two of the fingers on her right hand were sticking out at an impossible angle. They were broken in a way that couldn't possibly have anything to do with the car. She hadn't been there long; the blood hadn't dried.

The attack had been brutal—and deliberate.

"It wasn't me," the driver whispered. "I swear, I barely touched her with the fender." His face crumpled, and he sank to the ground, his back against the car.

Thomas crouched down to check for a pulse just as Nora arrived, panting. "She's alive," he said over his shoulder. "But she needs to go to the hospital. Has anyone called an ambulance?"

Nora inhaled sharply. "That's Anna-Maria!" she exclaimed, looking around. "She's the manager at Freya's Haven." She tugged at Thomas's jacket. "Kovač must be here—who else would have done this to Anna-Maria?"

"Call an ambulance and the police!" Thomas yelled to the onlookers as he began to run.

CHAPTER 116

Nora stopped behind a thick tree trunk around fifty yards from the white gate leading into Freya's Haven. "That's it," she whispered, pointing to a large wooden house surrounded by several small cottages. Everything looked peaceful. There were no lights showing in most of the rooms. Thomas narrowed his eyes, trying to spot anyone moving around inside.

"Stay here," he said to Nora as he drew his gun.

"Be careful!"

Thomas was well aware that Kovač was dangerous. He was certainly armed with a sharp knife, at least; presumably he was carrying a gun as well.

Dino Herco had been shot dead.

Nora grabbed his arm. "It's too risky to go in on your own—can't you wait for backup?"

There was no time, and they both knew it, given Mina's situation.

"Please?"

Thomas gently loosened Nora's grip. "Call Leila again and find out what's happening," he said. He climbed over the low fence, then crept across the damp ground hidden by the lilac hedge that ran along one side of the lawn, its bare branches outlined starkly against the gray sky.

The hedge was sparse, but he crouched down and hoped he would blend in with the darkness.

Was Kovač in there? Had he gotten hold of Mina?

He couldn't hear a sound—did that mean Kovač hadn't arrived yet? Or was it all over?

He avoided the gravel paths and stuck close to the wall until he reached the front door. He pushed down the handle, hoping that the door was locked and that Kovač hadn't been able to get in.

It opened smoothly into a dark hallway.

Thomas held the gun in front of him as he turned his head from side to side, scanning his surroundings with jerky movements. A sudden glint in the corner of his eye made him jump, but it was only his reflection.

He could hear his own breathing, and the hum of a refrigerator somewhere nearby—nothing else.

He moved on slowly, every muscle tensed and ready for action. The kitchen was empty, as was the next room, which must be the office. There was a computer in one corner, and a phone charging on the desk.

Something broke the silence and Thomas stopped.

A baby crying.

He followed the noise along a corridor. He turned a corner and saw light seeping out of a half-open door. He edged closer; a woman was sitting in an armchair, about to feed a baby with a bottle.

It had to be Mina.

At that moment she became aware of Thomas outside the door. She dropped the bottle and clutched the baby to her breast.

Thomas put a finger to his lips and mouthed "Police" to reassure her. He stepped into the room and closed the door. "Is your husband here?" he whispered.

Mina's hand flew to her mouth. "Andreis? Is he on the island?"

"You haven't seen him today?"

She shook her head.

"Come with me." He took her hand and pulled her to her feet. "Is there anywhere in the house where you can lock yourself in?"

"No. Yes—the bathroom."

"Go and lock yourself and the baby in there. Don't open the door until you hear my voice—promise."

Thomas waited until he heard the key turn, then he continued searching the house. When he'd gone through the ground floor, he crept over to the stairs, but paused on the first step. The upper floor was in darkness; it was impossible to see anything. If Kovač was waiting up there with a gun, Thomas would be an open target.

But if he switched on the light, Kovač would know that someone was coming, and that would give him the chance to get away.

Thomas hesitated, then released the safety catch and continued up the stairs.

Bosnia, May 1993

Dario was driving. Blanka was in the passenger seat with Nermin, their five-year-old son, on her lap. Selma, Zlatko, and the children were jammed together in the back.

Selma gradually began to grasp the extent of the tragedy as they passed one burned-out village after another. The fields that should have been turning green at this time of year were blackened and ravaged by shell blasts. The fruit trees were nothing but charred stumps, and there was no sign of the cattle that would normally be grazing peacefully in the pastures.

Dead bodies rotted in water-filled ditches.

Bearded soldiers in mud-stained uniforms trudged along the ruined roads. Every time Dario had to bribe his way through yet another roadblock, Selma was filled with terror.

They drove past columns of people with empty eyes walking in the same direction as they were traveling, carrying bundles of their possessions on their backs. Men with gray, haggard faces, mothers with babies in their arms. Someone was pushing a sick person on a two-wheeled cart, while others carried the elderly wrapped in blankets.

Every step was laborious, as if it were their last in this life.

The first time Selma saw a corpse, she was horrified and tried to stop Andreis from looking. After a while she learned to turn her head away, and in the end she didn't even notice anymore. Fear already had her in its grip; she couldn't feel any worse.

The boys stayed astonishingly calm.

Time passed. Selma didn't have a watch, but it was beginning to get dark. They'd been on the road all day; soon they would reach the border.

Both Andreis and Emir had fallen asleep from sheer exhaustion. Selma's legs ached from sitting in the same position for hours—the back seat was hot and cramped. She needed to pee, but knew that stopping the car was out of the question.

The sun was setting when they reached the last roadblock before the border. Several military vehicles barred their way. Four soldiers with machine guns were monitoring the single-track passage, which was lined with thick rolls of barbed wire. Each had a knife dangling from his belt.

They appeared to be drunk; one staggered sideways and fired his gun straight up into the air, laughing out loud.

Selma had never been so terrified.

Dario slowed behind a blue Volkswagen and stopped the car.

Chapter 117

Thomas made his way up the creaking wooden staircase as quietly as he could; every step sounded like a gunshot. He stopped when he reached the top and tried to orient himself. It was hard to see, even though the sun hadn't yet gone down.

There was a narrow corridor to the left, while a small landing opened out on the other side, with two closed doors opposite each other. Straight ahead lay an empty balcony with a couple of lounge chairs and a table.

Kovač could be waiting for him behind any one of the doors, ready to shoot him dead.

Thomas tried to listen for strange noises, something that didn't fit in, but he couldn't hear a thing, in spite of his best efforts.

Wait—was that a shuffling sound from the end of the corridor?

He waited for a minute or so but couldn't decide whether it was real, or just his imagination. He broke out in a sweat as he stared at the doors, holding his breath.

Maybe Kovač hadn't found his way to Freya's Haven?

A sudden clattering outside the balcony doors made Thomas jump, then he realized it was only the halyard lines on the flagpole, flapping in the wind.

He crept over to the nearest door and flung it wide open. Empty. He did the same with the one opposite and found himself staring into another empty room.

The old Mora clock in the corner was ticking much too loudly.

He decided to make himself known. "Police!" he roared. "Drop your gun and come out!"

Nothing. He listened for a few seconds, then yelled again:

"Police! Come out with your hands up!"

CHAPTER 118

Mina was still shaking when Nora walked into her room. She had a blanket around her shoulders, but it didn't seem to be helping. There was an untouched cup of tea on the table in front of her.

"How are you?" Nora said, sitting down in the other armchair.

"He's going to find me and Lukas. He's going to kill me."

Nora took Mina's hand. Thomas had searched the whole place. Andreis Kovač wasn't in the building. Backup had arrived; the island was crawling with cops. The air ambulance had picked up Anna-Maria some time ago.

"That's not going to happen," Nora assured her. "You don't need to be scared. I promise we'll protect you and Lukas."

"He knows where I am."

Nora hated the fact that Mina was right. "You can't stay here," she said. "We'll find another place where you can feel safe."

Mina pressed her clenched fist to her lips and turned her head away.

Nora had given her a brief account of what had happened to Anna-Maria, but hadn't mentioned Herman Wibom. The situation wouldn't be improved by making Mina feel even more afraid. Knowing that two people in her immediate circle had been attacked could easily make her give up.

Nora's phone rang: Leila. She excused herself and left the room.

"How's it going?" Nora asked. "Have you found somewhere for Mina and Lukas?"

"I've spoken to the witness-protection team, and they're on the case." Leila muttered something inaudible. "I mean, how hard can it be?"

Nora went over to the window and rested her head on the cool glass. It was dark now, with clouds hiding the stars. She could hear the barking of the police dogs searching for Kovač. "She can't stay here, Leila."

"I know. She'll probably end up in some crap hotel over the weekend."

"A hotel?"

"If they can't find room in a safe house, they usually go for a hotel as a temporary measure. They said they'd call back as soon as possible."

A movement behind Nora made her turn around. Mina was standing there.

"Will you come with me? To the hotel?" she whispered. "I don't want to be in a new place all by myself. Please?"

Nora didn't even know what she was going to say until she said it. "I'll take her to Sandhamn. She can stay the night in my guest room. Or she can have my old house—I don't have a tenant at the moment. No one will find her there."

Leila didn't say anything.

"Hello?"

"Are you sure that's a good idea?"

"Do you have a better suggestion?" Nora took a deep breath. "I can ask Thomas to take us over there in the Buster when he's finished; he can stay the night, too. No one will see Mina leave the island, or find out where she's gone. Besides, I'm sure they'll find Kovač before long. There are cops everywhere, and a warrant has already been issued for his arrest."

"Do you really want to take on the responsibility?"

Nora saw Anna-Maria's unconscious face in her mind's eye. The vicious cut on her cheek, the broken fingers.

Herman Wibom was in the hospital, seriously injured.

If only she'd managed to persuade the court to keep Kovač in custody in February, no one would have been hurt. This situation, all this suffering, was her fault.

The silence grew.

"It might work," Leila said hesitantly. "If you're really sure . . ."

Mina waited for Nora's answer with tears in her eyes.

"Let's do it," Nora said. "I'll go and speak to Thomas."

CHAPTER 119

Nora found Thomas on his phone outside the TV room, where an agitated hum of conversation could be heard from the other women who had returned from their excursion and been told what had happened.

"I've spoken to Leila," Nora informed Thomas when he'd finished his call. "They can't find a place for Mina tonight, so I'm going to take her to Sandhamn."

Thomas frowned. "To your house?"

"She can stay in our guest room, or in my old house—just overnight, until they can organize somewhere safe for her."

"Why would you do that?"

"She doesn't want to be alone. She's terrified and desperate; she's gone through hell over the past few days."

"She certainly has." Thomas sighed. He leaned on the wall and shook his head. "You're getting in way too deep. Mina isn't your personal responsibility."

"She asked me to stay with her. She's too scared to go to a hotel with Lukas by herself."

"You're not a police officer, you're not trained in the use of firearms, and you don't even have a gun."

Nora couldn't argue with that. "I thought you could take us over in the Buster," she said tentatively. "No one will know where we are. How would Kovač find out?"

"It's a terrible idea." Thomas pressed his palms together in front of his face and breathed through his nose. "Kovač is still out there, and he's extremely dangerous. Until we pick him up, the threat level against Mina and anyone who helps her must be taken seriously. Look what happened to her parents. What are you going to do if he tracks you down?"

There was a fresh burst of barking from the search dogs outside.

"Mina needs police protection," Thomas concluded.

Nora didn't need reminding of Kovač's brutality, but she wasn't prepared to give up. The thought of telling Mina that she had to leave Runmarö alone was unbearable. "If you come with us and stay the night, we'll have police protection . . ."

Nora knew she was pushing the boundaries of their friendship. She didn't want to see the disappointment in Mina's eyes, but the look on Thomas's face was almost as bad.

She couldn't cope with telling him why she felt so guilty about Kovač, yet she hated the position she'd put him in. "It's only for one night, Thomas. Kovač will never find out where she's gone." She placed a hand on his shoulder. "Please?"

Chapter 120

The wind was blowing straight in Nora's face as they set off from Runmarö, with the lights of Stavsnäs sparkling directly opposite. A little voice whispered in her ear that they were going in the wrong direction, that she should be heading home to her own family instead of sitting in a freezing-cold boat with a knot in her stomach.

Mina was crouched in the stern in a borrowed sailing jacket, staring blankly into space with Lukas in her arms. Nora could see the tears dripping onto the baby's head.

In the end Thomas had agreed to let Mina spend the night in Sandhamn. With a bit of luck, they would pick up Kovač before dawn. There was a warrant out for his arrest, and dog teams were searching for him all over Runmarö. As soon as he was in custody, the danger would be over. It couldn't take long.

Everyone realized that Mina couldn't stay at Freya's Haven, but Nora had almost fallen out with Thomas before he gave in.

They had just passed Eknö, where the illuminated sign on the jetty made it possible to orient oneself in the pitch darkness. The Buster was moving fast, and Thomas was concentrating hard, with the help of the lighthouses.

The boat jolted, and Nora shivered in the cold. She hoped she wasn't putting herself in danger by taking Mina and her son to the Brand villa, but there was no way she could leave Mina to her fate when she had failed so spectacularly to protect her from her husband.

Her throat contracted. *If Kovač had remained in custody, none of this would have happened,* she thought for the hundredth time. Her failure was too great to bear without attempting some form of recompense.

Jonas was due to land in Stockholm early tomorrow morning. Nora wasn't intending to tell him what had gone on until he arrived home. She thought it was best to avoid a discussion until Mina was safely installed in the house.

The children were in the apartment in town, so she wasn't exposing them to any danger.

Everything will be fine, she told herself. She knew she'd acted impulsively and compromised her professional integrity, but it was too late to change her mind now.

The islands whizzed by, dissolving into dark silhouettes against the night sky. The wind lashed her cheeks.

At long last the lights of Sandhamn came into view, and Nora allowed herself to relax a little. They would be safe on the island. There was no way Kovač would be able to track them down.

Thomas slowed to eight knots as they passed Västerudd and entered the zone where the speed limit applied. In a few minutes they would reach Kvarnberget and Nora's own jetty.

Her neighbor's exterior light showed them the way.

"Can you take the bowline?" Thomas shouted over the roar of the engine. Nora made her way forward and got ready. She could feel his displeasure; he'd hardly said a word since they left Runmarö.

This is for Mina. I have to do this for Mina.

And for myself.

CHAPTER 121

Nora put down her knife and fork. She hadn't had much of an appetite, but had put together an improvised meal of spaghetti with a jar of pasta sauce. Mina had only poked at her food, but at least Thomas had cleared his plate.

It was almost nine o'clock; she was so tired that her head was spinning.

"Shall we figure out where you're sleeping?" she said to Mina, who looked utterly exhausted. Her face was gray, and her head was almost drooping over the table. Lukas had fallen asleep long ago.

Nora hesitated. On the one hand it felt safer to have Mina under the same roof, but on the other, maybe the girl would prefer to be left in peace after the day she'd had.

"It's up to you," she said. "You and Lukas can have the guest room here, right next door to me, or we have another house just across the street. You can see it from the kitchen window." She gave an encouraging smile. "If you want to stay there, that's fine. Thomas will come with you, so you'll be perfectly safe. It's entirely up to you."

Mina rubbed her forehead. "I think I'd prefer the other house, if that's OK?"

"Absolutely. Whatever suits you." Nora got to her feet. "In that case I suggest we go over there and get you settled."

Nora unlocked the door and led the way in. She switched on the lights and turned up the heat.

She'd lived here with Henrik throughout their marriage. For almost ten years, the boys had spent their summers under this roof. Then she'd moved into the Brand villa, which she'd inherited from Aunt Signe; Jonas had rented this house, and they'd become a couple.

Nora showed Mina into the large bedroom upstairs, the one that used to be hers. This place was much smaller than the nineteenth-century Brand villa and nowhere near as elegant, but she'd always loved it.

Mina gently laid Lukas down on the double bed, then she went over to the window and looked out over the village. "It's pretty desolate," she said.

"Most of the houses are unoccupied at this time of year. There are only about ninety permanent residents on the island."

Mina ran her finger along the sill. "Is that all?"

"During the summer we have something like three thousand visitors; the harbor area is packed. Hard to believe on a night like this."

Nora opened a drawer and took out towels, sheets, and pillowcases. The faded floral pattern reminded her of Henrik and another life.

"You'll be fine here," she said. "I'm sure they'll have found you a new safe place by tomorrow."

Mina was still gazing out of the window.

"They'll have picked up Andreis long before that," Nora added as she began to make the bed. When she'd done one side, she moved Lukas across and made the other side. He was still fast asleep, with his pacifier in his mouth and fingers spread like starfish.

He was so beautiful. Nora gently stroked his cheek. "I promise we'll take care of you and your son," she said.

Mina let out a sob. "Why are you being so kind to me?"

Nora searched for an answer. "Sometimes you just have to . . . do the right thing."

Mina's gratitude embarrassed her. Mina thought Nora was doing this out of the goodness of her heart; she didn't know that the real reason was Nora's failure, the guilt she couldn't shake off.

"Anyway," Nora said. "I hope you can get some sleep." She slipped the pillow into its case and smoothed down the covers. "Don't worry about a thing. No one knows you're here, and Thomas will be sleeping in the other room. You won't be alone tonight."

Mina shook her head. "There's no need. I'll be OK."

"It's for the best."

"I'm sorry to be so much trouble," Mina whispered.

Nora had a lump in her throat. "You're no trouble. Thomas will be over soon. He's just making a couple of phone calls."

CHAPTER 122

Mina locked the front door behind Nora, but left the light on in the hallway. She almost changed her mind; maybe it would have been better to stay with Nora in the big house? And yet she longed to be alone, not to have to encounter a stranger every time she left her room.

The stairs creaked as she went back to Lukas. There were three bedrooms, and she'd been given the largest.

She switched on the lights in the other rooms, including the bathroom, which made her feel better.

Then she got into bed, curled up in the fetal position next to Lukas, and closed her eyes. She filled her lungs with air, but she still couldn't breathe properly. Her chest seemed to have shrunk, as if something heavy were crushing it.

This morning she'd thought that life was getting better, that all the bad stuff had already happened. Then disaster struck.

Mom.

She longed for her mother. There was no one left now, except for Dad. She had to take care of Lukas, but who would take care of her?

I can't do this, she thought, but she knew that wasn't an option. She had to find the strength from somewhere.

Her eyes were so swollen from crying that the skin around them was throbbing. Even though she was under the covers with an extra blanket, she was shivering so much that her whole body was shaking.

Dad.

Nora had stressed that she mustn't tell a single person where she was, but Anna-Maria had said that Dad was coming to Freya's Haven tomorrow to see her and Lukas. She couldn't let him make the trip in vain.

Mina slid out of bed and fetched her cell phone from the pocket of her jacket. It had been off all afternoon. She switched it on and keyed in the code. Then she sent a short text message to her father, explaining where she'd gone. Maybe he could come here instead?

She missed him so much that it hurt. It wouldn't take him much longer to travel to Sandhamn than to Runmarö. She'd do anything to see him tomorrow.

Just for a little while.

Mina went back to bed and drew Lukas toward her. He whimpered, but she had to feel the warmth of his small body.

Hold the only good thing in her life.

Her phone beeped; Dad must have answered right away. She immediately felt better.

The letters on the screen faded in and out before her eyes as she read the message from Andreis. She couldn't breathe.

I will find you, you fucking whore. You can't hide from me.

CHAPTER 123

When Nora got back to the Brand villa, Thomas was sitting on the glassed-in veranda with a cup of coffee in his hand. He seemed to have finished making his calls; his phone was on the table.

He'd lit the old kerosene lamp that had been there for as long as Nora could remember. It made her think of her beloved Aunt Signe.

The flame flickered.

Thomas was staring blankly out of the window, but turned his head when she joined him. "How's Mina?"

"What can I say? She's devastated." Nora sank down on the sofa. She was so tired that she felt as if her legs couldn't hold her any longer, yet the adrenaline was still coursing through her veins. "I think I'll have a whisky—would you like one?"

"I would, but I'd better not," Thomas said with a weary smile. "I need to keep a clear head, since you got your own way. I'll go over to the house in a few minutes."

He was right, unfortunately. Nora didn't want to be reminded that Thomas needed to stay sober in case anything happened during the night. She'd convinced herself that Mina was safe now.

The alternative was too awful to think about.

She went over to the big cabinet in the dining room where she kept her china and glasses. One shelf was set aside for Jonas's modest stock of booze. She found a half-full bottle of whisky and poured a measure into one of Signe's fine crystal glasses, then rejoined Thomas. The alcohol burned on her tongue, but she began to feel warm again.

Thomas was sitting in the wicker chair with his eyes closed. He was as exhausted as she was. "It would have been much better if Mina had been moved straight into a safe house," he said after a while.

"Well, she's here now." Nora tucked her feet under her body and reached for a cushion, which she pressed to her stomach. She took another sip of whisky to chase away her unease. "So how's the search going?" she said, changing the subject. "Have they found Kovač?"

"Not yet." Thomas ran his hands through his hair. "I've just spoken to Aram. The dog teams have been all over the island, but there's no trace of him. The theory is that he left Runmarö before they arrived. He probably couldn't find the shelter—he didn't have much time. He's not stupid; he must have realized that someone would find Anna-Maria and call the police."

"At least he didn't kill her." Nora hugged the cushion more tightly. Kovač hadn't shown the same mercy to Dino Herco. "I wonder why he let her live."

"Perhaps someone was coming down the lane, or maybe that car turned up and frightened him off."

"He didn't kill Herman Wibom either. They're both potential witnesses."

"It's impossible to understand why he's done what he's done."

"I wonder whether nothing else mattered once he'd gotten the information he wanted," Nora speculated. "Or has he lost control to the extent that he can only think about Mina? Everything else is irrelevant. He's incapable of taking a tactical approach at this stage."

Thomas shrugged and reached for his phone. "I'm sure he knows he'll do less jail time for assault than homicide."

"Where do you think he's gone?" Nora gazed out toward the sea. It was dark now, but she knew exactly what was beyond the windows: the islands she'd known since she was a child, the old jetties in a line. She'd always felt safe in this environment, never been afraid of the night.

"If he's smart, he'll be on his way out of the country," Thomas said. "He might try and get to the Balkans—he has both money and contacts there."

Nora was still mortified that Kovač hadn't been held in custody, but the net was tightening around him. He wasn't going to escape. "I just hope they pick him up soon."

Thomas was sitting with his face turned away. In the glow of the lamp, his profile cast a long shadow on the wall. "I hope so, too."

Friday

Chapter 124

Thomas's phone rang just as he closed the front door of Nora's old house behind him.

It had been a quiet night; he'd even managed a few hours' sleep on top of the covers. This morning the adrenaline was keeping him going. He wasn't as tired as he should have been under the circumstances.

It was only seven o'clock; Mina and Lukas were still asleep. It wasn't raining yet, but the sky was overcast.

He glanced at the display: *Aram.*

"A patrol has seen a guy matching Kovač's description outside his brother's apartment."

Of course Kovač wasn't dumb enough to go anywhere near his own home, but he should have realized that Emir's place would also be under surveillance. Or maybe not. A man on the run wasn't always on top of things.

"We're getting ready to go in," Aram continued. "With a bit of luck, we'll arrest him by lunchtime."

Thomas switched his phone to the other hand. If they were about to pick up Kovač, then he didn't need to worry about Mina or Nora. He could safely leave them for a few hours.

"I'm on my way over," he said.

"OK."

Thomas ended the call, and his phone immediately rang again. This time it was Leila Kacim.

"We have forensic evidence linking Kovač to the attack on Herman Wibom," she began. "The CSIs have found his fingerprints on a shard of glass, and on the front-door handle."

"Any news on Wibom?"

"He's not doing too well. He'd lost a lot of blood, and he'd also had a stroke."

"When will we be able to question him?"

"It's impossible to say. He's in intensive care, and he's unconscious."

Thomas set off toward the jetty without knocking on Nora's door. He would call her from the boat.

Bosnia, May 1993

The blue Volkswagen had stopped a few yards ahead of them. Selma could hear one of the soldiers yelling at the driver, telling him that everyone must get out. After only a few seconds he brandished his gun, fired it up into the air, then pointed it at the man in the driver's seat.

"What's happening?" she whispered to Zlatko.

"I don't know."

Zlatko's forehead was beaded with sweat, and he kept clenching and unclenching his fists. The children were sleeping, thank goodness.

Selma craned her neck, trying to get a better view. They'd already paid out so much in bribes at every roadblock; she hoped there was enough money left.

The Volkswagen driver got out, arms outstretched, palms upward. He was in his early forties, and had a thick black mustache. A woman of a similar age climbed out of the other side, along with a pretty girl who looked about thirteen. Her light-brown hair was gathered up in a ponytail, and she was clutching her mother's hand.

The soldier, who couldn't have been more than twenty, made a vulgar gesture; there was no mistaking its meaning. Then he waved his gun at the women, ordering them to go over to the other soldier. The girl began to cry, and flung her arms around her mother.

"Please, no," the father said, producing a wad of notes out of his pocket. "This is all we have. Take it, but please leave my wife and daughter alone. Be merciful."

The soldier took the money as if this were the accepted procedure. He turned and smiled at his fellow soldiers. The mother looked uncertainly from him to her husband, perhaps wondering whether they were allowed to get back in the car and continue their journey.

The soldier turned back and shot the man in the chest.

"Oh God," Selma gasped.

The woman screamed and dropped to her knees beside her husband, but one of the soldiers grabbed her by the arm and dragged her off in the direction of a grove of trees.

The girl stared at the blood pumping from her father's chest. She let out a howl like a wounded animal.

Another soldier dragged her away.

Blanka was weeping silently in the front seat, pressing Nermin's face to her breast so that he wouldn't see.

"We have to do something," Selma sobbed.

"Keep quiet—don't say a word," Zlatko whispered.

The first soldier began to walk toward their car.

CHAPTER 125

Nora knocked on Mina's door with some breakfast and a bag of groceries that she'd bought from Westerberg's, the local store.

Mina didn't look much better than she had the previous evening. The color hadn't returned to her cheeks, but she did manage a shaky smile when Nora asked how she was feeling.

They went into the kitchen; Nora made coffee and set out breakfast. Mina took a few tiny bites of the sandwiches Nora had brought.

The gray morning outside did nothing to lighten the atmosphere.

Mina tugged at her sleeves, even though she was wearing a thick woolen sweater that reached down over her thighs.

"Are you cold?" Nora asked. "I can turn the heat up if you like."

"Yes, please. I'm so sorry, I can't stop shivering."

"No need to apologize." Nora turned up the kitchen radiator. "Feel free to do the same in all the other rooms," she said, pointing to the thermostat before she sat down again. "How did you sleep, by the way?"

"Not very well."

Nora hadn't gotten much sleep either. She'd woken up several times, drenched in sweat, her heart pounding. Vague figures had chased her through her dreams.

She'd just been given an update on Herman Wibom's condition by Leila. Thomas had called to say he'd gone into town first thing and would be back later, if Mina was still there.

"They haven't tracked down your husband yet," she said to Mina, "but it's only a matter of time. Thomas will be in touch as soon as he has any news. They're expecting to pick him up today."

Mina nodded but didn't say anything. Nora's reassurances didn't seem to have helped much. Should she tell Mina about Anna-Maria? They'd operated on her broken fingers overnight, and she was in severe shock. However, she had managed to identify Andreis Kovač as her attacker.

Nora decided not to mention Anna-Maria unless Mina brought up the subject. She got up and began to unpack the food. Bread, milk, eggs, cheese.

"It's probably best if you and Lukas stay indoors today," she said over her shoulder. "Just to be on the safe side. You know you can't tell anyone you're on Sandhamn, don't you?"

Mina took another tiny bite of her sandwich but didn't answer.

"Mina?" Nora closed the refrigerator door and turned around. "Have you already told someone?"

"No. Yes." Mina ran her index finger around the rim of her coffee cup.

"Who?"

Mina couldn't look Nora in the eye. "I sent a text to my dad so he'd know where we were." She tugged unhappily at her sleeves again. "Sorry."

There was no point in berating the poor girl. What was done was done; telling her off wouldn't help.

"I'm sure it's fine," Nora said, against her better judgment. "But don't tell anyone else until your husband has been arrested. You have to be careful."

"I promise."

Chapter 126

Stefan Talevski closed the front door behind him and headed for the car. He'd hoped to get away much earlier, but there had been so many formalities to deal with before he could set off for Sandhamn.

Time passed both quickly and slowly. He was exhausted, but hadn't been able to sleep.

Today the funeral director was going to the morgue to collect Katrin's body.

The thought of her death knocked the air from his lungs once again. Everything flickered before his eyes, and he had to stop, put down his bag, and lean on the wall for support.

He punched the palm of one hand with his fist until his hands hurt more than his heart. It was several minutes before he was able to pull himself together sufficiently to pick up the bag and put it in the car.

He could hardly see through his tears when he got into the driver's seat. He wiped them away with the back of his hand, started the engine, and reversed onto the road. His progress was jerky, and he missed the first stop sign on his way out of the residential development.

His little girl was all alone in the archipelago. This time he was determined not to let anything stop him from seeing her and Lukas. She wouldn't have to struggle by herself anymore.

He'd made a promise to Katrin on her deathbed, and he was going to keep it. Whatever happened, he would be there for Mina and Lukas. He would protect them from Andreis.

What else did he have to live for?

Katrin was gone. Nothing he could say or do would change that. She was never coming back.

Stefan took the on-ramp to the freeway and continued toward Gustavsberg. There was very little traffic, thank God. The last ferry of the day was due to leave at six; he mustn't miss it.

Soon he would see his darling daughter and grandson.

He reached Mölnvik and dropped his speed to thirty miles per hour. In the rearview mirror, he noticed a black BMW pull in behind his Passat.

Stefan signaled right and joined the correct lane for the exit for Stavsnäs. It shouldn't take more than twenty minutes from here.

He was on his way. Mina wouldn't have to face her demons by herself.

Chapter 127

Nora was standing in the kitchen with a cup of coffee.

Things seemed better in daylight. Yesterday's fear had abated slightly; she no longer jumped at every sound. However, she was so restless that she couldn't sit still for more than a few minutes. She'd tried to do some work on her computer, but her concentration was poor.

From the window she could see her old house across the way.

She'd spoken to Leila several times during the morning, and the only other option for Mina and Lukas remained an impersonal hotel room. It looked as though they'd be staying for another night, but that was fine. Thomas had seemed pretty sure that Kovač would soon be under arrest. She had to stay positive.

It was raining, with a cold north wind whistling around the Brand villa.

After breakfast Mina had said she wanted to rest, so Nora had decided to leave her in peace during the day. She knew where Nora was if she wanted to talk. Sometimes it was nice to avoid the company of others.

Nora had sent her several texts to be on the safe side, and each time Mina had replied that everything was fine.

There had been no word from Thomas, in spite of his promise to keep Nora informed. She picked up her phone and called him.

"Have you found him?" she asked as soon as he answered.

"No."

Why couldn't they track him down, set her mind at rest?

"We thought he was at his younger brother's apartment, but we were wrong."

Nora grabbed a cloth and wiped down the already spotless counter.

"However, we have had a breakthrough in the investigation into Dino Herco's murder," Thomas continued. "We've found a fingerprint on Herco's shoe that belongs to Emir Kovač, so we've brought him in."

If Emir was anything like his brother, he wouldn't say a word. No doubt Ulrika Grönstedt would provide him with a legal representative cut from the same cloth as her, who would do his or her best to make life as difficult as possible for the police.

"What about the search of Kovač's house?" Nora asked.

"No sign of him." Thomas sounded stressed. "It's only a matter of time, though. We've got people in all his usual haunts."

"OK." Nora ended the call, then went onto the veranda with her coffee. The windows were streaked with raindrops, and the gray rocks below the house were treacherously slippery.

If Mina was staying tonight, Nora would have to call Jonas and explain why she couldn't come back to town.

She could already hear his objections.

Chapter 128

Mina stared at her cell phone on the kitchen table. She could hardly believe the text her father had just sent.

He would soon be here. She and Lukas wouldn't have to be alone anymore. He'd asked for the address.

Mina couldn't help laughing. She suddenly found it funny that there were no street names here on Sandhamn, just like on Runmarö. Andreis would never be able to find her here, even if he tried. He hadn't sent another message after last night, but Mina still gave a start every time her phone buzzed. She consoled herself with the thought that he was on the run and didn't have time for her.

I'll meet you on the jetty, she wrote quickly, grabbing her jacket. The boat was due in at seven o'clock—in fifteen minutes.

She pulled on her boots, then got Lukas into his snowsuit. She was going to have to carry him; the stroller had been left behind on Runmarö. That didn't matter, as long as she could see her father again.

Nora had told her not to leave the house, but it wouldn't take many minutes to run down to the harbor to meet him. That was easier than trying to explain where the house was in a text message.

She locked the front door behind her, hoping that Nora wouldn't notice she'd gone missing for a little while. Nora had been so kind, and Mina didn't want to worry her unnecessarily. She was only going to show her dad the way.

A cold rain was falling, but Mina didn't care. Soon they would be together again.

Chapter 129

Thomas was back at the police station. They'd had another tip-off about Kovač's whereabouts, but it had turned out to be another false alarm.

This wasn't good. Thomas had been convinced that they'd arrest him during the course of the day; now he had to reevaluate Mina and Lukas's safety. Nora had informed him that they would be spending a second night on Sandhamn.

He rubbed his eyes and drank a cup of cold coffee that was sitting on his desk. The day had been full to bursting point, but he felt somehow inadequate. He went over to Margit's office; she was absorbed in something on the screen.

"Do we have Kovač?" she asked without looking up.

"No."

"He can't stay under the radar for long." She turned her chair in Thomas's direction. "Don't you think you should go home and get some sleep? You look as if you need it."

Thomas considered telling her that Mina was still in Nora's house, but decided against it. They should have been able to provide round-the-clock protection for Mina, but the resources just weren't there. They'd already blown the overtime budget, and the staffing situation was at the breaking point as a result of the reorganization.

The murder of Dino Herco and the intensive search for Kovač on Runmarö hadn't improved things.

He knew exactly what Margit would say if he told her that he'd offered to look after Mina on Sandhamn—no point in bringing it up now.

He didn't think Mina was in any immediate danger. Even Kovač couldn't be so dumb as to stay in the Stockholm area when every cop in town was looking for him. However, he didn't want to leave Nora and Mina on their own. He had no intention of taking any risks at this stage.

He yawned; he wasn't looking forward to another sleepless night.

"Go home, Thomas," Margit said. "You look like shit."

CHAPTER 130

Mina couldn't take her eyes off her father. He was sitting opposite her at the kitchen table, with Lukas on his lap. Mina was so happy that they were together again.

And yet tears lurked just below the surface. She wished she could sit on her daddy's knee and have him tell her that everything was going to be all right.

At some point she would ask him to tell her about her mother's final hours, when he'd sat by her side—but not now.

Mina had made them both an omelet. She'd texted Nora, saying she was going to have an early night. She knew she ought to tell Nora that her father was here but didn't quite know how to explain it. It was easier to make an excuse, although of course the cat would be out of the bag when Thomas arrived later.

Lukas gave his grandfather a big, toothless smile, and Mina felt a lump in her throat. He was the image of her dad, with that same crooked grin.

He was hers and hers alone.

She would never let Andreis have him.

She reached across the table and squeezed her father's hand. The smell of his aftershave reminded her of the home she'd grown up in on

Körsbärsvägen, the bathroom she and Mom had quarreled about when she was a teenager.

Mom.

"Thank you for coming," she said quietly.

Stefan kissed Lukas on the forehead and bounced him up and down. "You have nothing to worry about now," he said. "I'm staying right here, and everything will be fine."

Mina really wanted to believe him.

Lukas yawned, showing his pink gums. It was almost nine o'clock—high time he was in bed.

Tiredness was making Mina's eyelids droop, too; she'd lain awake until the early hours. Maybe she'd be able to sleep tonight, knowing that her father was in the room next door.

A sound outside the house made them both jump.

Someone was tugging at the front-door handle.

Stefan frowned. "What was that?"

The handle moved again.

Chapter 131

Thomas wiped his mouth with his napkin and pushed his plate away.

"Thank you," he said. "It was good to have a hot meal. I really needed it."

He looked even worse than the previous evening, if that were possible.

"You must eat," Nora had said. "If I know you, you've had nothing all day."

She'd made a beef stew and laid the dining room table, candles flickering in the old silver candelabra. She wanted to create a cozy atmosphere, but the light made Thomas look even paler; his face had a greenish tinge.

Mina had texted to say that she was going to have an early night, and didn't want any dinner. Nora hadn't insisted.

She put down her knife and fork and shivered. There was a draft from the windows when the wind blew from the north. The halyard lines on the flagpole were clattering angrily in the storm.

It was the kind of evening when it was best to curl up indoors.

"Do you have to go into work tomorrow?" she said. "Can't you stay here and catch up on your sleep?"

"You know we're in the early stages of an investigation."

"Yes, but you need to take care of yourself." There was so much she wanted to say to Thomas. Life was short and fragile, and he looked worn out.

Wrong time, wrong place.

"By the way, what did Jonas say when you told him Mina was staying in your old house?"

Nora wished he hadn't asked. Jonas had been just as angry as she'd feared. They'd quarreled, and he'd accused her of being irresponsible and putting others before her own family.

No point in going into all that now.

"He reacted more or less the way you did at first," she said, turning her glass around in her fingers. "I'll talk to him later."

She'd allowed herself a glass of red wine with dinner. Thomas had decided to stick to water, but now he was looking longingly at the cupboard from which Nora had produced the bottle of whisky the previous evening.

"Would you like something?" she asked.

"Maybe a small one." He rubbed the back of his neck and blinked several times. "I know I shouldn't, but I'm so tired . . ."

Nora glanced at her watch. "I'm sure you can stay for a few minutes. Mina's already gone to bed."

Thomas had told her that both he and Aram were convinced that Kovač had left the country by this stage, and that Mina was in no immediate danger.

"Everything's under control," Nora added with an attempt at a smile.

CHAPTER 132

"Are you expecting anyone?" Stefan said quietly.

"No."

Nora had texted Mina to say that Thomas was going to eat with her before he came over—and he had a key.

Mina stared at the door.

The handle moved again.

Stefan stood up and passed Lukas to her. He went to the kitchen door, then stopped and listened.

A sound from the window made Mina turn her head. It was pitch-dark outside, and she hadn't closed the curtains.

Anyone could see in.

Nora had told her to be careful, but she hadn't thought about the fact that the sun had gone down and the lights were on in the house.

As if he'd read her mind, Stefan switched off the kitchen light.

"What are you doing?" Mina whispered.

"Trying to see who it is." He crept over to the front door and peered through the pane of glass. "There's no one there."

"Shh!"

Mina heard footsteps on the gravel. There was no lawn in the small yard surrounding Nora's house.

Someone was moving around out there. Her father remained in the hallway, while Mina focused on the other door. The kitchen had two entrances, one of which led onto the small glassed-in veranda. She'd sat there with a cup of tea in the afternoon, gazing out at the village's empty houses. The veranda had beautiful windows that had presumably been there since the place was built in the 1920s. Narrow strips of wood divided the glass, letting in light from floor to ceiling.

The front door was locked, but the veranda doors were old and far from robust. It wouldn't be difficult for a strong, fit man to kick them open.

A strong, fit man like Andreis.

Mina kept her eyes fixed on those doors as the seconds ticked by. Lukas sensed her unease and began to whimper. She held him tight; she couldn't let go.

Footsteps crunched on the gravel again.

A shadow grew before Mina's eyes. Someone dressed in black climbed the steps to the porch and met her eyes.

By the light of the streetlamp, she saw who it was.

She could hear her heart pounding.

He had found her.

"He's here!" she tried to yell.

Bosnia, May 1993

Andreis was woken by the sound of the gunshot. He sat up sleepily, wondering what was going on.

Mom didn't notice that he was awake. Her face was ashen, and she was gabbling incoherent prayers to herself. Emir was in her arms, still sleeping.

Dad was on the other side of Andreis, tense and on full alert. His shirt was wet with sweat.

Uncle Dario wound down the window. A bearded soldier had come up to the car and was shouting at him to get out. He swore and struck the hood with his gun.

"He's going to kill you, too," Aunt Blanka wept, reaching out to stop Dario.

"Stay here," Dario said as he opened the door. Andreis saw that he'd left the keys in the ignition.

The soldier pointed to Andreis's father. Mom was slumped in her seat, her lips still moving. Dad kissed Andreis on the forehead and whispered, "Look after Mom," before getting out of the car.

Through the open door Andreis could hear a girl screaming, but he couldn't see her. The noise seemed to be coming from a grove of trees a short distance away.

Then he saw the man lying on the ground, his chest covered in blood. His eyes were staring blankly into space, and his mouth was half-open. Andreis had seen dead bodies on TV and during their journey; they frightened him, but not as much as Dad's words.

A gust of wind carried the smell of blood and metal into the car, making him feel sick.

"Show me your papers!" the soldier yelled to Dario and Dad, who were standing in front of him.

Emir woke up and started to cry, which roused Mom from her paralysis. She began to rock Emir back and forth, trying to soothe him, but the child was having none of it. She pushed her finger into his mouth, hoping he would suck on it and settle down.

Another soldier reacted to the noise and leaned forward to peer into the car. Mom bent over Emir and put him to her breast to shut him up.

Out of the corner of his eye, Andreis saw the soldier walk away.

The man with the gun slowly read through Dario's papers and gave them back to him without a word.

Then he held out his hand for Dad's documents.

CHAPTER 133

Mina couldn't take her eyes off the tall figure outside the veranda doors. Andreis had found her. It ought to have been impossible, and yet he was standing just a few feet away.

"Dad," she whispered, clutching Lukas tightly. "He's here."

Lukas began to cry.

Andreis's eyes locked onto hers. His lips were moving, but she couldn't hear what he was saying.

Time stood still.

Then he drew back and kicked in the door. The sound of breaking glass was shockingly loud. The wooden framework shattered like matchsticks, and yet it wasn't until the cold air struck her face that Mina realized Andreis was in the house.

She knew she ought to get out, take Lukas and run for her life, but she couldn't move.

Her muscles refused to cooperate.

Andreis was breathing heavily. "Did you really think I'd let you have my son?"

"Please, Andreis . . ."

"You know me better than that." He held out his hands. "Give him to me."

Mina backed away. "No."

His voice hardened. "Give him to me and I won't hurt you."

"You're not having him."

Lukas stopped crying and whimpered against her breast, as if he, too, understood the danger.

"I'm leaving the country. Give me my son."

"No."

Andreis reached into his pocket and pulled out a black, gleaming gun, which he pointed at Mina. "I'm warning you," he said quietly. He came toward her, and Mina backed away even more, until she bumped into the kitchen counter. The room was in darkness, but she could see his face by the light of the streetlamp.

Eyes without mercy.

He raised the gun. "I'll shoot both you and the boy if you don't give him to me right now."

Mina closed her eyes as the shot was fired.

CHAPTER 134

The sudden bang made Thomas leap to his feet. He reacted instinctively, running for the door without thinking.

The noise could only have come from Nora's old house.

He raced across the road, yanked open the gate, and tugged at the front door. It was locked, and the place was in darkness.

Nora caught up with him. "The veranda doors!" she yelled.

They ran around the back. There was broken glass everywhere, and the wooden frames were smashed to pieces.

Where was Mina?

"Oh God," Nora gasped, dropping to her knees. "Kovač must have found them. He's shot her!"

Thomas pulled her to her feet. "Go and get your phone and call Leila—quickly! We need backup if Kovač is here."

Nora stared at him in shock, incapable of taking in what he was saying.

"Don't do this to me, Nora. Go and get your phone and call for backup!"

He pushed her toward the gate and turned back to the house. He could see something—someone?—lying on the floor inside the doors.

Was it Mina's body?

He removed the safety catch from his gun. Less than twenty-four hours ago, he'd been hunting for Kovač on Runmarö. The adrenaline was pumping just as hard now.

The sound of a child crying reached him. If Lukas was alone with Kovač, anything could happen. Should he go in, or wait for reinforcements?

Mina might still be alive; he had no choice.

He crept forward and positioned himself against the wall.

"Police!" he roared. "Drop your gun and come out with your hands up!"

Endless seconds ticked by.

"Police!" he yelled again.

"Don't shoot," said a faint male voice.

Thomas edged closer, crouching by the dark entrance to the veranda. It took a few seconds for his eyes to adjust, then he was able to make out the figure of a man on the floor. A large pool of blood was spreading from beneath the body, and the smell of blood and gunpowder filled the air.

Then he saw Mina, sitting by one of the cupboards, with Lukas in her arms. She was rocking him back and forth, not making a sound.

Another person was sitting with his back to the wall in the living room, staring blankly into space. There was a rifle beside him. That was where the smell of gunpowder was coming from.

Mina's father looked up as Thomas approached. "I had to kill him," he said hoarsely. "He was going to shoot my daughter."

Bosnia, May 1993

Selma could hardly breathe as the soldier read through Zlatko's papers. It was impossible to determine which army he belonged to. There were so many factions and paramilitary groups these days; she couldn't tell one from the other.

"Please, God, don't let them shoot him," she murmured to herself.

She'd often been afraid of Zlatko over the past year, but he represented the last vestige of security to her. His loyalty kept her going; she was overwhelmed by the fact that he'd chosen to come with her and the boys, to keep their family together.

The screams from the grove of trees were tearing her apart. She wished the poor girl would shut up. Every shriek heightened the atmosphere even more, reminding her of the fate that might well await her and Blanka.

"Give me all your money and jewelry!" the soldier demanded.

Zlatko and Dario handed over everything they had. The soldier turned his attention to the women in the car. Blanka held out her rings, and Selma quickly removed her wedding and engagement rings, along with the small gold chain she always wore around her neck.

The important thing was to save the children. Nothing else mattered. Her sons must be given the chance to create a new life in a land without war. Andreis and Emir must have a future.

A shot made Selma jump. The screams stopped.

Oh God.

The soldier looked Zlatko up and down. "Is that all?" he said.

"Yes, yes, I swear."

Suddenly the blade of a knife flashed in the soldier's hand. He pressed it against Zlatko's throat. "Don't lie to me."

Zlatko dropped to his knees. "We have nothing else. I swear on my mother's grave—I've given you everything we own."

The soldier ran the knife down Zlatko's cheek, then he jabbed the point into Zlatko's right eye. Zlatko yelled out in pain.

Selma bit her lip so hard that she pierced the skin in order to suppress her own scream.

"Have you given us everything?" the soldier shouted at Dario, without removing the knife.

"Daddy!" Andreis sobbed beside Selma.

Dario nodded in a state of shock.

The sky was illuminated by exploding shells, and the two-way radio on the soldier's belt crackled to life as one of his colleagues shouted that they had to leave. He pulled out the knife, altered the angle a fraction, and slid it deep into Zlatko's jugular vein. Blood spurted across the dusty road in a wide arc, and he smoothly withdrew the knife as Zlatko's lifeless body fell to the ground.

"You can go," he said to Dario, wiping the blade on his pants.

Selma stared openmouthed at the bloody stripes on the fabric. Andreis was screaming, trying to get out of the car to run to his father, but Selma grabbed him and held on to him as tightly as she could, digging her nails into his arms. He wriggled and kicked, desperate to get away from her.

Dario staggered back to the car and managed to start the engine.

Andreis bit Selma to try and make her let go, but the car was already moving. He twisted around and pressed his face to the rear window as they drove away.

They left Bosnia to the sound of Andreis's despairing cries: "Daddy! Daddy! Dadddeee . . ."

Monday

CHAPTER 135

Ulrika nodded to the practice's receptionist and hurried into her office. It had taken every scrap of self-control to behave normally. She had no intention of letting anyone see how shaken she was by the events of the weekend.

By what Andreis Kovač had done.

All her worst fears had been confirmed.

She'd spent the previous day feverishly going over everything she'd said and done over the past few weeks, in an effort to reassure herself that nobody could point the finger at her in her role as his defense attorney. The last thing she needed right now was for the Bar Association to open a disciplinary inquiry against her. It was bad enough that the practice's managing partner had called her to a meeting at ten o'clock this morning.

There was a knock on the door, and Nico came in.

"What a mess!" he exclaimed.

Ulrika raised an eyebrow. "What are you talking about?"

"Kovač, of course! Haven't you seen the headlines? SHOOTING DRAMA IN THE ARCHIPELAGO. It's all over the press. We ought to post something on social media," he said with a grin.

"Andreis Kovač is dead," Ulrika pointed out.

Nico didn't seem particularly bothered. He sat down in one of the visitor's chairs. "Mina's father's going to need a good defense lawyer— maybe we should offer him our services?"

Ulrika gave him a sharp glance. "Show a little respect, for God's sake!"

"Do you think he'll go to jail? The father?"

Ulrika hadn't given the matter any thought, but the case wasn't complicated. "I imagine he'll be acquitted on the grounds of self-defense," she said. "If worst comes to worst, he might get a short sentence."

She rubbed her temples with her fingertips; she already had a headache, even though she'd only been in the office for ten minutes. She needed two strong painkillers, and wished Nico would disappear.

She should have stayed at home.

"He took a hunting rifle to Sandhamn with him," Nico said. "It could be said that he intended to murder his son-in-law all along."

Ulrika sighed wearily.

There were many mitigating circumstances that could be brought up: Stefan Talevski had taken the rifle because he had wanted to protect his daughter and grandson. And if he hadn't intervened, Kovač would have shot Mina. A skilled lawyer would have no difficulty in convincing the jury that Stefan should walk free, or at least get a lenient sentence.

"There's no shortage of witnesses to testify that Kovač had threatened both Mina and her parents," she said.

"Yes, but the court might want to make an example of him."

Ulrika couldn't bear to listen to Nico's speculation. "I've got a lot to do," she said, rummaging in her briefcase. Nico left, and Ulrika dug out her painkillers.

Andreis Kovač's actions were incomprehensible and unforgivable. Herman Wibom had passed away as a consequence of Kovač's attack, as had Katrin Talevski, Mina's mother. The manager of Freya's Haven was badly injured and presumably traumatized.

Ulrika's client had left behind a bloody trail of death and destruction.

Her eyes were drawn to the photograph of Fiona on her desk. Stefan's bitter words came back to her, in spite of her efforts to shut them out:

How can you defend such a piece of shit? How can you live with yourself?

Chapter 136

The door of Anna-Maria's room was closed. Nora tapped gently before opening it.

Anna-Maria was lying in bed. Her right hand was bandaged, and a large dressing covered half her cheek. She was on a drip.

"Nora?" she said, clearly surprised.

"Am I disturbing you?"

"Not at all—come on in." Anna-Maria beckoned Nora in with her left hand. She looked surprisingly bright, considering everything she'd been through. Nora pulled up a chair and sat down. She was on leave from work for a week and still felt shaken, but she'd wanted to speak to Anna-Maria as soon as possible.

"How are you feeling?" she asked gently.

"I don't really know." Anna-Maria pulled up the covers a fraction. "I'm glad he's dead. That's a terrible thing to say, but it's true."

Nora didn't contradict her.

"The doctors say my fingers should heal well, and that's the most important thing. I've picked up an infection, so I'm on intravenous antibiotics." She touched the dressing on her cheek. "We'll see what happens with this . . ."

"You were so brave." Anna-Maria hadn't told Kovač where Freya's Haven was, even though he'd cut her until she fainted.

"I couldn't let him find her."

"Will you go back to your job as manager?"

"Absolutely." Anna-Maria sat up a little straighter. "I'm going to fight for our survival as long as I can."

That was why Nora had come. Anna-Maria's account of the local authority's actions had upset her deeply. "I've spoken to a good friend who works for one of Stockholm's top legal practices," she said.

"Oh?"

"She's an expert in public sector tenders. Her practice has a pro bono program."

"What does that mean?"

"It means they take on especially sensitive issues for free. For the good of the cause." Nora saw this as a kind of atonement for failing to keep Kovač in custody. She owed Anna-Maria. "My friend is prepared to take your case. She can help you fight the local authority, if you'd like to use her services."

Anna-Maria's left hand flew to her mouth. "And it won't cost anything?"

"Correct."

"You don't know how much this means to me. To us."

Nora managed a smile. "In that case I'll let her know she has a new client. She'll be in touch with you." She got to her feet and said goodbye. The nurse had warned her not to stay too long; the patient was still a long way from recovery. She took the elevator down to the entrance and continued to the parking lot, where Jonas was waiting for her.

"How did it go?" he asked.

"She was pleased."

Nora expected him to start the car, but instead he leaned over and gently stroked her cheek. "It could have been you who was attacked and ended up in a hospital bed," he said quietly. "Don't ever put yourself in danger like that again."

Nora leaned back against the headrest. The visit had taken its toll on her. Jonas was right; she'd acted with the best of intentions, but without thinking about the possible consequences.

And she still couldn't shake off the guilt.

When she saw Anna-Maria lying there, she'd felt even worse. Kovač might be dead, but life had changed forever for the people he'd hurt so much.

It was still her fault that he'd been released too early, and she was going to have to live with that for the rest of her life.

She just wanted to go home and curl up on the sofa with enough red wine to slow her racing heart and stop her thinking.

She had no idea how she was going to go back to work in only a week.

"Can we go now?" she said, fighting to hold back the tears.

CHAPTER 137

Thomas was waiting for Pernilla on Götgatan. They were due to meet at ten o'clock, and he was a little early.

The door opened and a man and a woman came out. They set off in the same direction, but a short distance apart. Not really together.

Thomas couldn't help wondering if they'd been to the therapist he and Pernilla were due to see. If so, they didn't seem very happy.

He wasn't looking forward to this. The idea of exposing his innermost thoughts and feelings to a total stranger was unbearable. He'd rejected the suggestion at first, but Nora had persuaded him.

"Think about Elin," she'd said. "Even if you and Pernilla can't find your way back to each other, you have to be able to talk. You'll never be able to cut the tie between you—not when you have a child together."

Thomas still hadn't been convinced.

"See it as a chance to be better parents to your daughter," Nora had pleaded, and in the end he'd agreed to at least try. Much to his surprise, Pernilla had said yes right away. Maybe that was a sign that he ought to give this therapist a chance? Not remain stuck in old patterns of behavior? For once he and Pernilla would be working toward a common goal.

The sun was warm, the air pleasant. Thomas saw Pernilla coming toward him without a coat. She had a slight tan, and new blond highlights in her hair.

From a distance she looked like the woman he'd fallen in love with one night when he was out with Nora and Henrik. He'd felt like the fifth wheel, and Pernilla had been in the same position.

He'd fallen like a pine tree in the forest.

Pernilla waved, and soon she was by his side. "Hi," she said. She hesitated for a moment, then gave him a cautious hug.

He inhaled her scent, the pure freshness she carried without any apparent effort. She was still just as beautiful as that first time they met.

"Shall we go up?" she said, opening the door.

Thomas nodded and followed her.

EPILOGUE

Mina opened the gate and pushed the stroller into the churchyard. The lilacs were in full bloom; it was only a few weeks to midsummer.

Lukas was fast asleep.

Slowly Mina walked over to her mother's grave. There was no headstone yet, and the earth was covered with wilted funeral tributes. They'd chosen a beautiful spot in the shade of a weeping willow.

She sank to her knees, brushed aside some leaves, and added fresh flowers. A few blades of grass had begun to appear.

"Forgive me, Mom," she whispered.

She had to be strong for Lukas's sake. And for her father; he was going to need her support during the upcoming trial. He was in custody at the moment. He'd looked so tired the last time she went to see him, his face gaunt and gray. The green standard-issue shirt and pants hung loosely on his body.

Mina ran her fingertips over the black soil.

It wasn't her father's fault that Andreis had followed him to Sandhamn and found her new hiding place. She would never blame him for that. He had sacrificed everything to protect his daughter and grandson.

He had saved her more than once.

He had finally admitted that he was the one who had anonymously tipped off the authorities about Andreis's business affairs. As an accountant he knew what the consequences would be if Andreis were convicted for tax evasion. He had understood the significance of the information Mina had sent him late one night in desperation. Andreis had been drunk and left out his black notebook, and Mina had photographed the pages.

Her father had done everything in his power to help her, and he had paid a terrible price.

His trial would soon be over, and he would be released, just as his defense attorney had promised. Then they would make a fresh start. Learn to live without Mom, and without threats and violence and constant fear.

It would be a different kind of life.

Her cell phone buzzed in her purse. Mina gave a start, even though she didn't need to be afraid of messages from Andreis anymore. It wasn't easy to forget.

She blinked away the tears and took out the phone.

It was a few seconds before she recognized the number.

The message came from Emir, Andreis's younger brother. He'd been arrested for the murder of Dino Herco, but he'd blamed everything on Andreis, and there wasn't enough evidence to convict him. Andreis was a convenient scapegoat.

Mina stared at the screen. The letters flowed together.

Lukas belongs to our family.

SUPPORT FOR VULNERABLE WOMEN

You can turn to any of the organizations listed below if you or someone you know needs support.

In the US

Numerous resources also exist at the city, county, and state level. The organizations listed below can direct you to them for help.

- **National Domestic Violence Hotline**

    1-800-799-7233 (SAFE) or 1-800-787-3224 for TTY
    thehotline.org or text LOVEIS to 22522.

- **Loveisrespect**

    1-866-331-9474 (call or text) or 1-866-331-8453 for TTY
    www.loveisrespect.org

- **National Sexual Assault Hotline**

    1-800-656-4673 (HOPE)
    www.rainn.org

- **National Center on Domestic Violence, Trauma & Mental Health**

    1-312-726-7020
    www.nationalcenterdvtraumamh.org

- **National Network for Immigrant and Refugee Rights**

    1-510-465-1984
    www.nnirr.org

In the UK

- **National Domestic Violence Helpline**

    0808 2000 247

- **Women's Aid**

    womensaid.org.uk

- **Victim Support**

  victimsupport.org.uk
  0808 506 6380

ACKNOWLEDGMENTS

In Bad Company began with the image of a mother with a stroller running for her life. Over time the narrative was expanded with the background story set in Bosnia. Writing these two strands, which are woven together throughout the novel, was an exciting, educational, and sometimes deeply upsetting journey.

As always I have taken certain liberties. Specially trained police officers are usually brought in to deal with crimes involving domestic violence, but I have allowed Nora and Leila to handle this case. I have also conflated certain police procedures, and given the Economic Crimes Authority greater responsibility than it would normally have with regard to violent crime. The local authority's approach to public sector tendering is entirely fictional in this instance.

Any resemblance to persons living or dead is entirely coincidental, and I take full responsibility for any possible errors. I hope there aren't too many!

Many people have generously helped me with this book, and I would like to thank them: Judge Cecilia Klerbro, who checked legal procedures in the manuscript; Detective Inspector Rolf Hansson, who answered countless questions on police work; Negra Efendić, an award-winning journalist with *Svenska Dagbladet*, who specifically looked at the parallel story in Bosnia; Sandhamn resident Gunilla Pettersson, who once again went through the manuscript with sharp archipelago eyes; lawyer Henrik Olsson Lilja, who provided valuable support in questions relating to the role of the defense attorney and the Swedish Bar Association's rules and regulations; Ambassador Björn Lyrvall, who lived in Sarajevo and was heavily involved in the peace process in 1995–97; Detective Inspector Annika Teckner, who explained the new police organization and the work that goes on in Flemingsberg; Peter Einarsson, Area Manager for Handelsbanken, who clarified the rules regarding money laundering and tax evasion; and Camilla Sten, my very best sounding board.

This novel is the result of teamwork. Without my fantastic publisher, Karin Linge Nordh, and Sweden's best editor, John Häggblom, it would have been a completely different and vastly inferior book. Thank you so much—it's a real privilege to work with you, and with the phenomenal Sara Lindegren and everyone else at Forum.

Annika, Sissel, and everyone at Bindefeld—thank you for your brilliant contributions!

Anna Frankl, you are my rock! I'm so grateful for everything that you, Joakim Hansson, and the gang at Nordin Agency do to promote my books all over the world.

Finally, to my family: Lennart, Camilla, Alexander, and Leo. I love you.

Sandhamn, April 4, 2018
Viveca Sten

ABOUT THE AUTHOR

Photo © 2016

Viveca Sten is the author of the internationally bestselling Sandhamn Murders series, which includes *In Bad Company*, *In the Name of Truth*, *In the Shadow of Power*, *In Harm's Way*, *In the Heat of the Moment*, *Tonight You're Dead*, *Guiltless*, *Closed Circles*, and *Still Waters*. Since 2008, the series has sold more than 5.5 million copies, establishing her as one of Sweden's most popular authors. Set on the island of Sandhamn, the novels have been adapted into a Swedish-language TV series shot on location and seen by eighty million viewers around the world. Sten lives in Stockholm with her husband and three children, yet she prefers spending her time on Sandhamn Island, where she writes and vacations with her family. Follow her at www.vivecasten.com.

ABOUT THE TRANSLATOR

Marlaine Delargy lives in Shropshire in the United Kingdom. She studied Swedish and German at the University of Wales, Aberystwyth, and she taught German for almost twenty years. She has translated novels by many authors, including Kristina Ohlsson; Helene Tursten; John Ajvide Lindqvist; Therese Bohman; Theodor Kallifatides; Johan Theorin, with whom she won the Crime Writers' Association International Dagger in 2010; and Henning Mankell, with whom she won the Crime Writers' Association International Dagger in 2018. Marlaine has also translated *In the Name of Truth*, *In the Shadow of Power*, *In Harm's Way*, *In the Heat of the Moment*, *Tonight You're Dead*, *Guiltless*, *Closed Circles*, and *Still Waters* in Viveca Sten's Sandhamn Murders series.